MOTHER'S RUIN

Kitty Neale was raised in South London and this working class area became the inspiration for her novels. In the 1980s she moved to Surrey with her husband and two children, but in 1998 there was a catalyst in her life when her son died, aged just 27. After joining other bereaved parents in a support group, Kitty was inspired to take up writing and her books have been *Sunday Times* bestsellers. Kitty now lives in Spain with her husband.

To find out more about Kitty go to www.kittyneale.co.uk

D1375591

By the same author:

KITTY NEALE

Mother's Ruin

AVON

AVON

A division of HarperCollins*Publishers*
77–85 Fulham Palace Road,
London W6 8JB

www.harpercollins.co.uk

This Paperback Edition 2012
1

First published in two hardback editions in Great Britain as
Another Time, Another Place and *No Time for Tears*
by Severn House Publishers, 2006

Copyright © Kitty Neale 2006

Kitty Neale asserts the moral right to
be identified as the author of this work

A catalogue record for this book is
available from the British Library

ISBN: 978-0-00792-615-2

Set in Minion by Palimpsest Book Production Limited,
Falkirk, Stirlingshire

Printed and bound in Great Britain by
Clays Ltd, St Ives plc

MIX
Paper from
responsible sources
FSC® C007454
www.fsc.org

In memory of my brother, Donald Underwood.

'Sometimes life is like climbing a hill, but when
you get to the top the view is wonderful.'
Anon

Author's Note

Many place and street names mentioned in the book are real. However, others and some of the topography, along with all of the characters, are just figments of my imagination.

Prologue

Battersea, London, 1961

Sally tossed in agony as waves of pain ripped through her. She screamed again and as time passed it felt as though she'd been screaming for hours. The midwife had arrived, but Sally was hardly aware of her voice. The pain was unrelenting, blotting out all other thought. 'Please! Make it stop!'

'Can't you do something?' Ruth, Sally's mother appealed.

There was a hissed reply, something about an ambulance, but the room was growing dim. 'Mum, Mum,' Sally whimpered.

'It's all right, love. Hold on. Just hold on.'

Pain shot through Sally again, pain that was tearing her body apart. She was dimly aware of other sounds now: a door banging, someone shouting excitedly, and then a voice she had never expected to hear again. No! It couldn't be! Sally knew then that she was hallucinating. She closed her eyes, heartbreak adding to her agony, but then that voice again, this time close to her ear.

'Sally, Sally, I'm here, darling.'

She opened her eyes. She could see him! 'Arthur?'

'Yes, Sally,' his mother, Elsie, cried. 'My boy has come home.'

Sally couldn't believe that Arthur was really here. He had emigrated to Australia with no idea that he'd left her pregnant, yet he was here just as she was giving birth to their baby. She reached out to touch him, but her hand just flopped back down onto the bed. She felt odd, strange, as though she was drifting away, and there was a ringing in her ears that almost blotted out the sound of her mother's voice.

'She's haemorrhaging! Do something! Stop the bleeding! For God's sake, stop the bleeding!'

'I'm trying! Get me some clean towels – lots of them.'

Arthur's voice sounded urgent, but distant. 'Sally, don't leave me! Please, don't leave me.'

There was a slithering, rushing sensation as the baby left her womb, but by then Sally was hardly conscious of anything going on around her. She felt cushioned, as though floating, the pain gone as a familiar golden light appeared just ahead of her. She drifted towards it, arms outstretched. Her friend had come, the one who always came to comfort her. 'Angel. My Angel,' she whispered.

Then there was nothing. Just darkness until . . .

'Oh, thank goodness. She's come round,' a voice said.

As the midwife's words penetrated Sally's foggy mind, she was also aware that she could hear her mother sobbing.

'Is she gonna be all right?'

'Yes, I think so, but she still needs to go to hospital.'

For a moment Sally was bewildered. She had vague memories of floating through a tunnel, surrounded by a golden glow and a light in the distance that seemed to draw her towards it. She struggled to remember, but then a hand gripped hers and she turned her head to see Arthur sitting beside her. 'You're here,' she gasped. 'You're really here.'

'Yes, and I promise I'll never, ever, leave you again. Look, Sally, here's our daughter.'

She saw the bundle nested in his arms, a wisp of red hair visible. 'Oh, please, let me hold her.'

Arthur placed their daughter into Sally's arms, saying softly, 'She's beautiful, just like you.'

Sally felt a surge of joy, but exhausted she only managed a

weak smile. She looked down at her daughter, her heart immediately swelling with love.

'You've given her a beautiful name.'

She raised her eyes to look at Arthur, puzzled. 'Name? What name?'

'Angela. You called out that name and stretched out your arms to hold her just before you fainted.'

Sally smiled softly as her daughter nuzzled into her breast. 'Angela,' she whispered. 'My angel.'

One

Battersea, South London, 1966

Sally Jones sat on the edge of the bath, gently splashing water over her four-year-old daughter. Angela's bright red hair curled in tendrils over her shoulders as she giggled, grey eyes, so like her father's, bright with merriment.

Suddenly the child's expression changed and she became strangely still. 'Mummy, we didn't bath like this before.'

'Didn't we, darling? What was different?'

'We used to sit in a tin bath in front of the fire.'

Sally was surprised to hear her daughter talking about the 'before time' again. At two years old when Angela had started to speak it had been a common occurrence that gained in momentum the more words she picked up. On one occasion Angela had insisted that washing was done in a big tub with a poss-stick before being put through a mangle. She had described ironing too, insisting that the iron was put onto the fire to make it hot. It was almost as if her daughter had lived before and was remembering a previous life, but was that possible?

Gradually it had petered out and when questioned Angela had no memory of the things she'd said, yet now she was talking about the 'before time' again.

'How do you know about tin baths?'

Angela shrugged. 'I dunno, I just do. Don't wash my hair, Mummy. It stings my eyes.'

Used to this nightly battle, Sally folded the flannel into a strip. 'Hold this over your eyes to keep the soap out.'

'No, Mummy!'

'Come on, I'll be as quick as I can,' Sally cajoled as she poured water gently over her daughter's head. She braced herself for the ensuing screams of protest, but for once Angela was surprisingly pliable.

Sally massaged soap into Angela's hair, wondering yet again if her daughter had inherited her spiritual gifts, but other than talking about the 'before time' there had been no other signs. Perhaps it was too early to tell, Sally thought, as she rinsed away the shampoo and quickly wrapped a towel around her daughter's head. 'There, all done.'

'Can I get out now, Mummy?'

'Yes, darling,' Sally agreed, hoping that soon she'd have Angela settled in bed.

It was over an hour later and Sally was sighing with relief. Angela was finally in bed, but would struggle to stay awake until her daddy came home. Sally was excited, anticipating Arthur's arrival too. He worked for his father who had his own removals company, but when moving people long distances the hours could be erratic.

Now, almost ready for his homecoming, Sally checked her appearance in the mirror. Her own red hair, a slightly darker shade than her daughter's, hung to her shoulders as her husband liked it. The black dress that she only wore on special occasions clung to her hips, but as she twisted this way and that, Sally frowned. She looked pale, but her skin, common to redheads, refused to tan. A touch of make-up would help so she applied a little rouge to her cheeks, mascara to her lashes, which emphasised her green eyes, and then applied coral lipstick.

That would have to do, Sally decided as she went into the kitchen. Surely Arthur wouldn't be home late tonight? No, of course he wouldn't, he'd promised, so she opened a bottle of Chianti and took it to the living room. The specially laid table looked nice, and taking two glasses she poured the wine, ears pricked for the sound of her husband's key in the door.

Only moments later she heard the street door open, footsteps on the stairs and with a flurry Angela ran out of her bedroom. 'Daddy!'

'Hello, sweetheart,' Arthur said as he swept her up into his arms.

'Did you like my present?'

'Yes, it's a lovely painting, and I seem to remember telling you that this morning.'

Sally watched the scene, feeling a frisson of pleasure as she always did when she saw her husband. Theirs was a happy marriage, and only the fact that there hadn't been more children caused a ripple in her contentment.

As Angela yawned, Arthur said, 'Let's get you back to bed.'

Sally kissed her daughter on the cheek, then went back to the living-cum-dining room. The flowers on the table were tweaked, the vase moved a fraction, and then Sally wandered to the window, looking down at the busy street below. Their flat was above a small shop on Wandsworth Road, and, though facing the factories, they had fallen in love with the spacious rooms.

At last Sally heard Angela's bedroom door closing and in readiness she picked up a glass, holding it up in a toast as Arthur appeared. 'Happy birthday, darling.'

His huge, gentle, bear-like bulk seemed to fill the doorway as he walked in. 'Thanks. Now come here, you.'

Sally put the glass down and flew into his arms, their kiss passionate. For a moment she melted against him, saying softly, 'I've made your favourite dinner.'

'Sod the dinner,' he growled sexily. 'You look and smell gorgeous and I've got other things on my mind.'

'Later,' she teased as she ran from the room with Arthur chasing after her. 'Shush, don't wake Angela,' she warned over her shoulder.

His head lifting, Arthur sniffed the air as they reached the kitchen. 'Do I smell stuffed hearts? Mmm, in that case I can wait.'

'It'll be ready by the time you've washed and changed.'

'And after dinner I'll be ready for you,' he said with a lewd wink as he left the room.

Sally was happy, pleased that they'd have the whole evening to themselves. Though their daughter's given name was Angela, with her wide, innocent smile she soon became Angel to most of the family. But by the time she was eighteen months old, it became apparent that this was no celestial being. Spoiled by her grandparents, and her father, Angela became adept at getting her own way. *You spoil her too*, a small voice whispered at the back of Sally's mind and she had to admit it was true. Yes, she spoiled Angela, but after her own rotten childhood Sally was determined that her daughter would know nothing but love.

With the dinner dished up, Sally carried the plates through to the dining room and had just placed them on the table when Arthur entered the room. She walked into his arms, her nostrils filling with the familiar smell of Brut aftershave. 'Come on, eat your dinner before it gets cold.'

'I'd rather eat you, but later,' he said huskily, then took a seat at the table.

Sally shivered at the look in his eyes, yet it was a shiver of pleasure. Her passion matched his, a passion that hadn't abated in over four years of marriage. She smiled now as a drop of gravy spilled onto his chin. He was so handsome and she was tempted to go over to him to lick it off.

8

'Now then, stop looking at me like that,' he said, chuckling, reading her well.

She laughed and for a while they ate in silence, until Sally finished her dinner and went over to the sideboard. She picked up Arthur's present, hopeful that he'd like it as she placed it in front of him. 'Happy birthday.'

Arthur quickly opened the box, his eyes brightening with pleasure when he saw the watch. 'It's great, Sally.'

'Do you really like it?' she asked, taking a seat again.

'Yes, I love it,' he said, 'and you.'

'I love you too,' Sally said, recalling the past, 'but didn't realise it until you met that girl and decided to emigrate to Australia with her.'

'You hid it well and seemed happy to see me go.'

'I didn't know then that I was having your baby. Do you ever regret coming back to England?'

'Sally, it's been over four years now yet you ask me the same question over and over again. I always give you the same answer too. Of course I don't regret it.'

'You left it a bit late. I was giving birth to Angela the day you arrived.'

'Yes, I know, but I married you as soon as I could, with a special licence three weeks after Angela's birth.'

'I still worry about her. When she grows up she'll find out she was born before our marriage. She'll carry the stigma.'

'Darling, this is the nineteen sixties and attitudes are changing. By the time Angel's an adult I don't suppose it will matter at all.'

'I doubt that. Having a baby before marriage will always be frowned upon.'

Arthur came to Sally's side and lifted her from the chair with ease. 'Stop worrying, woman, and enough reminiscing. It's my birthday and I think I've waited long enough.'

Sally snuggled against him, hoping as she always did that this

9

time she'd be able to conceive another baby. They'd been trying for so long, and though the doctor had assured her there was nothing wrong, so far it hadn't happened. She snaked her arms around Arthur's neck, felt his rippling muscles as he carried her to their bedroom and lowered her onto the bed.

Soon their clothes were discarded and they were a tangle of limbs, slick with perspiration as their passion mounted. Sally arched her back as Arthur entered her and she groaned in ecstasy.

As always Arthur gradually aroused her to fever pitch and Sally was writhing beneath him, almost at the pinnacle, almost at the point of release when he exploded inside her, her own climax following moments later and coinciding with the shrill sound of the telephone.

'Leave it, Sally, let it ring,' Arthur gasped as he collapsed on top of her.

Even as he spoke, Sally knew she had to answer it, her body covered in goose-bumps as she sensed without a shadow of doubt that something awful had happened. 'I've got to,' she cried, scrambling naked from the bed and running to the hall.

'Sally!' her mother shrieked down the line. 'Come quick! It's your gran. I think she's had a stroke.'

Arthur had been marvellous. While Sally had stood frozen, clutching the receiver, he had come to her side, gently unravelled her fingers and taken over.

The next thing Sally knew she was dressed, getting into a taxi that Arthur had ordered and was now sitting beside her mother on a hard bench at the hospital, both still in shock as they waited for news.

'I wish they'd get a move on, Sal,' Ruth said, wringing her hands.

'Me too, Mum,' Sally agreed and thinking of her mother's sister, she added, 'Did you ring Aunt Mary?'

'Yes, she's on her way.'

A young man in a white coat walked up to them. 'Are you relatives of Mrs Sadie Greenbrook?'

'Yes, I'm Ruth Marchant, her daughter, and this is her grand-daughter,' Ruth told him indicating Sally. 'How is my mother?'

'The stroke has caused some immobility and I'm afraid her speech is impaired.'

'Oh, Mum,' Ruth wailed.

'I've made arrangements for her to be admitted, but in the meantime you can see her now.'

Sally went with her mother to a small side room and after just one look at her grandmother's gaunt face on the pillow, tears filled her eyes. It made it impossible for Sally to focus on her grandmother's aura, her gift useless now; a gift she'd had since childhood, but one that had remained undeveloped until Arthur's mother, Elsie, had taken her under her wing.

Elsie had psychic abilities and had taught Sally how to under-stand the auras she'd always seen, but hadn't understood. Elsie had helped her to develop as a healer too and she had been able to ease her gran's arthritis, but now as she grasped the old lady's hand, Sally felt helpless, a stroke beyond her healing abilities.

There was an unintelligible sound, Sadie agitated as she tried to speak. 'Wha whaas . . .'

'I can't understand you, Mum. Say it again,' Ruth urged, hovering anxiously at her side.

She made another attempt, trying to formulate words to no avail, her eyes frantic with distress.

A nurse poked her head into the room. 'Doctor Ralston, there's a lady here asking to see Mrs Greenbrook.'

'That'll be my sister.'

'Very well, she can come in,' he said, 'but only for a few minutes. Your mother needs rest and she will shortly be moved to a ward.'

Mary was ushered in, and though she must have dressed in haste, she looked immaculate, as always. However, seeing Sadie, her usual formal manner collapsed. 'Oh, Mother . . .'

'Wha, whass . . .'

'She's trying to say something but I can't understand her. Can you?' Ruth asked her sister.

Mary shook her head, then raised her voice. 'Mother, what do you want? Is there something I can get you?'

'There's no need to shout,' Ruth admonished. 'The doctor didn't say that Mum's lost her hearing.'

Sally could see the distress in her grandmother's eyes and could sense her frustration. Though short and tubby, her gran was usually strong and wise, a tower of strength, but now, lying against the white pillows she looked grey, shrunken, a shadow of her former self.

'Sha . . . Sha . . .'

'I think she's trying to say your name, Sally.'

Sally sat carefully on the side of the bed. 'I'm here, Gran.'

Slowly, Sadie raised her good arm and touched Sally's cheek to wipe her tears away. 'Noo c cr . . .'

An involuntary sob escaped Sally's lips. Was her gran telling her not to cry? She felt so selfish. It was her gran who needed comfort. 'Don't worry, you'll be all right and talking again soon,' she said softly, hoping that her words would help.

'I'm afraid you'll have to leave now,' the nurse said as she returned to the room. 'Mrs Greenbrook is being taken up to a ward.'

Sally kissed her gran's papery cheek, Ruth then doing the same before saying, 'We've got to go now, Mum, but we'll be back tomorrow.'

Next it was Mary's turn. 'I'll see you in the morning, Mother.'

Sally could hardly bear to leave her gran, but her aunt took charge, putting an arm around her as they left the hospital. 'Don't cry, Sally. My mother is a strong woman and I'm sure she'll be fine. Now come on, get into my car and I'll run you both home.'

There wasn't a lot said as they drove back to Battersea, each with their own thoughts, Sally's a continuing silent prayer. *Please, God, please don't let my gran die.*

Two

Sally still missed her flat in Wandsworth, but the shop below had been sold and the new owners wanted to live on the premises. Arthur wasn't worried as he had saved the deposit for them to buy their own house, however their plans had to be delayed when Sally's prayers had been answered and her gran had recovered enough to return home.

The problem had been that Gran was still frail and she couldn't be left on her own. Sally knew that with her mother working full time at a local grocer's shop, and Aunt Mary employed as a doctor's receptionist, it only left her so she had offered to look after her gran.

Arthur wasn't keen on the idea, but as it was for a short while, he'd agreed. With their furniture going into storage at the family firm, they had moved in with her mother in Candle Lane. It wasn't easy for Sally. Her gran had changed so much. Most of the time she was bad-tempered, belligerent and moody, but on odd occasions her former personality shone through which made looking after her bearable.

It didn't take long for the cracks to show. Arthur hated living here, hated that they slept in the double bedroom with Angela in a single bed alongside them. It made lovemaking impossible and Sally could sense her husband's growing impatience. He wanted them to move on, but Sally just couldn't agree. She had studied her gran's aura, and though unable to see darkness other than that caused by arthritis, she couldn't shake off her fears. Something was looming, something awful waiting to happen, and Sally was worried that her gran was going to have another stroke.

Four months had now passed and sighing, Sally went to check on Angel. Gran was often snappy and found Angel tiring, which was why Sally had allowed her daughter to play outside.

As Sally's eyes roamed the lane, she felt a bolt of fear. Where was Angel? She had told her not to leave the front of the house, but there was no sign of her. Sally saw Jessie Stone, a woman who was known to be a gossipmonger, standing on her front step and called out to her, 'Have you seen my daughter?'

'She was around a few minutes ago, but if you ask me, the kid's too young to be playing outside.'

Sally bit back an angry retort as she saw Angel flying round the corner, her curly hair bouncing on her shoulders, free of the plaits that had been carefully arranged that morning. Tommy Walters and his gang were a few steps behind Angela, but as soon as she skidded to a halt in front of Sally they veered off, ending up on the other side of the road. Tommy lived next door, and though only seven years old he was a little hooligan, running wild on the streets.

'Are you coming out later?' Tommy shouted, his dark, auburn hair standing up like a brush.

'Nah, me auntie's coming so I've gotta stay in.'

Sally stared at her daughter in despair. Her freckled face was dirty, her dress smeared with mud, and socks that had been clean less than an hour ago, were hanging baggily around her ankles. 'Oh, Angela, your dress is filthy.'

'I don't like dresses. Why can't I wear trousers?'

'You're a little girl, not a boy, and how many times have I told you not to run with that gang?'

'But I like Tommy.'

'He's nothing but trouble. Anyway, I told you not to wander off.'

'But we was playing tag.'

'That's no excuse. Wait till your father comes home and we'll see what he has to say about it.'

'Daddy won't mind,' she said confidently.

Sally sighed. Yes, Arthur would probably side with his daughter, he always did, she could do no wrong in his eyes. She tried unsuccessfully to discipline the child, but with the rest of her family giving in to Angel's every demand, Sally felt she was fighting a losing battle.

'Goodness, there's Aunt Mary now,' Sally said as she saw her aunt's car turning into the lane. 'Quick, let's get you washed.'

'Mary's here, Gran,' Sally gasped, grabbing a damp sponge, and giving Angel a quick lick before her aunt marched un-ceremoniously into the house.

'What on earth has that child been doing?' were Mary Taylor's first words. 'She looks like she's been rolling in mud.'

'She's been playing outside.'

'Angela is rather young for that. You should keep her inside.'

'I can't keep her cooped up in this kitchen and she wanted to try out her new skipping rope.'

'The child wouldn't have got in such a state if she was only skipping. It's about time you took her in hand.'

'I do my best,' Sally said, her teeth clenched. She loved her Aunt Mary, but sometimes her hoity-toity ways were difficult to cope with.

Mary pursed her lips but changed the subject as she beckoned Angela towards her. 'Here, darling,' she said, delving into her handbag to pull out a packet of Spangles.

'Fanks, Auntie.'

'The word is *thanks*. Now, say it again.'

'No,' Angel scowled.

'Sally, you shouldn't allow her to be so cheeky,' Mary said, sighing heavily. 'And you really *must* do something about her diction.'

Sally grimaced. Yes, her daughter was cheeky, but at such a

young age how was she supposed to tackle the way she spoke? Gran, along with everyone else in Candle Lane, spoke in the same way, and ever since they'd moved back here Angel was like a parrot, repeating everything she heard.

'Give over, Mary. The child is fine as she is.'

Sally threw her gran a grateful smile, then sitting Angel down she again tried to brush her unruly locks, finding that it was like trying to pull a comb through a mop.

'Ouch! Ouch! Stop it. Tell her, Gamma.'

'It's not gamma. It's grandmamma,' Mary admonished.

'For Gawd's sake leave the kid alone. I've been Gamma since she first started to talk, and anyway, I rather like it.'

Pleased that Gran was sounding more like her old self, and giving up with the brush, Sally said, 'There, that'll do, Angel.'

With the grace of a gazelle the child jumped to her feet, her eyes wide in appeal. 'Mummy, can I go out to play again?'

'No, darling. Daddy may be home soon and it's time for your bath.'

Angel began to wail, and Gran's mood abruptly changed. 'Shut that kid up. She's giving me a headache.'

With no other choice, Sally took her daughter's hand to drag her kicking and screaming to the bathroom.

When Sally and Angel were out of earshot, Sadie sighed with relief. 'Thank goodness for that.'

'How are you, Mother?' Mary enquired.

'I'm fine. Why shouldn't I be?'

'I only asked, and though Angel can be a handful I'm glad you have Sally here to keep an eye on you. I'd hate for you to be on your own like poor Nelly Cox.'

'Nelly ain't been the same since she lost her husband, but she's a good sort and often pops in to see me. Anyway, I'm worried about Sally.'

'Why? Is she ill?'

17

'No, but it ain't right that she has to stay here to look after me. She and Arthur should be in their own place, and I've noticed that he's away from home more and more these days.'

'The removals firm is busy and they've just expanded again.'

'I know, but I can feel it in me water that something is wrong with their marriage.'

'Rubbish! Arthur adores Sally.'

'Yeah, maybe, but things don't seem the same since they moved back here.'

'I'm sure you're just imagining things.'

'Imagining what?'

Both women looked around as Ruth spoke. She had just arrived home from work, and as Mary studied her younger sister she saw a face drawn with tiredness. Ruth's short brown hair was untidy and her complexion pasty. 'You look washed out, my dear. Are you all right?'

'Yeah, I'm fine, but with a new manager joining soon we're doing a stock-take and it's a lot of extra work. Now, tell me, what is Mum imagining?'

'It's nothing really. She's just a bit concerned about Sally and Arthur.'

'Concerned . . . why?'

'I'll let Mum tell you while I make a cup of tea. You look like you could do with one.'

Blissfully, Ruth sank into a chair, pushing off her shoes before fishing for a packet of Embassy in her cardigan pocket. It was only after lighting the cigarette that she spoke. 'Right, Mum, what's this about Sally and Arthur?'

'I'm just worried that they're drifting apart, that's all.'

'Of course they aren't. I know Arthur's away a lot, but with the firm being so busy, Sally understands.'

'That's more or less what Mary said, but I still think they should be in a place of their own.'

18

'Maybe, but Sally doesn't mind staying with us until you've recovered.'

'I'm fine now.'

'Well, tell Sally that.'

'I have, but she won't listen, and she's forever looking at me aura. As a kid Sally used to say she was looking at our lights. Do you remember, Ruth?'

'Yes,' she murmured before turning away, her eyes veiled. She'd known that Sally was different, but it had been Arthur's mother who had recognised her gifts. Elsie had offered to help Sally to develop her abilities, and though concerned that the church was against things to do with clairvoyance, Elsie had swayed Ruth's decision. They are God-given gifts, Elsie pointed out, so how can the church say it's wrong to use them?

Ruth pursed her lips. There was no getting away from the fact that Sally seemed to have a natural ability to ease people's pain and surely it would have been a sin to waste such a gift? If Sally still sensed that her gran was unwell, she'd stay to look after her until it was safe to leave.

'Talking about lights,' Sadie said, 'seeing you smoking that fag, I could do with a pinch of snuff.'

Mary turned swiftly, the teapot poised in her hand. 'Mother! Surely you're not thinking of using that disgusting stuff again!'

'It's all right for you, miss goody two shoes, but I miss my snuff.'

'It's bad for you, especially now you've had a stroke.'

'Don't nag, Mary. I just said I fancied some, that's all.'

There was a shout, footsteps running down the stairs and, as Angel scampered into the room, she dived into Ruth's arms. 'Nanny, Nanny, got sweeties for me?'

'I might 'ave.'

Angel giggled as she settled on Ruth's lap, enjoying the nightly game. 'What did you get me?'

'Let me see. It might be a sherbet fountain, or maybe a gob-stopper and you could do with one of those,' she said, chuckling at her own wit. 'On the other hand it could be some black jacks or penny chews. You'll 'ave to guess.'

'I've already given her a packet of Spangles, Ruth.'

'Is that right?' Ruth said. 'Now then, Angel, if you've already had sweets from Auntie Mary, I'll save mine for tomorrow.'

'No, Nanny. I want them now!'

Ruth moved Angel from her lap, and when the child was standing she gave her a small pat on the bottom. 'You'll get them tomorrow, madam. Now off you go. Mummy's calling you, and I'm not surprised. It's not nice to run around in your birthday suit. Go and get your nightdress on.'

'Sweeties later?'

'We'll see. Now scat!'

Angel ran off with a giggle, but as her little white bottom disappeared, Mary said, 'I hope you're not going to give in to her as usual. One packet of sweets is quite enough and I hate to think what all this sugar is doing to her teeth.'

'Oh, and Spangles are sugarless are they?'

'Touché! Yes, I suppose I'm as bad as the rest of you, but she is irresistible.'

It was quiet for a while as Mary poured the tea. Just as she finished the door opened again and Arthur came into the kitchen.

'Hello, love, you're early,' Ruth said.

'Yes, it was a family moving to Farnham in Surrey today and they didn't have a lot of furniture. It was a lovely-looking little town and I wouldn't mind living there,' he mused, his voice sounding wistful. 'Still, it's nice to get home before seven for a change. Where's Sally?'

'She's just finished getting Angel ready for bed and as they'll be down in a minute you might as well take the weight off your feet. Mary's just made a pot of tea.'

'Great,' he said, drawing out a chair. 'Mum said to tell you she'll be popping in to see you on Tuesday.'

'Luverly. I still miss your family living next door. Elsie was the best neighbour we ever had, and that lot who moved in six months ago are nothing but trouble.'

'I agree the Walters are a rough lot, but they've only one child. It could have been worse.'

'Yeah, but Tommy's a little bugger,' Sadie said. 'Still, at least they're white so I suppose we should count our blessings. We've got West Indians in two houses now and it's getting like the bleedin' jungle round here.'

Mary was listening to the conversation, but at her mother's last words her temper flared. Angrily she stomped across the room, her face grim. 'Mother, don't talk about them like that! I can't believe you're so prejudiced.'

'Here we go again, the same old record. Now you listen to me, Mary. Before the 1961 Immigration Act we hardly saw a coloured man in Battersea. I can remember dads telling their kids they'd get a penny for every black man they saw, and they didn't get many I can tell you. Since the Immigration Act they've flooded in by the thousands, and nowadays kids round here could make a fortune in pennies. And not only that, they're taking our men's jobs and it ain't right.'

'Don't be silly. The jobs they're doing are ones that employers couldn't fill. They work on the railways, the buses, and in hospitals amongst other things. Our national health and public transport system would grind to a halt without them!'

'Poppycock! Anyway they ain't like us and should go back to where they came from.'

'They came here because our government encouraged companies to recruit them. You seem to forget that they're British, and many of the men fought alongside our soldiers during the war.'

'They ain't British!'

'Yes they are, and have British passports. For goodness' sake, they're just people with a different skin colour . . . that's all. They have the same feelings as us, the same dreams, and aspirations.

You should listen to yourself. Hitler's prejudice killed millions of Jews, and now it sounds like you're adopting his ideals!'

'How dare you say that!'

'Because it's the truth. Maybe you should think about joining the organised racists.'

'Someone's got to do something. Perhaps Mosley had the right idea.'

'Mother, as long as people think like you, things will never change.'

'I've got a right to my opinions.'

'Yes, but maybe you should keep them to yourself. I don't think it's right that my niece hears you spouting racial hatred.'

'Come on, you two, calm down,' Arthur cajoled.

'I am calm,' Mary said, fighting her feelings. 'But what about you, Arthur? Are you happy for Angela to hear my mother's claptrap?'

He slowly shook his head. 'No, I'm not happy about it, but if she doesn't hear it from Sadie, she'll hear it as soon as she goes to school. It's everywhere.'

'And are you of the same opinion as my mother?'

'No, I'm not. I hate the things Mosley stood for, and I think you'll find that the majority of working class people hate his ideals too. Yes, there are those who still follow the man, but these are just ignorant louts who can't think for themselves. Now, if you'll excuse me I've had just about enough of this conversation.'

On that note Arthur abruptly stormed out of the room, leaving the women staring after him open-mouthed. 'Blimey!' Sadie said. 'We certainly ruffled his feathers.'

'*We* ruffled his feathers! No, Mum, it was you,' Ruth said, speaking for the first time since the argument started.

'Yes,' Mary agreed, 'and every time I come to see you, Mum, it's to hear the same old rubbish. Like me, I think Arthur is sick of it. It's almost becoming an obsession with you and what next? Will you be hanging the Black Shirts flag out of the window?'

'Don't be ridiculous, and don't you dare talk to me like that! I'm your mother and you should show me some respect.'

'You have to earn respect. We've always looked up to you, come to you with our problems, and listened to your words of wisdom. Yet since those two West Indian families moved into Candle Lane you've changed, and nowadays you just sound like a bigot. And I'll say it again – I'm ashamed of you.'

'I ain't standing for that! You think you're so high and mighty with your sanctimonious preaching, but you're no better than the rest of us, despite talking as though you've got a plum in yer mouth. Now get out of my house, you cheeky bitch!'

'Don't worry, I'm going, and you seem to forget that the tenancy of this house is in *Ruth's* name, *not yours*,' Mary said, ignoring her sister's cry as she snatched up her bag before running out of the door.

As Mary marched down Candle Lane, her shoulders were stiff, but by the time she reached the corner they were slumped in despair. She shouldn't have lost her temper, yet the things her mother said made her blood boil. *Oh, what am I going to do?* she cried inwardly. *I've got to tell her, and soon.*

Three

'Daddy,' Angel cried as she bounced on the bed, bobbing along the mattress to reach him. Her foot caught in the hem of her nightdress and she squealed with delight when her father averted a nasty fall by swooping her up into his arms.

His expression soft now, Arthur kissed his daughter's cheek. 'You silly sausage,' he gently admonished. 'You could have hurt yourself. Now tell me, what else have you been up to? Have you been a good girl today?'

'Yes, I've been good . . . ain't I, Mummy?'

Sally raised her eyes heavenward at the 'ain't' but only said, 'Other than playing with Tommy Walters again, I suppose so.'

'I thought Mummy told you to stay away from that boy.'

Angel hung her head for a moment, but raised it, her eyes wide with innocence. 'I didn't mean to play with him, but he asked me and it would have been rude to say no, wouldn't it?'

Arthur laughed, but then trying to pull a stern face he said, 'Well, missy, don't do it again. If Tommy asks you to play, just tell him that you're not allowed.'

'Awright, Daddy.'

'Good girl. Now come on, hop into bed and I'll tuck you in.'

'But I haven't said goodnight to Gamma, Nanny and Auntie Mary.'

'All right, pop downstairs, but then come straight back.'

'No, I don't want to go to bed yet. Pleeease, Daddy.'

'I don't suppose an extra half an hour or so will hurt, but no longer.'

'Arthur!' Sally protested. 'Angel starts school on Monday and she needs to get used to early nights. I'm trying to settle her into a routine.'

'I've hardly seen her today and as I said, half an hour won't hurt.'

Sally was left looking at her husband's back as he carried Angel from the room. Arthur hadn't even given her a kiss on the cheek and she felt the gulf that had grown between them. In August they had celebrated Angel's fifth birthday, and now her daughter would be going to school. Five years had flown past, five wonderful, happy years that had come to an abrupt halt when they'd moved back to Candle Lane.

Sadly, Sally followed them downstairs, puzzled when she went into the kitchen. 'Where's Mum and Aunt Mary?'

'Mary's gone, and good riddance too,' Sadie snapped. 'I dunno who she thinks she is.'

'Are you cross, Gamma?'

Looking at her great-granddaughter, Sadie smiled wanly. 'Nah, I'm all right, ducks. Mind you, a cuddle might be nice.'

Angel scampered across to Sadie. She gave her a quick hug, but then rushed back to her father. 'Play horses, Daddy,' she appealed.

'Not tonight, princess. I'm afraid my back is playing up. Go and get a book and I'll read to you.'

Sally smiled at her gran, pleased that she had been nice to Angel for a change. When her daughter returned with a book, she climbed back onto her father's lap and Sally heaved a sigh of relief. No rough game, no hysterical giggles, just listening to a story and with any luck, Angel would fall asleep.

As the child was settled, thumb in her mouth, Sally went to find her mother. The front room had been turned into a bedroom for Gran a long time ago, and it was here that she found her. 'Are you all right, Mum?'

'I just wanted a bit of peace and quiet. Sometimes when your gran gets on her high horse it drives me mad.'

'I've been reading up about strokes and they're caused by a clot of blood touching the brain. It explains the changes to her personality and we must make allowances for her.'

'Tell me the truth, Sally. How is she?'

'Her aura doesn't look too bad, but her arm is still weak. I give her a bit of healing every day, but it only seems to ease her arthritis.'

'She was in fine fettle when she was arguing with Mary.'

'If Gran loses her temper it can't be good for her. We should all try not to upset her.'

'It wasn't me, I hardly said a word, but Mary really got out of her pram. She hates it that your gran is so against the blacks.'

'It's understandable. She works in a doctor's surgery and comes into contact with lots of immigrants. From what she's told me they seem to be having a rough time of it. Can you imagine what it must be like to face racial hatred every day?'

'There's no need to preach to me. Live and let live, that's what I say. Still, I'll tell Mary not to argue with her again.'

'Yes, good idea. Now, are you coming back to the kitchen? Angel will want to say goodnight. With her starting school soon I want to get her used to going to bed earlier.'

'I'll be there in a minute.'

'Are you sure you're all right?'

'You should know, Sal. Haven't you looked at my aura?'

'Of course I have and it looks fine, but you still seem a bit down in the dumps.'

'I'm fine, now just bugger off and leave me in peace for five minutes.'

'All right, I'm going,' Sally said. She hadn't seen anything to worry about in her mother's aura, but something was obviously wrong. Was it just that she was a bit fed up or was there more to it?

* * *

26

Alone again, Ruth stared disconsolately out of the window seeing a mean little terraced house identical to her own across the narrow, grey vista. Secretly she'd been pleased when Sally and Arthur had moved in. It was wonderful to have her grand-daughter under the same roof, a joy, but there was no getting away from the fact that the house was bursting at the seams. Oddly, despite this, there were times, like now, when she felt lonely, yet memories of the past always held her back from seeking another relationship. Her marriage to Ken had been a disaster, and when she remembered the way he had treated Sally, Ruth was, as always, swamped with guilt.

When Ken had been away during World War Two she'd had no news of him for a long, long time and had feared he'd been killed in action. In a moment of madness she'd walked into the arms of another man, and had an affair that left her pregnant.

Shortly after Ken had come home and despite her affair he had begged her to stay with him. He'd suggested that they tell everyone that the baby was his, had promised to bring Sally up as his own and Ruth had agreed. She had sent a letter to Andrew at his unit, told him that her pregnancy was a false alarm, and that as her husband had returned she could never see him again.

All Ken's promises came to nothing when Sally was born. He had hated her on sight, obviously seeing her as a constant reminder of the affair. He had changed so much that fearing his violence she had kept Sally confined to her room when he was at home, her daughter a virtual prisoner and a sad, lonely child.

Ruth closed her eyes as once again she was swamped with guilt. Instead of kowtowing to Ken, she should have put her daughter first. She'd been a selfish mother so was it any wonder that Sally clung to her grandmother?

When Ken had gone off with another woman and Sally found out that he wasn't her father the questions had begun. She had wanted to know who her *real* father was. All Ruth could tell her was that Andrew had been a soldier, married too, with a young

27

son, and after ending the affair she had no idea what happened to him.

Ruth slumped on the side of her mother's bed. She didn't even know if Andrew had survived the war. Stop it, she berated herself, stop thinking about him. It was all best left in the past, but why, oh why, did the memory of being in Andrew's arms still haunt her?

Angela had fallen asleep so Arthur carried her upstairs where he gently tucked her into bed.

For a while he stood gazing down at his daughter's innocent face and then his eyes flicked around the cramped bedroom. Angela shouldn't be in here with them, she should be in her own room again.

Arthur's thoughts turned to Sally and he wondered what was happening to their marriage. When he'd agreed to return to Candle Lane it was only supposed to be for a short while and he'd soon found the perfect house for them in Richmond. It was a bit pricey, but the firm was doing well and he could afford the mortgage. Huh, so much for that plan. Sally stubbornly refused to leave. Her gran was too ill, she insisted, and might never fully recover. Why not look for a house close to Candle Lane, Sally had suggested, one that allowed her to stay with her gran during the day. Arthur wasn't having that. He wanted them to live in or around Richmond where Angel could breathe clean fresh air instead of the muck that the factories churned out around here. As far as he could see, Sadie looked all right and, though testy at times, she was sounding more and more like her old self. It was time for them to move out, to move on. He intended to put his foot down.

'Is Angel asleep?' Sally whispered, entering the room.

'Yes, she's out for the count. Oh, and I've got to go out again after dinner.'

'Oh Arthur, this is the first time you've been home early all week. I hardly see you these days.'

28

'I know, but we've just heard about a larger yard in Clapham. It's just what we need and will hold eight vans. Dad's arranged to see it and he wants me with him.'

'Why can't he go on his own?'

'I'm his partner, Sally, and it's natural that he wants my opinion.'

'But you've been on the road all day. Can't you talk to your dad about your hours?'

'I've told you, we're exceptionally busy at the moment and it can't be helped,' said Arthur, glad to be going out again. They had no privacy now and if he stayed in it would be an evening stuck with Sally's mother and gran in front of the television. If Sadie was in a bad mood it was hell and woe betide them if they spoke while she was watching her favourite programme. It drove him mad and he didn't know how Sally stood it.

'I suppose you have to go then,' Sally said, 'but surely it won't take too long just to look at a yard.'

'I shouldn't think so, but I'm meeting an old friend afterwards.'

'What old friend?'

'A bloke I met in Australia,' Arthur said. He felt a bit rotten when he saw Sally's face fall, but then quickly decided that he had nothing to feel guilty about. She was putting her gran first, refused to move out of this dump and he'd had just about enough of it. 'Right then, I'm off for a wash and shave.'

Sally was despondent when Arthur left, her mood low as she went into the kitchen.

'I didn't expect Arthur to go out again,' Sadie said.

'Nor did I, but he and Bert are going to look at larger premises.'

'What! On a Saturday night?'

'They don't get time during the day. The firm has gone from strength to strength and I suppose I shouldn't complain, yet Arthur is rarely home these days.'

29

'I don't know why he still has to do the humping and driving. Surely they employ enough men now to do the heavy work.'

'Yes, but what else is there for Arthur to do? His dad's back has gone and so he handles all the office work.'

'Yeah, well, over the years I suppose Bert has done his share of hard work. He built up the business from nothing really and it was thanks to him that he and Elsie were able to buy their lovely house in Wimbledon.'

'Arthur wants us to move out of Battersea too.'

'I don't blame him. I miss Elsie, yet I don't blame her either for wanting to move away from this dump. We're being surrounded by huge blocks of flats and nearly all the old streets have been demolished, with this one no doubt on the list as well. And have you seen the way they build them tower blocks?'

Sally opened her mouth to reply but didn't get the chance to say anything. Her gran was off again, in full sail.

'Great slabs of concrete, Sally, that's what they use, lifted into place by massive cranes. Twelve floors are built in a jiffy, but I can't believe they're safe. You won't catch me living in one, I can tell you. I'll stick to good old bricks and mortar.'

'I expect they're lovely and modern inside.'

'Modern or not it'd be like living in a matchbox. Arthur's right, my girl, you should get away from this area. It's gone to the dogs. The factories are still here, belching smoke, and that peculiar smell that drifts in when the wind's in a certain direction makes my stomach churn. You'd think I'd be used to it after all these years, but no such luck.'

'I think with the hops, yeast and other paraphernalia used, the smell comes from the brewery.'

'Yeah, you could be right, but others blame Gartons Glucose factory, or Price's where they make candles. Now come on, cheer up and see what's on the telly.'

Sally forced a smile, pleased that her gran was feeling chatty.

'When Arthur came home early I hoped he'd take me out, if only to the pictures or something.'

'When was the last time the pair of you had a night out?'

'It was a couple of months ago.'

'No wonder you look a bit fed up. You're only young and shouldn't be stuck indoors all the time.'

Both heads turned as Ruth came into the room, her hair wrapped turban-style in a towel. 'I've used the hot water, Sal. If you want a bath you'll have to wait an hour for the immersion to heat up again.'

'Sally needs a break, Ruth, not a bath. She's stuck in all day, every day, looking after Angel and me. Arthur is rarely home before eight and he hardly ever takes her out.'

Ruth pursed her lips then said, 'Once married, men seem to think that their wives are happy to stay at home while they go off out to the pub. Still, things have changed and there's nothing to stop you going out on your own too, Sally. Take now for instance. Angel's asleep and if she wakes up I'm here to see to her.'

'Where would I go on my own?'

'You used to do a healing service in the hall down the road and as you've been keeping your hand in you could go back to it.'

A silence followed whilst Sally digested her mother's words. Now that Angel was starting school she'd be in bed early, and if her mother didn't mind keeping an ear out for her, there was no reason why she couldn't go out for a couple of evenings a week. 'I'd like to go back to healing, Mum, but I'll have to see what Arthur says about it.'

'He won't mind. It's not as if you'll be out all hours. The service is over by ten.'

'Yes, but if he doesn't arrive home before I leave, what about his dinner?'

'I can sort that out.'

'Are you sure you don't mind, Mum?'

'I offered, didn't I?'

'Right, that's sorted then,' Sadie said. 'Now shut up the pair of you and let me watch the telly in peace.'

Sally settled down for another night in front of the television, yet she hardly saw what was on the screen. Surely Arthur wouldn't object? No, of course he wouldn't, yet even as she told herself this, Sally felt a moment of doubt.

Four

Tommy Walters saw Angel's dad leaving his house, and dying to find out what it was like to ride in a car, he begged, 'Gis us a ride in yer motor, mister.'

Arthur Jones just shook his head, but then he paused, a funny expression on his face. 'Have you had any dinner today?'

'I had a bit of bread and dripping,' Tommy told him, wondering why he was asking. Mr Jones was huge, but there was a sort of softness about him too. Tommy envied Angel her parents who, unlike his, he had never seen drunk.

'Here, go and get yourself a bag of chips or something,' Mr Jones said, tossing him a coin.

Tommy caught it deftly, saw it was a tanner and his eyes lit up. 'Fanks, mister,' he called, his mouth salivating at the thought of chips smothered in salt and vinegar as he ran off. It didn't take him long to reach the chip shop and soon he was licking the last remnant of fat from his fingers. He screwed up the paper, chucked it in the gutter, scowling when he turned back into Candle Lane to see his mother on the doorstep.

'Tommy, get in here!'

'Yeah, I'm coming,' he said, reluctantly following her indoors.

'Here, take this and go and get me a bottle of cider.'

If anyone else had seen inside the Walters' house they might have been appalled, but Tommy was used to the grime. His mother

33

was swaying, her breath reeking as she gave him some money. He grimaced. 'Do I have to? You're already pissed.'

'You cheeky little bugger,' his mother said, raising a hand as if to strike him. 'Do as you're told.'

'I'm going,' and with that Tommy snatched the coins and left, used to these regular trips to buy his mother's booze.

Arthur was thinking about Tommy Walters as he drove to see the premises. He knew the boy could be a menace, but he couldn't help feeling sorry for him. The lad looked undernourished, his thin legs like sticks, but despite his obvious lack of parental care Tommy's cheeky grin was never far away.

An hour later, Arthur and his father, finding the yard to their liking, decided to go ahead with the deal. When they parted, Arthur drove to the pub to meet his old friend, Joe. He parked, walked into the bar and grinned at the man sitting just inside the door.

'Hello, stranger,' Joe said.

Arthur was chuffed to see him again. He and Joe had hit it off from the start and had become close mates as they travelled around Australia. 'It's great to see you, Joe.'

'And you, mate.'

'What are you drinking?'

'I'll have another pint of bitter.'

Arthur got the drinks in and then sat beside Joe, smiling. 'You could have knocked me down with a feather when you got in touch. How on earth did you know my mother's address?'

'You were down in the dumps in Australia, but wouldn't tell me what the problem was. I wanted to help, and though I know it was out of order, I read your mum's letter.'

Arthur was surprised, but he had a lot to thank Joe for and found that he wasn't annoyed. He had liked Australia, but after reading that Sally was pregnant he'd been desperate to get back to England. He didn't have enough money for the fare, but Joe had stepped in. 'By the time I'd found the money you'd slipped in my wallet, you'd gone. I wanted to pay you back, but I had no way of contacting you. Until now of course and I'm glad that I can return it at last.'

'It wasn't a loan. I gave it to you.'

'I'd still prefer to pay you back. How long are you here for?'

'For good, but I'm not sure if I've made the right decision. I came home because my mother was taken ill and apparently pining for me. She's on the mend now while I'm finding it freezing. I'd forgotten how awful the weather can be.'

'It's early September and mild,' Arthur protested.

'Mild! You must be kidding,' Joe said as he clutched his coat closer to his body. 'What have you been up to since leaving Australia?'

'I'm a partner in my father's furniture removals business.'

'Sounds good, and what about the girl you couldn't wait to get home to?'

'I married her and we have a five-year-old daughter.'

'That's great. I'm glad it worked out for you.'

'What about you, Joe? Now that you're back, are you working on your father's farm?'

'No, nothing has changed and we still don't get on. I've got plans for starting something up but it's only in the early stages.'

'Such as what?'

'There's no point in going into it now, but if it's viable financially and I can get it up and running, I'll tell you about it.'

'Sorry, mate, I didn't mean to sound nosy.'

'It's not that, Arthur, it's just sort of all pie in the sky at the moment.'

'Fair enough, but where are you living? Are you staying with your parents?'

'As I didn't fancy being in the sticks, I've found myself a little flat in Earls Court, though I pop home most weekends to see my mother.'

Time passed quickly as they began to reminisce, laughing as they remembered the things they had got up to on their travels. Then of course the subject of football came up and Arthur went into great detail about England winning the World Cup. The choice of players came under review, their position on the field and the choice of goalkeeper.

Arthur lifted his pint of bitter and took a long swig before saying with a grin, 'With Gordon Banks we had the best goalkeeper in the world. I can remember watching a match when a dog invaded the pitch. Banks showed his all-round skills by catching the dog with a flying tackle. You should have heard the cheers.'

'It was great that England won, but rugby's more my game.'

'I don't mind watching a bit of it now and then, but the rules do my head in.'

'What don't you understand?'

'Well, the offside law for one.'

Joe launched into an explanation which Arthur did his best to follow, and then finishing his pint he ordered another round. They downed them, still talking sport until Joe said, 'Sorry, mate, I've got to go now, but can we meet up again?'

'Of course. And anyway as I said, I owe you some money.'

Joe still protested, but Arthur was determined to pay what he saw as a debt and they arranged to meet up the following week.

Arthur was a little tipsy as he made his way home. Joe sounded like he had big plans for starting up a business and Arthur found that he was envious. The man would make his own way in life and, unlike him, he wouldn't be hanging on to his father's coat tails.

When had his dissatisfaction started, Arthur wondered. At first he'd enjoyed the removals game, enjoyed travelling around the country, but now he'd come to hate it. He might be a partner, but his father was the boss and made that plain, almost as if he was frightened that his son would usurp his position.

All Arthur could see was years of doing the same thing, years of being no different from the other men his father employed. He was still just a driver, a humper, with no responsibilities and no say in the running of the business. Arthur continued his journey home, finding that his good mood on seeing Joe again had evaporated.

Sally was still awake, waiting for Arthur to come home, hoping he wouldn't object to her taking up healing again. Her hopes were dashed.

'I don't like the idea, Sally. I know I'm often late home, but at least you're here when I arrive. I don't fancy being stuck with just your mum and gran while you're at the hall.'

'I'd be home just after ten.'

'Why take up healing again? You've got enough to do with looking after your gran.'

'I need a change, a chance to get out of the house and you're too busy to take me anywhere. My days are spent looking after Angel and Gran.'

'And *you* don't seem to appreciate that I work all hours and hardly get any time off to take you out. Oh, poor Sally, stuck in front of the telly. What a hard life,' Arthur drawled sarcastically.

'I do appreciate how hard you work, but I'm twenty-three, not eighty-three and I feel as though life is passing me by. The swinging sixties! What do I ever see of the bloody swinging sixties? All I ever see is Candle Lane and the local shops.'

'Don't swear, Sally. It doesn't become you.'

'Do you know what, Arthur? You sound pompous and old before your time. When was the last time we had a bit of fun? Tell me that. I'm fed up, bored, and not only that, when was the last time you made love to me?'

As soon as those words left her mouth, Sally flushed. Shame filled her and she lowered her eyes. Why had she spoken to Arthur like that? Yes, she felt frustrated, but suddenly realised

37

that it wasn't the only reason for feeling so low. For weeks now she'd been on tenterhooks, almost as if instinctively waiting for something awful to happen.

'We have no privacy and I refuse to make love to you whilst my daughter is in the same room,' Arthur retorted. 'What if she woke up? After all, you aren't exactly quiet, are you?'

Sally coloured again. How could he throw *that* in her face? What was happening to them, to their marriage?

'I'm sorry,' Arthur said contritely. 'I shouldn't have said that. I was in a bad mood when I came in but I've shouldn't have taken it out on you.'

She saw how shamefaced he looked and flew into his arms. 'I'm sorry too. It's all right, I won't take up healing again.'

'Don't be daft. You go to the spiritualist hall, and if I can get home early I promise I'll take you dancing.'

Arthur's arms tightened around her and Sally pushed her body closer to him. She felt his desire mounting too, hard against her, and, turning, she led him towards the bed.

Angela was asleep, thumb in her mouth as always, and as Arthur's eyes flicked towards her he said, 'No, Sally. We can't.'

'Please, Arthur, I'll be quiet. I promise,' she begged, her frustration almost unbearable as she again pressed herself against him.

His eyes became dark with passion and with a soft groan he unbuttoned her blouse, his eyes feasting on her breasts. In moments they fell on the bed, both now frantically pulling off their clothes and Sally groaned softly as Arthur's lips found her nipple. It had been so long, so very long, and unable to wait she whispered urgently, 'Please, darling. Please, take me.'

As Arthur entered her, Sally arched her back, matching his passion and mindlessly forgetting her surrounding as he pounded into her. The frantic coupling was quick, Sally's nails unconsciously digging into her husband's back. She was nearly there, almost on the point of release, her mouth wide as she screamed, 'Yes, yes! Now, Arthur! Now!'

At that very moment a small voice intruded, 'What are you doing?'

Sally frantically pushed Arthur off and they were left unspent, panting. She saw her husband's eyes were wide with horror as he desperately tried to cover himself, but it was too late, Angela asking, 'What's that, Daddy?'

'See what you've done,' he growled, as at last he managed to pull the sheet over his rapidly diminishing erection.

Sally scrambled off the bed, hastily wrapping the spread around her naked body. 'It's all right, darling. Come on now, go back to sleep,' she urged.

'You was screaming, Mummy. Was Daddy hurting you?'

'Of course not, we were just playing, that's all. Now be a good girl and go back to sleep.'

'I want some milk.'

'All right, Daddy will get you some,' Sally said, her eyes holding an appeal as she looked at Arthur.

He glowered at her, but as Sally blocked Angela's view Arthur was able to pull on his dressing gown, tightening the belt angrily as he left the room.

That was it! The thing Arthur dreaded had happened and he would never attempt lovemaking again while Angela slept in their room.

How much longer could this situation go on? It was hell for both of them. As Angel drifted off to sleep again, Sally was left wondering and worrying about what the future held in store for them.

Five

Sally's thoughts drifted whilst waiting for a client in the spiritualist hall. Angel's first day at school had initially proved to be traumatic. She had refused to enter the building, clung desperately to Sally's hand until Tommy Walters had come to the rescue.

The boy had told Angela not to be a baby and Sally had been amazed when she went off with him without further protest. Tommy was dressed like a ragamuffin while Angel had been scrubbed and groomed to within an inch of her life, the two making an incongruous pair. It surprised Sally that Tommy had taken Angel under his wing, especially as the boy was two years older and she doubted it would do much for his credibility with the gang he ran with.

Thankfully, since that day, Angel had gone to school without a murmur, which had been such a relief. However, despite his initial help, Sally still didn't want her daughter mixing with Tommy, the boy an unsuitable playmate, and she continued to warn Angel to stay away from him.

Now, as September drew to a close, Sally was in despair over her marriage. On their fifth wedding anniversary there had been flowers from Arthur, but no card and he hadn't taken her out. She had pushed the disappointment away, told herself that Arthur was too busy, but he had begun to act strangely and she was sure he was hiding something.

Worse, on occasions Arthur had gone out in the evenings with what sounded like feeble excuses and Sally wondered if he was seeing another woman. She felt nauseous at the thought, wondered if she should confront him, face him with it, but dreaded what she might hear. No, no, she was being silly. Arthur would never be unfaithful. It was living in Candle Lane that was the problem, but every time Sally thought about moving out, fear for her gran held her back. It was as though she could feel that something dreadful was looming on the horizon. Was her gran going to have another stroke?

It helped to be out of the house for a couple of evenings a week and Sally now came to the hall to join three other healers, two of whom she already knew and liked. Yet even so her thoughts constantly turned to her gran and though her mother had promised to ring the hall immediately if she became ill again, Sally was unable to completely relax. It affected her healing powers and she had to pass a number of people to the other healers.

A woman now approached Sally and, after inviting her to sit down, Sally gently questioned her to find out that she suffered from migraine attacks. Sally kept her voice soft, told the woman to relax and then stood behind the chair, lifting her eyes in silent prayer. Her hands hovered over the woman's head as she tried to concentrate, opening the channel and allowing the healing energy to flow through her palms.

Elsie, her mother-in-law, had been so patient when teaching her and Sally would always remember her first attempt at healing. After the session, which had eased her gran's arthritic pain, she herself had been left feeling dreadfully tired. Elsie had explained that she must allow the energy to flow through her, not *from* her, and once Sally had mastered this technique her healing energies had flowed more naturally.

As her hands continued to hover, Sally could feel the familiar tingle that radiated from her palms and closed her eyes in added concentration. It was quiet, the atmosphere peaceful and calm,

41

but then the double doors swung open and Angel catapulted into the hall.

'Mummy!' she shouted as she ran full pelt across the wooden floor, then skidded to a halt in front of Sally. 'Mummy, you've got to come! Gamma's shouting and Nanny is crying.'

Sally spoke urgently to her client, 'I'm so sorry, I must deal with this. Do you mind if I pass you on to another healer?'

The woman was smiling at Angel, an effect her daughter usually had on people the first time they saw her. 'No, of course not, and your daughter looks adorable.'

'Looks can be deceiving,' Sally said ruefully seeing that Angel's coat had been thrown over her nightclothes and she was wearing slippers on her feet. 'Margaret,' she called, 'would you mind taking over for me?'

The healer nodded, taking her place while Sally crouched down in front of her daughter. 'Why aren't you in bed? And who is Gamma shouting at?'

'She's shouting at the black man.'

'What black man?'

Placing her hands on her hips, her stance like that of a miniature adult, Angel sighed with exasperation, 'The one wiv Auntie Mary of course.'

Sally wondered what her aunt was doing with a black man, but at the moment she was more concerned that Angel had left the house on her own. 'Does Nanny know you've come to the hall?'

'No, I ran out before she saw me. Mummy, please come home. I'm frightened.'

If Angel was frightened, the situation at home must be bad. Sally grabbed her daughter's hand and called a hasty goodbye to the other healers before running from the hall.

'Slow down, Mummy, pleeease,' Angel cried, but Sally hardly heard her daughter's protest as they almost skidded around the corner into Candle Lane, at the same time seeing the door to

42

number five flying open. A man shot out as though propelled by a cannon, landing in a heap on the pavement.

Mary came dashing out to solicitously help him to his feet and close behind came Sally's gran, her voice raucous as she cried, 'Get him away from here or there'll be murder done!'

'He's got a name, Mother! It's Leroy and I can't believe you're behaving like this!'

'And I can't believe that you're going to marry *him*! He . . . he's . . .'

'Black! Yes, Leroy is black, but unlike my first husband, he's a decent man.'

'Why couldn't you find a decent *white* man? It ain't right, Mary, and if you go ahead with this I'll wash my hands of you!'

'Very well, Mother, if that's how you feel there's nothing more to say. Oh, except that I'm pregnant! Yes, that's knocked the wind out of your sails, hasn't it?'

The neighbours were now on their doorsteps, obviously enjoying the spectacle, with only Nelly Cox looking at them sympathetically. Tommy Walters and three of his gang were watching too, their eyes bright with excitement.

Sally pushed her way between her aunt and gran, hissing, 'For goodness' sake, do you want the whole street to know our business?'

'They can't bleedin' miss it when she turns up with the likes of *that*!'

'What do you mean *that*?' Mary cried. 'Leroy is a human being and as I said, a decent one.'

'He's a soddin' nigger!'

'Mother, don't call him that!'

'What's a nigger, Gamma?'

On hearing her great-granddaughter's question, Sadie had the grace to look shamefaced. 'Its not a nice word and I shouldn't have said it. Take no notice of your Gamma.'

Sally saw her mother hovering in the doorway and said, 'Mum, didn't you notice that Angel had left the house?'

'No, love, and I'm sorry. Mind you, with all this going on it ain't surprising that she was able to run off.'

Sally then looked on in amazement as her impossible, yet sometimes sensitive daughter walked over to Leroy, and taking his hand, gently stroked it. 'You've got a cut. Does it hurt?'

'No, darlin', it's just a graze and I'se fine.'

'Look, she's touching a sooty,' Tommy shouted. 'I bet she catches something bad now.'

'Shut up!' Angel said, rounding on him.

To Sally's surprise the boy didn't say anything more, but Angel did, looking up at Leroy to ask, 'Why is your skin black?'

''Cos I comes from Jamaica.'

'Where's that?'

'Angel, that's enough. There's no need to interrogate the man,' Sally gently admonished.

Leroy smiled. 'It's all right, I don't mind.'

'Get away from him, Angel!' Sadie demanded.

'Why, Gamma?'

'Just do as I say!'

'Mother, he isn't contagious,' Mary snapped.

'Come on, it's best we go,' Leroy urged, taking her arm.

'Yes, you're right. It's obvious we aren't welcome here.'

'There ain't many places we is,' Leroy murmured sadly.

With a sniff of derision, Sadie turned on her heels to march back indoors, but not without a parting shot as she shoved Ruth to one side. 'I'm warning you, Mary. Don't bring the likes of him to my house again.'

The door then slammed shut and with a groan Ruth turned to her sister. 'You shouldn't have brought him here. I warned you about upsetting Mum and why on earth upset her even more by saying you're pregnant?'

'Because I am.'

44

'What, at your age! Don't be stupid.'

'Don't call me stupid!'

'If you think you're having a baby, you must be, but I ain't standing here arguing with you. I dread to think what effect this will have on Mum's health so I'm off to see if she's all right.'

'Huh,' Mary snorted, 'she can't be that ill. You saw the way she shoved Leroy out of the door.'

'In that temper I think she could've shoved a bus outside, but it can't have been good for her blood pressure,' Ruth argued, her nostrils flaring with anger. 'Sally, come on, let's get inside.'

'In a minute, Mum. I'd like a word with Aunt Mary first.'

'Your gran probably needs you so make it quick,' and on that sour note, Ruth turned away.

Mary heaved a sigh. 'Leroy, this is Sally, my niece, and you've already met her daughter, Angela.'

'Pleased to meet you.'

'Hello, it's nice to meet you too,' Sally said shaking his hand. Leroy was tall, with very dark brown eyes and black, tightly curled hair. His suit was grey and double breasted, with very wide-legged trousers that bagged into narrow turn-ups at the ankles. There were several West Indian families that had settled in Battersea and all the men seemed to adopt this same style of dress. Sally was amazed at her aunt's bravery. If a white woman was seen with a black man she was scorned, but her aunt must think a lot of Leroy if she was prepared to face becoming an outcast.

'It seems at least one member of my family is prepared to take your hand, Leroy.'

'I'm not prejudiced, Aunt Mary, but you know what people are like around here and it's going to be hard for you.'

'Yes, we know, and others before Leroy have run the gauntlet of landladies with signs saying "No Blacks" on their doors.'

'When are you getting married?'

'As soon as we can arrange it. Will you come, Sally?'

45

'Of course and I'm sure my mother will.'

'I doubt it. She won't go up against your gran and no doubt you'll be put under pressure to stay away too.'

Before Sally could answer, Angel tugged at Mary's sleeve. 'Can I be a bridesmaid, Auntie?'

'I'm sorry, darling. We aren't getting married in a church so there'll be no bridesmaids.'

Sally saw the rebellious look forming on her daughter's face and quickly intervened. 'Angel, go indoors now, there's a good girl.'

'No, don't want to.'

'Do as I say, and now!'

Angel's lower lip began to tremble, but knowing her daughter's wily ways, Sally kept her expression stern. Angel huffed like an old woman, and Sally had to suppress a smile, thankful when her daughter did as she was told. However, no sooner had Angel gone inside than she was running out again.

'Mummy, Gamma said you've got to come in now.'

'Goodness, Aunt Mary,' Sally complained, 'you'd think I'm still a child to be ordered around. Still, it's best that Gran stays calm.'

'Goodbye, my dear,' Mary said as she took Leroy's hand, her head held high as they began to walk away.

Tommy and his gang followed, dancing around them in imitation of a tribal dance, and Mrs Stone from number nine spat at Mary's feet as she passed. Sally's temper flared. Kids didn't know any better, but there was no excuse for adults. She wanted to shout at Mrs Stone, but knowing it would take a miracle for someone like that to overcome their prejudice, she remained where she was, standing stiffly until her aunt and Leroy turned the corner.

No sooner had Sally gone indoors than her gran started, her voice thick with venom as she said, 'I can't believe it! My daughter marrying a flaming black man! She said she's pregnant too and that'll mean she'll give birth to a half-caste.'

46

'I doubt she's pregnant,' Ruth said. 'Are you forgetting how old she is?'

'In the club or not, I'm finished with her. From now on she's no daughter of mine. In fact, if she comes to my house again she'll get the door slammed in her face.'

Sally, still upset by the treatment her aunt had received, found her temper flaring again. 'This isn't your house, Gran, it's my mother's, and if you don't mind I'd rather you stopped spouting racial hatred in front of my daughter.'

'If you don't like it, my girl, you know what you can do!'

'Don't speak to Sally like that,' Ruth shouted, her temper in evidence too.

'I'll speak to her how I bloody well like!'

'Don't shout . . . please, don't shout . . .' Angel cried.

Sally saw the distress on her daughter's face and was flooded with shame. It was bad enough that Angel had to cope with Gran's mood swings, but now she was seeing them arguing too. She stroked the top of her daughter's head, saying softly, 'It's all right, darling. Come on, let's go upstairs to find a nice jigsaw puzzle and we'll do it together.'

It wasn't long before Angel's tongue was poking out in concentration as she tried to fit a piece of blue sky into the puzzle. Sally helped, but she was still inwardly seething, determined now that it was time to move out.

Six

It was mid-October and Ruth was glad to get home from work. There was no sign of Arthur before Sally went to the spiritualist hall and with Angel tucked up in bed she faced a quiet evening with her mother. However it was interrupted when there was a knock on the door.

It was Elsie, and Ruth's eyes widened. 'Well, this is a nice surprise. Is everything all right?'

'Yes, fine. I just want to talk something over with all of you.'

'Come on in, love,' Ruth urged.

'Watcha,' Sadie said, looking pleased to see Elsie as they walked into the kitchen.

'Hello, Sadie, and how are you?'

'I'm as fit as a fiddle.'

'Good, but where is everyone?'

'Sally's doing a healing service at the hall and I've no idea where Arthur is,' Ruth told her.

'That's odd. Bert said he only did a local job today and I expected him to be home by now.'

Ruth glanced at the clock, frowning. It was eight o'clock. What was keeping him?

'Perhaps there have been a few problems, or the van broke down.'

'If that was the case, I'm sure Bert would have mentioned it when he came home. I should have rung first to check that you were all in, but with Bert hovering, it was impossible. He has no idea I was coming here. I just hope Arthur arrives home soon.'

'What's this all about, Elsie?'

'Its Bert's birthday in January and I thought we could arrange a surprise party.'

'Blimey, Elsie, ain't you being a bit premature?'

'Not really. There's a lot to sort out and I'll need to rope Arthur and Sally in with the planning. Fifty, Ruth, my Bert's going to be fifty. Where has all the time gone?'

'He's just a whippersnapper,' Sadie commented. 'Where are you thinking of holding this party?'

'I thought I'd book the hall. I know we don't live around here now, but most of our friends are still in this area.'

'Right then,' Ruth said. 'Arthur may not be here, but we can make a start. Let's draw up a list of what's needed.'

'Yes, all right. I know Ann would have wanted to help, but it's impossible with her living in Milton Keynes.'

'With three kids and two of those twins, your daughter certainly has her hands full.'

'She does, and living so far away I can't do much to help her. Still, she's arriving on Friday night to stay for the weekend and it'll be lovely to see her.'

'I hear you're having Angel over for the night too. Talk about a glutton for punishment,' Ruth said, smiling wryly.

'It'll be lovely, and to be honest one more won't make a lot of difference.'

'Rather you than me.'

'Have you heard about my Mary?' Sadie asked.

'Yes, Arthur told me.'

'I'm not gonna stand for it. She'll marry that black man over my dead body.'

'Arthur said you're against it, but would it be so bad? Mary has been alone since her husband died, and after what she went through she deserves a bit of happiness.'

Ruth saw her mother's eyes darken and quickly changed the subject. 'Come on, we're supposed to be planning a party.'

Sadie ignored the comment, livid as she shouted, 'Elsie Jones, if you're going to take Mary's side you can get out of my house!'

'Now there's no need for that,' Elsie protested. 'I'm not taking sides.'

'It sounds to me like you are.'

Elsie moved across to Sadie and bending over she took the old woman's hand, saying softly, 'Come on, love, I don't want to fall out with you. Let's forget I said anything and start again.'

'Yeah well . . . just don't mention Mary's name.'

'I won't,' Elsie said, her eyes full of sympathy as they met Ruth's.

Things were a little subdued at first as they sat down to make plans, but the tension soon eased. Food was the first thing they discussed, then drink, music, and a second list was drawn for guests. 'It's funny,' Ruth commented. 'I seem to remember helping you out with another party some years ago. The one you threw for Arthur before he left for Australia.'

'Our first grandchild must have been conceived that night. Maybe lightning will strike again at Bert's party,' Elsie said, chuckling.

Ruth smiled and soon they were reminiscing, until at nine-thirty, Elsie said she had to leave.

'I'll ring for a cab, but while I'm waiting can I pop upstairs for a peek at Angel?'

'Of course you can, but for Gawd's sake don't wake her up.'

Elsie was soon back downstairs again, smiling softly. 'Angela looks so sweet, but don't worry, she's out for the count. I'm surprised that Arthur still isn't home. I can't imagine where he is.'

Ruth managed a nonchalant shrug. 'He knew Sally would be at the hall this evening so perhaps he went to a pub for a drink.'

'Yes, that's probably it,' Elsie agreed, and then they heard the toot of a horn.

'That's the cab,' Ruth said, and though she went with Elsie to the front door, then waved as the taxi drove off, her mind was churning. She'd been sure for a while now that Arthur was up to something, and though hiding her concern from Elsie, she was swamped with suspicion.

Sadie was dozing, but Ruth kept glancing at the clock, until at last, half an hour later, Arthur came home. 'Hello there,' she said, doing her best to act normally. 'You're late. Have you had a busy day?'

'Yes, a delivery to Devon. A big load too and I'm bushed.'

As she lit a cigarette, Ruth looked at Arthur from under her lashes. He was lying of course, but why? All these late nights, and the lame excuses pointed to one thing. Arthur was being unfaithful to Sally. He was having an affair. Should she say something? Confront him? Ruth opened her mouth, about to have it out with him, but then the door flew open and Sally entered the room with a flurry.

'Hello, darling,' she said, her eyes on Arthur before anyone else.

Ruth watched her son-in-law's reaction, saw the fondness in his eyes as he wrapped his arms around Sally and berated herself. No, Arthur would never be unfaithful. He obviously loved Sally, but Ruth was still sure he was up to something, though what it was remained a mystery.

When everyone had gone to bed, Ruth sat alone in the kitchen, her face set in sadness. When her sister had turned up with a bloke, albeit a black man, she had felt her own loneliness. There were times when Ruth craved to feel a man's arms around her again and lighting yet another cigarette, she wondered if she dare take the chance. Yet what hope did she have of meeting anyone? Her life revolved around work and home. Not only that, women just didn't go into places like pubs on their own.

Taking a final drag on her cigarette, her shoulders slumped, Ruth at last went upstairs to her lonely bed.

Seven

On Saturday morning Sally was humming as she absent-mindedly flicked a duster over the furniture. Angel had stayed overnight with Elsie and alone at last, she and Arthur had spent most of the night making love. It had been wonderful, Arthur's eagerness matching hers and after waiting so long, the first time had been over quickly, so much so that it had proved to Sally that she had been silly to suspect Arthur of having an affair.

'What's that bleedin' racket?' Sadie complained.

Sally moved across to the window, her lips set in a grim line when she saw Tommy Walters being thrashed by his mother. Angel was close by, watching the scene and obviously distressed as the boy screamed out in agony. Sally had no time for the lad, but no matter what he'd done, there was no need for Laura Walters to lay into him with a belt.

'I won't be a minute, Gran,' Sally said before rushing outside.

A few neighbours were on their steps, all looking uncomfortable, but none intervening. Sally rushed up to Laura to grab her arm and the woman turned, spitting abuse.

'Get your hands off of me!'

Sally was sickened by the stench of alcohol on the woman's breath. She'd heard rumours that Laura Walters was a drinker, but this was the first time she'd seen it for herself. 'Let Tommy go,' she demanded.

'Mind your own business. He deserves a good hiding and that's what I'm giving him.'

'Why? What had he done?' Sally asked, relieved that at last the woman was distracted enough to stop laying the belt across Tommy's legs.

'He defied me, that's what,' Laura spat, but in the process she had let go of Tommy's ear and in a flash the boy was gone, his little legs pumping like pistons as he fled.

'You won't get away from me. I'll get you later, you little bugger,' Laura screeched.

'It's disgraceful, that's what it is,' Mrs Stone commented after Laura had staggered back indoors. 'It's only one o'clock on a Saturday afternoon and the woman's as drunk as a skunk.'

Other women nodded, joining in the gossip, but Sally took her daughter's hand. 'Come inside now.'

'No, I don't want to. I want to wait for Tommy to come back.'

'He won't show his face for a good while,' Sally told Angela, unable to help feeling sorry for the boy again.

'What was all that about?' Sadie asked as soon as she saw them.

'Laura Walters was giving Tommy a hiding.'

'Yeah, well, no doubt he deserved it.'

'No child deserves to be thrashed with a belt, Gran. I think the woman was drunk.'

'Yes, as a skunk,' Angel said. 'What's a skunk, Gamma?'

'It's an animal,' Sadie said and on an aside to Sally asked, 'Where did she pick that saying up from?

'Jessie Stone.'

'I might have guessed, but I'm not surprised. Nelly told me that Laura likes the booze, her old man too, and from what she said it sounds like they're both alcoholics.'

'What's an al . . . alco . . .?' Angel asked, struggling with the word.

Sally didn't want her daughter to hear any more of this kind of conversation. 'It's nothing important, darling. Now run upstairs to fetch a jigsaw puzzle or another toy to play with.'

Thankfully Angel did her bidding and when she was out of earshot Sally said, 'If Tommy's parents are both alcoholics, no wonder the boy runs wild. It also explains why his clothes are like rags.'

'Yeah, well, if his mother's on the booze she won't live to see old bones.'

'Dreadful though that sounds, I'm more concerned about Tommy. Maybe I should report this to someone in authority that can help.'

'Keep your nose out of it, Sally. It's none of our business and do you really think the boy would be better off in care, in some sort of kids' home, 'cos that's where he'd end up.'

'If getting beaten by his mother is a common occurrence, then yes.'

'What makes you think it's common? Have you ever seen her beating him before?'

'Well no.'

'There you are then, and it's probably something the boy did that drove Laura over the limit. There's no getting away from the fact that he's a naughty little tyke. One thrashing isn't enough to stick your oar in.'

Sally was still unsure. She just hoped that Tommy stayed away until Laura calmed down and now understood why the lad was allowed to roam the streets at all hours. His parents were probably too drunk to care. It was little wonder that Tommy had learned to be streetwise, but at only seven years old it wasn't safe to be out so late at night.

As Sally sat down she felt a flush of guilt. There had been so many occasions when she had chased the boy off, yet what choice had she had? Tommy's language was dreadful and only recently he'd been caught trying to pinch apples from a market stall. He was a bad influence, and she still didn't want her daughter mixing with him.

* * *

At three o'clock Mary came to see them, but as she walked in, Sadie said, 'You ain't bringing that black geezer in here again. If he's with you, bugger off.'

There was no curt response, no argument and instead Mary looked at them with pain-filled eyes. It was Ruth who spoke now, asking worriedly, 'Mary, what's wrong?'

She just continued to stand there, trembling, and worried too, Sally focused on her aunt. There were no dark patches in her aura, no signs of illness.

'Mary, what's wrong?' Ruth asked.

'I . . . I'm not pregnant.'

'I told you that,' Ruth said smugly.

Sadie pursed her lips. 'Does this mean you won't be marrying that nigger?'

'Please, Mother, please don't call him that, but yes, it's over and Leroy has gone.'

With a smile of satisfaction Sadie said, 'Good riddance to bad rubbish.'

At last Mary reacted as she'd have done in the past, fire in her eyes as she glared at her mother. 'Leroy is a wonderful man and I won't have you calling him rubbish.'

'If he's so wonderful, how come he's buggered off?'

'Because I told him to.'

'But why?' Sally blurted out.

Mary crumbled again, her eyes flooding with tears, and jumping up she fled the room. Ruth was about to follow her, but Sally quickly said, 'I'll go, Mum.'

'Yes, all right. You two were always as thick as thieves and no doubt she'd prefer to talk to you.'

Sally found her aunt in the bathroom, perched on the edge of the bath, leaning forward with her arms wrapped around her waist and rocking as though in pain. She looked up at Sally, crying in anguish, 'Oh, I've been such a fool.'

'Why?' Sally said softly, hoping to draw her aunt out.

Her voice cracking with emotion, Mary said, 'Since your uncle's death, I've occasionally been out with men, but I've never been able to – to, be, err, intimate with them. Leroy changed all that and somehow he managed to break through my barriers. He was wonderful, but now I've had to send him away.'

'I don't understand.'

'No, of course you don't, but you see when I thought I was having a baby, I almost burst with happiness.'

'I'm so sorry, Auntie. It must have been awful to miscarry,' Sally said as she sat down next to her on the edge of the bath.

'I didn't miscarry. Your mother was right and I've been a stupid, stupid woman,' Mary cried. 'I'm eight years older than Leroy, but it didn't seem to matter and like me he was thrilled when he thought I was pregnant. But I'll never be pregnant, Sally. I'll never be able to have a baby. It . . . it's too late.'

'But why?'

'Instead of confirming my pregnancy the doctor told me that I'm going through the change of life. It was only then that I realised what an idiot I'd been.'

Sally did a rapid calculation of her aunt's age and realised that though she always took great care of her appearance, she was actually in her late forties. 'It must have been awful for you, but I don't understand why you sent Leroy away.'

Mary took another deep breath as she again fought for composure. 'Leroy couldn't wait to have a family, so when I found out I wasn't pregnant, how could I marry him? He needs to meet a young woman, not a dried-up old prune like me, one who can give him the children he wants.'

'Did you tell him that?'

'No, I just told him that the pregnancy was a false alarm and then went on to say that I didn't want to marry him after all.'

'If you had told him the truth, it might not have mattered.'

'He may have stayed, but eventually Leroy would have grown to resent me.'

'Oh, Auntie, I'm so sorry,' Sally sighed.

Visibly straightening, Mary managed a lopsided smile. 'I was mad to come here expecting any sympathy from my mother. I'll get over it given time, and for now it's time to put on a brave front.'

When they went downstairs, Mary's assessment of her mother proved to be right when after telling her what had happened, the old lady said, 'Yeah, well I hope you've learned your lesson now. In future I suggest you stick to your own kind.'

'I guessed you'd say that,' Mary commented, 'and it's best I leave now.'

'You don't have to rush off,' Ruth protested.

'I think it's better to go before I say something that I might regret.'

'Huh, if you've got something to say to me, let's hear it.'

'No, Mother. Some things are better left unsaid and anyway, knowing how you feel it would be a waste of time.'

With that Mary marched out and Sally followed her, saying urgently, 'She didn't mean it, Aunt Mary. The stroke changed Gran, and she really can't help being the way she is now.'

'Oh Sally, I know, and I shouldn't argue with her. It's just that I came round hoping to see my old mum, the one who was wise and tolerant, the one I could always run to with my problems.'

'She's still in there somewhere.'

A loud bang made Mary jump and with her hand on her heart she said, 'Oh goodness, I hate the run-up to fireworks night. There are children everywhere, throwing bangers or asking for a penny for the guy. I don't know why their parents allow it, after all it's tantamount to begging.'

Mary suddenly halted in her tirade, her face paling. 'Listen to me, Sally. I'm complaining like an old woman, yet since finding out that I'm going through the change I feel like one. I feel as though I've aged overnight.'

'You're not old, Auntie.'

'I'm past having children,' she said sadly, leaning forward to give Sally a kiss on the cheek. 'Bye, my dear.'

Sally stood on the step as her aunt walked straight-backed down the lane. She didn't look back, but Sally remained where she was until her aunt turned the corner. She then went back to the kitchen to hear her mum and gran talking about Mary, both pleased that she had broken up with Leroy, both forgetting the pain her aunt was in.

For a moment Sally wondered if this was what her intuition had warned her about, her aunt's unhappiness and pain. Yet even as the thought crossed her mind she dismissed it as a shiver ran down her spine.

What was coming would be worse, much worse, and Sally's heart filled with dread.

Eight

It was November fifth and Sally was outside with Angel, smiling as her daughter squealed with delight, a sparkler held in her gloved hand reflecting bright pinpoints of light onto her face. 'Why can't we have a bonfire, Mummy?'

'We've only got the yard and it isn't big enough.'

'But Tommy's having one. He's got loads of stuff piled in his backyard.'

Sally hardly listened, her eyes peeled for Arthur.

As though in understanding, Angela said, 'I wish Daddy was here.'

'Me too,' Sally murmured as her eyes continued to scan the lane. Arthur had promised to bring home some fireworks, and though there wouldn't be a bonfire, they were going to set them off in the yard. The lane was smoky, and the occasional rocket could be seen as it whooshed up into the air to explode in a cascade of bright, twinkling lights.

'Will Daddy be home soon?'

'I hope so.'

A group of small boys ran into the lane, one throwing a penny banger in their direction. Just as it exploded Sally grabbed Angel's hand, pulling her daughter inside before she had time to protest.

Angel ran into the kitchen, her tone wheedling. 'Nanny, I want to go out again. You take me.'

'Let's wait for your daddy to come home,' Ruth placated.

Sally glanced at the clock. 'Mum, I'm supposed to be standing in for one of the other healers at the hall.'

'Get going then. This little madam will be fine with me.'

'All right, but don't give in to her. There are kids outside throwing bangers and I don't want her hurt.'

'Sally, I've been at work all day and the last thing I want is to stand outside. It's always the same around here on fireworks night and last year a little bugger tied a jumping jack to a cat's tail. The poor thing was terrified and it bolted down the lane with it going off behind him every few seconds.'

'That was cruel,' Sally said, wondering yet again where Arthur was. She leaned down to kiss her daughter. 'I've got to go, darling. Be a good girl for Nanny.'

Sally hurried down the lane, her brow furrowed. After that wonderful night when Angela had slept over at Elsie's Arthur had soon become distant and distracted. Most evenings he still came home late and sometimes she could smell alcohol on his breath. When asked he just said he'd popped into a pub for a drink, but he failed to meet her eyes and Sally was sure he was hiding something. Was Arthur having an affair?

The hall was almost empty, with only one healer working on a client when Sally walked in. Perhaps the smoke and fireworks had kept those needing healing indoors, Sally thought.

By nine o'clock she'd only had one client, and, still worried about Arthur, Sally asked the other healers if they'd mind if she left early. The smoke was dense as she turned into Candle Lane and Sally coughed before tugging her scarf over her mouth. A fire engine drove past, heading away from the lane, but why had it been there in the first place?

Sally's pace quickened, the pavement wet under her feet now and as she hurried into the kitchen it was to find her mother cuddling a small, sobbing form. 'What's the matter with Angel?' she cried.

The small form unwound itself and Sally saw that it wasn't her daughter. It was Tommy Walters, the boy's face streaked with dirt and his eyes red. 'Tommy burned his hand and as his mother wasn't in a fit state to look after him, I fetched him in here to have a look at it,' Ruth said. 'It isn't too bad but it's giving him a bit of gyp.'

'How did he burn his hand?'

'The silly sod lit a bonfire in his backyard, but the flames were bigger than he anticipated. Blimey, Sal, you've missed all the excitement. Luckily for Tommy, Mrs Stone saw the blaze over her back wall and she called the fire brigade.'

'But where were Tommy's parents? Didn't they see the fire?'

'His dad wasn't in, and his mum was in her front room with no idea what was going on,' Ruth said, throwing a look at Tommy before mouthing silently, 'Drunk.'

The boy was too astute. 'Yeah, me mum was pissed.'

'That isn't a nice word,' Ruth told him, unable to hide a smile of amusement. 'Sally, it's just as well your gran's in her room or I'd be getting it in both ears.'

'Is Arthur upstairs?'

'No, he didn't turn up. Angel was disappointed and it was a right old job to get her off to bed.'

'Is she asleep?'

'I haven't heard a peep out of her, so yes, I should think so.'

'I'll go and check,' Sally said, turning to hurry upstairs. There was no sign of Angel when she walked into the bedroom, both the double and single beds empty. 'Angela, where are you?'

There was a muffled cry and then the wardrobe door flew open. Her daughter came tumbling out and buried herself in Sally's arms. 'Mummy, Mummy, there was a fire and Tommy got burned!'

'I know, but it's only a small burn on his hand and he's fine now.'

'No, Mummy! I saw his bonfire from the window and it got really big. Tommy was on top of it and . . . and he fell in,' Angela sobbed.

'Of course he didn't.'

'He did! He got all burned up,' she insisted, her voice verging on hysteria.

'Come on, darling. Come with me,' Sally said, disengaging her daughter's arms to take her hand.

They went downstairs, Angel's eyes rounding with surprise when she saw Tommy sitting on the sofa. 'I . . . I thought you fell in the fire.'

'Of course I didn't, but look at me hand,' Tommy said, holding it out like a trophy.

'But . . . but you was on top of the bonfire and . . .'

'Nah, you silly sod. It was a guy that I dressed in me old clothes. You can't have a bonfire without a guy on top.'

'Mum, I found Angel in the wardrobe,' Sally admonished, 'and she was very upset.'

'I thought she was asleep,' Ruth said, flushing with guilt. She then turned to Tommy. 'Come on, lad, I think it's time you went home.'

'But what about me hand?'

'It isn't a bad burn and doesn't even need a bandage. I've rubbed some margarine on it and it'll be better in no time.'

Tommy reluctantly rose to his feet, but paused on his way out to say to Angel, 'You daft bugger. Fancy thinking I fell into me bonfire.'

Sally hated his language but held her tongue as the boy left. 'Say goodnight to Nanny,' Sally told her daughter before taking her upstairs again.

'Why didn't Daddy come home?' Angel asked as Sally tucked her into bed.

'I expect he got held up at work,' she replied, yet thinking there was more to it than that.

'But he promised to buy me some fireworks.'

'I know, darling. I'm sure he'll make it up to you,' Sally placated as she began to hum a lullaby, relieved when at last her daughter

63

settled down. Angel had been badly frightened, and Sally's anger was aimed at Tommy's parents. How could they let the boy light a bonfire without supervision?

It was fifteen minutes later when Sally crept from the room, her mother saying as soon as she walked into the kitchen, 'I had no idea that Angel was still awake. Is she all right now?'

'Yes, but I'm worried about Arthur. He was supposed to be home by seven and now it's gone ten.'

Just at that moment Arthur walked in. 'Well, well, it's about time,' Ruth drawled.

'Where have you been?' Sally asked. 'You said you'd be early and that you'd buy Angel some fireworks.'

'Did I? Sorry, I forgot.'

'I don't see how when you must have seen endless fireworks going off.'

'Look, I've got a lot on my mind. Now just leave it, will you.'

Sally was unable to believe his attitude and now watched as Arthur took a seat by the fire, gazing into the flames. It was as though his mind was elsewhere. What was he thinking about, or who? One thing was certain; he obviously didn't want to talk. 'If that's how you feel, fine. I'm going to bed.'

'Are you all right, Sal?' Ruth called.

'Yes. Goodnight, Mum,' she managed to say, aware as she left the room that Arthur was still staring into the fire.

With one foot on the stairs, Sally paused as tears filled her eyes. She and Arthur were growing further and further apart. If only Gran wasn't so ill, if only they could find a place of their own. Suddenly Sally was struck by another thought. Arthur hated living here, but he hadn't mentioned moving out for some time now. Why?

Was he going to leave her? With a sob, Sally ran upstairs feeling as though her life was falling apart.

* * *

A few minutes later Sally heard their bedroom door open and through tear-filled eyes she asked, 'Arthur, are you seeing another woman?'

'What? Of course I'm not. Whatever gave you that idea?'

Angel stirred and worried that she would wake, Sally kept her voice low. 'It isn't just work that keeps you out late. You often arrive with the smell of beer on your breath and you never mention moving out now.'

'I've got a lot on my mind and buying a house has been put on the back burner.'

'So if it isn't a woman, what is it?'

'It's to do with work and if you must know, Sal, I've been looking for a way out.'

'What! Surely you don't mean a way out of your father's firm?'

'That says it all, Sally. *His* firm. Not mine.'

'But he's your father and takes it for granted that one day the business will go to you.'

'Yes, *one day*, but he isn't yet fifty and he'll carry on running the place for at least another fifteen years. He doesn't need me, Sally. I just do deliveries, the same as the other men, and he can easily replace me.'

'I thought you liked the removals business.'

'It was all right at first. I enjoyed travelling around the country, but now it's just a daily grind and I've come to hate it.'

Sally thought about her father-in-law, a man she had grown to love. Bert, like Arthur, was a gentle giant and she knew that if Arthur made up his mind to leave the firm, he wouldn't be happy about it. 'So have you found a way out?'

'Yes, I think so,' he said, and sitting down on the side of the bed he spoke quietly. 'I told you a while ago that an old friend of mine, Joe Somerton, was back in the country. He's asked me to go into business with him and I've been looking into it. There's been a lot to sort out and we've been meeting as often as we can to discuss the details.'

'You're not thinking of going back to Australia, are you?' Sally asked worriedly.

'No, silly, the business is in England. We're going to build houses, though we won't be involved in the actual construction,' Arthur explained, then went on to tell her about their plans, from the plot of land they'd buy to the actual sale of houses and the projected profits they'd make.

To Sally it sounded plausible, but risky. Arthur sounded so enthusiastic and she hated to burst his bubble, but felt she had to voice her concerns. 'I'm not sure about this. You'd be leaving your father's firm and the security it offers. Are you sure you'd be doing the right thing?'

'Yes, after giving it a lot of thought, I'm sure, though of course I intended to mull it over with you before I gave Joe my decision. I was going to talk to you in the morning, but then you came out with this ridiculous idea that I've been seeing another woman.'

'I'm sorry, but you have to admit you've been acting strangely.'

'As I said, I've had a lot on my mind. I'll have to invest all our savings into the venture and that will mean we won't be able to buy a house for the foreseeable future.'

'That wouldn't worry me. We can stay here.'

'No, Sally, we still need a place of our own again. I know you feel that your gran needs you to look after her, but there's no reason why we can't rent a flat close by. You can look after her during the day, but in the evenings we'd be in our own home again.'

Sally refrained from pointing out that she'd already suggested they buy a house locally. 'If you use all our savings, what would we do for money?'

'Joe and I are going to pay ourselves a small wage until the houses are sold, but it'll be nothing like the money we're used to. It'll be enough to pay the rent on a small flat, but we'll need to pull our horns in.'

'It sounds like you've already made up your mind.'

'Yes, I have, but I'd like to think you're with me in this.'

Sally began to realise how lucky they had been. Arthur was well paid and they had never had to worry about money. Now, for the first time, she would have to economise. Well, she'd had a good teacher in her mother and though she had never had to resort to it, she knew how to make nourishing meals from cheap cuts of meat. Not only that, Elsie had been supportive of Bert when he had started up the removals business, and she would do the same. 'If this is what you really want to do, then yes, I'm with you.'

Sally was rewarded by the way Arthur's face lit up as he hugged her. 'I'll tell my father tomorrow, clear it with him and then tell Joe.'

When Arthur undressed and climbed into bed, Sally snuggled into his arms. There'd be no lovemaking while they remained here, but with any luck she'd shortly find the perfect flat close by.

Nine

Ruth had seen how upset Sally was and couldn't sleep that night. She lay awake, wondering what Arthur was up to, but then heard someone shouting outside in the lane, followed by a door slamming.

It was probably that lot next door, Ruth decided, closing her eyes again. The room felt clammy, airless and she wondered if there was a storm brewing. With an impatient sigh, she threw back her blankets and padded to the window to open it a little wider.

Ruth was just about to return to her bed when she heard a faint noise that sounded like muffled sobs. Puzzled, she looked up and down the lane. At first she saw nothing, but then, in the dim light from a street lamp, Ruth saw a small figure sitting on the kerb, feet in the gutter. A child! What was a child doing outside after midnight?

Careful not to make any noise, Ruth threw on her dressing gown to go out into the lane. Shocked, she saw that the small figure sitting hunched in a thin jumper was Tommy Walters, his head bent as Ruth approached. 'Tommy, what on earth are you doing out here at this time of night?'

'Me muvver chucked me out,' he said, cuffing his face with his sleeve to wipe away tears.

Ruth found herself angry. What sort of mother threw a child onto the streets? 'Why, Tommy?'

"Cos of me bonfire."

'I don't understand. That happened earlier so why wait until now to throw you out?'

His thin shoulders lifted in a shrug. 'She's had a few more bottles of cider, that's why, and she gave me a right old belting too.'

'Come on,' Ruth said, holding out her hand. 'I think it's time for you to go indoors and I'll have a few words to say to your mother.'

'No, missus!' he cried, scrambling to his feet. 'You can't do that. She'll go mad.'

'I can't leave you out here all night.'

Tommy straightened his shoulders, now saying bravely, 'I'll be all right. I'll wait until she's asleep, me dad too, and then I'll sneak back in.'

'Have you got a key?'

'Nah, of course not, but me bedroom's at the back. I can climb over the wall into the yard and then shin up the drainpipe.'

'But you might fall,' Ruth said, horrified by the danger.

'Course I won't. It's a piece of cake and I've done it loads of times.'

Ruth shivered, clutching her dressing gown closer to her body as she eyed Tommy's inadequate clothing. All right, the boy had lit a bonfire in their backyard, but it didn't warrant being thrown out. Despite Tommy's protests she wanted to give the woman a piece of her mind and said, 'No, you're not climbing drainpipes. Come on, we're going to knock on your door.'

'No! No, don't do that! If you do, I – I'll run away.'

Ruth could see the fear in the boy's eyes and hear it in his voice. She touched his shoulder. 'All right, but it's freezing out here so you had better come into my house for the time being.'

All might have been well, but as they stepped inside, Sadie came out of her room. In other circumstances her appearance might have been comical as she stood, her blue hairnet askew and her dressing gown gaping to reveal a long, flannelette nightdress. Toothless, and lisping, she demanded, 'Why are you bringing that hooligan in here again and at this time of night?'

'Because his mother chucked him out.'

'Yeah, well, after what he's been up to he deserves it. Now get him out of my house.'

'No, Mum. I'm not leaving him on the streets.'

'But look at the state of him. He's probably alive with fleas and as I said, I want him out of my house.'

'This isn't *your* house, Mum, it's mine, and *I'll* say who comes in and out of it.'

'Don't you dare talk to me like that!'

Ignoring the indignant look on Sadie's face, Ruth spoke to Tommy. 'Go into the kitchen and I'll find you a bite to eat.'

'What! You're going to feed the little bugger too?'

'It's all right. I don't want nuffin',' Tommy said, his eyes glistening with tears.

'Go into the kitchen,' Ruth urged again, giving him a gentle shove. When he was out of sight she turned back to her mother. 'He's only two years older than Angela and I'd like to think that if she was in trouble, someone would help her. Now go back to bed, Mum, and keep your nose out of it.'

Perhaps it was something her mother saw in her face, Ruth didn't know, but instead of arguing Sadie huffed loudly. 'Sod you then. Do what you like.'

Ruth went into the kitchen and in no time she had cut a doorstep of bread, spreading it liberally with margarine and strawberry jam. With a reassuring smile she gave it to Tommy, and wide-eyed he took it, cramming it hurriedly into his mouth as though scared it would be snatched away again. ''Cor thanks, missus. That was bleedin' lovely.'

Tommy was perched on the edge of the sofa, his face pinched with cold and Ruth's heart ached for him. She poured him a cup of milk and then sat beside him, her questions gentle. 'Do you get many beltings, Tommy?'

'Nah, most of the time I keep out of my muvver's way.'

'What about your dad?'

'He's all right. When he's had a skinful he just goes to sleep.'

Seven, he's only seven, Ruth thought, yet already he sounded so streetwise. She was about to offer him another slice of bread when she saw him sinking back into the sofa, his eyelids drooping. As he drifted off to sleep Ruth studied his face, finding that in sleep he looked so sweet and innocent.

Ruth stood up and taking her cigarette packet from the mantelpiece she lit one, taking a deep drag. There was something about Tommy that drew her to him, and seeing an old blanket on her mother's chair she gently tucked it around the child. He stirred, but didn't wake and she decided to let him stay. Sally wouldn't be happy to see him there in the morning, nor would her mother, but there was no way Ruth was going to turn the boy out to climb drainpipes in the dark.

Once again Ruth studied the boy's face and found that there was something about him that tugged at her maternal instincts. The poor kid. What a life he had, with both parents it seemed fonder of booze than their son. What sort of future did Tommy have? Not much of one, Ruth decided, but there was little she could do about it. She stubbed out her cigarette, lay down on the sofa, and tired now Ruth joined Tommy in sleep.

Sally woke the following morning and stretched, aware of sounds drifting up from the kitchen. Her mother must be up already and soon after Arthur and Angel stirred. It was Sunday morning and usually leisurely but Angel seemed anxious to go downstairs.

Unwilling to get up just yet, Sally helped her daughter into her dressing gown and let her go, but shortly after Angel was back again. 'Mummy, Daddy, come and see who slept here last night!'

Sally now threw on her dressing gown, but Arthur said, 'If we've got company I'd best get dressed first.'

Puzzled about their overnight visitor, Sally wasn't pleased to see that it was Tommy Walters. He was perched at the table, tucking into a bowl of cereal, his ragged clothes rumpled. Hissing at her mother, Sally asked, 'What's he doing here?'

'His mother chucked him out. I found him outside after midnight so I let him sleep on the sofa.'

'She threw him out! But he's only a child.'

'I know, and if you ask me Laura Walters is a bloody disgrace. She isn't fit to be a mother.'

Angel scrambled onto a chair beside Tommy, grinning as she said, 'Tommy, I knew you'd be here. I had a dream that you were living with us,' and then looking at Ruth she asked, 'Can he stay forever now, Nanny?'

'Well now, I don't know about that, ducks.'

'No, of course he can't,' Sally said and moving closer to her mother she whispered, 'I think you should report what happened to Tommy. Anything could have happened to him if he'd been left on the streets and his mother needs sorting out.'

'No, Sally, if I make waves Tommy might end up in care.'

'Yes, *care*, and that's what he'd get instead of neglect.'

'I don't want the poor kid to be shoved in a kids' home. I'll have a strong word with his mother, and I'll also keep an eye on him from now on.'

'But . . .'

'Shut up about it, Sally,' she said, then smiled at Tommy. 'Now lad, would you like some more cereal?'

'Yes please, missus,' he said with a wonky-toothed grin.

'I bleedin' well told her she shouldn't bring him in here,' Sadie said as she stepped into the room, her face set in disapproval.

Arthur appeared as well, looking surprised to see the lad, but unlike Sadie, he smiled. 'Hello, young man, and what are you doing here?'

'Me muvver chucked me out and she,' he said pointing at Ruth, 'fetched me in here.'

'She,' Arthur gently admonished, 'is Mrs Marchant. Now tell me, why did your mother throw you out?'

''Cos of me bleedin' bonfire, but it wasn't that bad and didn't set our house on fire.'

Arthur roared with laughter, obviously finding the boy amusing, but Sally's lips were pursed in an expression of disapproval. 'Don't swear, Tommy.'

'Swear? But I didn't swear.'

'Yes you did. You said, *bleeding*.'

'But that ain't swearing, and she just said it,' he protested, looking at Sadie. 'Now if I'd said fu—'

'Don't you dare!' Sally cried before the boy had time to finish. 'Where on earth did you learn such bad language?'

'Me dad says it all the time. He calls me a little bugger too.'

Arthur roared with laughter again, but Sally's smile was thin and once again she spoke quietly to her mother. 'I don't like Angel hearing this bad language. Look at her. She's drinking in every word that Tommy comes out with.'

'I know, but you've got to feel sorry for the boy,' and turning to Tommy she said, 'Come on, love. It's time you went home. I'll come with you.'

'No, no, there's no need for that,' Tommy said as he hastily stood up to make a run for the front door, calling out as though on an afterthought, 'Fanks for 'aving me.'

The door slammed, followed by silence for a few moments, and then Ruth said, 'It was nice that he thanked me. He's not such a bad kid really.'

'How can you say that, Mum? You heard his appalling language.'

'You can't blame the boy for that. He's only repeating what he hears at home.'

'I feel sorry for Tommy, but I still don't want Angel mixing with him.'

73

'Mummy, I like him,' Angel protested.

'Like him or not, I want you to stay away from him.'

'Sally, you should listen to yourself,' Ruth commented. 'You sound as snobbish as your Aunt Mary. Tommy is no different from the other kids around here.'

'I know that, and I don't want her mixing with them either.'

'Both you and Arthur grew up in Candle Lane and it didn't do you any harm. Now you act as though the place isn't good enough for you.'

'There weren't children like Tommy Walters around then.'

'Yes, there were, but you seem to have a selective memory. As for bad language, Angel has heard swearing before, and mainly from my mother, but she hasn't picked it up.'

'Here, Ruth, you swear too,' Sadie protested, 'yet Sally has a point, neither of us use the *f* word.'

'You always take her side,' Ruth complained.

'Look, the boy's gone home so can we drop the subject now,' Arthur said. 'We have something else to talk about, something we want to tell you.'

'Spit it out then,' Sadie ordered.

Sally left it to Arthur, her mother saying nothing until he came to the part about moving into a place of their own. Sally braced herself as her mother turned to look at her, saying worriedly, 'But what about your gran? Who is going to look after her?'

'I'll still come here every day. When you come home from work, you can take over and I'll go home.'

Sadie commented, 'It's about time you found your own place again, and I don't see why you'd have to come here every day. I don't need looking after any more. I keep telling you that.'

'I don't mind, Gran, and I'm going to look after you until the doctor gives you the all clear.'

'He's an old fusspot and hell might freeze over before he does that.'

'Are you trying to get rid of me?' Sally asked, trying to introduce a bit of lightness into the conversation.

'Of course not, you silly mare.'

'What's a silly mare, Gamma?' asked Angel.

'It's a funny horse, me darling.'

'Can I have one?'

Arthur picked Angel up and swung her high before putting her down again, laughing as he said, 'If you ever have a horse of your own, you won't want a silly one. Now, Sally, how about feeding me? After that I'm off to see my dad to break the news and it's not something I'm looking forward to.'

'He isn't going to like it,' Sadie observed. 'Are you sure you're doing the right thing? You've got security working for your father and it isn't something to be sniffed at.'

Sally hadn't realised how unhappy Arthur had been, and though she knew her gran was right, she was once again determined to support Arthur in his decision. She began to cook his breakfast but suddenly a cold shiver ran up her spine and her hands shook.

Something was going to happen, something terrible she was sure, and Sally's eyes shot to her gran. Was she in danger?

Ten

Arthur drove to Wimbledon wondering if he should delay telling his father. His hands were tight on the steering wheel, but he wouldn't wait, he'd get it over with, and at least this way there'd be nobody at the yard to overhear what might turn into a heated argument.

As he parked in his parents' drive, Arthur's eyes roamed over the house, appreciating why they had chosen it. The mellow red bricks added warmth to the facade and though the front garden was bleak now, he knew that in the summer it would be ablaze with his mother's favourite flowers.

Arthur rang the bell to see that his mother looked harassed. He could hear the sound of children screaming with laughter and shortly after he saw his nephews tumbling into the hall. The terrible twins, he thought, grinning. No wonder his mother looked frazzled.

Ann, his sister, chased behind them and seeing him her face lit up. 'Arthur, how lovely, but where are Sally and Angela?'

'Back in Battersea. I've only called in for a quick word with Dad,' Arthur said, thinking that after the trendy clothes she used to wear, his sister now looked almost matronly. 'If we had known you were here, Sally would have insisted on coming.'

'It's a surprise visit. Mum wasn't expecting me.'

There was an awful howl, and then Bert's loud bellow, 'Darren, Jason, stop that!'

Arthur saw that they had a hold of the cat's tail, its hackles up. They let it go and the cat hissed at them before running off. 'It would have served you right it he had scratched you,' Bert told them, but then he smiled at Arthur. 'Hello, son. What brings you here today?'

'I want to talk to you, but with this lot around I don't think there's a hope in hell.'

'We'll go to my study, and woe betide you lot,' he said with a mock frown, 'if you disturb us.'

'Surely whatever it is can wait until you've had a cup of coffee,' Elsie protested.

'Of course it can,' Arthur said, finding that now the moment had arrived he was relieved to put it off for a while.

His mother's usually immaculate sitting room was strewn with toys, but it didn't seem to bother her as she smiled happily at her grandchildren. 'What a shame that Angel isn't with you. She'd have loved to see her cousins.'

'Yes, and I'd have loved to see Sally,' Ann said. 'She's my best friend but I hardly see her these days.'

'Well, you chose to move out to the sticks, sis.'

'I know, but it wouldn't hurt you to drive her down to see us more often.'

'Give me a break. I only have Sundays off and by then I'm sick of driving.'

'It isn't that far and you know my husband can't drive.'

'Then it's about time he took lessons.'

'You drove here to see Dad.'

'Only because I need to talk to him. It isn't for pleasure.'

'Now then, you two, if you don't stop this will turn into an argument. Arthur, can I get you something to eat with your coffee?'

'No thanks, Mum. I had a big breakfast before I left.'

'How's Sadie? She didn't look too bad the last time I went to Candle Lane.'

'She's all right, except for her changeable moods. I don't know how Sally puts up with her.'

'Nor do I, but I saw in the tarot cards that things are going to change for both of you and it's imminent.'

Arthur saw that his mother was looking at him with a strange expression on her face, almost as if she knew what his plans were. He blanched. 'What sort of change did you see?'

'It wasn't clear, but I think we're about to find out. Isn't that why you've come to talk to your father?'

Unable to meet his mother's eyes, Arthur lowered his head, relieved when she left the room to make the coffee.

When Arthur looked up it was to see his father gazing at him, brow furrowed, but then the children began to squabble over a toy and chaos reigned for a while. Ann managed to sort them out, but then the baby woke up, squalling in her carry-cot.

'Arthur, bring your coffee to my study,' Bert said brusquely when Elsie carried it in. 'We might as well have this talk now and perhaps by the time we're finished this lot will have quietened down again.'

The small study was at the back of the house and as his father settled behind his desk, he indicated the chair that sat in front of it. 'Right son, what did you want to talk to me about?'

'I . . . I'm leaving the firm. I want to strike out on my own and I've been given a great opportunity to take on a partnership with an old friend of mine.'

'But you're already in partnership with me!'

'It isn't official, Dad, and in reality I'm no different from the other men you employ.'

'What do you mean, no different? You're my son!'

'Dad, I'm sorry, but I'm fed up with it – fed up with lugging furniture around every day, along with being on the road all the time.'

'We're a removals firm, Arthur. That's what we do.'

'Yes, but it's *your* firm, one *you* built up and I had little hand in it. I want to achieve something for myself, something I can be proud of.'

'I see, and just what do you intend to do?'

'I'm going into the construction game,' Arthur told him, knowing that he'd have to repeat everything he'd said to Sally. 'Joe Somerton will be my partner and we're buying a plot of land. We'll be building houses for first-time buyers.'

'But you know nothing about the building game.'

'Joe and I won't be involved with the actual construction, we've got a builder on board for that. We'll be the project managers and it will be up to us to market the houses.'

'But if they don't sell, all you'll be left with is a pile of debt.'

'They will, Dad. We've looked at this from every angle and the market is out there. Things are changing, and instead of renting, young couples are looking to get onto the property ladder. The time is ripe for this.'

'It all sounds too risky to me. Have you forgotten that you've got a wife and child to support?'

'Of course I haven't, but Sally is with me on this.'

His father pursed his lips, but then the questions came, one after another. 'I see, but what about this friend of yours? You're talking about going into partnership with him, so have you checked him out? How much is he putting into the venture? Is it an equal amount?'

'Joe is a great bloke and he's risking far more money than me. He's putting in the lion's share.'

'Where did he get the money from? Has he borrowed it, because if so, once the partnership is drawn up you'll be responsible for half of the debt. Has *he* got any experience of the building game?'

Arthur was getting fed up with this interrogation, but nevertheless he managed to keep his tone even. 'Joe inherited money

79

from his grandparents, and no, having been brought up on a farm, he hasn't had much experience.'

'A farm! Christ, son, this just sounds worse and worse. Your only experience is in doing removals and Joe is a carrot cruncher, a farm boy. What do the pair of you know about running a business?'

'Dad, you started yours in virtually the same boat with no idea if it would succeed. You uprooted us to live in Battersea and sank every penny you had into the venture. It worked for you, so why shouldn't it work for me?'

'At least I'd worked in removals and knew the game back to front.'

'What we don't know, we'll learn, and that will stand us in good stead for the next lot of houses we build. It's what I want to do, Dad, and I'm sorry, but I've made up my mind.'

'Yes, I can see that, but I need a bit of time to take this in. Go back to the sitting room and I'll join you in a minute.'

Arthur knew his father was trying to hide his true feelings and felt awful as he sadly left the study.

When Arthur went into the sitting room it was to see Ann nursing her baby daughter. The boys were absorbed with crayons, drawing quietly, and as he met his mother's eyes she said, 'What have you done, son?'

'I told Dad I'm leaving the firm.'

'How did he take it?'

'Not very well.'

'Why are you leaving?'

Arthur perched on the arm of his mother's chair to explain his reasons, ending with, 'I have to try this, Mum. I just can't let this opportunity pass me by.'

His mother sighed, whilst Ann said nothing, though her eyes were wide in surprise. 'I saw changes in the cards,' his mother said at last, 'but somehow I wasn't expecting this.'

'Mum, I think it might be for the best if I go now. Dad said he needs time to take it in, and no doubt you do too.'

'Yes, you're probably right. I just hope it all works out well for you, darling.'

Arthur hugged his mother and his sister, but his father remained in the study and all he could do was to call out goodbye. When there was no reply, he left with a heavy heart, flinging himself into the car and gunning the engine to life.

As he drove off, Arthur couldn't get the hurt he'd seen in his father's eyes out of his mind and found himself on autopilot as he sped down West Hill. Had he done the right thing? Was this venture too risky? Should he please his father and stay with his removals firm? No, no, he needed a change, needed to venture out and achieve something for himself.

With his mind all over the place, Arthur hadn't seen the traffic lights turn to red nor had he realised that he'd jumped them until he heard the screech of tyres. He swiftly turned his head, just in time to see the lorry almost on top of him. Unable to react, his eyes wide with horror, he felt the lorry hit his car with a deafening thud.

Arthur was thrown violently sideways, his body slamming against the door as the car slewed across the road. There was more deafening noise and then he became aware of pain. Agonising pain. He screamed, but then mercifully there was nothing but blackness.

Eleven

Tommy had been unable to get into his house that morning, so he shinned the drainpipe to find his parents still in bed, snoring loudly and the bedroom stinking like a brewery. His stomach was still pleasantly full and he smiled at the memory of waking up to find Ruth asleep beside him. He envied Angela. Her house was nice and he wished Ruth was his nanny too. She had taken care of his hand when he had burnt it, and then taken him in again when he'd been chucked out. Angela's mum was all right too, though a bit stuck up, but he wasn't keen on that grumpy old woman, Sadie. She was a right misery guts.

When Tommy went downstairs it was to find the usual chaos, the kitchen a mess with empty bottles of cider on the table along with an overflowing ashtray. Tommy found himself wanting to make it look nicer and started to tidy up, stuffing the bottles into the bin.

'Now there's a good boy.'

He spun round to see his mother, face puffy and bleary-eyed, yet she was smiling. It seemed she had no memory of chucking him out, and relieved he said, 'I thought I'd clear the place up a bit.'

'Were all those bottles empty?'

'Yeah.'

She moved to the sink, poured herself a cup of water and drank it greedily before plonking her bottom on one of the rickety kitchen chairs. She then lit a roll-up, picked a speck of tobacco from her lip before beckoning him towards her. 'It's good to see that you've tidied the place up a bit. Come and give me a cuddle.'

Tommy scrambled onto his mother's lap, savouring this rare moment. He treasured the occasions when his mum was sober, and despite having a skinful last night she seemed to be in a good mood. When his mum stroked his hair, Tommy snuggled into her, wishing it could always be like this.

'I ain't much of a mother, but I do love you. I know I've got to stop this boozing and I will, you'll see.'

Tommy had heard it all before and knew it wouldn't happen, content for now just to feel his mother holding him. If his mates could see him sitting on her lap they'd call him a cissie, yet right now Tommy didn't care.

At one o'clock Sally was humming as she finished peeling the potatoes, smiling at the antics of her daughter sitting perched on a cushion at the kitchen table and playing cards with Sadie. It was lovely to see her gran in such a good mood, happy to amuse Angel, though Sally wasn't sure how long it would last.

'Snap!' Angel yelled, giggling as she grabbed the cards.

'Gawd, you're too good for me,' Sadie said, holding up her hands in defeat.

'Play again, Gamma?'

'All right, though just one more game.'

Ruth looked up from basting the roast lamb, her face pink from the heat of the oven. 'Do you think Arthur's going to be home in time for dinner?'

'He left before eleven so should be back in plenty of time. Would you like me to peel some parsnips?'

'Yuk, no, Mummy!'

Sally grinned. Angel hated parsnips, but Sadie smacked her lips, her reply an affirmative. She set to the task, her mind now on Arthur again. He'd sounded so excited, but should she have tried to talk him out of it? He was sinking so much money into this new business, in fact every penny they'd saved over the last five years. What if it all went pear-shaped?

'No more now, Angel. I'm fair worn out,' Sadie complained.

'Gamma doesn't want to play, Mummy. Can I go out?'

'No you can't.'

'Pleeease, Mummy.'

'I said, *no*.'

'Half an hour won't hurt, Sally.'

'Gran, the last time I let her play outside she went off with Tommy and his gang.'

'She won't do that again, will you, sweetheart?' Sadie said winking at Angel.

'No, I'll stay by the door.'

'See, she's learned her lesson. Let her go out for a while, Sally. She'll be fine and it can't be a lot of fun for her to be stuck in here.'

Sally sighed heavily as her mother joined in, also taking Angel's side. 'Go on, Sal, let her go out for a while.'

If the backyard wasn't so full of junk, Angel could play out there, but her mother was a hoarder, the yard and every cupboard in the house stuffed with things that would never be used. Now that the decision had been made to live in a place of their own again, Sally found herself itching to find a flat, hopefully one with a garden for Angel to play in.

'Please, Mummy,' Angel appealed again.

'All right, but for half an hour and no more. And woe betide you, my girl, if you leave the front of the house.'

'Yippee!' Angel yelled as she made to run outside, coming to an abrupt halt when Sally grabbed her.

'Put your coat on,' she demanded. A scarf was then tucked around her daughter's neck, followed by a bobble hat, and when she was wrapped up to Sally's satisfaction she let her go, watching as Angel grabbed her skipping rope before flying out of the door.

'You mollycoddle that child,' Sadie said.

'It's freezing outside.'

'Blimey, when I was a kid we were lucky if we had shoes on our feet, let alone hats and scarves.'

'Yes, well, that was a long time ago. I don't want Angel to catch a cold.'

'See, mollycoddling her,' Sadie murmured.

Sally closed her eyes in exasperation, but kept her mouth shut. She had learned that it was pointless to contradict her grandmother.

It was an hour before Sally called Angel inside, her mind elsewhere as she ignored her daughter's protests. Dinner would be ready soon and there was still no sign of Arthur. She glanced along the lane, hoping to see his car, and then decided to ring Elsie to see if he was still in Wimbledon.

When they had first moved back to Candle Lane Arthur had insisted on paying to have a telephone installed, and now she thankfully reached for the receiver. It was a luxury few other families in the lane had, but one that acted as a lifeline should Sadie be taken ill again.

Sally replaced the receiver, frowning. Elsie said that Arthur had left them at twelve-thirty, so where was he? Her frown then turned to an expression of annoyance. Had he gone off to see his friend again? If so he could have at least rung to let her know. God, he drove her mad sometimes. There was a knock on the door, and composing herself she opened it, her complexion paling when she saw a police constable on the doorstep.

He didn't need to speak, didn't need to tell her, she just knew. Something awful had happened to Arthur! The hall spun, strange pinpricks of light floated before her eyes, and then her knees caved under her.

Sally became aware that the policeman had prevented her from falling, his arms holding her up, but she felt light-headed. The kitchen door then opened, Angel appearing on the threshold, her eyes wide as she took in the scene.

'Nanny, Nanny, there's a policeman!'

'What's going on?' Ruth cried.

'She took one look at me and her legs went,' the constable told her.

With the man's help, Sally was able to stagger to a chair, her heart thumping. She had been living in dread; feared something awful was going to happen, but not this, not Arthur!

For a moment the policeman just looked at her, but then he cleared his throat. 'Are you Mrs Jones?'

'Ye . . . yes,' Sally croaked.

'I'm afraid your husband has been injured in a traffic accident.'

'Oh no, no! Arthur's been hurt? How . . . how badly?'

'He's been taken to hospital, but I'm afraid I don't know the extent of his injuries.'

Sally sprang to her feet. 'What hospital has he been taken to?'

Sally sat by Arthur's side, thankful that the news hadn't been worse, thankful that he was still alive, yet worried too that he was still unconscious.

'Why won't he wake up, Sally?' asked Elsie who had rushed over to the hospital as soon as she'd heard the news.

'I don't know, but I wish the doctor would get a move on.'

'Surely it shouldn't take this long to look at Arthur's X-ray results,' Elsie complained, both looking up expectantly as the curtains drew back.

It wasn't the doctor; it was Bert, his face grey. 'Hasn't Arthur come round yet?'

'No,' Elsie told him. 'And if that bloody doctor doesn't come back soon, I'll find him myself.'

'I wish I could get out of here. I hate hospitals,' Bert growled.

Elsie said crossly, 'Look, I know you've got a phobia about them, but that's our son lying there.'

'Yes, sorry, love. I'll try to pull myself together. I just can't work out how this happened. Arthur's a good driver and I intend to find out how he got hit by a lorry.'

A nurse appeared, her stiffly starched, white apron rustling as she took Arthur's blood pressure. 'There really shouldn't be three of you in here,' she murmured.

Bert ran a hand through his hair, his voice echoing their frustration. 'Look, we've been here for an hour now and still don't know the extent of my son's injuries.'

'The doctor will be here shortly,' was the nurse's only comment, as she picked up Arthur's notes from a clipboard at the end of the bed, and wrote down his blood pressure results.

Bert was about to speak again, but then the doctor arrived, motioning to them to step outside. He spoke quietly, his eyes on Sally. 'I've made arrangements for your husband to be admitted to an orthopaedic ward. The porters will be here shortly to move him.'

'Is . . . is he going to be all right?' Sally croaked.

'We're concerned that he hasn't regained consciousness, but the X-ray results only show a hairline fracture to his skull. There are no symptoms of compression and his pupils are equal. His leg is badly damaged with a fracture to the tibia, and fibula. There is also a nasty flesh wound near his ankle.'

Sally hardly took in one word, gasping again, 'Yes, but is he going to be all right?'

'Your husband will be closely monitored to make sure there are no signs of pressure to the brain. However, as I said, the X-ray results show no indication of compression.'

'And if there is pressure on the brain?' Bert now asked.

The doctor continued as though Bert hadn't spoken, 'Ah, here are the porters. You can follow them up to the ward.'

'Wait. What are the symptoms of compression?' Bert insisted.

Seemingly annoyed the doctor rattled off a list. 'Noisy breathing, flushed face, pulse strong and slow, pupils unequal and a high temperature. Now I understand your concern, but as I said, none of these symptoms are present.'

Elsie laid a hand on Bert's arm, saying softly, 'Calm down, love.'

'Calm! How can I be calm when my son's lying unconscious on a hospital bed?'

For another agonising hour they sat outside the ward, only allowed in one at a time for a brief glimpse of Arthur. The ward sister advised them to go home, but they refused, until finally, when Sally was by his side, Arthur opened his eyes, groaning softly.

'Nurse!' Sally cried.

Both a doctor and nurse responded. They ushered Sally away but she hovered outside the drawn curtains around Arthur's bed. When the doctor emerged with a smile on his face, Sally felt a surge of relief. So great was it that her knees gave way again and she was aware of a hand on her elbow, guiding her to the ward sister's office. Elsie and Bert came in, but with a ringing in her ears Sally was hardly aware of what was going on. At last, Bert's questions penetrated her fuddled mind. Arthur hadn't sustained any brain damage, but now they were going to operate on his leg.

'How bad is it?' Bert asked.

'The compound fracture needs immediate surgery. We wouldn't normally operate so quickly following a concussion, but I'm afraid it can't wait.'

The doctor then left and they were allowed to see Arthur. He managed to smile tiredly at them, his attention drifting shortly after the ward sister came to their side. 'I suggest you all go home,' she said. 'There's nothing you can do and he'll be going down to theatre soon. You can ring the ward for information on his condition, and then return tomorrow.'

'Can't I see him after his operation?' Sally asked as she released her grip on Arthur's hand.

'Mrs Jones, it will be very late by the time your husband returns to the ward.'

'I don't care . . . I want to stay.'

'Very well, but you will only be able to see him for a minute or two.'

Sally bent to give Arthur a kiss, but he hardly seemed aware of her presence.

Elsie too kissed her son on the cheek. 'Don't worry, son. You'll be all right,' she choked.

As Arthur was given his pre-med, all three were again asked to leave, and not knowing what else to do they made for the canteen.

'Sally, do you want a sandwich or something?' Elsie asked.

'No, I'm not hungry.'

'We could be here for hours and you need to keep up your strength. Try to eat something.'

'Later . . . maybe later.'

'I can't believe this has happened and why didn't I see something in the cards?' Elsie blurted out, her face lined with distress.

Sally gripped her hand. 'I've had a feeling for some time that something awful was going to happen. I thought it would be my grandmother not Arthur. Oh, Elsie.'

'Come on now,' Bert cajoled, 'you heard the doctor, he said Arthur's going to be fine.' This remark was followed by a wide yawn.

'Why don't you both go home?' Sally suggested. 'I can ring you as soon as there's any news.'

'What, and leave you on your own! No, we'll stay and Bert is just missing his Sunday snooze, that's all.'

'I must ring my mother and should have thought of it before,'

Sally said. 'Angel was upset when I left and as I doubt I'll be home before her bedtime, I'll be able to at least say goodnight.'

'Have you got any change for the telephone?' Bert asked.

'I didn't bring my handbag. I . . . I didn't think.'

'Oh course you didn't. Here, take this and there's a phone over there,' he indicated.

Sally spoke to Angel, reassuring her daughter that her daddy was going to be fine. Then her mother came back on the line. 'When will you be home?' she asked.

'I don't know . . . I suppose soon after Arthur returns from theatre.'

'All right, but I'd better ring work and tell them I won't be in tomorrow.'

'Why?'

'Sally, wake up. I expect you'll want to return to the hospital in the morning so you won't be able to look after your gran. It's a bloody nuisance and I'll lose a day's pay.'

Her pay, Sally thought. With all that had happened her mother was worried about a paltry few quid. She fought to quell the tide of hysterical laughter that bubbled up inside her, but found it impossible and doubled over with mirth, leaving the telephone receiver dangling by its cord.

'Come on, come and sit down,' Elsie said, rushing over to lead Sally back to her chair. 'Bert, if Ruth is still on the line, have a word with her.'

'Yeah, all right.'

'Now, Sally, what brought that on?'

'My mother,' she spluttered, hiccupping as she gained her composure. 'Arthur is in the operating theatre, yet all my mum seems worried about is money.'

'Don't take any notice of what your mum said. I'm sure she spoke without thinking and is just as worried about Arthur as we are.'

'Oh, Elsie, you always see the best in people, but my mother

90

can be very selfish at times. And what about me, laughing like that when Arthur's in the operating theatre?'

'We all react differently to stress and I'm sure it was just nervous tension that needed an outlet. As for your mother, she spent years when your father left worrying about money, and it's a hard habit to break.'

'Ken Marchant isn't my father.'

Bert came back to the table, and sitting down he reached across to take Sally's hand in his. 'I told your mother that you're all right. You are, aren't you?'

'Yes . . . thanks, Bert. Oh, how much longer will we have to wait to find out how Arthur is?'

'It's only been an hour since he went down to theatre, but if you like I'll pop up to the ward to see if there's any news.'

'We'll all go,' Elsie said firmly.

There was no news yet but the ward sister allowed them to wait in a small side room where they sat quietly, each with their own thoughts and prayers.

Another hour passed, then another, until at last, a nurse poked her head around the door. 'Mr Jones is back from theatre and sister says you can see him for a minute or two.'

All stood up quickly. 'I'm sorry, but one at a time please.'

Sally tiptoed into the ward, her face registering distress when she saw Arthur. He looked so pale! She took his hand and he briefly opened his eyes, yet it was obvious that he was hardly aware she was there. His leg was encased in plaster, but he seemed unaware of that too as his eyes closed again. She bent forward, kissing his cheek, her voice a murmur as she said, 'I love you, darling.'

After her in-laws had been to see Arthur the ward sister came out of her office, saying kindly, 'The operation went well, and he'll look a lot better in the morning.'

'Thank you,' Sally said, feeling faint with relief and, she now realised, hunger.

They were on their way home again, exhausted, yet happy to know that Arthur was going to be all right. 'I'm so tired,' Sally murmured.

'It's stress, love, but you can relax. The worst is over.'

Sally registered Elsie's words and they played a drumbeat in her mind as her eyelids drooped. Yes, the worst was over, and she thanked God for listening to her prayers.

When they arrived in Candle Lane, Sally wasn't surprised to see her Aunt Mary sitting in the kitchen, all three women looking at her expectantly as she walked into the room. Like in most families, past rows were forgotten when an emergency arose, and Sally asked, 'How did you know about the accident, Aunt Mary?'

'Your mother rang me of course. Now tell me, how is Arthur?'

Sally managed to say that he was going to be all right, but then to her surprise she found the room spinning. She swayed on her feet, Bert rushing forward to help her onto the sofa.

'She's as white as a sheet and it's probably delayed shock. I think she needs to be in bed,' Elsie said.

'Yes, and a drop of brandy wouldn't hurt,' Bert added.

The room came back into focus again, the dizziness passed, and as a cup of strong tea laced with brandy was placed in her hands, Sally began to feel better.

'I think Sally should eat something,' Elsie put in. 'She's eaten nothing, no wonder she felt faint.'

'I'll make you a sandwich,' Ruth said, bustling over to the cupboard.

It was Bert who answered their questions about the accident and Arthur's condition, but then he smiled gently at Sally. 'I'll have to go to the yard in the morning to sort out drivers and deliveries. After that I'll be down to run you to the hospital.'

'I'll be with him,' Elsie said, and after Sally assured her again that she was all right, they said their goodbyes.

Sally ate her sandwich, suddenly alert when her Aunt Mary

spoke. 'I thought for a while that I might have to change my plans, but thankfully as Arthur is going to be all right, I can go ahead.'

'With what?' Sadie asked.

'I'm going to be away for a while. I . . . I'm going on a cruise.'

'What!' Sadie spluttered. 'Have you won the pools or something?'

'No, Mother, but I have savings. I've always wanted to travel and as I'm not getting married now, or getting any younger, I felt that this is as good a time as any.'

'When are you leaving?' Ruth asked.

'In just over a week. I managed to get a late booking.'

'What? That soon! What about your job?'

'I've been allowed extended leave.'

'You jammy cow,' Ruth said sourly.

It was obvious that her mother was jealous, but Sally couldn't blame her. She doubted her mother had ever had a decent holiday, her life a hard one, but Sally was pleased for her aunt. 'I'm sure you'll have a wonderful time, Aunt Mary,' she said, 'and I'll expect a postcard from every port of call.'

'And I'll see that you get one,' Mary said, smiling warmly.

Sally was unable to stifle a yawn, tiredness washing over her again.

'Why don't you get yourself off to bed?'

'Yes, Mum, I think I will,' Sally replied, saying goodnight and going upstairs.

The bed felt empty without Arthur beside her and Sally clutched a pillow to her chest, finding that despite her exhaustion it was impossible to sleep. For an hour she tossed and turned, her mind refusing to still. She should have known that Arthur had been in an accident, should have sensed something. So much for intuition. Yet even as this thought crossed her mind she felt a shiver run up her spine again. No, no, surely there wasn't more to come?

Sally's heart was full of fear, sleep still impossible and her head began to ache as she turned onto her back. It happened then, a familiar glow appeared, something she hadn't seen since Angel's birth. The room began to glimmer with a strange but beautiful translucent light. Her friend was here, the lovely presence had come, and as the soft light began to spread, she smiled with joy.

Slowly it seemed to drift towards her, and then Sally found herself enfolded, cocooned as wonderment replaced her tormented thoughts. She closed her eyes, a smile still on her lips, and as soft fingers seemed to caress her hair, she finally drifted off to sleep.

Twelve

When Sally awoke the next morning she was smiling as she recalled her dream. She'd been flying, free as a bird, skimming low over the rooftops. The dream had been so real, so vivid that she could still feel the exhilaration coursing through her veins.

She turned over, luxuriating in the warmth of the blankets, but then little niggles of worry began to pick at her mind. Last night the spiritual presence had come, one that as a child she had called her friend. When she was upset, hurt, or worried, this friend had come to comfort her as it had last night. Since her marriage to Arthur, she no longer saw it, sensing that perhaps it had disappeared because she no longer needed it.

So why now? Why had it come back now? Suddenly frightened, Sally shivered and flung back the blankets. Had Arthur taken a turn for the worse? Without stopping to put on a dressing gown or slippers, she ran downstairs, frantically dialling the number of the hospital. Come on, come on, she thought impatiently as she waited to be put through to the ward.

'What are you doing up so early?' Sadie asked as she came out of her room.

'I could ask you the same thing,' Sally said, but then pressed the phone closer to her ear as she was finally put through. She was aware of her grandmother listening as she spoke to a nurse, and then her shoulders slumped with relief as she replaced the receiver. 'He's all right, Gran. Arthur's still all right.'

'Sally, you're shaking with the cold. Put your dressing gown on and crikey, your feet are bare. Do you want to get chilblains?'

She smiled happily at her grandmother, her footsteps light as she ran back upstairs, calling, 'I'll be back in a minute.'

In no time Sally returned to the kitchen, wrapped up warmly. She wondered again why the spiritual presence had returned. 'Are you feeling all right, Gran?'

'Yeah, I'm fine. Ain't you looked at me aura?'

Sally adjusted her eyes, studying the halo of light surrounding her grandmother. There were dark patches, but these were familiar ones caused by her arthritis. 'I think you need a bit of healing. I can see your arthritis is playing up.'

'You always know when I'm in pain and it still gives me the willies.'

Seeing nothing else to worry about, Sally was perplexed. Why had she felt there was worse to come?

She glanced at the clock, deciding to get ready before getting Angel up for school. However, at that moment there was a flurry of movement as her daughter scampered into the room, hair tousled and a worried look on her face.

'Where's my daddy?'

'He's still in hospital, darling, but don't worry, he's fine.'

'I want to see him.'

'Not today, but soon, I promise.'

'But I want to see him now!' And as Ruth walked into the room, Angel cried, 'Nanny, tell Mummy.'

'Tell Mummy what?'

'That I want to see my daddy.'

'Come here, pet.'

Angel ran to her nanny, and leaning forward Ruth gently stroked her granddaughter's cheek. 'Your daddy is a bit poorly and needs to rest. When he feels better you can go to see him, and when he comes home you can be his nurse. We'll get you a nurse's uniform. Would you like that?'

96

'Yes, Nanny, and can I give him medicine?'

'Of course you can.'

Peace reigned then, and just after Ruth left to take Angel to school, Bert and Elsie arrived. 'You're earlier than I expected,' Sally said as she opened the door.

'Elsie came to the yard with me, pestering me to get a move on. The drivers have been sorted out and the rest can take care of itself for a while. Are you ready to go?'

'I don't like to leave Gran so do you mind waiting until Mum comes back? She's just taken Angel to school and won't be long.'

'Of course we don't mind waiting. It'll give us a chance to say hello to Sadie.'

Sally took them through to the kitchen, hardly listening as they chatted to Sadie, her thoughts again on Arthur. The ward sister had said he was comfortable, but was she just being kind?

As Ruth left Candle Lane, Angel's hand gripping hers, her mind was on her sister. She envied Mary going on a cruise, but then Tommy Walters fell into step beside them, his cheeky grin in place.

'Watcha, Angel. Where's yer muvver?'

'My daddy's in hospital and she's gone to see him.'

''Ospital! Why's 'e in 'ospital?'

'He got run over.'

'No, he didn't, Angel,' Ruth said. 'Your daddy was involved in a car crash, but thankfully not a bad one.'

'Has he got broken bones?' Tommy asked, his eyes wide.

Puffing with importance, Angel said, 'Yeah, loads of them.'

'Angel, that isn't true!' Ruth protested. 'He's broken his leg, that's all.'

Tommy fixed Angel with an accusing glare. 'Gawd, you ain't 'arf an effing liar.'

'Now that's enough of that language!' Ruth snapped, cringing and hoping that Angel didn't repeat the word in front of Sally.

She hastily changed the subject. 'Do you have school dinners, Tommy?'

'Nah.'

'Have you got a packed lunch then?'

Tommy shook his head, but before she could question him further he shouted, 'Come on, Angel, race yer to the end of the lane!'

Like a flash they were off, both skidding to a halt when Ruth screeched, 'Come back here!'

She hurried towards them, crouching down to take one of Tommy's grubby hands in her own. 'If you don't have school dinners, or a packed lunch, what do you get to eat?'

'Stuff,' he said. His eyes lowered. 'I manage.'

'I always save him some of mine, Nanny.'

'Oh, is that a fact? And how do you get it out of the dinner hall?'

'I shove it in my pocket.'

'What! If you've ruined your coat your mother will do her nut,' Ruth exclaimed, pulling Angel to one side and hastily checking her pockets.

'It's all right, Nanny. I don't put any runny stuff in there.'

'She gave me her jam sponge on Friday, and even though there wasn't any jam left on it . . . it was smashing.'

Ruth sighed heavily. 'Here,' she said, taking some money out of her purse. 'This week you'll have school dinners.'

His large eyes rounded. 'Cor, fanks, missus. Blimey, I wish you was my nanny too.'

Still holding his hand, they began to walk again, and as Tommy looked up at her, Ruth's heart flipped over. Dirt and all she was still drawn to the child.

When they reached the school gates, Ruth bent to kiss Angel. 'Now, be a good girl.'

Tommy's little chest puffed, and with a look of importance he said, 'Don't worry, missus. I always look out for her.'

Unable to resist, Ruth pulled him into her arms. 'You're a good kid.'

Shooting her a look of surprise, but pink with pleasure under the grime, Tommy gave Angel a shove. 'Come on, that's the bell.'

Ruth watched the two of them as they ran into the playground, then turning she made her way home again, wishing that she could do more for Tommy.

As soon as they reached the hospital it was obvious to Sally that Sister Moody wasn't pleased to see them. She frowned as they approached, saying, 'It isn't visiting hours yet and the consultant will be arriving soon to do his rounds. We have a strict routine that must be adhered to.'

Bert, already well over six feet, towered over the woman. 'We would like to see our son, if only for a few moments.'

At first it looked like the woman would refuse, but then with an impatient nod of her head she said, 'Very well, but only for five minutes. Visiting time is between two and three in the afternoon, and between seven and eight in the evenings. If Mr Jones were in any danger there would be leniency. However his operation was successful, and in future there is no reason why you can't keep to visiting hours.'

'Thank you, Sister,' Elsie whispered as they all moved towards Arthur's bed, Bert hovering anxiously at the foot whilst Sally and Elsie took a side each.

'Hello,' Arthur said, his voice weak.

Sally forced a smile, thinking that he still looked awful and not a lot better than last night. 'Hello, darling.'

'How are you feeling, son?' Elsie asked.

'Not so bad, Mum.'

Sally focused her eyes, her vision just slightly off centre as she studied Arthur's aura. His head area still showed slight darkness, but there was an improvement. Her eyes now moved over his body, and she saw a lot of darkness around his leg that worried her.

There was a slight groan as Arthur tried to adjust his position in the bed and, determined to show a cheerful face, Sally said, 'That'll teach you to argue with a ten-ton truck.'

'Yes, you were lucky to get off so lightly,' Bert said, now moving to stand next to Elsie. 'How did it happen? The lorry driver says you jumped a red light. Is that true?'

'To be honest, Dad, I can't remember. I was driving down West Hill, but other than that my mind's a blank. Is the other driver all right and what's happened to my car?'

'He's fine, but I'm afraid your car is a write-off.'

The ward sister approached the bed, her white starched cap as stiff as her body as she said firmly, 'You'll have to leave now. Mr Hardcastle has arrived to do his rounds.'

'Mr Hardcastle?' Bert queried.

'The surgeon who operated on your son's leg.'

'I'd like a word with him please.'

'I'm afraid that won't be possible at the moment.'

'Huh, we'll see about that,' Bert said, then marching down the ward to the surgeon.

Sally turned back to Arthur, grasping his hand. He smiled wanly, but his eyelids were beginning to droop. Their visit was obviously exhausting him.

'You really must go now,' the ward sister insisted a few minutes later. 'Your husband needs to rest.'

Sally bent to kiss Arthur, finding his lips unnaturally dry, but then Bert returned to say goodbye too and soon they were leaving the ward.

'What did Mr Hardcastle say?' Elsie asked.

'He said it would be some time before Arthur will be able to use his leg.'

'Some time! What does that mean? Weeks? Months?'

'He couldn't say for sure. It depends on how well the injuries heal.'

'Oh, dear,' Sally gasped.

'Now then,' Bert cajoled. 'Last night we were worried that Arthur might have brain damage, so let's count our blessings. His leg is broken, but it'll get better, even if it takes a while. Let's look on the bright side.'

'Yes, you're right, love,' Elsie said. 'What do you say, Sally?'

'I was so worried last night, but feel reassured today. He was hit by a lorry, shoved yards along the road, his car is a write-off, yet all he sustained is a couple of fractures.'

'Someone up there must have been looking after him,' Elsie commented.

For a moment Sally's steps faltered as she found herself thinking about the spiritual presence again. Why had it come to comfort her? Stop worrying, she told herself, and as Bert said, count your blessings. Arthur was going to be fine, and that's all that mattered.

Thirteen

If only the hospital was nearby, Sally thought as she once again prepared to visit Arthur. Just over a week had passed since his accident, her aunt had left for her cruise, and unable to leave her gran, she could only visit Arthur in the evenings. A few of the neighbours had offered to sit with Gran, one being Nelly Cox, but Sadie would have none of it, saying she didn't need a babysitter. With no other choice, Sally wouldn't leave her gran, but Elsie went to see Arthur every afternoon.

Sally had been to the hall to tell the other healers that she wouldn't be able to join them for a while, gratified when they offered to put out absent healing for Arthur. She had assured them that he wasn't in any danger and was recovering well, adding that she would be back to join them as soon as possible.

It was nearly time to leave and she dreaded the journey, the buses few and far between, but maybe Arthur would be able to come home soon. She heard a knock at the door, but left her mother to answer it as she grabbed her shoes before making her way downstairs, surprised to see a man on the doorstep.

'Sally, this man says he's a friend of Arthur's.'

'Hello,' she said hesitantly, struggling to see the man in the dim light.

'My name is Joe Somerton. Could I have a word with your husband?'

'Joe! The Joe that Arthur met in Australia?'

'Yes, that's me.'

'You'd better come in,' Sally said, and as he stepped into the light she saw that he was a handsome man with blond hair above chiselled features. 'I'm afraid Arthur had an accident in his car and he's in hospital.'

'Strewth! I wondered why he hadn't been in touch, but didn't expect this. Is he all right?'

'He's got a badly damaged leg, but he's on the mend.'

'Would it be all right if I visit him?'

'I don't see why not. As a matter of fact I'm just on my way to the hospital now.'

'May I join you?'

'Err . . . yes, I suppose so. I get a bus at the end of the lane and then change at Clapham Junction.'

'I have my car and can drive you.'

'Oh, wonderful, it will save us so much time.'

Angel came running into the hall. 'Mummy, can I come to see Daddy too?'

'Not tonight, darling, but I'll take you on Sunday.'

'But I want to see my daddy!'

'Come on, Angel. Come with Nanny,' Ruth said. 'I think we might find some sweeties in my handbag.'

'Thanks, Mum,' Sally mouthed as a placated Angel ran back to the kitchen. She then followed Joe outside to his car, glad for the lift.

'She's a little beauty,' he commented, unlocking the passenger door.

Sally climbed into the Jaguar, admiring the leather upholstery and walnut dashboard. As Joe climbed in beside her she said, 'Yes, it is a lovely car.'

He laughed, a deep, pleasant, rumbling sound. 'I was talking about your little girl.'

They drove to Putney, talking mainly about Arthur, and as they walked into the ward he managed to smile brightly.

'Joe, great to see you. I guessed you might wonder where I'd got to and was going to ask Sally to ring you tonight.'

'I pipped you at the post then. How's the leg?'

'Not too bad.'

'How did it happen?'

'I'd made up my mind to go into business with you and went to tell my father. Unfortunately, on the way back it seems I tangled with a lorry, but to be honest I can't remember much about it. It seems there were no witnesses, so it's probably down to the insurance people to sort it out.'

'At least you're all right, and its great that you're coming in with me.'

Arthur frowned. 'I could be laid up for some time, Joe. It might be better if you find another partner.'

'If you haven't changed your mind, there's no need for that. I can carry on without you for a while and once you're up and about you can get involved. I've also got a bit of good news.'

'You've found some land?' Arthur asked, his eyes lighting up with enthusiasm.

'Yup, and it's going for a fair price. It's just outside Reading, in Berkshire, ideal for commuting to London, and once the deal's been finalised we can get to work.'

'What about planning permission?'

'The outline permission is in place, but a lot will depend on our architect's drawings. I've an appointment to see the planning officer tomorrow.'

'Good luck, mate.'

Feeling like an appendage, Sally settled down beside Arthur, listening as they discussed the project until at last Joe said, 'Sorry, Sally, I seem to be taking all of Arthur's time.'

'That's all right,' she said graciously as Arthur took her hand and squeezed it gently.

'I'll come to see you again as soon as there's any news, Arthur, but now I think I'll leave you two lovebirds alone. I'll wait outside to run you home, Sally.'

'Thank you.'

'Bye for now, Arthur.'

'See ya, mate.'

They both watched Joe leaving the ward and then Arthur asked, 'Well, what do you think of him?'

'He seems nice.'

'He's a good bloke, and I'm relieved that he still wants me to go into the partnership. I just hope I'm out of here soon.'

'You will be,' she said, and after talking for a while longer, the bell sounded to signal the end of visiting time. Reluctantly Sally stood up. 'I'll see you tomorrow, love. Is there anything you need?'

'How about a kiss?'

Sally leaned across the bed, and as she kissed Arthur there was the sound of wolf whistles from several beds. Arthur grinned, enjoying the camaraderie. 'None of us in this ward are ill, it's mostly broken bones so we have a few laughs.' He then turned away from her, shouting, 'Shut up you lot. You're just jealous.'

Pink with embarrassment Sally hurried out of the ward, with more wolf whistles accompanying her. It was lovely to see that Arthur was recovering well, and she wondered how long it would be before he could come home. It couldn't come soon enough for Sally.

Fourteen

On a Saturday morning, with Christmas only a few weeks away and her mother finding an excuse to take the day off work, Sally had taken the opportunity to do a bit of shopping, but as she returned to Candle Lane the sound of yelling and screaming reached her ears.

She saw a circle of women, all shouting, and as she drew nearer, Sally could see two women in the centre. She blanched. One was her mother, the other Laura Walters, both with outstretched arms and gripping each other's hair as they grappled like wrestlers.

'Mum!' she called, trying to force herself through the ring of neighbours. 'Stop it. What on earth are you doing?'

Laura Walters suddenly released Ruth's hair and with a cry of anger she raised her fist, punching her opponent full in the face.

'Ouch!' Ruth cried. 'Why . . . you . . . you,' and lunging forward she kicked out, her shoe making contact with Laura's shin.

'That's it, Ruth. You give her what for,' Nelly Cox encouraged. She then saw Sally looking at her with outrage, and smiled ruefully. 'Well, it's no more than Laura deserves. Tommy went to your mum in an awful state. He's got a black eye, and bruises all over his body.'

Sally looked around frantically, wondering where her daughter was. Her mother was supposed to be looking after her. There she was, looking out of the window, Gran beside her as they watched the spectacle.

'That's enough, Mum,' Sally shouted as Laura Walters again squared up for the fight. She was wasting her breath.

Both women lunged forward. They grappled again, panting, but then with a huge shove from Ruth, Laura Walters found herself on her back, the wind knocked out of her.

She looked up as Ruth stood over her, her stance threatening as she spat, 'If you lay a hand on that boy again you'll be sorry, you drunken slut.'

Gasping for breath Laura wasn't ready to give in. 'He's *my* son, not yours. Keep your nose out of my business.'

'I know full well he isn't my son. In fact I'm old enough to be his grandmother. You're a disgrace, Laura Walters, and you should think yourself lucky that I ain't reported you to the authorities. Mind you, I could still do it, so think on that.'

'I'm not scared of you, *or* the so-called authorities. The boy deserved a thrashing, and I gave him one.' She scrambled to her feet, her chest heaving, and pressing a hand on her heart she made for her door, ignoring the jeers of her neighbours.

Ruth looked on, her eyes still dark with anger. As the crowd began to break up, hands patted her on the back. 'Good on yer,' one said. 'She's been asking for it,' said another.

Sally turned away from the scene and with a shake of her head she left her mother to her admirers.

'Nanny was fighting, Mummy,' Angel said, scrambling from her vantage point at the window.

'I know.'

'No doubt your mother will bring the kid in here now. For some reason she seems to be getting overly fond of that boy. When you're at the hospital she often has him in here for a bite to eat,' Sadie said.

'This is the first I've heard of it.'

'Yeah, well, I kept my mouth shut. You've got enough on your plate at the moment with Arthur.'

Ruth came in then, the boy with her. Crouching in front of him she said, 'Now then, Tommy, if your mother touches you again I want you to tell me.'

Tommy nodded, his eyes wide, and Ruth added, 'I don't think it's safe for you to go home yet. You'd best stay here for a while.'

Sally opened her mouth to protest, but the look her mother gave her was ferocious. Instead she said, 'Come on, Angel. Let's get you ready for the hospital. Daddy will be looking forward to seeing you.'

Angel followed her upstairs without demur and, as Sally bathed her daughter, she wondered what it was with her mother and Tommy Walters? She had never seen her involved in a street fight before. Her mother had been like a lioness protecting her cub.

Sally let go of Angel's hand as they went into the ward, her daughter running ahead to Arthur's bed while Sally smiled at the other patients as she passed them. They were nearly all young men and, though suffering broken bones, they weren't ill. The ward was a lively place, with jokes flying around, and goodness knows how some of the young nurses coped.

'Daddy's poorly,' Angel said as she walked to Arthur's side.

'Hello, love,' Arthur said, his usually bright greeting sounding weak.

'You look a little flushed. Are you feeling all right?'

'Not really and I'm hot.'

Sally focused on Arthur's aura and was immediately worried by what she saw. There was a huge patch of darkness around his lower leg and moving to the bottom of the bed her eyes were drawn to his foot where it stuck out from the plaster. Sally wasn't looking at his aura now; she was looking at the strange blisters that had formed over his toes. They were almost black, as though filled with blood, and she stared at them worriedly. 'Arthur, has anyone said anything about these blisters on your foot?'

'No, but my leg has been feeling uncomfortable since you left yesterday.'

'Angela, wait here. I'm just going to have a word with Sister Moody,' Sally said, then hurrying to the office.

The woman looked a little annoyed when Sally barged in without knocking, but after listening to her blurted explanation, Sister Moody rose to her feet.

'Black blisters, you say,' she said sharply. 'I'll come and have a look.'

From the moment Sister Moody saw Arthur's foot, panic seemed to set in. She almost ran back to her office and in what seemed like seconds, a doctor appeared.

'What's going on?' Sally demanded as the curtains were hurriedly drawn around Arthur's bed.

'Your husband has developed an infection,' Dr Willis said, and then immediately instructed the sister to give Arthur what, to Sally's ears, sounded like a dose of penicillin. 'We'll get this plaster removed and then he'll have to be put in an isolation ward.'

'Isolation! But . . .' Sally gasped.

'If you wait outside, I'll see that someone talks to you as soon as possible,' the doctor said dismissively, and at his words a nurse came to Sally's side, leading her and Angel from the ward.

They sat on hard wooden chairs, Angel confused and Sally doing her best to reassure her. She was very relieved and felt less alone when Elsie turned up to visit Arthur, but had only just told her about the infection when porters wheeled him out of the ward. Sally saw panic in Arthur's eyes and rushed forward. 'Wait, where are you taking him?'

'It's all right, Mrs Jones. We're just taking your husband to have his plaster removed,' a nurse said. 'Sister Moody is coming to have a word with you.'

Sally didn't know what to do. Should they follow Arthur?

Should they wait for the sister? The decision was taken out of her hands when Sister Moody appeared, indicating that she should come into the office, though she insisted that Angela should remain outside with Elsie.

'Mrs Jones, as the doctor told you, your husband has developed a very nasty infection.'

'What sort of infection?'

'He has developed what is commonly called, gas gangrene.'

'No . . . Oh no!' Sally cried. Oh, God, Arthur!

'Your husband will be put in a side room, given antibiotics to treat the condition, and of course analgesics for the pain.'

'Will . . . will he be all right?'

'We've caught the condition early so the prognosis is good, but now I suggest you go home.'

'Home! But I want to see him.'

'Very well, but you will have to wear a surgical mask at all times, and I'm afraid you will be the only one allowed to visit him for the time being.'

'But his mother is here . . . and my daughter, she will want to see her daddy.'

'I'm sorry. I'm afraid not.'

Sally slumped in the chair, the full impact and seriousness of Arthur's condition sinking in. She felt sick; she was going to be sick, and hand over her mouth Sally fled to the toilets.

Everything had happened so quickly that Arthur's mind refused to function. One minute he was in the ward, Angel and Sally were visiting, and the next it seemed that all hell had broken loose.

He lifted his head as the plaster was removed, and gagged. God, the stench! What had been a flesh wound now resembled a huge hole, one that he could fit his fist into. Arthur grew more anxious. He'd seen other patients in the ward with broken legs, many of whom had recovered enough to go home, and until this moment he'd expected to do the same. 'Doctor, just what sort of infection is this?'

'Don't worry, Mr Jones,' he replied without really answering the question. 'We'll soon sort you out.'

Arthur was given a local anaesthetic, and soon they began to tend the wound. The process took a long time and after they'd finally finished, the doctor said, 'Right, young man. We'll put a new plaster on now, this time with a lift-up flap over the wound.'

Instead of being wheeled back to the ward, Arthur was put in a side room. He wanted to know what was going on and was determined to ask questions, but then his usual doctor came in with a new nurse and Arthur noted that both were wearing masks.

'Mr Jones, this is Nurse Trimble and she'll be looking after you.'

'Why are you wearing masks?'

'You have gangrene in your wound, Mr Jones. It's been caught early and should respond to treatment. However, until then you have to be kept in sterile conditions. Now your wife is waiting outside to see you, but for the time being you won't be allowed to see any other visitors.'

Arthur had more questions, but then the nurse opened the door to beckon Sally in, saying as she appeared, 'I'm sorry, Mrs Jones, but I'm afraid you can only stay for five minutes.'

Though wearing a mask too, Arthur could see the anxiety in his wife's eyes as she approached the bed, her voice sounding muffled as she said, 'Oh, Arthur, are you all right?'

He made a supreme effort, saying, 'Yes, I'm fine, but get that mask off so I can give you a kiss.'

'Now then, Mr Jones, you know that isn't allowed,' Nurse Trimble said. 'In fact, no contact at all please.'

'It was worth a try,' he replied, forcing a grin.

As the doctor left the room Arthur was struck by a thought. 'Sally, where's Angel?'

'She's outside with your mother and as you can imagine, playing up because she can't see you. Your mother sends her love.'

'I'm sorry, Mrs Jones, but I must ask you to leave now,' Nurse Trimble said, 'and for the time being, would you please restrict your visits to one a day for half an hour.'

Blimey, Arthur thought, thinking that Nurse Trimble reminded him of one of his old school teachers. He half-expected Sally to reply with a 'Yes, Miss' but instead she just nodded, her eyes clouded with worry.

'I'll leave you to say your goodbyes,' the nurse said brusquely, at last leaving the room.

'Sally, don't worry, I'll be fine,' Arthur said, once again forcing a cheery note into his voice.

Sally reached out to touch him, but then remembering that she wasn't allowed, snatched her hand back. 'Oh, Arthur.'

'I know, love, but just make sure that when I get out of here you've found us a flat to move into,' he said with a cheeky wink, 'we've got a lot of time to make up for.'

'Yes, we have and I've started looking already.'

The door opened, Nurse Trimble back again. 'Bye, Sally, see you tomorrow,' Arthur said, trying not to sound too despondent.

'Bye, darling,' she whispered, and then with a small wave she was gone.

It hadn't been easy to keep up the pretence and a wave of exhaustion washed over Arthur. Gangrene! He had gangrene, and in truth he was quaking with fear.

Sally found herself shaking on the journey home, thankful that Elsie was there to give them a lift. The dreaded word gangrene kept going around in her mind, and it was all she could do to placate Angela. The child was still upset and she had now become petulant. 'Angela, that's enough. You can't see him for a while and there's nothing I can do about it.'

'Sally, I can understand how she feels,' Elsie said. 'I'm his mother and I wasn't allowed to see him either.'

'I know, and I'm sorry. I shouldn't have snapped at her, but I'm worried sick about Arthur.'

'Why, Mummy?'

Sally felt a wave of despair as she struggled to find the right words. 'He's got a bad headache, darling, and he needs quiet until it gets better.'

Angel settled down at last and soothed by the motion of the car she was fast asleep by the time they arrived in Candle Lane. Sally lifted her daughter gently from the car, and with Elsie's help she managed to put Angel onto Gran's bed downstairs. When they walked into the kitchen, their faces must have said it all.

'Sally, Elsie, what's the matter?' Ruth cried. 'Your faces are like lint!'

Sally broke, all her pent-up fears and anxieties rising to the surface and tears spurting from her eyes. 'Oh, Mum, Arthur's got gangrene.'

'No!' Ruth gasped.

'Stone the crows!' Sadie said. 'They'll have to take his leg off.'

'Don't say that!' Elsie begged.

'Well, you might as well face it now as later. Lots of blokes lost their limbs to gangrene during the war. It's inevitable.'

'No, it isn't,' Sally protested. 'The ward sister said that Arthur should respond to treatment.'

'Huh, who's she kidding?'

'She may be right, Mum,' Ruth said.

'Poppycock! I've told you once you get gangrene they take your leg off. It's the only way to stop it spreading.'

Sally couldn't bear it. Her gran had to be wrong . . . she just had to. 'Stop it, Gran! Stop talking as though it's a foregone conclusion. The doctor didn't mention amputation. Medical science has come a long way since the war, and Arthur is going to get better. I just know he is.'

'All right, love, I'm sorry and now calm down. Ruth, make a pot of tea. Elsie looks like she could do with a cuppa too.'

Sally laughed then, but it was hysterical laughter. Tea! Her mum and gran's cure all for everything. Oh, if only life was as simple as that.

Fifteen

Ruth made a decision on Monday and was relieved when her boss agreed to her request. If he hadn't she may have had to pack the job in, but it seemed he was happy to employ a Saturday girl to take her place. She'd miss the day's pay, but with Arthur in danger of losing his leg, Sally would have the weekend free to spend more time with him.

It came as no surprise to see that Tommy was hanging around outside when she arrived home from work. At least he looked a little more nourished now and uncaring of what his mother might say, Ruth would continue to feed him up. As usual Tommy was inadequately dressed, but during her lunch break she had been on a little shopping trip.

'Hello, missus,' he said, his nose blue with the cold.

As always Ruth's heart went out to him. 'Hello, love. I've got something for you,' she said, pulling the grey, hooded, duffel coat from the bag. 'Here, this will keep you nice and warm.'

'For me? It's for me?'

'Yes, love, and though it isn't brand new there's hardly a mark on it.'

'Cor, fanks!' he cried, hurriedly putting it on and then flinging his arms around Ruth.

She held him for a moment, fighting tears. It was just a coat and hadn't cost much from the second-hand shop, but Tommy was acting as if she'd given him a pot of gold. The difference between Tommy and Angel was marked. Angel had always been able to take it for granted that she would be fed and kept warm, whereas Tommy had to learn to survive with barely any parental care. Not that Ruth begrudged Angel her comforts, and though spoiled, her granddaughter had a sensitive side to her. Gently, Ruth pushed Tommy back. 'Sorry, love, I've got to go in, but come back around seven and I'll give you a bite to eat.'

He nodded, looking up at her for a moment before running off. 'I'm gonna show me mates me coat.'

Ruth was still smiling as she went indoors, and said straight-away, 'I've had a word with my boss, Sally, and from now on I'll be home on Saturdays. It'll give you more time with Arthur.'

'Mum, I'm only allowed to visit him for half an hour.'

'You didn't tell me that.'

'Didn't I? I'm sorry, Mum, with all the worry I didn't realise.'

'Never mind, love, it'll be nice to have my weekends off, so no harm done.'

'Nanny, have you got any sweets for me?' Angel said, running up to her.

'Not tonight, pet.'

'Blimey, that makes a change,' Sadie commented.

Ruth saw that Angel looked disappointed, but the child didn't go short, which was more than you could say for Tommy. 'I'll buy you some tomorrow,' she said.

The telephone rang and Sally went to answer it, while Ruth kicked off her shoes and rubbed her toes, hoping that a pot of tea was ready. Sally had already got the dinner on and the aroma of lamb stew filled the room, making Ruth's mouth water. 'That smells good.'

'Yeah, she's learning how to cook cheap but nourishing meals. I told her to add lots of pearl barley.'

Sally was soon back, saying as she walked in, 'That was Joe Somerton. He wanted to visit Arthur, but I had to put him off.

He was disappointed, but said he had some good news. Apparently they've got planning permission for the site.'

Frowning, Ruth said, 'I can't see Arthur up to working for some time yet, and if he loses his . . .'

'Mum,' Sally warned, nodding at Angela.

'Blimey, I nearly put my foot in it,' Ruth said, and hoping to distract the child she added, 'Go into Gamma's room and find the cards, Angel. After dinner I'll give you a game of snap.'

Angel ran out of the room and at the same time there was a knock on the door. Ruth answered it and Nelly Cox said, 'Can I have a word with Sally?'

'Yeah, come on in.'

'Hello, Sadie, how are you doing?' Nelly asked as she walked ahead of Ruth into the kitchen.

'I'm fine, Nelly. Why shouldn't I be?'

'I only asked,' she said, then turning to Sally, 'Are you still looking for a flat?'

'Yes, but with all that's happened to Arthur I'm afraid I've been too preoccupied to put much effort into it.'

'Right then,' Nelly said. 'I've heard of a flat going in Maple Terrace. Ted Johnson, the tobacconist, bought a house there recently, one divided into maisonettes and he's done them both up.'

Ruth bit her lip. If this flat came off, she'd miss them.

'Mind you,' Nelly continued. 'I can't see them hanging round for long so if you fancy one you'd better get yourself off to see Mr Johnson. He doesn't usually close up until seven.'

'Mum,' Sally appealed as her daughter came back into the room. 'Will you keep an eye on Angela?'

'I suppose so.'

'I won't be long. Angel, be a good girl,' Sally said as she grabbed her coat.

As the door closed, Sadie said, 'You should have told Sally not to take the upstairs flat.'

'Why?'

'I can't say it in front of *you know who*,' she said, looking at Angel. 'But what if a certain someone won't be able to climb the stairs?'

Nelly looked puzzled, but Ruth knew what her mother was hinting at and prayed she was wrong.

Sally was breathless by the time she reached the top of Long Street and rushed into the tobacconist's gasping for air.

'My goodness, where's the fire?' Ted Johnson said, his eyebrows lifting.

Sally fought for breath. 'Nelly Cox told me that you have some flats to let.'

'Yes, that's right, though there's only the downstairs one left. Are you interested?'

'Has it got two bedrooms?'

'It has, and a small back garden too.'

'How much is the rent?'

'It's eight pounds a week.'

'Eight pounds!' Sally squeaked.

'It's a fair rate for such a nice flat, and if you can't afford it there are others that can. I'd want a month's rent down as a deposit too.'

Could they afford to pay that much? Sally wondered. She had no idea how much Arthur and Joe were going to pay themselves.

'There's another couple interested in looking at it,' the man warned.

Sally glanced at the clock hanging up behind the counter and saw it was six-fifteen. She could still go to the hospital afterwards, even if it meant missing dinner. 'Can I go to see it now?'

'Yes, but I can't leave the shop so you'll have to go on your own,' he said, taking a set of keys from his pocket and handing them over. 'It's number seventeen, and when you've had a look at it, make sure you return those keys.'

Once again Sally found herself running, but unable to keep it up, she had to resort to a rapid walk until at last she turned into Maple Terrace. It was tree-lined and not only that, each house had a small front garden. Most of the properties looked well cared for, and at number seventeen, Sally was impressed by how neat the house looked. The window frames had been freshly painted, and she saw two front doors, one for the upstairs flat and the other for the down. Both were painted dark blue with brass letterboxes.

With her heart thumping in anticipation, she walked up the small path, hoping the flat would be just as nice inside. The door was a bit stiff, but when Sally pushed it open, it was love at first sight.

The front room had a bay window, and she even liked Ted Johnson's choice of pale blue, embossed striped wallpaper. Unlike the garish patterns that were in vogue at the moment, this décor would look lovely with the antique furniture she and Arthur loved, all of which was still in storage.

Sally hurried to the kitchen and found it modern with frosted glass wall cupboards. The kitchen window, just above the sink, had a view of a small back garden, perfect for Angel to play in. With time pressing, Sally was anxious to get back, but she gave the two bedrooms a cursory look, finding both fine. The bathroom was newly fitted, half tiled with a lovely big Ascot that would supply plenty of hot water.

With a last glance over her shoulder, Sally locked up and hurried back to see Mr Johnson. 'I'll take it,' she said.

'I thought you would,' he said, smiling smugly. 'As I said, I need a month's rent in advance, along with your first weekly payment.'

Sally was glad that she had automatically picked up her handbag and now fumbled inside for her cheque book. Arthur usually saw that she got her housekeeping funds in cash so she rarely used it, but soon she was writing one out with a flourish.

'I see you've given me the deposit and a month's rent on top of that. When are you moving in?' Ted Johnson asked.

'I'm not sure, but until I do, I'll see that the rent is paid on time.'

'Good, because if you get into arrears you're out,' he said. 'I'd normally ask for references, but I've known your family, and your husband's, for years. I heard on the grapevine that he's in hospital at the moment and no doubt that's why you aren't moving in yet. I hope he's on the road to recovery.'

'Yes, he is,' Sally said dismissively, sure that she was right. 'Now can I keep the keys?'

'Of course, and if you have any problems with the flat, let me know and I'll see they're put right.'

'Thanks, I'll do that,' Sally said, saying goodbye whilst thinking that Mr Johnson seemed a fair man and she hoped a good landlord.

Once again Sally found herself hurrying, this time to get home. As soon as she walked in the door her mother asked, 'Well, how did you get on?'

Sally threw off her coat, saying with a smile, 'It's a smashing flat and I took it.'

'How much is the rent?'

'Eight pounds a week.'

'Bloody hell,' Sadie said. 'It's a flat in Maple Terrace, not Buckingham Palace.'

'Sally, the rent does sound a bit steep,' said Ruth, 'but tell me what it's like while you get that dinner down you.'

'I'll eat when I get back, Mum. I've got to get to the hospital now. The flat is worth the rent and I can't wait to tell Arthur. It's bound to cheer him up,' Sally said, bending down to kiss Angel. 'Be a good girl for Nanny.'

As usual Angel started to protest, saying she wanted to see her daddy, but with no time to mollify her, Sally was off, leaving her mother to calm her down.

Had she looked back Sally would have seen her mother quickly ushering Tommy inside, but intent on seeing Arthur her eyes were fixed ahead. She couldn't wait to tell him about the flat. He was going to be thrilled.

Sixteen

Though another week had passed, there was still no sign of Arthur responding to the treatment. Despite this, Sally was determined to have the flat ready for when he came home. Bert had his men deliver their furniture from storage and now Sally looked around the living room with delight, running her hand over the oak sideboard. She could remember how excited Arthur had been when they'd found it.

The second-hand shop in Northcote Road had mostly been full of junk, but they had spotted it against the back wall. It was filthy, but under the grime they could see that the doors were carved oak. After a bit of bartering they got it for a good price, and flushed with success they spent many happy hours scouring second-hand shops for other choice pieces. The brown leather three piece suite had been a good find too, the hide cracked and worn in places, but they loved it nevertheless.

There was a knock on the front door and, wondering who it was, Sally rushed to open it. On the step she saw a slim young woman, with short, straight blonde hair that framed her elfin face. She had heavily made up eyes, amazingly long eyelashes, and an almost childlike, innocent smile. My goodness, Sally thought, she looks like a porcelain doll.

'Hello,' she trilled, 'I saw your furniture arriving and thought I'd better introduce myself. I'm Patsy Laurington and I live upstairs.'

'Oh, hello,' Sally said, liking this young woman on sight. 'I'm Sally Jones, please, come on in, though I'm sorry I'll have to leave soon. My husband is in hospital and I'm going to see him this afternoon.'

'Oh dear, what's wrong with him?'

'He had a car accident and broke his leg, which unfortunately has led to complications,' Sally told her. 'What about you? Are you married?'

Those large blue eyes now darkened with pain. 'I was,' Patsy said quietly, 'but not any more.'

Sally bit back her questions. Not any more – what did that mean? Was Patsy a widow? Or perhaps her husband had left her? Instead she said, 'How are you finding the neighbours?'

'I haven't met any yet, but I've seen that there's a young couple living next door. On the other side I reckon a young bloke lives in the upstairs flat and an elderly couple downstairs.'

'Do you work?' Sally now asked, then kicked herself. God, she sounded like a right old nosy parker.

'I work for myself. What about you?'

'I have a five-year-old daughter, and I also stay at home to look after my grandmother,' Sally told her, tempted to ask what sort of business Patsy had.

'What does your husband do for a living?' Patsy asked, forestalling Sally's question.

'Until recently he was a partner in his father's removals company, but now he's investing in building houses.'

'Goodness, that sounds impressive!'

'It isn't really,' Sally said, then glanced at her watch. 'I'm sorry, but I've got shopping to do before I go to the hospital so I must get back. I hope we can get together again when I move in.'

'Yes, that would be nice. Give me a knock and I'll show you my flat.'

'Thanks, I'll do that,' Sally said, and grabbed her coat to go back to Candle Lane. Her thoughts turned to Patsy as she walked.

She would like to get to know her better. Perhaps they could become friends.

Sally got everything on her shopping list and found that thanks to the furniture arriving early, she still had time before she went to see Arthur. 'Hello, I'm back.'

Angel ran up to her, brandishing a painting. 'Are you going to see Daddy today?'

'Of course I am, darling.'

'I want to come. I want to give him this.'

'I'm sorry, pet, you can't. I'll give your painting to Daddy. I know he'll love it.'

'No, I want to come with you.'

Sally knew that unless Angel was distracted she'd go on and on so she said, 'Listen, when Daddy comes home from hospital we're moving into a nice new flat. You'll have your own bedroom and there's a garden for you to play in.'

Angel's brow furrowed. 'Is Nanny coming too?'

'No, she'll stay here with Gamma. Don't worry, the flat isn't far away and you'll still see each other every day.'

'I want to stay here too.'

'I can't see you moving out before Christmas, Sally.'

'I can't either, Mum,' she said, sighing.

'Come on, Angel,' her mother said. 'I've got someone coming round with a Christmas tree soon and you can help me find the decorations.'

'Like last year, did it fall off the back of a lorry?' Sadie asked.

'That's for me to know,' Ruth said, with a cheeky wink.

Christmas, Sally thought, just over a week away and then it would be a new year. Would it be a good one? Yes, of course it would. Her gran was fine, and before long she and Arthur would be in their own home again.

An hour later and Sally was about to get ready for her Saturday visit to the hospital when there was a knock on the door. With

124

her mother and Angel still searching for Christmas decorations, she expected it to be the man with the tree, but instead she found herself shoved to one side as Laura Walters barged inside.

'Where is he?' the woman spat as her eyes darted around.

'Where's who?'

'Don't play games with me. Where's my son?'

'I don't know.'

'Don't give me that. The little bugger is always in here.'

'I doubt that,' Sally protested, 'and he isn't in here now.'

Laura ignored her and staggered through to the kitchen, snarling when she saw Ruth. 'Oi you, where's my boy?'

'Get out of my house!' Ruth cried.

'Not until Tommy's with me!'

'He ain't in here.'

'You're lying! Where is he?' she shouted, her eyes wildly looking around the room.

'You heard my daughter,' Sadie said, joining in the affray. 'She told you to get out!'

'Shut up, you old witch,' Laura spat.

Sally could see that Angel was frightened, and riled she grabbed Laura's arm. 'I won't have you upsetting my daughter or my grandmother. If you don't go I'll call the police.'

'All right, miss high and mighty, I'll go, but I'm not finished with your mother yet. I've told my boy to stay away from her, and if he comes in here again I'll flay him alive.' On that note Laura stumbled outside, shouting as she went, 'Tommy! Where are you, you little sod!'

Sally closed the door swiftly behind her and then marched back to the kitchen. 'Mum, you know I don't like Angela mixing with that boy. I hope this fiasco stops you fetching him in.'

'I'm sick of hearing you say that. Even if he didn't come in here, she still sees him at school.'

'Yes, but they're in a different year and I doubt they mix.'

'I like Tommy,' Angel wailed. 'He . . . he stuck up for me.'

125

'Did he now,' Ruth said, pulling Angel into her arms, 'and when was this?'

'It was last week, in the playground. Some boys were pulling my hair, calling me a ginger-nut, but Tommy sorted them out, though his coat pocket got ripped.'

Sally's stomach lurched at her daughter's words. She too had suffered bullying at school, and knew how awful it was. 'Why didn't you tell me, darling?'

Angel shrugged. ''Cos Tommy sorted them out.'

Sally closed her eyes. She took a good look at herself and didn't like what she saw. Tommy had stood up for Angel, but she had judged the lad and found him wanting. When had she turned into a snob? A snob who'd decided that the boy wasn't good enough to associate with Angel. 'Oh, Mum, I'm sorry. I've been awful to Tommy, and now I realise that he doesn't deserve it.'

'I've been telling you that all along but you wouldn't listen. He may swear, but that isn't his fault. He really is a good kid when you get to know him.'

'Yes, I see that now, and in future, if Angel wants to play with him, that's fine with me.'

'Good, I'm glad to hear it, and I *am* trying to do something about his language.'

'Well, I ain't happy about the bleedin' kid being in here, and you heard Laura Walters, it's got to stop,' Sadie said, her face stretching with amazement when both Sally and Ruth dissolved into tears of laughter. 'What's so funny?'

'Mum, you're worse than him,' Ruth gasped.

'I flippin' well ain't.'

'You flippin' well are,' Angel told her, arms akimbo.

Sally doubled up again, her eyes watering with mirth. At last able to pull herself together, she said, 'I'd best get ready for the hospital, Mum.'

'Yeah, off you go. Now come on, Angel, we still haven't found those decorations.'

Sally left, feeling lighter as she got ready. All right, Arthur might not be home for Christmas, but the New Year looked bright and she found herself looking forward to 1967.

Seventeen

Christmas wasn't the same without Arthur, but Sally tried to make it a happy one for Angel. She was still missing her daddy, but it was worse for Arthur in isolation with only a half an hour visit from Sally every day. He still wasn't responding to the treatment, and doped up with pain medication, he wasn't very communicative.

They were into the January of the new year when Sally opened the door to a surprise visitor. 'Ann!' she cried, seeing Arthur's sister. 'How lovely to see you.'

'I'm at Mum's for the weekend, and, bless her, she offered to look after the kids while I came to see you.'

'Come on in,' Sally invited.

'I wish I could see Arthur, but Mum said he's still in isolation.'

'Yes, I'm afraid so.'

'Isn't there any sign of improvement?'

'Not really, but hopefully there will be soon.'

They walked into the kitchen then, Ann saying, 'Hello everyone, and Angela, how about giving your auntie a cuddle?'

Angel hesitated for a moment, but then ran up to Ann. 'Where are them boys?'

'If you mean your cousins, Darren and Jason, they're with your Nanna Elsie.'

'But I want to see them.'

128

'You will, darling. Your granddad is coming to pick me up at two o'clock and you're coming back to Wimbledon with us for a little tea party.'

'Am I? Oh goody.'

'You don't mind do you, Sally?'

'No, of course not.'

'I think Mum would like her to stay overnight too. What do you think?'

'It's fine with me,' Sally said, sadly remembering the last time that Angel had stayed over with Elsie. She and Arthur had spent nearly all night making love. That seemed such a long time ago now.

Ruth smiled at Ann. 'It's nice to see you, why don't you and Sally go out on your own for a while?'

'Mum, thanks,' Sally said, touched by her mother's thoughtfulness.

'You could take Ann to see your flat.'

'I want to go too,' Angel said.

'But I'm making cakes and I need you to help me.'

Angel looked perplexed for a moment, but then said, 'Can we put icing on the top?'

'Yeah, I suppose so.'

'All right, Nanny, I'll stay with you.'

'Thank goodness for that. I couldn't manage without you,' Ruth said, with a sly wink at Sally.

Taking the cue, they left quickly, and as they walked Ann hooked her arm through Sally's. 'It seems strange to be out with no kids in tow. It reminds me of our teenage years.'

'Yes, it does, days when we were young, free and single.'

'I don't regret getting married and having kids, but sometimes I'm so worn out I feel old before my time.'

'I envy you having three. I'd love another baby.'

'It's sure to happen one day, but you might regret it if you have twins like me,' Ann said, going on to describe some of the boys' antics. When they turned into Maple Terrace the subject changed. 'Sally, I'd forgotten what a nice street this is.'

'Unlike nearly everything else around Candle Lane, at least it isn't scheduled for redevelopment,' Sally said, and reaching the flat she opened the front door with a flourish.

'It's lovely in here,' Ann enthused.

'I'll light the gas fire. Blast, I haven't got any matches. Hang on, I'll give Patsy a knock.'

'Who's Patsy?'

'She lives upstairs. I won't be a mo,' Sally said, hurrying out, hoping she was in.

There were footsteps, and as she opened the door Patsy smiled with delight. 'Hello, come on up,' she said, gesturing Sally inside.

'Sorry, I can't. I've just brought my sister-in-law round to see my flat, but I couldn't light the fire. Could you possibly lend me some matches?'

'Yes, but even then your flat will take a while to warm up. Why not come up to my place instead and it'll give me a chance to show you what I've done with it?'

'Well . . . maybe just for a little while,' Sally said, hoping that Ann wouldn't mind.

She didn't, and after a quick look around Sally's flat, they hurried up to Patsy's. It was a complete contrast to Sally's, all vibrant colours and modern furniture. The suite was made of black vinyl and scattered with bright orange, shaggy fur cushions and the wallpaper was predominately orange too. The psychedelic, swirling pattern made Sally's eyes swim, but Ann was enthusiastic. 'Oh,' she said, 'I love this.'

'Please, sit down,' Patsy invited, her coal-effect fire welcoming after the coldness downstairs.

Patsy made them coffee in glass cups, and while at first conversation was a bit stilted, gradually the ice broke, especially when Ann found out that Patsy was a mobile hairdresser.

'Before I got married I did hairdressing,' Ann told her, 'and when my children are older I'd like to go back to it. Going mobile sounds ideal, but I must admit, I'm a bit out of practice.'

'I mostly get elderly, housebound clients so I don't get the chance to keep up with modern styles. I can't see my old ladies wanting a Vidal Sassoon cut,' Patsy said, laughing at the thought.

'I just love his geometric five point cut,' Ann enthused.

While they were talking, Sally took in Patsy's striking outfit. She was wearing a black, polo neck sweater, under a black and white check, mini-pinafore dress. She looked great.

As though becoming aware of Sally's scrutiny Patsy looked down at her legs, exclaiming, 'Oh, no, I've got a ladder in my tights.'

'Are they comfortable?' Sally asked.

'Yes, and with miniskirts at least you don't show your stocking tops when you sit down,' Patsy replied before abruptly changing the subject. 'How's your husband, Sally? Is he still in hospital?'

'He developed an infection in his wound, though I'm hoping he'll be better soon.'

'That's good. I'm looking forward to you moving in downstairs.'

'You might regret it when my brother starts playing his records,' Ann warned. 'He prefers Frank Sinatra to any of the modern stuff.'

'It won't bother me, but tell me, Ann, do you live around here?'

'Not now. I used to, but when I got married we moved out of London. Anyway, back to hairdressing. Tell me, how did you build up your clients?'

'It was easy really. I just put an ad in a local newspaper and cards in newsagent shop windows.'

Sally could see that Ann was impressed, but with three young children it would be some time before she could follow Patsy's lead. While they continued to chat, Sally's eyes roamed the room, and seeing a photograph of a child on the long, low, sideboard, she wondered who it was.

'I can't wait to see your little girl,' Patsy said, drawing Sally's attention back to her.

'You may not say that when you meet her. Angel can be a proper little madam.'

'Take no notice of Sally,' Ann protested. 'Her daughter is adorable.'

'Angel. What a lovely name.'

'It's Angela really,' and plucking up the courage Sally added, 'I see you have a photograph of a little girl on your sideboard.'

'Yes, that's right,' she said, offering nothing further.

'Are you married, Patsy?' asked Ann.

'I was, but not any more.'

'I'm so sorry. You're so young to be a widow.'

'He isn't dead. We're divorced.'

Sally felt that Ann was asking too many questions, and said, 'Thanks for the coffee, Patsy, and I just love these cups.'

It was no good. Ann had risen to her feet and was now studying the photograph. 'She looks just like you, Patsy. Is she your daughter?'

'Yes.' The answer abrupt.

'She's lovely, but where is she?'

'Look, I don't usually talk about it, but if you must know she lives with her father.'

'Goodness. That must be hard for you.'

There was a small pause and then Patsy said, 'It was the court's decision.'

'They awarded custody to your husband! But why?'

'Ann,' Sally warned, 'this is none of our business.'

'It's all right,' Patsy said. 'You might as well hear the rest. You see I married young and quickly became pregnant, but soon found out it was a mistake. I met and fell in love with another man, but when he refused to take on my daughter, I had to leave without her. Yes, I can see you're shocked, and no doubt you'll be pleased to know that I got my come-uppance. He left me two years later and my husband wouldn't take me back. I had abandoned him and my child, hence he got custody.'

Both Sally and Ann were left speechless. Patsy then said, 'Now you can see why I usually don't talk about it. By the look on your faces I can see that you're both judging me and no doubt find me wanting.'

'No, no, of course not,' Sally said, but it did little to ease the atmosphere.

'I'm sorry for quizzing you, Patsy,' said Ann.

'Let's just forget it,' she said, 'but instead of going back to hairdressing you could consider becoming a copper. You'd be good at extracting confessions.'

Ann smiled hesitantly, but as Patsy laughed at her own wit, both she and Sally joined in. The tension in the room melted away and soon they were all chatting freely again, until Sally said, 'I'm sorry, Ann, but we'd best get back to Candle Lane. I want to dress Angel up a bit if she's going back to your mum's, and then get ready to see Arthur.'

They said their goodbyes, but as they walked home Sally found Ann quiet. 'What's up?'

'I'm not sure about Patsy. She seemed nice enough at first, but then she told us about abandoning her little girl.'

'I admit I was shocked, but we don't know what it's like to be stuck in a loveless marriage. She must have been really desperate to have run off like that.'

'Maybe, but think about it, Sally. Can you imagine abandoning Angel?'

'No, I can't, but maybe there's more to Patsy's story.'

'Yeah, maybe,' Ann said doubtfully.

'Come on, enough about Patsy. I want to pick your brains about what to get your dad for his birthday next week.'

'Blimey, search me. I haven't got a clue and had enough of a problem finding him something for Christmas.'

'What about cuff-links?'

'They'd do, but it's a shame that Mum cancelled his party. She said with Arthur still in hospital it wouldn't be the same without him.'

'I know. I feel the same.'

When they arrived home it was to find Angel covered in flour. It was daubed on her face and showing starkly white in her red hair. She excitedly pointed at the fairy cakes. 'Look, Mummy, I made them, and Nanny said I can take some for Darren and Jason.'

Angel looked thrilled, and smiling, Sally lifted her from the chair. 'I'm sure they'll love them, but come on, let's get you cleaned up and changed for when your granddad arrives. I won't be long, Ann.'

'There's no hurry, I'll be fine with your mum and Sadie.'

Sally nodded, but with one foot on the stairs she felt it again, that awful feeling of apprehension. Her stomach did a somersault, but then seeing that Angel was looking at her worriedly, she managed to force a smile. It was all in her imagination, that was all. *It had to be.*

Eighteen

It was towards the end of the month that Sadie's prediction came true, Arthur the first to find out when the surgeon came to see him. He was told that despite the aggressive treatment he'd been receiving, he had now developed another infection, one called osteomyelitis.

'What's that?' he asked.

'In layman's terms it's a disease of the bone marrow and it's preventing your fracture from healing. I'm sorry, young man, but we now have two alternatives, the first being a sequestrotomy.'

'A what?'

'To put it simply again, we'd cut away the dying bone and hope then that the wound will heal, but as the gangrene hasn't been brought under control I can't guarantee success. If it doesn't work it will mean another operation, again with no guarantee of success, and even if successful, you'd be left with one leg considerably shorter than the other. It would mean wearing a surgical boot for the rest of your life.'

'What's the other option?'

'I don't want to risk the infection spreading above the knee and to prevent that happening I would recommend amputating your leg now, while the infection is still below the joint.'

Arthur's stomach flipped and feeling nauseous at the thought he managed to gasp, 'I don't fancy that.'

The surgeon ignored his comment. 'A below the knee

amputation is easier to adapt to, and once you're fitted with a prosthetic you would soon learn to walk again.'

'I still don't like the thought of losing my leg,' Arthur protested as his mind railed against the surgeon's words. Why is this happening to me, he thought as self-pity engulfed him.

'I'll let you think about it,' the surgeon said, leaving Arthur alone in the room.

With his forearm flung across his eyes, and for the first time in many, many years, Arthur gave way to tears.

Sally had arrived at the hospital earlier than usual to see Arthur, but as she walked to his room an awful feeling engulfed her. Something was wrong. She began to run, only just remembering to get a mask before going into his room.

Arthur looked at her, his eyes red. His attempt at a brave smile didn't fool Sally. 'What is it? What's wrong?'

'I . . . I've just agreed to have my lower leg amputated.'

'Oh, Arthur,' she said, rushing forward and forgetting the rules she grasped his hand.

The pretence dropped and Arthur said in a choked voice, 'With only one leg, I'll be a burden, less than a man.'

Sally fought for words. 'Don't be silly. Think about Douglas Bader, he lost both his legs during the war, but still managed to fly a plane.'

Arthur was silent, his expression morose and Sally didn't know how to comfort him. 'I . . . I'm so sorry, darling, but don't worry, we'll get through this.'

'We! Don't you mean me? I'm the one who is going to be a cripple,' he said, almost shouting, but then his expression changed. 'I'm sorry, Sal, I shouldn't take it out on you, but I'm having the operation in the morning and my guts are churning.'

'Tomorrow! That soon!'

'The surgeon wants to do it before the infections spread any further.'

Sally blinked rapidly. Arthur needed her support, not her tears. She continued to do her best to comfort him, but she felt useless, the fear in Arthur's eyes apparent when she had to leave. 'I'll be here in the morning,' she said, 'and no doubt when I ring your parents to tell them, they'll be here too.'

With a heavy heart Sally left the hospital, and unable to face waiting for a bus she waved down a taxi. Tears were close to the surface, waiting to spill, and she arrived home to find her mother and gran watching the television. They were barely aware that she was there until Sally cried, 'Mum, Arthur has got to have his leg amputated.'

'What? Blimey, love, that's awful.'

'It's rotten luck, but I warned you this would happen,' Sadie pointed out.

'I'm scared, Gran, he's in an awful state and I don't know how he'll cope.'

'Now you listen to me, my girl. Arthur is a strong man, just like his father, and once he comes to terms with this he'll be fine.'

Sally tried to draw strength from her gran's words, and wiping tears from her cheeks she said, 'I'll ring Elsie.'

It was extremely hard to pass on the news. Elsie burst into tears and then Bert came to the phone, his voice cracking when he said they'd see her at the hospital in the morning.

The rest of the evening passed, but unable to stop thinking about Arthur, Sally found her head aching when she went upstairs to bed. *Where are you?* she begged inwardly as her eyes roamed the room. Oh, she wished her friend would come, the lovely angelic presence who brought her such comfort. No, she was being selfish. Arthur must be going out of his mind and more in need of comfort than her.

Go to him, please go to him, she begged, and as Sally whispered these word, her worry suddenly eased.

* * *

Arthur too was lying awake, his stomach churning. He tried to picture what it would be like with half a leg, but his mind shied away from the image. He felt that he'd been talked into having it done – that maybe he should have opted for that request . . . whatever the word was.

'Can't you sleep?' his night nurse asked, as she came into the room.

'I can't stop thinking about having my leg off tomorrow.'

'The surgeon said it's the right course of action and he's one of the best in the country. Here, take these, it'll help you to sleep.'

'Thanks,' Arthur managed to murmur before swallowing the pills.

The nurse left the room and now laying in darkness, Arthur was still in despair. Soon though a strange feeling began to engulf him, a feeling of being cocooned, enfolded, as though in someone's arms. It must be those pills, he thought as a profound feeling of peace washed over him.

Arthur closed his eyes, at last able to sleep.

Nineteen

The operation had been successful and during the following ten days Arthur began to take an interest in his surroundings again. He was taken out of isolation and allowed visitors, but when Sally took Angel to see him, she felt his attempts at cheerfulness were false. Sally had kept Joe Somerton up to date, and he was going to see Arthur within the next few days.

That morning, Sally had just taken Angel to school, and was almost home again when she felt a shiver of intuition as she reached Tommy's house. She paused to gaze at his front door, the feeling or foreboding so strong that she rattled his letterbox. Something was wrong, she was sure of it.

The door opened a crack and a small voice said, 'What do you want?'

'Tommy, is that you?'

'Yeah.'

'Why aren't you at school?'

'My mum ain't well.'

'What's wrong with her?'

'I dunno, but I'm staying home to look after her.'

'Where is your father, Tommy?'

'I dunno.'

Sally crossed her fingers, hoping Gran would be all right for a few more minutes. 'Perhaps I can help. Can I come in to see your mother?'

'No, she'll kill me if I let anyone in.'

'Tommy, if your mum's ill she may need to see a doctor.'

There was a pause, but then the door opened a few more inches. 'All right, come in.'

As Sally walked inside, she gagged at the smell of the place, for a moment wanting to run out again, but then Tommy led her upstairs. In the bedroom she saw what looked like a bundle of rags on the bed and, amongst them, Laura Walters. The woman's eyes were closed and she looked awful, her lips tinged blue. 'How long has she been like this, Tommy?'

'She was all right last night, but she won't get up this morning.'

'Laura . . . Mrs Walters,' Sally said loudly.

There was no response, and though frantic with worry, Sally tried to keep her voice calm. 'Listen, Tommy, I'm going home to call the doctor. I can't leave my gran for long, so I'm going to find someone else to stay with your mum until he arrives.'

Tommy stared up at her, his eyes round with fear, and Sally's heart went out to the boy. 'Don't worry, everything will be all right. Wait here, and I'll go and get Nelly Cox.'

Sally shot out of the house and as soon as she got indoors she called the surgery. She then rattled off a quick explanation to her gran before hurrying down the lane to fetch Nelly.

Thankfully the old lady took in the situation straight away, and in no time they were standing by Laura's bed. 'Blimey, she looks rough,' Nelly said as she gazed down at the woman.

'I told the receptionist that it's an emergency, so the doctor should be here shortly.'

'The sooner the better,' Nelly said as she endeavoured to straighten the bed covers. 'What about the boy?'

'I'll take him home with me.'

'No, I want to stay wiv me mum.'

'All right, don't get upset, love. You can wait with me if you want to,' Nelly said, adding, 'Go on, Sally, you'd best get back to Sadie. I'll give you a knock after the doctor's been.'

Sally reluctantly left, but once indoors she hovered at the window, looking out for the doctor's car. 'Laura Walters looked awful, Gran.'

'Are you sure it isn't just a hangover?'

'It's more serious than that.'

'Did you look at her aura?'

'Yes, briefly, and I think it's her heart. Oh good, the doctor has arrived.'

Sally turned away from the window, but shortly after there was a knock at the door, the doctor asking to use the telephone.

'Of course, come in,' Sally said, stepping to one side.

She hovered whilst he rang for an ambulance, and when the call ended he turned to speak to Sally. 'I need to get in touch with Mrs Walters' husband. Do you by any chance know where he works?'

'No, I'm afraid not. In fact, I'm not sure if he has a job.'

'He needs to be found. The child can't be left alone, and he's too young to go to the hospital with his mother.'

'It's all right. I'll look after him until his father comes home.'

'Good, well, I'd better get back to my patient.'

Things happened quickly after that. The ambulance came, and with the neighbours watching, Laura Walters was carried out. Tommy was yelling, trying to get into the ambulance too, and it took Sally, along with Nelly Cox to restrain him until finally he was led sobbing into number five.

Nelly sat opposite Sadie, both of them saying nothing as Sally did her best to soothe the boy. When Tommy finally stopped crying, he closed his eyes, obviously so emotionally exhausted that he fell asleep.

'Blimey, with the way Laura Walters treats the boy, and the state they live in, I'm surprised he's so upset,' Nelly said softly.

'I've seen it before,' Sadie said. 'The bond is strong. Kids can be beaten, abused, half-starved, but they still cling to their mothers.'

'I've never had kids so I wouldn't know, but then again my old mother was a strict and taciturn woman, and I still loved her.'

'It's the only life Tommy knows, and so he's clinging to it.'

'The poor kid,' Nelly said. 'I hope for his sake that Laura recovers.'

'I've got a feeling she's going to be all right,' Sally murmured.

'Have you, love?' Sadie said. 'That's good. Now I don't know about you two, but I'm spitting feathers.'

'I'll make a pot of tea, Sally,' Nelly offered. 'You've got your hands full.'

Sally smiled her thanks as she continued to hold Tommy. Yes, something was telling her that Laura Walters was going to be all right this time, but if she didn't keep off the booze, Sally feared it wouldn't be for long.

Tommy's father still hadn't turned up when Sally left to visit Arthur that evening. She found him sitting in a chair by the side of the bed, a blanket over his knees and his expression glum. She pulled up a chair beside him, her attempts to cheer him up unsuccessful, but then Joe Somerton arrived.

'Well mate, how are you doing?' Joe asked Arthur.

'Not so bad, but I expect you'll want to find another partner.'

'Why?'

'I'll be no good to you or anyone else with half a leg.'

'Leave it out. Now if you said you only had half a brain that might be a problem, but with a prosthetic you'll be walking in no time. Like it or not, you're my partner, mate.'

'What if I'm unable to drive?'

'We'd find a way round it and stop putting obstacles in the way before you know the score. Take one step at a time or should I say hop?'

Sally stiffened, but to her surprise Arthur laughed. 'Yeah, and you can call me Skippy.' Both men then broke into song, 'Skippy, Skippy, Skippy the bush kangaroo.'

'That's the spirit,' Joe chuckled. 'Arthur, you're young, you're strong, and I'm sure you'll adapt to a false leg in no time. Anyway, our job is to sell houses, not build them, and with the show house taking shape we'll be able to start marketing them when you get out of here.'

'Thanks, Joe, but I wouldn't hold it against you if you'd prefer to find someone else.'

'No, Arthur, we're in this together. All you've got to worry about for now is getting on your feet – or should I say foot?' Joe joked.

Arthur laughed again, and Sally was thrilled to see him looking so much happier. There was a brightness in his eyes and as he and Joe continued to chat, she sat there holding Arthur's hand.

'I must say I'll be glad to get out of here,' Arthur told Joe.

'Yeah, I can understand that, but if you want something to keep you occupied, how about having a go at designing a brochure to market the houses?'

'I suppose I could give it a try.'

'I'm having a board put up at the site soon so we'll need a name for the development. Any ideas?'

Arthur's brow furrowed in thought, and then said, 'It's in the countryside, surrounded by fields, so how about "The Meadows"?'

'Yes, I like it,' Joe said, smiling. 'See, I knew you had a brain in there somewhere. It's just as well it wasn't in your foot.'

'You cheeky sod,' Arthur joked back.

Sally loved to see Arthur so happy, but all too soon visiting time was over. Joe rose to his feet. 'I'll leave you two to say your goodbyes, but would you like a lift home, Sally?'

'Yes, please.'

'Right, I'll be in the car park. Bye, partner, and get on with that brochure,' he said to Arthur.

As Joe left the ward, Arthur said, 'He's a great bloke, Sally. I thought that he would want to find another partner and where would that have left me? I'd be no good to my dad now, unable to drive a lorry or to hump furniture.'

'Your dad would have found something for you to do.'

'I wouldn't have agreed to that. I'd just be a burden, taking pay for doing sod all.'

'Well, Joe is happy to keep you as a partner so all you've got to worry about now is getting on your feet.'

Arthur smiled. 'Foot, as Joe said. If he can joke about my leg, then so can others, and though I expect it's been my fault, it's been lousy in this ward. All the other patients seem to avoid talking to me, but I know what to do now. I'll make a joke of having one leg and that'll surprise them.'

'Good for you.'

'Sally, I've been meaning to tell you something, but sometimes I think it's all in my imagination.'

'Tell me anyway.'

'It was the night before my op, and at first I thought it was the pills, but I've had them before and since without the same effect. I don't really know how to describe it, and I've never taken any notice of this spiritual mumbo jumbo that you and Mum get up to, even if the pair of you have unnerved me at times. But that night . . . well . . . I sort of felt something around me.'

'Can you describe it?'

'It's going to sound daft but it was like a presence, and for a while it felt as though I was wrapped in cotton wool. The feeling was so comforting, and suddenly I wasn't scared about the op any more. I could still sense it the next morning and sort of felt at peace when I went down to theatre. They gave me an anaesthetic and the next thing I remember was waking up in the ward.'

Sally gave silent thanks, smiling as she said, 'I've had that same feeling in times of trouble and I'm so pleased to think you experienced it too.'

'It was a bit strange, but watch out, love, visiting time was over a while ago and the battle-axe is on her way. You're the last one here and had better scarper.'

Sally glanced to her side, saw the ward sister and then hurriedly leaned forward to kiss Arthur. 'Bye, darling. See you tomorrow.'

He waved as she left, and finding Joe's car in the car park, Sally got into the passenger seat. She felt much more optimistic now. 'Thanks, Joe.'

'There's no need to thank me. It won't take me long to drive you home.'

'I meant for cheering Arthur up.'

'I didn't do anything, really. Arthur's a fighter and won't let this beat him.'

'I know, but it was good to see him laughing. I think he needed that.'

'Losing a leg below the knee isn't the end of the world, and I'm sure he realises that.'

Sally smiled at Joe. He was a lovely man, not only Arthur's partner, but also a good friend. She sighed and leaned back in the seat, thinking that the future looked brighter than it had for what seemed such a long, long time.

Joe dropped Sally off and she walked in to find that Tommy was still there. It was eleven o'clock before they heard noises coming from next door, Tommy's father obviously home now, but Ruth had already put the boy to bed.

'I ain't waking the kid up now,' she complained.

'All right, but his father needs to know what's going on. I'll go and tell him,' Sally offered.

'I'll come with you,' Ruth insisted, but when Denis Walters opened the door he was drunk, bleary-eyed and barely able to take in what they were telling him.

'You wanna see my wife? What for?'

Ruth sighed with exasperation. 'We don't want to see her. We're telling you she's in hospital.'

He swayed and clutched the stanchion for support. 'Hospital? She ain't in hospital.'

'Oh, this is hopeless. Let's leave him to sleep it off and we'll come round in the morning.'

'All right,' Sally agreed and, talking as though to a child, she enunciated her words, 'Tommy's in our house, Mr Walters.'

'Wh . . . what?'

'This is a waste of time. Come on, Sally, let's go.'

'Oi, jush . . . jusht a minute,' Denis Walters slurred. 'What was you shaying about an 'ospital?'

'For Gawd's sake go to bed,' Ruth shouted and taking Sally's arm she ushered her away.

'What are we going to do, Mum?' Sally asked when they were back home again. 'Denis Walters doesn't seem fit to look after the boy, and we have no idea how long his mother will be in hospital.'

'They may have family in the area he can go to. If not, he'll just have to stay with us,' and seeing the worried expression on her daughter's face, she added, 'It won't be so bad. He'll be at school all day.'

'Yes, but what about when he *isn't* in school? He's used to running the streets and I'm not sure I could control him.'

'Of course you can. He isn't a bad kid, just one that craves a bit of love and attention, that's all. I'll have a word with him and I'm sure he'll do as you say.'

'But what about Gran? She won't be happy about this.'

'Until Laura Walters comes home she'll just have to put up with it.'

'Mum, we still have to be careful that we don't upset her too much. I feel sorry for Tommy, I really do, but Gran has to come first.'

'Sally, your gran is all wind and water. Once she knows the circumstances, she won't mind, you'll see. I'll give the lad a good talking to. He'll behave, you wait and see.'

'I hope you're right, but I'm off to bed. Let's hope we can get more sense out of Mr Walters in the morning.'

'All right. Night, love.'

Sally kissed her mother on the cheek before going upstairs. The bathroom was freezing and she shivered as she washed, glad to jump into bed. Oh, how she wished she could cuddle up to Arthur. She missed the warmth of his body, but surely he'd be home soon, and then there would be the joy of moving into their own flat. It would make things a bit difficult if Laura Walters was still in hospital, but as long as her mum got Tommy ready for school before she left for work, it should be all right.

In the light of a full moon, Sally looked at her daughter. It was odd really. From the day they had moved back to Candle Lane, Angel had taken to Tommy, and though older, the boy in turn had taken her under his wing. Then there was the dream Angel had had, the one in which she saw Tommy living with them. It was strange, and once again Sally wondered if her daughter's gifts were manifesting.

At last Sally settled down, pulling the blankets up to her chin. Tommy wasn't living with them, just staying for the time being. Angel's dream wasn't accurate, but maybe as she grew older, her abilities would develop. On this thought, Sally at last fell asleep.

Twenty

At eight o'clock the following morning Sally was busy getting Angel ready so it was Ruth, with Tommy hovering behind her, thumping on Denis Walters' front door.

'Wassa matter,' he said gruffly, his eyes fuddled with tiredness as he opened the door.

'Mum's in 'ospital,' Tommy said, darting forward.

Denis Walters shook his head in bewilderment, but managed to focus on his son. 'What are you talking about?'

'Mum was ill and she went in an amlance.'

'Ambulance, Tommy,' Ruth corrected. 'I did try to tell you last night, Mr Walters, but you obviously don't remember.'

'Did you? Look, you had better come in.'

Ruth followed the man inside and though Sally had described it, she was still shocked by the state of the place. The sink was piled high with dirty dishes, the table strewn with all kinds of rubbish; old newspapers, an empty jam-jar, crushed cigarette packets, and an overflowing ashtray. The hearth was as bad with old ashes thick under the grate, and carelessly thrown fag-ends.

'Why was my wife taken to hospital?' Denis asked, at least sounding sober now.

'She had a heart attack.'

'No! Where did they take her?'

'I don't know. You'll have to ask the doctor. Anyway, it's Tommy

148

I've come to see you about. Have you got anyone who can look after him?'

'There's only my wife's brother, but he lives in the North and we haven't seen him for years. Still, I suppose I could send Tommy there.'

'No, Dad, I wanna stay here.'

Ruth watched as Denis sank into a chair. Placing both hands over his face, he groaned softly. 'I can't seem to think straight.'

Deciding to take him in hand, Ruth said, 'It hardly seems worth sending the boy away until you know how long Laura's going to be in hospital, so in the meantime he can stay with me. Why don't you find out where she was taken to, and for the moment my daughter will see that Tommy goes to school.'

'Yes . . . yes, good idea.'

Ruth studied the man's face, realising that if it wasn't for the effects of alcohol, he could be good-looking. But, as it was, she could see his hands trembling, a sure sign of a heavy drinker, and so said briskly, 'Say goodbye to your father, Tommy. He'll come round later to tell you how your mum is. That's right isn't it, Mr Walters?'

'Yes, I'll do that, and thanks.'

'Dad, can I come with you to see Mum?'

'No . . . you get yourself off to school.'

'But . . .'

'You'll be able to see her soon,' Ruth consoled, taking the boy's hand. 'Perhaps this evening if you're a good boy.'

'Is that right? Will you take me later, Dad?'

'I dunno, maybe.'

Before Tommy could protest, Ruth said, 'We're off, Mr Walters, and if there's anything else I can do, let me know.'

'Yes, thanks, and you'd better behave yourself, Tommy, or else.'

Tommy nodded, reluctantly following Ruth outside, where out of his father's hearing he said, 'He won't take me to see her, he'll be too pissed.'

149

'Tommy! What have I told you about your language?'

'But he won't!' he cried, and Ruth saw tears welling in his eyes.

'Listen, darling, I know you're worried about your mum, but if your dad doesn't take you to see her, I will. That's a promise. Now come on, you don't want Angel to see you crying, do you?'

The boy cuffed his face with his sleeve and sniffing loudly, he shook his head. Smiling gently and ruffling his hair, Ruth led him back to her house.

'What did he say?' Sally asked as soon as they walked in.

'He said there's only a brother up North somewhere and agreed that Tommy should stay with us for the time being.'

'So we're stuck with him,' Sadie commented.

'Yes, Mum, we are, and try to be nice for a change. The boy won't be any trouble.'

'Huh!'

Ruth shook her head, but said nothing further. Crouching down she pulled Tommy into her arms. 'Sally will take you to school, and bring you back here afterwards. I've got to go now, but I'll see you later.'

She felt Tommy's arms snaking around her neck, and felt tears forming in her own eyes when he said, 'I don't want you to go.'

'You'll be all right with Sally. She'll look after you.'

'I . . . I want me mum.'

'I know you do, love, and I'm sure she'll be home soon.'

'Kiss me too, Nanny!' Angel cried.

'Come here then, pet.'

Angel ran across and, as she disengaged Tommy's arms, Ruth cuddled her granddaughter. 'I'll see you later too.'

'You're *my* nanny, not his,' Angel said petulantly.

'Of course I am, and I always will be.'

'See, she's *my* nanny, not yours!' Angel said, scowling at Tommy.

Ruth was surprised by Angel's behaviour. This was the first time she had shown jealousy towards Tommy, and she hoped it wasn't going to be a problem. She glanced up at Sally and saw the worried expression on her face. Letting go of Angel, Ruth rose to her feet. 'It'll be all right, don't worry,' she told her daughter.

'If you say so,' Sally replied doubtfully.

'I must go. Denis Walters may call round after he's been to see his wife. If he does, tell him to take Tommy with him when he goes to see Laura again this evening.'

'Yes, all right. Bye, Mum.'

Ruth left, worried by her promise to Tommy. If his father didn't take him to the hospital, she would have to do it, but with Sally going to visit Arthur, she had no idea how.

When her mother left, Sally piled the breakfast dishes in the sink, all the while keeping an eye on the children. Angel had been the centre of attention for so long, and was now seeing Tommy as a usurper. It would make matters worse if she fussed over him too, so though she felt sorry for the boy, Sally decided to keep her distance. 'Right, you two, it's time for school,' she said briskly.

'I don't want *him* to come with us,' Angel said.

'Now then, that's enough of that. Have you forgotten who stands up for you in the playground? Tommy stops you being bullied.'

For a moment Angel hung her head. She then looked at the boy from under her lashes. 'Sorry, Tommy. You can share my nanny if you want to.'

'Fanks,' Tommy said, a smile lighting his face at last.

Sally buttoned her daughter's coat, saying gently, 'Good girl. Now say goodbye to Gamma.'

Angel ran across the room, gave Sadie a quick hug, and then said, 'Tommy, you can cuddle my gamma too if you like.'

Tommy looked momentarily panic stricken as he stammered, 'No . . . no, I don't fink so.'

'And why not, young man?' Sadie asked.

'Err . . . err . . .'

Sadie held out her arms. 'Come on, I don't bite.'

'Go on, Tommy. I don't mind,' Angel urged.

Looking decidedly reluctant, the boy walked towards Sadie, his little body stiff as he gave her the briefest of hugs.

'See, I told you I don't bite. Here, have a Fox's Glacier Mint,' she said, pulling one out of her apron pocket. 'Here's one for you too, Angela.'

'Fanks, missus,' Tommy said, his eyes wide.

Sally saw his surprise. Angel was used to her great-grandmother's mood swings and mostly took them in her stride. Tommy, however, was new to them. She called a quick goodbye, bundled the children out in front of her, and soon they were safely in school.

For the rest of the morning, Sally kept busy by doing the housework, and it was two-thirty before Denis Walters knocked on the door, grinning crookedly and obviously drunk. 'I've been to see me wife. She's in Bolingbroke Hospital.'

'Will you be taking Tommy when you go to see her this evening?'

'Nah, he doesn't need to go.'

'He's upset and I think it would help if he could see that his mother is all right.'

'I'm not going again this evening. I'm meeting a mate in the King's Arms.'

Sally could see it would be pointless to argue with the man. He could hardly stand, let alone take in what she was saying. Her temper flared at his selfishness. 'Go to the flaming pub then, and *we'll* look after your son.'

When Ruth arrived home to find that Tommy's father wasn't taking the boy to see his mother, she had to ask Sally to forgo her usual visit to Arthur. Thankfully Sally had guessed as much and had rung Elsie, asking her mother-in-law to take her place.

'Are you sure you don't mind, love?' Ruth asked after sprucing Tommy up as best as she could.

'Arthur is a lot better now, and I'm sure he won't mind if I miss just one visit.'

'Right then, come on, Tommy, we're off,' Ruth said, rewarded by the delighted smile on the boy's face.

It wasn't far to go to catch a bus, though Tommy was unusually quiet during the journey. When they got off, Ruth held his hand and in no time they were walking into the old Victorian hospital.

Ruth had to ask what ward to go to, and as they walked in Laura saw them almost immediately. Tommy let go of Ruth's hand to run up to her.

'Hello, love, I wasn't expecting to see you.'

'Are you all right, Mum?'

'I'm fine,' and looking sheepish she smiled hesitantly at Ruth. 'After the way I've behaved towards you it's good of you to bring him, and I know I owe you an apology.'

Ruth could scarcely believe her ears. Sober, Laura Walters was like a different woman. 'Yeah, well, that's in the past and I ain't one to bear grudges.'

'Denis told me that you took Tommy in and I'm very grateful.'

'That's all right. He's a good kid and we don't mind having him.'

'When are you coming home, Mum?'

'Soon, love. But until I do, be a good boy.'

Ruth took a seat at the side of the bed. 'Is there anything you need?'

'No, but it's kind of you to ask.'

'Here, Mum,' Tommy said, obviously anxious to get her attention, 'Angel's dad's had his leg cut off.'

'Is this true, Mrs Marchant?'

'I'm afraid it is.'

'How awful. Did he have an accident?'

153

Obviously events in Candle Lane had passed Laura Walters by so Ruth told her about the car crash. Tommy scrambled up onto the bed, and as Laura cuddled him his little face lit up with pleasure until the ward sister sourly told him to get down.

He looked sulky, but his mother held his hand until visiting time was over. They were just about to leave when Laura took Ruth's hand too, pulling her forward until their faces were almost touching as she whispered, 'This heart attack has made me take stock of myself. I'll stay off the booze from now on.'

'For Tommy's sake, as well as your own, I hope you mean that.'

'I do. I wasn't always like this you know, but after losing my little girl to polio, the pain was so bad that I turned to drink.'

Ruth saw the agony in the woman's eyes. She couldn't imagine how awful it must be to lose a child. 'Oh, I didn't know, Laura, I'm so sorry. When did it happen?'

'How could you know? It was over a year ago, just before we moved to Battersea. Bessie was a beautiful little girl, and the youngest. When . . . when we lost her, I just didn't want to go on.' She smiled wanly at her son. 'Poor Tommy, he's had it rough since then, and when I think about my behaviour . . .' Pausing she let go of Ruth's hand to hold out her arms. 'Come here, son, and give me a hug.'

Tommy looked worried for a moment, but seeing that the ward sister wasn't in sight he scrambled onto the bed again and wrapped his arms around his mother's neck. She buried her face in his hair, saying, 'I haven't been much of a mother to you lately, but that's all going to change.'

Ruth watched the scene, saw the love on Laura's face, and hoped to God that this was the start of a new chapter in the woman's life.

During the journey home, Ruth said gently, 'You've never said that you once had a little sister, Tommy.'

'Mum doesn't like to talk about her so I've learned to keep me mouth shut. She was pretty though, like Angel.'

So that's it, Ruth thought. That's why Tommy was so protective of Angel. She reminded him of his little sister and putting an arm around the boy she hugged him tightly.

Twenty-One

Days had passed and Denis Walters had only called to see his son once, until at last he turned up after eleven one morning. Though slurring his words, Denis managed to tell Ruth that his wife was coming home the next day. She was surprised that Laura was coming home so soon after being admitted, but Denis said that she'd refused to have any tests and was therefore being discharged.

Ruth went to bed after that, sick at the thought of Tommy going home to that filthy house, a house that wasn't fit for a sick woman to return to either. Her mind turned until at last she decided on a plan of action.

When Ruth awoke the next morning she rang in sick, telling her boss she had an upset stomach. He didn't sound too pleased, but Ruth didn't care. What she had to do was far more important. She waited until Sally returned from taking the kids to school before breaking the news.

'Why didn't you say something earlier?' Sally asked.

'If Tommy knew his mother was coming home you'd never have got him to school and we've got a lot to do without having him under our feet.' Ruth told her, going on to say what she had in mind.

'What about Gran?'

'Sally, we'll only be next door and one of us can pop back every half an hour or so.'

'You don't need to do that,' Sadie protested.

Ruth didn't argue. No matter what her mother said they would still check up on her. And now, armed with brooms, a mop, bleach, disinfectant, and other cleaning paraphernalia, they knocked on Denis Walters' door. Thankfully he opened it, and when Ruth told him what they were going to do he didn't protest, instead scurrying off and saying he was going to work.

Sally looked around the kitchen, her expression one of dismay. 'Mum, this is awful.'

'I know, but we can't let Tommy, or Laura, come home to this.'

They tackled the kitchen first, Ruth saying as they worked, 'I still don't know where Denis works. I tried pumping Tommy, but the kid hasn't got a clue.'

Sally gasped, a hand covering her mouth as she heaved. 'Christ, Mum, look at this.'

Ruth saw that she was pointing to a part loaf of bread, thick with green mould, along with a dish of dripping, also covered in a layer of fur. She saw what looked like a remnant of cheese, hard and cracked with age and, as Sally lifted the lid of another dish, she stood back in horror.

'I don't know what this is –' Sally gasped '– but it's crawling.'

'Chuck the lot out, dishes and all. I'm sure I've got some old ones I can replace them with.'

Sally gingerly cleared the cupboard and then, with a bucket of soapy water and bleach, cleaned the inside. She then left to check on her gran, but bumping into Nelly and explaining what they were doing, the old woman said she'd go and sit with Sadie.

It took another hour to finish the kitchen and then they were thankful to find that the living room looked hardly used. It only needed dusting and the floor swept. The two of them then went upstairs.

Tommy's bedroom looked a pitiful sight, his bed coverings no more than a thin blanket and a couple of old coats. Laura's room wasn't much better and, sighing heavily, Ruth said, 'It's just as well I'm a hoarder, Sally. You strip the beds and I'll pop home to sort out some sheets and blankets. I'll find a few other bits and pieces while I'm at it.'

Ruth hurried next door and after making up a bundle of sheets and blankets, she rooted out a couple of bowls, some spare china and a nice clean tablecloth.

'What are you up to?' Sadie asked.

'I'm sorting some stuff out for next door.'

'We ain't a bleedin' charity you know.'

'It's my stuff, Mum, and I'll do what I like with it,' Ruth said as she put some tea, milk, sugar and a pint of sterilised milk into a shopping-bag. To that she added a fresh loaf of bread, some margarine and a jar of jam before saying to Nelly, 'We shouldn't be much longer, but if you need us you can bang on the wall.'

'Hold on, did you put Nelly up to sitting with me?'

It was Nelly who answered, 'No, she didn't. I just popped by.'

'That's all right then,' Sadie said.

Ruth threw Nelly a grateful smile and then hurried next door again to find Sally with a sheen of perspiration on her forehead. The beds had been stripped, and Sally had made a start on the dusting, but she frowned saying, 'I daren't touch the curtains, Mum. They're so old they'll fall apart if I try to take them down.'

'I've got some spare ones somewhere, but we can't do everything today. As long as the beds are made up and the place is clean and tidy, that's the best we can do for now.'

'The bathroom's a mess too.'

'As I said, we can't do everything. We'll just chuck some bleach down the toilet for now.'

They put in a last burst of effort and, going downstairs, added the finishing touch, Ruth's nice clean cloth on the table. With a final look around Ruth said, 'Well, it ain't perfect but it looks presentable. Let's hope Denis doesn't come back drunk or he might muck it all up again.'

'I wouldn't bank on it, Mum,' Sally replied, as they made their way home.

When the hospital transport arrived with Laura an hour later, Ruth went outside. 'Welcome home, love.'

Laura looked tired. 'Thanks,' she murmured.

'When Tommy comes home from school, he's going to be chuffed to see you.'

'I can't wait to see him and thank you so much for looking after him. I'd invite you in, but I dread to think what my place looks like.'

'Don't worry about that. I think you'll be pleasantly surprised,' Ruth told her.

Laura seemed to sag, and the driver asked, 'Are you all right, missus?'

'Yes, I'm fine and thank you. I didn't expect to be given transport home.'

Unconvinced, Ruth said, 'Come on, let's get you inside. I don't think Denis is in, so have you got a key?'

'Yes,' Laura said, taking it from her pocket, but she seemed so weak that Ruth took the key from her hand.

Laura didn't argue, and she held on to Ruth's arm as they stepped inside. 'My goodness,' she gasped, 'don't tell me that Denis did this.'

'Well, no, Sally gave me a hand to tidy the place up a bit, but it's nothing really.'

Laura lowered her eyes, but when she raised them again, Ruth saw they were moist with tears. 'You've been so good.'

'We're neighbours,' Ruth said dismissively. 'Now, would you like me to make you a cup of tea?'

'I don't think there'll be anything in the cupboards, but thanks for the offer.'

Ruth picked up a battered kettle, filling it with water before taking out the cups and saucers.

'Where did they come from?' Laura asked. 'Don't tell me. You provided them.'

'Yes, but don't worry, I don't need them. Sally is always complaining that I'm a hoarder and these haven't been used in years. I had a bit of a turnout and it's nice to have some room in my cupboards now.'

The moisture in Laura's eyes now turned to tears, but Ruth decided to pretend she hadn't noticed as she made a pot of tea. By the time it had brewed and she carried a cup over to Laura, the woman had managed to pull herself together, though Ruth was worried by her pallor. 'You look worn out,' she said. 'When you've drunk that why don't you go for a little lie down?'

'Yes, I think I will.'

Ruth waited until Laura had finished the last dregs of her tea and then said, 'Come on, I'll help you upstairs.'

When Laura saw her bedroom, there were fresh tears. 'I just don't know what to say,' she sobbed.

'There's no need to say anything. Just rest until Tommy comes home,' Ruth said. 'Now, are you sure you can manage, or would you like him to stay with us for another night or two?'

'No, but thanks anyway,' Laura said tiredly as she threw back the blankets and got into bed, fully clothed. 'I can't wait to see him and to show him that things are going to be different. I was lucky, the heart attack didn't do much damage and once I've had a bit of a rest I'll be fine looking after him.'

Ruth wasn't convinced. If Laura's heart was all right, why did she look so awful? She didn't like to leave her all alone and asked, 'When will your husband be home from work, Laura?'

'He's a casual labourer and works when the mood takes him, or when he's sober enough. If he's at work today I doubt he'll show up until after six. If he isn't working, well, your guess is as good as mine,' she said, her eyes closing.

'But he knew you were coming home,' Ruth protested.

She got no reply. Laura was already asleep.

Later that day, Sally went to collect the kids from school. As expected, Tommy was thrilled to hear that his mother was home. Sally had no choice but to let him run ahead of her, and by the time she reached Candle Lane, the boy was already out of sight.

Her mother had said that Laura seemed overly tired, so to make sure that she was all right and could cope with Tommy, Sally knocked on her door.

'Sally and Angel, please, won't you come in.'

Angel didn't need asking, she was already over the threshold, so with no other choice, Sally went inside. Everything was still spick and span, and Tommy was obviously delighted, his little face glowing with pleasure.

'Me mum's got it really nice in here now,' he said.

Laura looked about to protest, but Sally forestalled her, 'Yes, she has.'

'Thank you, Sally, for everything that you and your mother have done.'

'We were pleased to help,' she replied, worried by Laura's aura. As her mother had said, the woman looked far from well and unaware that she was echoing her words, Sally asked, 'Will your husband be home soon?'

'As I told your mother, search me. No doubt he'll turn up when he's good and ready.'

Sally felt it then, a flash of intuition that told her that Denis wasn't coming home, not today, not tomorrow; in fact she felt he wouldn't show his face for a long time.

Closing her eyes, Sally prayed she was wrong.

Twenty-Two

Over a week had passed and while Sally was at the hospital, Ruth was gazing into space. Denis Walters still hadn't turned up, but at least Laura was getting money from the National Assistance.

Despite having been deserted by her husband, so far Laura had kept her promise to stay off the booze, but just in case, when she got the chance, Ruth kept an eye out for Tommy, though she had to admit he seemed as happy as a lark, unaffected by his father's desertion.

It was silly really, but now that Tommy didn't need her, Ruth felt obsolete, and she had to admit she was missing him.

She sighed heavily, prompting Sadie to ask her, 'What's the matter? You sound as though you've got the weight of the world on your shoulders.'

'I was just thinking about Tommy. I don't see much of him now.'

'He's with his mother and that's how it should be.'

'Yeah, I suppose so,' Ruth murmured as she stood up to take Mary's letter off the mantelpiece. It had arrived that morning and as though unable to believe the contents, she read it again. Mary had travelled to so many places, but on her way home she had been offered a job in a hotel in Spain, which it seems she had decided to take for a while. It sounded so daring, yet exciting too, and while Ruth didn't like to admit it, she was envious.

162

'Why are you reading that letter again?' Sadie asked. 'She's not coming home yet and that's that.'

Ruth tucked the letter back into the envelope and as the theme music for *The Avengers* began to play, she sat down again to watch the television.

'I ain't keen on this programme,' Sadie complained.

'I think it's good.'

'I don't know what's good about watching a woman prancing about in tight, black leather and fighting like a man.'

'Diana Rigg looks great, and why shouldn't women be strong?'

'All right, don't go on about it or we'll miss the plot.'

Ruth sighed in exasperation. If her mother didn't like the programme, why was she watching it? However, not wanting to miss the action, she said no more.

'Hello, darling, how are you?' Sally said as she walked up to Arthur.

'I'm fine.'

She leaned forward and, as their lips touched, wolf whistles rang out as they had once before. Arthur's reaction was the same. 'Shut up, you lot!' he called, laughing as he looked along the ward. 'You're just jealous.'

'Can we have kisses too?'

'No chance.'

Sally grinned happily. 'What have you been up to today?'

'I've been practising on my crutches.'

'How did you manage?'

'It was a doddle.'

'Any news about coming home?'

'Missing me, are you?'

'Of course I am.'

'Well, the news is that I'm to be let out of here on Monday.'

'Oh . . . Oh that's wonderful!' Sally cried.

'I can't wait to see our flat.'

'We won't be able to move in until you're back at work,' Sally warned him.

'Of course we will. What's to stop us?'

'Arthur, think about it. I still need to be with Gran until Mum comes home from work, but I can't leave you to cope on your own either. I can't be in two places at once.'

'I'm *not* coming back to Candle Lane, Sally. I'll be fine on my own while you're with Sadie, and anyway, once I get my artificial leg, I'll be going to work.'

'You make it sound simple, but it isn't. What about your meals?'

'For goodness' sake, stop making mountains out of molehills. I'll have breakfast before you leave in the mornings, and you can leave me a sandwich or something for lunch. Don't treat me like a cripple.'

'I'm not, at least I didn't mean to. If you're sure you can manage, then fine.'

'Good, I'm glad that's sorted. Have you arranged to have a telephone installed?'

'Yes, it's already in, and despite having been in storage the television is OK,' Sally assured him, but then she frowned. 'I wonder if I can persuade Mum to have Monday off.'

'Why should she have the day off?'

'I should have thought that was obvious. I want to be at the flat waiting for when you come home.'

'Home! Sally, you don't know how good that sounds.'

When Sally arrived in Candle Lane, she was smiling. She would have to leave Arthur alone during the day, but he was adamant that he could cope, and thinking about it whilst sitting on the bus, she was sure that Elsie would pop down regularly to see him. He was coming home! Arthur was coming home, and it was wonderful.

'Hello, love, you look happy. Have you got some good news?' Ruth asked.

'Yes, Arthur will be leaving the hospital on Monday, and that means we'll be moving into our flat at last. I know it's a lot to ask, but can you take the day off work?'

'What for?'

'I want to be at the flat when Arthur arrives.'

'Flaming hell, Sally, I've had so much time off lately and I'm not sure my boss will put up with it for much longer. Oh, all right, don't look at me like that. I'll take the day off, but if I get the sack it's down to you.'

'Thanks, Mum.'

'Angel may not be too happy about leaving here.'

'She'll be all right, especially when she sees her daddy.'

'I hope you're right, Sally, but I can see feathers flying when you try to move her out.'

'She'll soon adapt, especially as we'll be here every day during the week, and we won't be leaving until you come home.'

'Yeah, but I'll just get a glimpse of her when you arrive, and then another before you leave.'

'Ruth,' Sadie warned, 'they need to be in their own home again, yet all you seem worried about is that you'll see less of Angel.'

'Yeah, yeah, you're right. I'm sorry, Sal, but I still think Angel is going to kick up.'

'No, she'll be fine,' Sally insisted, crossing her fingers and hoping that she was right.

Twenty-Three

The time seemed to drag by, but Sally filled the weekend by getting the flat aired and ready for Arthur's arrival. She insisted that Angel wasn't told that her father was coming home for two reasons. One – there was always the last-minute chance of Arthur's release being delayed. She didn't want to think about that, but with so many setbacks in the past, she was nervous of counting her chickens. And two – she had decided that the easiest way for Angel to accept the move, was by taking her straight to the flat after school. When she saw her daddy waiting for her, there was little chance she would want to leave him, making the transition easier.

At last it was Monday and Sally was almost hopping with excitement as she waited for Arthur's arrival. It was the last day of February and soon spring would arrive, heralding new beginnings, which to Sally seemed apt.

There was the toot of a horn and rushing to the window, Sally saw Bert's car. With a smile of delight she ran to open the door but, remembering how Arthur was adamant that he didn't want to be treated like a cripple, she stood on the step as he carefully climbed out of the passenger seat.

Elsie clambered out of the back and, with a little assistance from his father Arthur adjusted his crutches under his armpits as he stood gazing at her. There was an air of expectancy about him, as if gauging her reactions, and Sally, seeing one trouser leg pinned up, found that she had to fight tears.

Now, clenching her fists with determination, she forced her eyes away from his leg, saying flippantly, 'Well, are you going to stand there all day, or are you coming in?'

'I'm coming in of course,' Arthur said, carefully moving forward.

'I hope you've got the kettle on,' Bert said, his voice equally light. 'I could do with a cup of coffee before I go back to the office.'

'This is nice,' Elsie said, as she walked into the sitting room. 'What do you think of it, son?'

'From what I've seen so far it looks great,' and, turning a little clumsily on his clutches, he added, 'I'll have a look at the rest of the place.'

'We'll just have a quick drink and then we'll go,' Elsie said. 'I'm sure you two want to be alone.'

Sally, though silently agreeing with Elsie, shook her head. 'There's no need to rush off.'

'Bert has to get back to work, but I'll pop down to see Arthur tomorrow. I know you'll be with Sadie, so is there anything I can do while I'm here?'

'Just make sure he has something to eat, though I wish I could stay with him.'

'He's a grown man, love, and he needs to feel that he's capable of taking care of himself.'

'Talking about me, I hear,' Arthur said, as he returned to the room. 'The flat is great, Sally.'

'I'm glad you like it. Now, I'd best see about making us a drink.'

Bert and Elsie stayed for another half an hour, and then rose to leave. 'Don't get up, son. We can see ourselves out,' Bert said.

'I won't argue with you, Dad, and have to admit that I feel a bit whacked.'

'That's understandable, but you'll feel stronger as each day passes.'

Sally accompanied her in-laws out, but when she went back to the sitting room it was to find Arthur slumped in the chair with his eyes closed. 'Are you all right?' she asked worriedly.

He opened his eyes and for a moment they hardened. 'I'm fine, and don't mollycoddle me. Save that for Angel.'

'Yes, sorry.'

'Oh, love, it's me that should be sorry. I've got a horror of being treated differently and I'm being oversensitive. After being in hospital for such a long time, I feel a bit disorientated, but it's wonderful to be in our own place again. Come here and give me a proper kiss.'

Sally ran to his side and, kneeling by his chair, she threw her arms around him, her kiss passionate. Yes, he was being a bit snappy, but that was understandable if his stump was still painful. Despite her feelings to the contrary, she would be careful not to make a fuss of him.

Later that afternoon, Sally left to pick Angel up from school and, as her daughter ran out of the gates, she said, 'Come on, I've got a lovely surprise for you.'

'Where are we going?' Angel asked as they turned in the opposite direction from Candle Lane.

'You'll see,' Sally said, gently squeezing her daughter's hand.

As they turned into Maple Terrace, Angel looked puzzled. 'I don't want to see that place again. I want to go home.'

'I think you'll change your mind, darling,' Sally said as she opened the street door. 'Go into the sitting room and see who's waiting for you.'

'Daddy!' Angel screamed, dashing across the room.

'Hello, princess,' he said, holding out his arms.

Arthur pulled his daughter up onto his good leg, and Sally held her breath, worried that Angel might knock his stump. Angel gazed up at her father for a moment, and then looked down at his missing limb. 'Daddy, when will your leg grow again?'

With a chuckle, Arthur said, 'It won't grow again, darling, but I'm getting a new one made for me. In the meantime I'll have to get about on those things.'

Angel looked at his crutches, her eyes alight with interest. 'Can I have a go on them?'

'They'll be too big for you. Now come on, tell me how you're getting on at school?'

'It's all right, but Tommy doesn't play with me now.'

'When I was a little boy, I didn't want to play with girls, and I expect Tommy feels the same. Surely you've made other friends?'

'Yes, and they're nice. Rita is my bested friend.'

'Best friend, not bested,' Arthur said.

'Can we go home now, Daddy?'

'We're going to live here. You, me, and Mummy.'

'I want to go back to Nanny's house.'

'What and leave me on my own?'

'You can come too.'

'No, Angel, this is our home now. Anyway, I need my princess to look after me. I thought you were going to be my special nurse?'

'But . . .'

'You'll see Nanny every day, Gamma too.'

Angel sat quietly for a little while, her head cocked to one side and, for a moment, Sally thought her daughter was going to cry. But then she placed her hand on Arthur's cheek saying haughtily, 'Have you had your medicine today?'

'No, nurse, I think you'd better get it for me.'

'Mummy, where's Daddy's medicine?'

'In the kitchen. I'll go and get it for you.'

Sally quickly emptied a half bottle of cough syrup down the sink and then, rinsing out the bottle she filled it with cold tea. Returning to the sitting room and winking at Arthur, she said, 'Here you are, Angel, give him a spoonful of this.'

'I'll have to put my nurse's uniform on first,' she said importantly, and then frowned. 'Oh, no, it's at Nanny's house.'

'No, it isn't, pet. It's in your new bedroom.'

'Wait there, Daddy,' Angel said as she scrambled off his lap, and ran out of the room, Sally following close behind.

The play outfit had been a Christmas present, but for some reason Angel had refused to wear it until her daddy came home. Now, with Sally's assistance, she eagerly put it on, adding the white cap as the final touch. There was a little case to go with it, containing plastic instruments, including a pair of scissors, thermometer, stethoscope, and tweezers. A few bandages completed the kit, and now Angel grabbed it before running back to the living room.

'Hello, nurse,' Arthur said.

Angel picked up the bottle of medicine, and Sally forced herself not to intervene as she poured the liquid into a teaspoon, spilling some in the process. 'Open wide,' she said.

Arthur swallowed the cold tea and pulled a face of disgust. 'Yuk, nurse! That's awful.'

'I know, but it's to make you better.' Angel then took out the plastic thermometer, and asking Arthur to open his mouth again, she popped it inside. Obviously, this was an impatient nurse, as seconds later she pulled it out again, her little face screwed up with importance as she read the gauge. 'You have a temture,' she said, putting the stethoscope around her neck.

Arthur hid a smile, this time not correcting his daughter's mispronunciation of *temperature*.

She placed the stethoscope on his chest, and after listening to her daddy's heart, she adopted a haughty pose. 'I can't hear anything so I think you should lie down and have a rest.'

It was too much for Arthur, as while he'd fought valiantly to hold in his mirth, Angel's mannerism was the final straw and he roared with laughter.

Sally found it infectious and joined in, her heart swelling with happiness. Arthur was home at last, they were in their new home, and as their laughter subsided, their eyes met.

'I love you,' Arthur murmured.

'I love you too,' she replied.

'What about me?' Angel asked.

'And we *both* love you,' Arthur said, dragging Angel onto his lap again.

Sally smiled at the scene, pleased that the transition to Maple Terrace hadn't been too difficult. It was only the first day, but if this was anything to go by, things could only get better.

That evening, Sally said, 'Come on, Angel, it's time for your bath.'

'Daddy, you do it,' Angel begged.

'All right,' Arthur said as he clumsily stood up and tucked his crutches under his arms.

Worriedly, Sally said, 'Are you sure you can manage?'

'Of course I can. There's no need to treat me like an invalid.'

'Sorry,' Sally said hastily, but still watched nervously as they left the room. Their daughter could be a handful, and if the bathroom floor became wet, it would be slippery. Would Arthur be safe? She forced herself to stay where she was, but ten minutes later there was a yell.

'Angel!'

Heart thumping, Sally flew to the bathroom. 'What is it? Are you all right?'

Arthur was sitting on the side of the bath, his trousers and shirt soaked. 'There's no need to panic. We're both fine. Well, apart from this little minx soaking me with water.'

White bubbles formed a small crown atop Angel's red hair and, as she stood up, more coated her body. She held out her arms imperiously. 'Get me out now.'

'I'll do it,' Sally said hurriedly.

'Right, that's it,' Arthur growled as he reached for his crutches. 'As you seem to think I'm incapable, I'll leave Angel to you.'

Clumsily he left the bathroom, whilst Sally grabbed a towel and wrapped it around her daughter.

'Daddy's cross,' Angel said as they went to her bedroom.

'He's just tired, darling. Now come on, let's get you dry and into your nightclothes.'

'But I'm Daddy's nurse.'

'It's past your bedtime, and even nurses have to sleep. Now come on, be a good girl,' she said rubbing her daughter dry.

Angel consented to put her nightclothes on, but when Sally picked up a book and suggested a story, she shook her head, pouting. 'No, I want Daddy to read it.'

'I told you. He's tired, darling.'

'No, he isn't.'

Sally held back the blankets as her daughter scrambled into bed, saying, 'All right, I'll get him.'

When she walked into the living room, it was to find Arthur slumped in a chair. 'Angel wants you to read to her.'

'Are you sure I can manage it?' he asked, his voice dripping with sarcasm.

Sally's face fell. When Arthur had arrived home that morning, he seemed fine, but as the day wore on she could sense a growing tension. 'I'm sorry, love. I know I'm being overprotective, but it's your first day home and I don't want you to overdo things.'

'I don't need fussing over. If I can't cope with something, I'll tell you.'

'All right,' she said, but as Arthur stood up she thought she saw him wince. Was he in pain? With her eyes slightly unfocused, she used her spiritual gift to gaze at his aura, but before she could concentrate sufficiently, Angela burst into the room.

'Daddy, come on.'

'All right, but only one story.'

He left the room, but not before Sally noticed that he really did look tired, perhaps another reason for his tetchiness. Once

Angel was asleep she'd see that he relaxed and maybe he'd allow her to give him some spiritual healing.

At last we're alone, Sally thought. Angela was asleep, and Arthur was sprawled out on a fireside chair with his eyes closed. She focused on his stump, frowning, yet seeing only a little darkness in the aura that looked nothing to worry about.

He opened his eyes, saw her looking at his leg, and his lips tightened. 'Judging by the look on your face, you must find it repugnant, Sally?'

'Don't be silly. Of course I don't,' Sally protested.

'All right, forget it then and switch on the television. There's a programme I want to see.'

Sally did his bidding, and as Arthur stared at the screen, she remained silent. He hardly said a word for the rest of the evening, just thanked her briefly when she made him a cup of cocoa.

'Arthur,' she began, hoping he'd tell her what the problem was, but he cut her off, struggling to his feet and saying that he was going to bed.

'Are you coming?' he asked, not waiting for a reply.

Sally followed behind him, but in the bedroom one of his crutches caught on a bedside rug and he stumbled. She blanched as she rushed to his side. 'Are you all right?'

'Yes,' he snapped, regaining his balance.

He then seemed to stand awkwardly by the bed and thinking that he didn't want her to see his fumbling attempts to undress, Sally went to her side of the room, turning her back as she removed her own clothes. She then flung on her dressing gown, still not looking at Arthur as she headed for the bathroom. It was cold and Sally shivered, but to give Arthur time she washed slowly before cleaning her teeth.

Arthur was in bed when she returned, his eyes closed. He had always slept on that side, and had chosen to do so again, but that meant his stump would be next to her. She wanted to snuggle up to him, but what if she knocked it, causing him pain?

She eased herself carefully into bed, keeping a little distance between them and tentatively reached out to touch him. It was then that she heard a soft snore. Poor Arthur, he must have been exhausted and had already gone to sleep.

He was sure to feel better tomorrow, and as they had been apart for so long they were sure to make love soon. Angel had her own room again now and there was nothing to stop them. For now, Sally closed her eyes, smiling at the thought as she drifted off to sleep.

Twenty-Four

When Sally awoke in the morning she stretched out her arms. It was early, still dark, and as Arthur didn't stir she guessed that he was still asleep. Careful not to wake him, she got up and tiptoed from the room, the house silent as she washed and dressed.

With the sun just beginning to rise, Sally made a pot of tea and sat sipping it, relishing being in her own home again. All too soon she would have to leave it to spend the day at Candle Lane.

After drinking another cup of tea, Sally stirred herself and went into Angela's room. 'Come on, sweetheart, wake up,' she said, giving the child a gentle shake.

Sleepy eyes gazed up at Sally. 'I was flying, Mummy.'

Sally's eyes widened. She too had dreams of flying, vivid ones of skimming low over rooftops, the moon casting a translucent glow on the tiles. It felt so real, so joyful, and now Angel was experiencing it too. She gazed at her daughter, sure now that Angel had inherited her spiritual gifts, though how they would manifest, was yet to be seen. 'Did you enjoy flying?'

'Yes, and I want to go back to sleep so I can do it again.'

'Sorry, darling, you've got to get up.'

Angel pouted a little, but scrambled out of bed and in no time Sally was getting her ready for school.

Later, just as she was preparing breakfast, Arthur appeared, slowly walking across the room on his crutches, his hair tousled and looking to Sally, deliciously sexy.

'Hello, love,' she said. 'You're up then.'

'Daddy!' Angel cried.

'Morning, princess.'

'What do you fancy for breakfast?' Sally asked.

'What are you having, Angel?'

'Porridge.'

'Then I'll have the same,' Arthur said, his eyes avoiding Sally's.

'Are you all right, love?'

'I'm fine. Why shouldn't I be?'

Sally hid a frown. Arthur still seemed tetchy, but maybe his wound was painful. 'Does your leg hurt?'

'I'll get your medicine, Daddy,' Angel said before he had a chance to answer, and as Arthur indulged her, Sally made breakfast, though with no appetite herself she just poured two bowls.

Sally was all too aware of the strained atmosphere, though she had no idea what had caused it. Thankfully Angel seemed blissfully unaware, her chatter filling the silence, until glancing at the clock Sally saw that it was time to leave. She put the bowls in the sink, rinsed them out and then said, 'Right, it's time we were off. Come on, Angel, get your coat on.'

Angel did as she was told, and then ran to kiss her daddy goodbye. Sally went to do the same, but Arthur leaned away. Though hurt, she said, 'I'll be back as soon as I can. Your mother will be down later to see if you need anything.'

'There's no need. I'm perfectly capable of looking after myself. In fact, I'm going to ring Joe to tell him that I'm ready to start work.'

Sally wanted to argue, to tell Arthur that without his prosthesis it was too soon, but managed to hold her tongue, only murmuring, 'All right. I'll see you later.'

He smiled thinly, calling to Angel as they left, 'Bye, sweetheart, and be a good girl at school.'

'Bye, Daddy,' she called back.

Holding her daughter's hand, Sally made her way to Candle Lane, arriving to find her mother hovering in the hall. 'You're here at last. If I don't get a move on I'll be late for work.'

'Nanny, have you got any sweeties for me?'

'No, sorry, darling, but I'll fetch some home. Now come on, give me a kiss before I go.'

Angel ran into Ruth's arms, clinging to her nanny for a moment, obviously bewildered by this new routine. Ruth was finally able to extract herself, saying as an afterthought, 'How's Arthur?'

'He's fine. See you later, Mum.'

As the door closed behind her mother, Sally went into the kitchen, Angel on her heels. 'Hello, Gran.'

'Hello, love, and what are you doing here?'

'You know why I'm here, Gran. I'll be staying with you until Mum comes home from work.'

'What on earth for? You should be with Arthur.'

'Arthur is fine on his own,' Sally said, frowning. Since Gran's stroke she was often forgetful, but until now there had been signs of improvement. Surreptitiously Sally looked at her gran's aura, but she couldn't see any signs of deterioration. 'Did you sleep well last night?'

'No, not really, my hips were playing up.'

'I'm taking Angel to school now, but I'll give you a bit of healing when I get back.'

'Thanks, love. That always does the trick. Now then, Angel, before you go to school, ain't you gonna give me a kiss?'

The child ran to her side, grinning widely. 'I'm Daddy's nurse now, Gamma.'

'That's nice, and do you wear your uniform?'

Angel puffed with importance as she answered Sadie, 'Yes, and I take my daddy's temture.'

'Temperature,' Sadie corrected, 'and my, ain't you a clever girl.'

'Come on, Angel, it's time to go,' Sally urged.

Angel reluctantly left Sadie's side, but not before Sally called, 'I'll be back soon, Gran.'

Sadie pursed her lips as her granddaughter left the room. It wasn't right that Sally had to come round here every day to look after her, yet despite protesting, nobody listened. She didn't need nursing, and even if she did, it wasn't Sally's place to do it.

Ruth had to work, Sadie knew that, and though she loved her daughter, there was no getting away from the fact that she had a selfish streak. All right, it would be a bit humiliating to apply for National Assistance, but surely that was better than laying the burden of her care onto Sally.

Her elder daughter was as bad, going off on a cruise and then deciding not to return for what sounded like some time. Sadie sighed heavily. Though her daughters were similar in looks, both pretty with brown hair and blue eyes, they had very different personalities. As children, Ruth had been the needy one, whilst Mary had always been self-sufficient, growing into an uppity and bossy adult.

Sadie had no idea where Mary got that from, but then she smiled and finally chuckled. If truth be known, Mary was the daughter who was the most like her. She might appear hard, but it was just a veneer that hid a soft and vulnerable core.

With a wriggle, Sadie shifted in her chair to ease a cushion behind her back and then dozed lightly until Sally returned.

Sally smiled when she saw her gran having a nap, but she soon woke up and the rest of the day passed as normal. When Ruth came home from work and it was time for them to leave, Angel looked bewildered. 'Can't I stay here?'

'Don't you want to see your daddy? After all, it must be time for his medicine.'

That did the trick and running up to Ruth, Angel said, 'Sorry, Nanny, I've got to go.'

'I know, darling. Give me a kiss and I'll see you in the morning.'

Angel flung her arms around Ruth's neck, kissed her cheek and then ran to Sadie to do the same. Sally hovered impatiently, anxious to see Arthur, until at last they were hurrying home. Tentatively she opened the door. Arthur grinned when he saw Angel.

'Well, there's my girl.'

There was no such greeting for Sally, but as their eyes met, he managed a tight, little smile. 'I rang Joe and invited him round. He said he'd call in on his way home from the site, so he should be here soon.'

'If he's coming straight from work, he might be hungry. Do you think I should ask him if he'd like some dinner?'

'Yes, good idea.'

Angel, obviously feeling left out, wormed her way onto Arthur's lap. 'I got a star for my drawing today, Daddy.'

'Well done, sweetheart.'

'Arthur, before I make a start on the vegetables, can I get you anything?'

'No, thanks,' he said without raising his head. 'Now then, Angel, what else did you do at school today?'

It was silly really, but Sally felt oddly rejected as she made her way to the kitchen. She began to prepare the food, thankful that there was an extra pork chop, and it was almost ready when the doorbell rang.

'Hello,' Joe said when she went to answer it. 'I hope you don't mind me calling.'

'No, of course not. In fact, I've prepared extra so you can stay for dinner,' she told him, thinking that at least Joe's visit might help with the tense atmosphere.

This proved to be true. When they walked into the living room, Arthur grinned at Joe, and greeted him with a cheery, 'Hello, mate.'

'Can I get you a drink, Joe?' Sally asked.

'A coffee would be great.'

'What about you, Arthur?'

'Yes, the same please.'

Sally went through to the kitchen, relieved that Arthur had spoken civilly to her. Was it just because Joe was here, or would he keep it up?

Joe made a fuss of Angel, but Arthur saw that she was a little shy with him. It wouldn't last, but for now she was being unusually quiet. Sally came back into the room and as she handed them the drinks, Arthur asked, 'How are things going on the site, Joe?'

'We're progressing well. The foundations for the first row of terraces are in and so far we're keeping to schedule.'

'That's good. I can't wait to start work. You've waited long enough and it's time I pulled my weight.'

'There's no hurry, and it's amazing what you managed to achieve from that hospital bed. The brochure you designed is great, along with the name of the development. "The Meadows", it has a nice ring to it.'

'Have you had the brochures printed?'

'I had to get an artist's mock-up first, but yes, have a look,' Joe said, reaching into his briefcase to pull one out.

Arthur was pleased with the artist's impression. The site was in Reading, the houses clustered around a central green. 'It looks good, but I'd like to see the site.'

'If you feel up to it I'll drive you there tomorrow. Well, that's if Sally doesn't mind.'

'You don't need to consult my wife. This is my decision, not hers.'

'Fine, I'll pick you up around seven.'

'I'd best get back to the kitchen,' Sally said. 'Dinner is nearly ready.'

As Sally left, Arthur took a sip of his coffee and then asked Joe a few more questions about the housing development. He tried to take it all in, but with no experience of the construction game he felt out of his depth. There was so much to learn. Was he up to it?

'Do you mind if I have a bit of a wash up, Arthur?'

'Help yourself, mate. The bathroom is just across the hall.'

As soon as Joe was out of sight, Angel chirped, 'Daddy, you haven't had your medicine.'

'You'd best go and get it then,' he said as Angel scurried off.

It wasn't long before Arthur had dutifully taken his mock medicine, and after Sally laid the table for dinner, they all tucked in. Arthur found that with Joe's lively conversation his tension had eased. It could be that Sally was fine about his leg and last night he'd been imagining things. He was probably being over-sensitive and later, when they went to bed, things would be different.

At seven-thirty, Angel was tucked up for the night and Sally was about to wash up when she heard a ring on the doorbell. She dried her hands and went to see who it was. 'Hello, Patsy.'

'I just popped down to say hello. I thought it was a bit much when you had just moved in yesterday, but hope it's all right now.'

'Of course it is. Come on in,' Sally replied as she took in Patsy's outfit. Her upstairs neighbour was wearing a navy and white striped mini-dress, with white knee-length boots. Blonde hair framed her pretty face and her make-up had been skilfully applied. 'I love your dress, Patsy.'

'It's from Biba in Kensington. I couldn't resist buying it.'

Sally looked down at her own outfit, feeling frumpy beside Patsy as they walked into the living room. 'Arthur, Joe, this is Patsy Laurington. She lives upstairs.'

Joe jumped to his feet, his hand outstretched. 'Pleased to meet you.'

'It's nice to meet you too,' she said, her neck craning as she looked up at him, their hands still clasped.

Sally could see that Patsy was flushing prettily, but she wasn't surprised. Joe was a good-looking man and if she wasn't mistaken, there was an instant attraction.

'Put her down, Joe,' Arthur joked.

Their hands dropped and Sally then introduced Arthur. 'Patsy, this is Arthur, my husband.'

'Hello,' Patsy said. 'I expect you're pleased to be home after all that time in hospital.'

'Yes, I am,' he said.

'Patsy, sit down,' Sally invited. 'Can I get you something to drink?'

'A coffee would be nice.'

'I'd like one too,' Arthur said. 'What about you, Joe?'

'Yes, great.'

'I'll give you a hand,' Patsy said, following Sally through to the kitchen. 'Joe seems nice.'

'Yes, he is.'

'Is he married?'

'No, he's single and as far as I know he hasn't got a girlfriend.'

'What does he do for a living?'

'I think I told you before about my husband getting involved in building houses. It's a new venture and Joe is his partner.'

'Is he now,' Pasty said. 'That's interesting.'

For a moment Sally thought she saw a calculating look in her eyes, but then Patsy smiled at her without guile, saying, 'Well, I wish them the best of luck.'

The rest of the evening was pleasant, and when asked by Joe about her line of work, Patsy told him she was a mobile hairdresser.

'Do you cut men's hair?'

'Err yes, but I don't get many male clients.'

'Did you hear that, Arthur? Patsy here could give you a bit of a trim.'

'What's wrong with my hair?'

'Well, mate, you've got to admit it's a bit long.'

'Maybe, but no offence, Patsy, I'd rather stick to the barbers,' Arthur said, then yawned widely.

Joe glanced at his watch and then rose to his feet. 'It's nearly eleven and as we've got an early start in the morning, I'd best be on my way.'

'Yes, I'll be off too,' Patsy said.

Sally saw them out and returned to the living room to see Arthur standing with his crutches tucked under his arms. 'I'm going to bed,' he said. 'Are you coming?'

She had seen him yawning and though tired too, Sally said, 'I've got a stack of washing up to do first. I'd rather do it now than tackle it in the morning.'

'Suit yourself,' he said abruptly.

Sally put his attitude down to tiredness and found she had to scrub the plates extra hard to remove the stuck on residue of gravy. At last it was done and when she went through to the bedroom, she saw that Arthur was already asleep. If he was going to the site with Joe tomorrow it meant an early start, so careful not to wake him she climbed in, again resisting the urge to snuggle close.

It was another night without the warmth of Arthur's arms around her, and feeling a twinge of disappointment, Sally chided herself. Arthur had only just come out of hospital, and he probably still needed time to recover. She would just have to be patient, that was all.

Twenty-Five

Though late, Joe had accepted Patsy's invitation for coffee and was upstairs in her flat.

'Just in case you're wondering, it's only coffee I'm offering,' Patsy said as she carried in two cups.

'That's fine with me.'

She sat down beside him, her skirt riding up and Joe couldn't help admiring her shapely legs. He dragged his eyes away and looked around the room, not really liking the garish décor. His eyes then settled on a photograph of a little girl that was displayed on the sideboard. 'Nice-looking kid – is she a relative?'

'Yes,' Patsy said shortly, offering no further explanation.

Joe felt he had said the wrong thing, but then Patsy blurted, 'I'm a divorcée.'

'Are you?' he said, surprised. Patsy looked so young, too young to have been married and divorced.

'I was only seventeen when I married and soon found it was a dreadful mistake.'

'What went wrong?'

'I'd rather not talk about it.'

Joe shifted uncomfortably. They'd been fine in Arthur and Sally's company, but now the atmosphere was tense. Perhaps Patsy was worried that he'd try it on. Hoping to alleviate her fears he moved along the sofa, putting a little distance between them.

Patsy was the one to look surprised now and leaning forward she placed her cup on the coffee table. She then shuffled close to him again, her expression soft and her eyes inviting as a small smile curled her lips.

Joe's brow rose and, hoping he hadn't misread the signs, he placed his cup next to hers before pulling her into his arms.

Their kiss was passionate, and as it deepened Patsy's tiny teeth nipped his lower lip. Joe groaned, becoming aroused as his hands began to roam her body, one coming to rest on a small, but pert breast.

She stiffened instantly, pushing him away, her voice sharp as she said, 'Joe, I think you'd better leave now.'

'I'm sorry,' he said.

'Just because I'm divorced, it doesn't mean I'm that sort of girl.'

'I didn't think you were, but well, you are rather lovely and you can't blame a chap for trying.'

Small dimples appeared on her cheeks as she smiled. 'Thanks, but it's time you left.'

Joe rose to his feet. 'Can I see you again?'

'Yes, I'd like that.'

'How about tomorrow night? Dinner? Or a movie?'

'Dinner would be nice.' She stood on tiptoe, kissing him swiftly on the cheek, and then led the way downstairs. 'Goodnight, Joe,' she whispered as he stepped outside.

'I'll pick you up at eight tomorrow night.'

'That's fine,' she said, adding before closing the door, 'I'll look forward to it.'

Joe climbed into his car, but as he drove home there was a worried frown on his brow. He liked Patsy, and there was no denying that she was a looker, but there was something he couldn't put his finger on, something not quite right.

He'd asked her out, but now hoped he hadn't made a mistake.

* * *

Arthur had little to say to Sally the next morning. Last night she had taken ages to come to bed and it confirmed his suspicions. He hadn't been imagining things, nor was he being oversensitive.

At seven Joe arrived and Arthur was relieved to leave for the site. He settled back in his seat and began to enjoy the journey, turning his head when Joe spoke.

'By the way, I'm taking Patsy out to dinner tonight,' he said.

'Blimey, that was quick work, though I can't say I blame you. She's a bit of all right.'

'Yes, she is, but I'm not sure she's my type,' Joe said, and then turned the conversation to more serious things to do with the project.

Arthur was enjoying himself, feeling at least a little useful again. As they drew closer to Reading a soft rain began to fall, a thin veil that obscured his view as they arrived at the site. Joe parked and Arthur got out of the car, now able to see what looked like thick mud in the centre of the site. To one side building materials were stacked high, and the first row of houses was emerging.

'Well, Arthur, what do you think?'

'It's good to see that the houses are going up.'

'Come on,' Joe said, motioning towards a prefabricated hut. 'Such as it is, that's our site office. I'll give our foreman a shout and he can bring us up to speed.'

Arthur saw planks of wood leading to the door and gingerly swung over them, doing his best to hide his feelings. The site was a quagmire, impossible to manoeuvre on his crutches, and glancing around he saw some of the men looking at him. They quickly lowered their heads, but not before he saw the pity in their eyes.

As they went inside, Arthur's eyes roamed the hut. The plans and charts attached to the wall meant nothing to him.

'One sugar or two?' Joe asked, as he started to make them a drink.

'Two, please,' Arthur said as he sat down on a wooden chair, placing his crutches to one side.

Soon after Joe handed him a tin mug, and then took a seat at the makeshift desk. 'It's good to have you on board, mate.'

'Doing what?' Arthur asked.

'Blimey, mate, what do you think? The site doesn't run itself. To maintain the schedules there are materials to be ordered, and as project managers it's our job to keep things running smoothly. The bricklayers will do their job, as will the roofers, but there are all the other tradesmen to sort out; the plasterers, plumbers, carpenters and electricians. They all need access at different stages, and it's up to us to see that they have all the materials they need, *and* that they don't overlap with each other.'

'I thought you said we have a foreman.'

'Yes, we do, and Billy does a good job with the men, but he isn't the one who does the ordering, or the marketing.'

Arthur shook his head doubtfully. 'Christ, Joe, until I get my leg I won't be able to navigate the site.'

'If you want to start work now, you won't have to. There's plenty of stuff that needs doing in this office, such as making up and paying the men's wages, along with marketing the houses and as I said, ordering materials. I could certainly do with a hand.'

'I haven't got a clue where to start.'

'Neither did I at first, but like me, you'll learn. We may make a few mistakes, but what we pick up in experience here, we'll take on to our next project. I must admit there have been a few cock-ups, but nothing too serious, and we're on schedule. Well, so far that is.'

The enormity of what they had undertaken hit Arthur, and he wondered what they had got themselves into. They had sunk all their savings into the venture, and if it all went pear-shaped, they'd be left with nothing but a pile of debts.

Arthur took a deep, steadying breath. As Joe said, he'd learn, and he'd do just that, putting everything he could into making this work. Their future depended on it.

Twenty-Six

Sally chewed worriedly on her lower lip. Arthur hadn't complained about working on the building site, yet she was sure that something was wrong.

Two weeks had passed and in that time Arthur had grown more remote. Sally feared he found the job too much, especially as every night he fell asleep as soon as his head hit the pillow.

A good night's sleep didn't help, and as always he had got up that morning terse and moody with hardly a word spoken between them. Sally was at a loss to know what to do.

It didn't take Sally and Angel long to reach Candle Lane, and after taking her daughter to school she had only just returned when there was a knock on the door. 'Hello, Nelly.'

'Wotcher, Sally. What sort of mood is Sadie in?'

'She's much better nowadays. Her mood swings aren't as bad.'

'Right, I'll come in then.'

Sally only half listened to the conversation as the two ladies chatted, but her ears pricked up when she heard Laura Walters' name. 'What did you say about Laura?'

'I was just telling Sadie that she might be drinking again.'

'No! I can't believe it.'

'Jessie Stone saw her yesterday and said she was acting a bit odd.'

'Jessie is nothing but a gossip,' Sally protested. 'Just because

Laura wasn't herself, it doesn't mean she's drinking. She might have been ill.'

'I don't think so. Jessie said that Laura was furtive, sneaking home with something hidden under her coat. She spoke to her, and when Laura answered, her voice sounded slurred.'

Sally frowned. 'Oh dear. I don't like the sound of that.'

'Me neither, but I ain't surprised. There's still no sign of her husband, and it must be hard on Laura that Denis walked out like that.'

'That's no excuse,' Sadie snapped.

'Maybe not, but if you're an alcoholic just one drink puts you back on the slippery slope.'

'Oh, and since when did you become an expert on the subject, Nelly Cox?'

'Now then, Sadie, there's no need to be sarcastic. I'm only repeating what I've heard.'

'I'm not being sarcastic and I'll say what I like in my own home. If you don't like it, then you know what you can do.'

Sally jumped to her feet, surprised by her gran's sudden mood change, and tried to change the subject. 'Do you fancy a cup of tea, Nelly?'

'No, thanks. I'm off.'

With no other choice, Sally escorted Nelly to the door where the old woman said, 'Sorry, love, but I could see that Sadie was on the turn and I didn't fancy being in the line of fire. When she gets in a two and eight she's impossible.'

'It's all right, I understand, but it's rare nowadays.'

'If you say so. Maybe I'll pop along to see her again tomorrow.'

'Do you think Jessie is right about Laura?'

'I dunno, love, but no doubt we'll soon find out,' Nelly said, lifting a hand to wave as she bustled off.

The rest of the day passed slowly for Sally, but at last her mother arrived home, and she was surprised to see Tommy Walters with her.

'I found him sitting on his doorstep. The poor little sod's hungry.'

'Nelly came round earlier with a bit of gossip,' Sadie told her. 'She said that . . . well . . . *you know who*, might be back on the booze.'

The boy was too astute, and with an adult-like nod of his head, he said, 'Yeah, I fink me mum's pissed again.'

Ruth didn't rebuke Tommy, only smiled at him fondly. 'Sit down, love, and I'll get you something to eat.'

Sally's eyes narrowed as she watched her mother. She looked pleased to be looking after Tommy, as though glad that Laura was drinking. Surely that wasn't the case? Surely she was imagining things?

Arthur arrived home after Sally, and as always Angel ran up to him. 'Daddy, Tommy's having his dinner with Nanny.'

'Is he, well, that's nice.'

'His mummy is pissed.'

'Angel!' Sally exclaimed. 'Don't use that word!'

'Tommy said it.'

Arthur forced his voice to sound stern. 'Little girls shouldn't swear. It isn't nice and I don't want you copying Tommy.'

'All right, Daddy.'

'Did you have a good day, Arthur?' Sally asked.

As Angel was around, Arthur managed to keep his voice pleasant. 'It was all right.'

Sally glanced at the clock and frowned. 'With Joe and Patsy coming to dinner tonight, I'd best get a move on.'

Arthur said nothing, and when she left the room Angel began to chatter. He did his best to answer her, yet in truth his mind was elsewhere. When he came home from hospital Arthur had expected everything to be wonderful, and as far as work was concerned, other than the occasional pitying look from some of the men, it was. However, he couldn't say the same about his relationship with Sally. It had gone wrong from day one when he had sensed her withdrawal after just one kiss. In bed, rather than face rejection, he pretended to be asleep, though aware when Sally climbed into bed, that she kept a careful distance.

Every night now followed the same pattern and Arthur knew why. Sally found his stump repulsive and didn't want it near her. She was making him feel less than a man, and he hated it.

At seven-thirty, Sally put Angel to bed and then laid the table for dinner. Arthur hardly spoke again and once again Sally was determined to talk to him, to get to the bottom of what was wrong, but with Joe and Patsy due to arrive soon it would have to wait.

Patsy as usual looked lovely when Sally let them in, this time in a bright red miniskirt and white roll-neck jumper. As they walked into the living room, Arthur perked up. 'Blimey, Patsy, you're a sight for sore eyes,' he said, looking the girl up and down.

'Thank you, kind sir,' she replied, and as she sat down her skirt rode up to reveal more of her shapely legs.

Sally saw that Arthur was looking at them with appreciation and was surprised to feel a surge of jealousy. When was the last time he had looked at her like that? She forced a smile, shaking off the feeling as she asked if they'd like a drink.

It was the start of an evening that seemed full of undertones. Arthur focused most of his attention on Patsy, almost, Sally thought, as if he was deliberately trying to make her jealous. But why?

Joe was good company, chatting to her throughout the evening and acting as a counterbalance, yet even he seemed tense as he watched Patsy laughing and giggling her way through the evening.

Sally decided to play Arthur at his own game, and flirted a little with Joe, but her heart wasn't in it and it made her feel foolish, especially when Arthur didn't seem to care. She tried another tactic. 'How's business, Patsy?' she asked, drawing her attention away from Arthur.

'It isn't too bad, but I could do with a little car and would love to learn to drive. It's a bugger carting my stuff on and off buses.'

'But I thought you said all your clients are local.'

Patsy flushed. 'Yeah, well, they are, but I've just picked up a couple of new clients in Streatham.'

Sally wondered why Patsy sounded so flustered, but only said, 'Oh, did you advertise there?'

'No, they came by way of a recommendation.'

'I wouldn't mind having my hair restyled. How much do you charge?'

'Leave it out, Sally, I wouldn't charge you anything. What sort of style are you thinking of?'

'I don't know really. Perhaps a cut like yours. What do you think, Arthur?'

'Do what you like,' he snapped.

Sally flinched at his tone, hurt and bewildered by his behaviour, while Joe glanced pointedly at his watch. 'I didn't realise it was so late. Come on, Patsy, we'd best be off.'

They said goodbye to Arthur, his reply short, and as Sally showed them to the door, Joe said quietly, 'Is Arthur all right?'

'He isn't himself and he seems dreadfully tired.'

Joe frowned. 'In that case, I could suggest he takes a bit of time off. At least until he gets his prosthesis. I think he said he's going for his first fitting next week.'

'Yes, that's right.'

'Come on, Joe,' Patsy urged.

'Yes, yes, all right,' he said. 'Bye, Sally, and don't worry, I'll have a word with Arthur.'

Relieved, Sally waved to Patsy and then closed the door, only to find when she went back to the living room that it was empty.

She went through to the bedroom and in the darkness heard Arthur snoring.

Sadly she got undressed, hoping that Arthur would agree to take some time off. He'd be less tired then and maybe, just maybe, they could regain the intimate side of their marriage.

Twenty-Seven

The following morning, Sally was in despair. She had prepared
Arthur's breakfast, his manner again distant, but just as she was
about to talk to him about it, Angel appeared.

'I had a bad dream,' she said, rubbing her eyes.

'Come here, poppet,' Arthur said, pulling her onto his lap to
comfort her. 'What was your dream about?'

'I can't remember now.'

Arthur hugged her to him and Sally found herself wishing he
would do the same to her. It had been so long, so very long since
he had held her.

'Sorry, sweetheart, that'll be Joe,' Arthur said, urging Angel
off of his lap when the doorbell rang. 'I've got to go.'

Sally waited, but all she got was a short goodbye and then
Arthur was gone. Sadly she got Angel ready, to find as they left
the flat over an hour later, that Patsy was just going out too.
'Good morning,' Sally said. 'Have you got an early
appointment?'

'Yes, one of my ladies is wanting a cut and set. Thanks for
dinner last night. It was great.'

'You're welcome,' she said, walking with Patsy to the corner,
where they parted to go off in different directions.

Angel was unusually quiet, but when they drew close to Candle
Lane she suddenly said, 'I don't like Patsy.'

'But she's nice. Why don't you like her?'

'Dunno, just don't,' Angel said and, letting go of her hand as they turned the corner, she ran ahead to number five.

Sally was unable to think of a reason for her daughter's dislike of Patsy, and was frowning when she walked into her mother's kitchen.

'Hello, love,' Ruth said. 'What's up?'

'It's nothing.'

'That's good because I've got to go or I'll be late for work. Bye, Angel, see you later, pet,' she called, the door slamming behind her.

'Blimey, where's the fire?' Sadie complained.

'What fire, Gamma?'

'Oh, it's just a silly saying for someone in a rush.'

Sally returned from taking Angel to school to find her gran waiting to question her. 'As your mother said, what's up, Sally?'

'It's nothing, Gran.'

'Don't give me that. It's been obvious for a while now that something's worrying you.'

Sally sat down, saying nothing for a moment, but then found that she wanted to confide in someone, the need to unburden overwhelming. 'Since Arthur came home from hospital, he seems tired all the time, but it's not just that, he's acting strangely. He seems distant, remote, and hardly talks.'

'That's to be expected.'

Sally was surprised by her gran's answer. 'Is it? But why?'

'He was in hospital for months, and in that time the ward became his insular little world. He was cut off from outside worries, with everything done for him. Now he's had to adapt to ordinary life again, and is doing a job he's unfamiliar with. He's got a lot to learn and must be worried that if it all goes wrong, he'll lose everything. That's a lot of responsibility on his shoulders and perhaps the burden of it is wearing him down.'

'I hadn't thought of that, and yes, you could be right,' Sally said. 'Poor Arthur, I'll have to be more supportive. Thanks, Gran, I'm so glad I confided in you.'

'And I'm glad I come in useful for something. Now how about putting the kettle on?'

'It wouldn't suit me, Gran.'

'Yeah, very funny, but I don't suppose it would look any worse on you than the daft fashions youngsters are wearing nowadays. It's all mini-dresses, long boots, straight-cut hair and black-rimmed eyes that make them look like pandas.'

'I keep meaning to get myself some new clothes and I rather fancy a miniskirt, but I just never seem to have the time.'

'Leave it out, Sally. You look fine as you are and I can't see Arthur letting you wear a short skirt.'

'Oh, you'd be surprised, Gran. My upstairs neighbour wears them all the time and Arthur ogles her legs with great appreciation whenever he sees her.'

'Yeah, well, that's typical of men. They like to see women in sexy clothes, as long as it isn't their wife who's wearing them.'

Sally chuckled, 'Yes, you may be right.'

As she waited for the kettle to boil a smile remained on Sally's face. She felt so much better after talking to her gran about Arthur, and berated herself for her lack of understanding.

When Sally arrived home she was determined that no matter what sort of mood Arthur was in, she would keep smiling. What he needed was a cheerful environment to come home to, a haven where he could leave all thoughts of work and worry behind.

However, when Arthur walked in half an hour later his expression was thunderous, and even Angel was ignored as he spat, 'Joe denied it, but it was you, wasn't it? You who got him to suggest that I take some time off.'

'I told him that you seem tired. I . . . I was worried about you.'

'I am *not* tired,' he yelled. 'I'm a grown man, Sally, not a child and if I want time off I can speak for myself!'

'Why are you shouting, Daddy?' Angel cried, her eyes wide with fear.

Her voice must have penetrated Arthur's anger, and the rigidness went out of his stance. 'Sorry, sorry, pet,' he murmured.

As Arthur sat down and urged Angel onto his lap, Sally slipped through to the kitchen, trying not to cry as she busied herself with finishing off their dinner. In her concern for Arthur she had put her foot in it again, and now she dreaded his mood for the rest of the evening.

Thankfully he made an effort to be amenable in front of Angel, and soon after she was tucked up in bed, Arthur's parents paid them a visit.

'How are you feeling, son?'

'I'm fine, Mum.'

'Sally, how about you all coming to us on Sunday for a nice roast dinner? In fact spend the day and stay for tea too.'

'What do you think, Arthur?'

'It's fine with me.'

'Good, and your dad will pick you up.'

'Right, I've had my orders, and now tell me, Arthur, how is work progressing on the site?' Bert asked.

'It's going well.'

Sally offered them a drink and as she went through to the kitchen to make it, Elsie followed her. 'I was hoping to get here before Angel went to bed, but persuading Bert to get a move on is impossible. How is she?'

'She's fine and doing well at school.'

'Does she still talk about the before time?'

'Not recently.'

'It was certainly unusual, but some eastern religions believe in reincarnation.'

'I must admit it was like she was remembering a previous life, but it sounds so far-fetched.'

'No more than heaven and hell, or angels and demons.'

'When you put it that way, no, I suppose not.'

'Who's to know which teachings are right, Sally, and if you ask me, religion seems to be a matter of geography and nationality.'

Sally frowned. 'What do you mean?'

'If I had been born, say, in Tibet, I may have been brought up a Buddhist. In India, maybe a Hindu, but because I was born here and my parents were Christians, that's the doctrine I was taught. If you ask me, as long as the religion you practise makes you a better person and gives you something to cling to in time of trouble, that's all that matters.'

Sally nodded. 'Yes, I agree, but it's a shame that there's so much intolerance.'

'Oh, Sally, I do miss our chats. Bert thinks it's all a load of tosh and I've given up talking to him about spiritual subjects. I used to love it when you visited me, or I you, but since you've had to look after Sadie, you're so tied down.'

'I know, but she can't be left on her own.'

Elsie sighed and then said, 'Changing the subject, I was doing the cards the other day and something strange came up. I saw your father in the spread.'

'Oh no! I hope he doesn't turn up again after all these years.'

'I don't know, Sally. I'm afraid the cards weren't clear on that.'

Sally continued to make the drinks, her mind racing. She didn't want Ken Marchant to show his face again, in fact she hated the thought. Not only that – what sort of effect would it have on her mother?

* * *

'Tommy, run down to the off-licence and get me a bottle of cider.'

'What for?' he asked, scowling at his mother. 'You're already pissed.'

'You little sod,' she slurred, rising unsteadily to her feet.

As she walked towards him, her hand ready to strike, Tommy backed away. Why? Why had she turned to booze again? He'd been good, had kept out of mischief, and with his dad gone, he'd tried to look after her. She'd been fine for a while and he'd loved the affection showered on him, loved how with his help she had kept the house clean. Now it was a mess again, a dump, a stinking, smelly, dump.

His mum was almost on top of him now, but Tommy turned and fled, the street door slamming behind him as he ran down Candle Lane. With his mother in a drunken temper, Tommy knew he would have to keep out of her way and so he began to wander aimlessly. He'd had no dinner and was hungry, but with the shops closed there was no chance of nicking anything. Kicking a stone, he continued to amble, until finally he'd walked a full circle and was back in Candle Lane. The lights were still on in his house, but Tommy knew that if he went in now he was sure to get a belting.

With his stomach growling, Tommy bit hard on his lower lip as tears welled in his eyes. He was a boy and mustn't cry. Big boys don't cry, his dad had always told him. He wondered where his father was, and why he'd buggered off. Tommy choked back a sob. Had he caused that too just as he had caused his mother to start drinking again?

He looked with longing at Ruth's door, and, though his mother had warned him to stay away from her, Tommy rattled the letterbox.

The door was opened, the smile of welcome warm. 'Come in, love, and don't tell me, I can guess. Your mum's been boozing again.'

Tommy nodded and nestled into Ruth's arms. 'I expect you're hungry,' she said.

He nodded and, despite all his efforts to stem them, tears flowed. Ruth might not be his real gran, but he had come to love her, along with seeing her home as his refuge.

Twenty-Eight

On a Saturday evening towards the end of March, Joe rang Patsy's doorbell, dreading the conversation he was about to have with her and just wanting to get it over with. He'd taken her out a good few times now, along with joining Joe and Sally for dinner, but there was something about Patsy that he didn't like. Something false. When he'd first met her she had seemed sweet and innocent, but it hadn't taken him long to decide that it was all an act, a veneer covering a hard centre. She was too pushy, too eager to take the relationship further, and lately much too interested in his finances.

'Well, well, Joe. This is a surprise. I haven't heard from, or seen you since Monday and I was beginning to think you've been avoiding me.'

Patsy was Sally's friend and it could make things awkward, but nevertheless he wanted to nip this in the bud before it went any further. After a moment's hesitation, he decided that honesty would be the best policy and said, 'I've been busy, and to be honest, I don't want to get into anything serious at the moment.'

Her eyes hardened. 'So, why did you ask me out?'

'That's just it, Patsy. It was just meant to be casual, nothing serious, but after a couple of dates you started getting proprietary. I'm not ready for that.'

'Bugger off then. There's plenty more fish in the sea and I know of one just waiting to be caught.'

202

Joe was pleased to go and hurried downstairs, happy to drive off. From Patsy's reaction it was obvious he hadn't broken her heart. In fact it sounded like she already had her eye on someone else.

Unaware of what had just transpired upstairs, Sally did her best to be cheerful. She had kept up this facade since talking to her gran, but it hadn't made any difference. The atmosphere at home was still strained, but at least they still managed to act normally around Angel, and Sally was consoled that at least her daughter was happy.

When Patsy rang the doorbell, Sally could see by the expression on her face that something was wrong. She urged her in, and as Patsy flopped onto a chair, she said, 'Joe has just been round. He said he doesn't want to see me any more.'

'I'm so sorry,' Sally said, moving forward to lay a conciliatory hand on Patsy's shoulder. She looked so miserable and Sally's heart went out to her. 'Would you like something to drink?'

'Yes, please, a coffee would be nice,' she said, dabbing at her eyes with a handkerchief.

It didn't take Sally long to make Patsy a drink and she returned to the living room where her eyes widened with surprise. In the short time she'd been in the kitchen Patsy had recovered, no longer looking sad as she sat relaxed and laughing at something Arthur had said.

'Oh, you are funny,' Patsy sputtered. 'It's good that you can joke about your leg. And when do you get your artificial one?'

'I've had two fittings now and I'm going to Roehampton to collect it on Monday morning.'

'One of my clients has a false leg, but you can hardly tell. He barely limps at all, but he's quite elderly and uses a stick.'

'One of your clients? Somehow I can't imagine you cutting an old man's hair.'

Patsy flushed. 'I do his wife's hair and one day he asked me to cut his.'

Arthur nodded and then said, 'I'm determined to walk without a stick.'

'Good for you,' Patsy said, uncrossing her own legs and reaching out to pick up her coffee.

At nine-thirty, Patsy still hadn't left. She laughed and giggled with Arthur until Sally felt like screaming. His eyes continually strayed to Patsy's legs, and in such a short skirt, there was a lot of them on show.

'Bye, Arthur,' Patsy said, with a cheeky wink when at last she rose to leave.

Sally managed to keep her feelings in check and said at the street door, 'I'm sorry about you and Joe.'

'Don't worry about me, I'll soon get over it, in fact, after this evening I already have.'

Sally was puzzled by her words, but soon forgot them when she returned to find Arthur struggling to his feet. It was before ten, yet he was going to bed. Impulsively she said, 'Arthur, please, I know that something is wrong. Won't you stay up for a while to talk about it?'

'I'm not in the mood for talking,' he said curtly.

With that he turned and hobbled away leaving Sally staring at his retreating figure.

When Sally awoke the next morning, she found the bed empty beside her. Surprised that Arthur was up at half past eight on a Sunday she threw on her dressing gown and went to the kitchen. Arthur was sitting at the kitchen table, deep in thought and seemed unaware of her presence. 'Arthur, won't you tell me what's wrong?'

His face was taut. 'Nothing's wrong.'

'I can see you're upset about something. Is it to do with the site?'

'No, it isn't, in fact it's closer to home. I was just sitting here thinking that unlike you, Patsy doesn't see me as less of a man.'

204

'What's that supposed to mean?'

His face suddenly reddened with anger and he yelled, 'If you don't bloody know, then I'm not about to tell you.'

'Daddy, why are you shouting again?' Angel cried.

Neither of them had noticed that she had come into the room and, after a brief, shocked silence, Arthur held out his arms. 'Take no notice of me, princess. I must have got out of bed on the wrong side this morning. Come on, give me a hug and that will make me feel better.'

She scrambled onto his lap, saying, 'Are you cross with Mummy?'

'No, of course not. Now then, we're going to see Nanny Elsie today, and as your granddad is coming to collect us in an hour, I think we should get ready, starting with breakfast.'

Angel nodded and Sally began to make toast, her mind on Arthur's comment. He'd said that Patsy didn't see him as less than a man, but what did he mean by that?

'Can I wear my bestest dress, Mummy?'

'Yes, all right,' Sally said, hurrying to get her daughter bathed and ready after breakfast.

Alone in the bathroom, Angel said, 'Daddy said he isn't cross with you, but he is, Mummy. He isn't nice to you.'

'He's just tired, darling,' Sally said.

'But he shouts at you and . . . and it makes you sad.'

Oh no, Sally thought, upset that Angel had seen through the façade. Her own childhood memories were of rows, yelling, and she didn't want her daughter affected in the same way. At least today would be a happy one, full of laughter at Elsie's, and she found herself looking forward to it. In fact, though it was hard to admit, Sally found that nowadays she'd rather spend the day with anyone other than Arthur.

Twenty-Nine

Arthur was waiting impatiently for his father on Monday, and looking out of the window, he saw Patsy leaving her flat. He eyed her appreciatively. Patsy didn't seem repulsed by his leg, and he had lightly flirted with her, hoping to make Sally jealous. He shouldn't have done it of course and had been surprised when the girl flirted back. He was also surprised that Joe had broken up with her, and wondered why, but no doubt he'd soon find out.

Patsy disappeared from view just as he saw his father's car drawing up outside, and Arthur hurried to let him in. 'Hello, Dad.'

'Hello, son, I've sorted the men out so are you ready for the off?'

'Yes, let's go.'

As they travelled to Roehampton, they mainly spoke about the removals business, but more than once Arthur saw his father glance around, until finally he said what was on his mind. 'Are you worried about adapting to an artificial leg, son?'

'No, I can't wait to get rid of the crutches.'

'Don't expect miracles, son. It'll take you a while to adapt to a false leg.'

'I've had practice in the gym and they were right, with a below the knee amputation it wasn't too bad. The leg just needed a bit of adjustment, that's all,' Arthur told him, his thoughts turning to Sally. She was repulsed by his stump, so would having the false leg make any difference?

* * *

'When we get home, Daddy should be there and he'll have his new leg,' Sally told Angel.

Angel smiled, as she skipped along beside Sally, and when they walked into the living room it was to see Arthur standing by the hearth. Her eyes travelled straight to where his trouser leg was usually pinned up to see that he looked whole, two black shoes now visible.

'Well, what do you think?' he asked, for once his tone soft.

'It's amazing,' Sally told him.

'Daddy . . . Daddy, show me,' Angel cried, and running up to her father she began to tug at the leg of his trousers.

'Leave it, Angel. Let me sit down,' Arthur said, and taking a cane he limped towards a chair where he flopped down.

Angel looked puzzled. 'Does it hurt, Daddy?'

'Yes, a bit, but it's my own fault. I've been trying all day to walk without a cane,' he said, as he pushed up his trouser leg to show Angel his prosthesis.

'It looks funny, Daddy.'

Sally focused on Arthur's aura and frowned. Surely it was a bit soon to go without crutches, let alone a cane.

'You might find it funny, Angel, but from the look on your mother's face, she doesn't feel the same.'

'But . . .' Sally began to protest, but Arthur cut her short.

'Don't worry, I'm used to it,' he said bitterly, covering the prosthesis again.

'Arthur, please, what do you mean? Used to what?' Sally asked.

'Forget it,' he said, turning his attention back to Angel.

'I can't just forget it.'

'Tough, I've got nothing more to say.'

'What's wrong?' Angel asked worriedly.

'Nothing, darling,' Sally said hastily, moving towards the kitchen. 'I'll make a start on dinner.'

They made the effort for Angel's sake, but as soon as the child was put to bed Sally got the silent treatment from Arthur. When she asked if his stump was hurting she got little more than a grunt in reply, and was about to offer him some healing when Patsy paid them a visit.

Arthur perked up as soon as he saw her. 'Hello, Patsy, you look nice.'

'Well thank you, kind sir,' she said. 'I see you've got your prosthesis. How are you getting on with it?'

'All right, except it's a bit sore at the moment. I think I'm going to have to take another day off work tomorrow.'

'Never mind. It's early days yet and sure to get easier,' she consoled.

On hearing that, Sally was worried. Arthur's stump must be more than just sore for him to take another day off and she'd take a look at it as soon as Patsy left.

'Any chance of a coffee?' Patsy asked as she sat down.

It seemed Patsy intended to stay for a while so any chance of looking at Arthur's leg would have to wait. 'Yes, of course. Do you want a coffee too, Arthur?'

'No,' he said shortly.

At his tone, Patsy's eyes met hers, but Sally just shrugged before leaving the room. She returned to find that for the next two hours all Arthur's attention was focused on their neighbour, his eyes frequently straying to the yards of leg Patsy had on show again.

Unable to help feeling jealous, Sally rose to her feet, and picking up the cups she marched into the kitchen.

Pasty smiled as Sally walked out of the room, the stupid cow playing right into her hands. As she had told Joe, there were plenty of fish in the sea, and from what she'd seen, this one was definitely ready to be caught. Joe may have slipped from her fingers, but she'd make sure that Arthur didn't. He was a good-looking bloke, tall, with a bear-like build and his missing lower leg didn't bother her. She was more interested in the money he was going to make from the building game and the good life that would be on offer. Patsy crossed her legs, making sure that Arthur got a good view, and smiled when she saw his eyes darken with lust.

'Do you like what you see?' she quietly asked.

'Who wouldn't?'

'Joe for one,' she said.

'He must be blind.'

'Who must be blind?' Sally asked, as she came back into the room, her back rigid.

'Arthur's talking about Joe.'

'I see,' Sally said stiffly, then affecting a wide yawn.

'I should go,' Patsy said, saying goodbye prettily to Arthur. 'It's time for my beauty sleep.'

'You don't need it, but bye for now,' Arthur called.

As Sally walked with her to the street door, Patsy could see that she was annoyed. She didn't want to alienate her yet, not while she still needed time and access to work on Arthur. 'Sally, I hope you haven't got hold of the wrong idea. I could see that Arthur was a bit down in the dumps and there's nothing like a bit of harmless flirting to cheer a man up. It can't be much fun for you when he's in that sort of mood and I was just trying to help.'

'Oh, I see,' Sally said. 'I feel silly now. I was actually jealous.'

'Really? That makes me feel awful.'

'It's all right. Now that you've explained I'm fine about it.'

'Thank goodness for that, after all, I wouldn't want to lose my new-found friend.'

'You haven't,' Sally said. 'In fact I should thank you for trying to help.'

What a mug, Patsy thought as she went up to her flat. Taking Arthur from Sally would be like taking candy from a baby.

Sally was feeling a lot better as she closed the door. She hadn't liked the way Patsy had flirted with Arthur, but knew now that it had been harmless.

'I'm going to bed,' Arthur said as soon as Sally went back to the living room, wincing with pain as he gripped his cane tightly.

Determined to check his stump, Sally was about to follow him when an awful premonition washed over her. Something was going to happen, something dreadful. Other than his stump, Arthur was fine, and panicking now she rushed to the telephone.

Sally's fingers trembled as she dialled her mother's number, her voice high as she said, 'Mum, it's me. Is Gran all right?'

'Yeah, and we're just off to bed. What is it? Have you had one of those funny feelings again?'

'Yes, so keep an eye on her, Mum.'

'All right. See you in the morning, love.'

Sally replaced the receiver, finding that despite her mother's reassurance, the awful feeling remained with her. Sick with worry she turned the lights off and went to the bathroom to brush her teeth. In their bedroom the lights were off and she whispered, 'Are you asleep, Arthur?'

There was no reply and with his stump so sore she got into bed, careful to keep a distance between them. Sally lay on her back, the feeling of foreboding still with her as her eyes closed on a prayer for all those she loved.

Ruth was sitting on the sofa beside Tommy, the boy sound asleep now. She was fuming. It was bad enough that Laura was back on the booze and the boy unfed, but tonight he had turned up with bruises on his face. She'd been ready to go round to have it out with Laura, but Tommy had insisted that he'd got into a fight with a rival gang.

Ruth stroked Tommy's hair. She had grown so fond of him, wanted to keep him safe, but if she made waves with the authorities they'd just take him from Laura and put him in a home.

Her thoughts turned to Sally and the earlier telephone call. She had to admit to being a bit worried, especially as nine times out of ten Sally's premonitions turned out to be right. Her mother had been fine when she went to bed, but deciding to check on her, Ruth went to her room and quietly opened the door.

'Bugger off. I ain't dead yet.'

'Oh, Mum.'

'Look, I'm all right, now go and get some sleep.'

'Tommy's still here.'

'If you keep this up, Laura will find out and then there'll be trouble.'

'If she doesn't keep her hands off of Tommy, the trouble will be from me. Goodnight, Mum,' Ruth said, leaving the door slightly ajar.

She wasn't going to wake Tommy, he could stay where he was for the night and she'd doze beside him on the sofa, close to her mother's room in case she was needed.

Thirty

Arthur had been uncommunicative again the next morning, yet as always he was fine with Angel. He hadn't yet put on his prosthesis, and worriedly, Sally asked, 'Is your stump still sore?'

'Yes,' he said curtly.

Angel went into nurse mode again, demanding he took his medicine, and at least her constant chatter made the strained atmosphere a little more bearable.

Sally thought about her premonition as they walked to Candle Lane, surprised to find Tommy there, her mother telling her on an aside that the boy had stayed the night.

'Tommy,' Angel said, running up to him. 'My daddy's got a false leg.'

'Blimey, what's it made of?'

'I dunno.'

'I should fink it's made out of wood,' Tommy said. 'You can carve wood into all sorts of shapes.'

'You're clever, Tommy. I wouldn't have thought of that,' Angel told him.

His little chest puffed with pride, but then they all heard someone thumping loudly on the front door. 'Who the flaming hell is that?' Sadie complained.

'Tommy!' a voice yelled. 'I know you're in there and I'll give you five minutes to come home or else.'

'I'd best go,' Tommy whispered.

'I'll come with you,' Ruth said.

'No, don't. I'll be all right. She's all talk when she's sober.'

'Oh, love,' Ruth whispered sadly, but once the boy had gone she became all hustle and bustle, soon leaving for work.

'Mum looked tired, Gran.'

'Yeah, well, she spent the night on the sofa.'

'It's my fault. I shouldn't have rung her, but I was worried about you.'

'Sally, you've got to stop this. I keep telling you I'm fine, but you just don't listen. I really don't need looking after any more.'

'Does the doctor agree?'

'Well, no, but you shouldn't take any notice of him.'

'Gran, I've told you before. When he gives you the all clear I'll stop coming round, but until then you'll just have to put up with me.'

'You're as stubborn as your mother.'

'Yes, but where do we get it from?' Sally asked.

The morning passed, and Sally was surprised when her mother came home at twelve-thirty. 'Mum, what's wrong?'

'I'm just tired that's all, and I must look a bit rough 'cos old misery guts agreed to let me have the afternoon off.'

'Yes, you are a bit pale and dark under the eyes.'

'A bit of smudged mascara goes a long way,' she said, sitting down to spit on a hanky and rubbing the dark rings away, 'and I always look a bit washed out without any lipstick.'

'Mum!'

'Don't look at me like that. Faking it is hardly the crime of the century and to be honest I really am bushed.'

'That's my fault. Sorry, Mum, when I rang last night I really was worried.'

'Yeah, well as you can see your gran is fine.'

Sally nipped her lower lip, wondering now if she should be more worried about Arthur. His stump was sore. Was it infected?

'Now that you're here do you mind if I go home? Arthur has taken the day off work and maybe he feels worse than he's letting on.'

'Of course I don't mind, and looking at your gran, like me, I reckon she's ready for forty winks.'

Sally didn't need telling twice and called goodbye, hurrying to Maple Terrace, hoping she was worried about nothing. Her stomach was churning with anxiety by the time she arrived, and rushing in she made straight for the living room. She flung open the door then froze on the threshold by the tableau before her. No, no, it can't be, she agonised, her mind refusing to accept what she was seeing.

With eyes rounded like saucers now, Sally baulked as she finally took in the scene. Bile rose in her throat and her hand rose to cover her mouth in horror. Arthur was sitting on the sofa with Patsy straddled across his lap, both naked from the waist down. The two were heaving and panting, Arthur's hands gripping Patsy's hips as he pumped her up and down.

His eyes were closed in ecstasy, but hearing her horrified gasp they suddenly flew open. 'Sally!'

Patsy turned, a look of triumph on her face, and that was all Sally saw as she turned and fled the room.

She didn't hear Arthur's frantic call, she couldn't hear anything for the blood pounding in her ears. Leaving the door open, she fled, heading for Candle Lane.

'Get off me, Patsy!'

'That wasn't what you were saying a few minutes ago.'

Arthur groaned as he pushed her away and, recalling the look on Sally's face, he felt sick. Christ, what had he done?

He'd been surprised when Patsy knocked on the door, saying she'd just popped in to see how he was. He'd invited her in and they'd sat on the sofa chatting, just small talk at first, but then Arthur found himself unburdening to Patsy, telling her that Sally no longer fancied him. She had been sympathetic, said he was gorgeous and that Sally was mad, whilst moving ever closer to him. As Patsy's body touched his, the atmosphere became charged and the next thing he knew, her hand was seductively running up the inside of his leg. He'd responded immediately, and Patsy had seen that, her smile knowing as she raised an eyebrow.

Arthur groaned. He should have stopped her, but felt powerless with lust as she had peeled off her short skirt. Skimpy little knickers followed, and then she was astride him, her tiny hands unzipping his trousers.

It had been all her. She had guided him in, aroused him to fever pitch, but just as he was reaching a frantic climax Sally had walked in.

'Get dressed, Patsy,' he growled.

'Don't you want to finish what we started?'

'No!' he shouted. 'My wife just caught us, and you saw the look on her face. Haven't you got any shame?'

'You said yourself that Sally doesn't want you now. In fact, I think she's got her eye on Joe. When we're alone she never stops talking about him.'

'Don't talk rot. Joe's not only my partner, he's my friend, and I trust him.'

'Yes, but do you trust Sally?'

Arthur pondered her words. Joe was a good-looking bloke, and unlike him he was whole. It was no wonder that Sally was attracted to him, and no doubt Patsy still felt the same about him too. In fact, it was possible that she was annoyed that Sally fancied him and so this was payback. 'What is this really about, Patsy? Is it jealousy? Do you still want Joe? Is that it?'

'No, I don't. We didn't really click, and maybe it's because from the first time I saw you, I fancied you something rotten.'

'I doubt that. Just get dressed,' he said, unable to help watching as Patsy slowly began to pull her knickers over her hips. He licked his lips, despite everything, tempted again, but then heard a sound in the hall. 'For God's sake, Sally's back! Quick, get your skirt on!'

Patsy had just stepped into it when the sitting-room door opened, and Arthur's breath left his body when he saw who was standing on the threshold. 'Mum,' he gasped. 'What are you doing here?'

He saw his mother's eyes narrow, saw the way her lips tightened, and then she advanced across the room, her face livid as she marched up to Patsy. 'You, miss, finish putting your skirt on and then get out! And you, Arthur, I suggest you zip up your fly!'

Arthur looked down in horror and quickly fastened his trousers.

'Get out!' he heard his mother say again and, hastily pulling up her skirt, Patsy walked out.

'How could you, Arthur! And with a tart?' she cried, as soon as the door closed.

'She isn't a tart, Mum. Patsy is a mobile hairdresser and she lives upstairs.'

'Oh, and that's supposed to make a difference, is it? She knows you're a married man, and as far as I'm concerned that makes her a tart. How could you do this to Sally?'

'Sally doesn't want me and she's made that plain.'

'Don't give me that as an excuse. I've known Sally since she was ten years old and she's like a daughter to me. She loves you, and doesn't deserve this,' she said, wringing her hands. 'Don't you realise that if Sally finds out this could be the end of your marriage?'

'She already knows.'

'What! Sally knows? But . . .'

'She caught us and ran out. I can't believe you didn't bump into her.'

'Well, I must admit I was surprised to find your street door wide open. I rang the site, but Joe told me you were taking the

216

day off. I thought it the ideal opportunity to talk to you about your father.'

'Talk about what?'

'It's just that I'm a bit worried about his health. His back's playing him up but he won't see anyone about it.' Elsie then shook her head impatiently. 'That hardly seems important now, not after what I've just seen. Arthur, what on earth possessed you?'

'Patsy doesn't find me repulsive and . . . well . . . she offered.'

'She offered!' Elsie spluttered.

'Yes, Mum, and she made all the moves. Unlike Sally, she doesn't see me as a cripple.'

Elsie's eyes narrowed again and Arthur could have kicked himself. He wouldn't put it past his mother to have a go at Patsy, and quickly said, 'I've been home for ages now, but Sally has hardly been near me. In bed she keeps her distance, and she can't bear to look at my leg.'

'If Sally is keeping a distance between you, there must be a reason, and I can't believe it's because she finds you repulsive. Are you sure you aren't imagining it?'

'Yes, I'm sure. Sally makes me feel less than a man and I can't stand it.'

'All right, maybe she is having trouble adjusting, but that's still no excuse for what you've done. Look, I'll go round to Candle Lane and talk to her.'

'No, Mum, keep out of it, and anyway, what makes you think she'll be at Candle Lane?'

'Where else would she go?'

'I said keep out of it.'

'Why? Don't you want her back?'

Arthur pondered his mother's words. Yes, of course he wanted Sally back, but if she couldn't stand the sight of him, what was the point? His thoughts turned to his daughter, and he groaned. If he and Sally didn't patch things up, when would he see Angel?

217

He couldn't think straight. 'Mum, I don't know what I want at the moment, and to be honest, if Sally can't accept me the way I am, there's no future for us.'

'I can't believe you, son. Sally caught you with Patsy, she must be heartbroken, and all you're thinking about is yourself.'

'I doubt she's heartbroken,' Arthur retorted, pushing away the memory of the horror on Sally's face when she had seen him with Patsy. 'She's got her eye on someone else.'

'Rubbish! You're just saying that to salve your conscience.'

'No, I'm not. Patsy told me that she fancies Joe and that she never stops talking about him.'

'I don't believe it. I'm going to see Sally.'

'No, Mum,' Arthur called, but he was wasting his breath.

Elsie stormed from the room like a ship in full sail, calling, 'I'll be back.'

Thirty-One

By the time Sally had reached the lane, she had slowed to a crawl, her earlier horror now replaced by anger. How could he? And with her! Bile rose again as she recalled the scene, the ecstasy on Arthur's face imprinted on her mind.

She was his wife, the one who was beside him in bed every night, but Arthur hadn't made love to her since he came home from hospital. She had made all sorts of excuses for him in her mind, his tiredness, his worries about the building project, his painful stump, but it hadn't stopped him when it came to Patsy.

When Sally reached number five she paused to draw breath, once more feeling tears flooding her eyes and wanting only the comfort of arms around her. 'Oh, Mum,' she cried, as she ran into the kitchen.

'What on earth's the matter?'

'Arthur . . . Arthur. Oh, Mum,' and sobbing, she ran forward.

For a moment her mother's arms enfolded her, but then abruptly she was pushed away. 'What is it? Has something happened to Arthur?'

Sally's throat was so constricted with emotion that she could hardly speak. 'No, but . . . he . . . he . . .'

'Come on, Sally, pull yourself together. Tell me what's happened.'

Hearing the stern tone of her mother's voice, Sally felt as if she'd been doused with a bucket of cold water. 'I caught him with another woman.'

Her mother's eyes widened, and for a moment there was silence, but then she said, 'Sally, start at the beginning.'

She sank on to a chair, fumbling with her words at first, then gradually able to recount the scene. Nausea rose again, and with her hand over her mouth she rushed to the toilet where bending over the bowl she was violently sick. When there was nothing left, she perched on the rim of the bath, brow beaded with perspiration and her throat burning.

Her mother appeared in the doorway. 'Sally, are you all right?'

'I don't think I'll ever be all right again.'

'Of course you will. Now come downstairs and let's talk about this.'

'What's there to talk about?'

'Come on,' she repeated. 'I'll make you a cup of tea.'

Tea, Sally thought, her mother's answer to every crisis, as though the brew had some sort of magical qualities. Not this time, she thought as she followed her mother into the kitchen.

Whilst her mother set the kettle to boil, Sally sat down, her gran asking, 'What are you going to do now, love?'

'I don't know, but as far as I'm concerned my marriage is over.'

'Listen, Sally, I know you're hurt, and I don't blame you, but don't make hasty decisions. Men are different to us. They're ruled by what's in their trousers and can sleep with a woman without emotions being involved. Why else do you think there are prostitutes?'

'That's no excuse, Gran. And anyway, Arthur wasn't with a prostitute. He was with our upstairs neighbour.'

'You're not listening to me, girl. Arthur may have slept with another woman, but I'm sure it's you he loves.'

'But he betrayed me, Gran. He betrayed my trust and our marriage. I . . . I can't forgive him.'

'You're in a state, and perhaps it's too soon to talk about it.'

220

Sally glanced at the clock, surprised to see that it was only just after three. She felt that her life had fallen apart, that nothing would ever be the same again, and it had all happened in less than two hours. Closing her eyes, she felt a rush of weariness. She knew that she didn't want to think about it any more, that her mind wanted to shut down. Her mother spoke, but her voice seemed to come from a great distance.

'Why don't you go and have a lie down? I'll pick Angel up from school.'

Sally wanted to be alone, to crawl into a shell and never come out again. 'All right, Mum,' she said, rising to her feet.

'Wait, Sally. What if Arthur comes round?'

'He won't do that. He's too busy with Patsy.'

'Don't be silly. He's bound to want to talk to you.'

'Well, I don't want to talk to him! If he comes round, as far as I'm concerned you can shut the door in his face.' And on that note she left the room, climbing upstairs like a weary old woman.

Only five minutes later there was a knock on the door. Ruth was surprised to see Elsie on the step. 'Blimey, that was quick! Did Arthur ring you?'

'He didn't need to. I turned up just after Sally ran off and he was still with that tart. Is Sally here?'

'Yes, but she's upstairs having a lie down. This has knocked her for six, Elsie.'

'Do you mind if I go up to talk to her?'

'Of course not, but at the moment I don't think it'll do any good.'

'Maybe not, but I'd still like to see her.'

'Go on up then. I've got to collect Angel from school, but I'll see you when I get back.'

Elsie knocked softly on the bedroom door and opened it to see Sally sprawled on the bed, one arm flung over her face. 'Can I come in, love?'

'Elsie, what are you doing here?' Sally asked, her eyes bruised with pain as she raised herself into a sitting position.

'I know what Arthur has done and had to talk to you. You're upset and I don't blame you, but I've spoken to Arthur and he said some funny things.'

'Like what?'

'Are you repulsed by him now that he's lost part of his leg?'

'No, of course not.'

'He said you keep a distance between you in bed?'

'How would Arthur know that?' Sally said bitterly. 'He falls asleep as soon as his head touches the pillow.'

'He also said that you've got your eye on his friend Joe.'

'What!'

'Is it true?'

'No,' Sally said, but then her eyes narrowed in thought. 'Once, when Joe and Patsy came to dinner, Arthur was flirting with Patsy. I was annoyed, so much so that I got my own back by flirting with Joe.'

'I see . . .'

'It meant nothing, Elsie, and it's no excuse for sleeping with another woman. I love Arthur, and until now I thought he loved me.'

Elsie sensed that Sally was telling the truth, and even if Arthur thought Sally was repulsed by his leg, it didn't excuse what he had done. However, the thought of them breaking up was awful, and she fought for words that might mend bridges. 'If you ask me, Arthur was led on by that girl. He said that she made all the moves, and I reckon she's nothing but a slut. Please Sally, don't let this break up your marriage. Can't you find it in your heart to forgive him?'

'I don't think I can, and if anything, his excuses have made things worse. I can't believe he's blaming me, and I can't believe he said that I'm repulsed by his leg. That's utter rubbish, and he knows it. And as for Patsy leading Arthur on, well, he's got a tongue and could have said no.'

It's too early, Elsie thought, Sally's wound deep. 'Give it a few days, love, and maybe then you'll see things differently.'

222

'I doubt it, Elsie. I doubt it. Can I ask you a favour?'

'Of course you can.'

'I left without bringing anything with me, and both Angel and I will need clothes. When you go to Maple Terrace again, can you pack a few things for us?'

'Yes, all right,' Elsie said and, after stroking Sally's hair for a moment, she left the room. Oh, son. What have you done?

Ruth had been to fetch Angel and was just coming in the street door as Elsie came downstairs. With an expectant expression she said, 'Did Sally talk to you?'

'Yes, but if anything I think I've made things worse. Where's Angel?'

'I let her play outside for a while. What did you say to Sally?'

Elsie recounted her conversation, ending with, 'So you see, she now thinks that Arthur is blaming her for what happened.'

'It sounds like he is to me,' Ruth snapped.

'None of this makes sense. Arthur says that Sally doesn't go near him and makes him feel less than a man. But Sally says he's been distant and cold with her since he came home from hospital. If you ask me, it seems that the two of them have got their wires crossed.'

Ruth frowned. 'That still doesn't excuse what he's done, Elsie.'

'I know, believe me I know. Anyway, I'd best be off. I told Sally I'd pick up a few things for her and I want another word with my son.'

'Tell him not to come round here, at least for the time being,' Ruth said hurriedly. 'Sally is adamant that she doesn't want to see him, and not only that, I'm so mad at him that I wouldn't trust myself not to give him a piece of my mind.'

Elsie's eyes clouded with distress. 'Oh, Ruth, I'm so sorry.'

'You don't have to apologise,' Ruth said as she laid a hand on Elsie's arm. 'It isn't your fault.'

'But he's my own flesh and blood and I'm so ashamed of him.

Not only that, what on earth is Bert going to say? He'll probably disown the lad.'

'I doubt that,' Ruth consoled.

Elsie left with a heavy heart. She saw Angel playing, and stopped to give the child a kiss and a hug, but her thoughts were elsewhere as she made her way to Maple Terrace.

Please God, she prayed, *don't let this be the end of Sally and Arthur's marriage.*

Thirty-Two

It was seven-thirty in the evening when Arthur heard a knock on the door. If it was his mother again she could clear off. He'd had just about enough of her lecturing.

Sally had told his mother a pack of lies, and he was fuming. She'd accused him of being distant and cold, when in truth it was the other way round. She also denied being repulsed by his leg and it seemed his mother believed her. Before leaving she had packed a suitcase of clothes for Sally and Angel, saying that he should stay away from Candle Lane for the time being. Bloody cheek! He wasn't a child to be given orders. He'd go to Candle Lane if he wanted to, if only to give his wife a piece of his mind.

There was another rap on the door and with his stump still too sore to wear his prosthesis, he fumbled for his crutches and went to see who it was. 'Come in, Joe,' he said shortly.

Joe's brows rose at his tone and as they walked into the living room, he said, 'What's up, mate?'

'Sally's gone back to her mother's. We've split up.'

'Split up! But why?'

'If you must know, she caught me having it off with Patsy.'

'You and Patsy? No . . . I can't believe it. Bloody hell, Arthur.'

'Don't look at me like that. Patsy made it obvious that she was available, making all the moves, and well, it just happened.'

'And Sally caught you. She must be in a right state.'

225

'I doubt it,' Arthur said, choosing to forget the look he'd seen on his wife's face. 'If you must know, things have been bloody awful since I came out of hospital. Sally can't stand the sight of my leg, and has made it plain that sex is off the menu.'

'I reckon you're imagining things.'

'Is that so, and have I imagined the pitying looks I've been getting from our labourers too?'

'You can't blame them for feeling sorry for you, but if you must know from what I've heard they admire you for getting to work so soon after coming home from hospital.'

Arthur ignored the comment, only saying what was on his mind. 'Patsy told me that Sally fancies you.'

'Bloody hell, mate, can't you see how juvenile this sounds? If you ask me Patsy's still peeved that I ditched her and is stirring things up. You're mad to listen to her. She's nothing but trouble.'

'You took her out a few times.'

'Yes, but unlike you, I'm single.'

Arthur scowled. 'All right, so I shouldn't have had it off with her, but, well, it was there, offered to me on a plate and—' There was a knock on the door and somehow Arthur knew who it was. Did he want to see her again? For a moment he floundered, but then remembering Sally's lies, his anger reasserted itself.

Once again he tucked his crutches under his arms and went to the door. It was Patsy.

'Hello, Arthur. I had to come down to see you. Are you all right?'

'I'm fine,' he said, leading her into the living room.

'What do you want?' Joe snapped.

'I've come to see Arthur.'

'Don't you think you've done enough damage?'

'Joe, keep out of it,' Arthur said. 'If I didn't want to see Patsy I wouldn't have invited her in.'

Joe looked angry, his face reddening, but he only said, 'Fine. I'm off then. Are you coming to work tomorrow?'

'If you can do without me for another day, I could do with staying home. My stump is still giving me gyp,' he said, flopping heavily onto the sofa.

'I can manage and for longer if necessary. Just let me know when you want picking up again,' Joe offered, and then throwing Patsy a look of disgust he saw himself out.

Arthur was aware of the front door slamming, but then Patsy perched on the arm of the sofa beside him, her expression one of regret. 'I'm sorry that Sally caught us, Arthur.'

'Yes, so am I.'

'I'm so ashamed of the way I threw myself at you. I was brazen and it's not like me at all. It's just that I fancy you so much and I just couldn't help myself. You're such a handsome man, and the fact that you're missing a little bit of leg doesn't worry me.'

'It worries Sally.'

'Yes, I know. She told me she finds it revolting.'

Arthur felt vindicated and wished his mother could hear this. She'd know then that Sally had been lying through her teeth. She *was* repulsed by him, and now the pain of her rejection twisted his guts. As if aware of how he was feeling, Patsy slid onto his lap. She leaned forward to kiss him and Arthur didn't resist.

Patsy got to work, smiling secretly. She had hoped that Joe would be her way out of her present life, but he'd rejected her. Not about to give up she'd seen the way things were between Sally and Arthur. Most men were so easy to manipulate and it had been a simple thing to feed Arthur's paranoia.

She mounted Arthur now, her thoughts distant from the act and set only on the future. Patsy as always felt nothing, but had learned to be a good actress, finding that a few groans here and there sufficed. Sex to her was just a means of making money, but unbelievably, as Arthur drove into her, she found herself responding. Feelings she thought dead rose to the surface and she gasped with pleasure. Her hands reached up to pull off her jumper, and with no bra on she leaned forward to bury her breasts in Arthur's face.

Patsy's mind now became oblivious to anything but the sensations that ripped through her body. How long had it been? How long since she had felt like this? She eased up, moving slowly, loving the feeling and for once wanting it to last. 'Wait, darling,' she urged, 'take it slowly.'

Despite that, soon after it happened, a sensation deep inside, one that left her gasping. 'Oh, Arthur, ohhh!' she cried, and as Arthur exploded inside her, they climaxed together.

For a while they just clung to each other, drawing breath, Patsy astounded by what had happened. She thought about her clients, the old and sometimes crippled men that she serviced, and grimaced. Mind you, they paid well, and were pathetically grateful. None of them lasted for more than a few minutes; she made sure of that, ensured that with a few tricks the act was soon over. Now though she wanted out of the game and was determined to snare Arthur. What she hadn't expected was to find the sex enjoyable, this an added bonus.

'I'm sorry, Arthur, I couldn't resist you again. You're so handsome and I can't believe that Sally doesn't fancy you any more. She must be mad.' Patsy leaned across Arthur again, making sure that her breasts were in his face as she stroked his hair. 'Still, don't worry, I'm sure she'll get used to it. You'll just have to give her some time.'

'Huh,' he murmured, his lips now brushing her nipples. 'Why should I? My leg doesn't bother you, and if Sally doesn't like it now, she never will. Anyway, after the frustration she's put me through, I'm not sure that I want her back.'

Patsy smiled. That was just what she had wanted to hear, and triumphant, she kissed him passionately. He was soon aroused, as ready as she was. 'Oh, yes!' she cried as he entered her. He was hers now, and if there was any sign of him trying to get Sally back, she'd find a way to put a spoke in the wheel.

Thirty-Three

For Sally the days were filled with moments of agonising pain at Arthur's betrayal, interspersed with moments of anger. She knew that Angel was confused and she constantly asked to see her father, but so far she had fobbed her off with excuses.

It was the first Sunday in April, but the day had started bleak, the sky dark and heavy to match her mood. Then, by three in the afternoon, the sun broke through and Angel begged to be allowed outside to play.

'No,' Sally said, her eyes fixed on the sparse fire burning in the grate.

'Pleeease, Mummy!'

'Sally,' Ruth urged, 'she's been cooped up all day and it won't hurt to let her go out for a while.'

She sighed heavily, too caught up in her own misery to fight. 'All right then.'

Angel squealed with delight, but Sally hardly heard her. Her gran's words kept going round in her mind, but they failed to comfort her. So men could sleep with women without becoming emotionally involved, but to her that was no excuse. When she fell in love with Arthur, she'd found real love, deep love, and had thought he felt the same. How wrong, how blind she'd been.

Time ticked by slowly and desperate for diversion, Sally listened to her mother and gran as they talked about Tommy.

'That boy seems to be staying away.'

'Yes, and when I saw him playing outside earlier he looked all right. To be on the safe side I'll go on keeping an eye on him, and if he turns up at my door again, whether Laura likes it or not, I'm taking him in.'

'That'll just get her back up and make things worse for the boy.'

'What choice is there? If I don't take him in he'd be out on the streets all night.'

Sadie sighed heavily. 'Yeah, I suppose you're right.'

Half an hour had passed since Angel had gone out to play and Sally decided to check on her. She scanned the lane but there was no sign of her daughter. Tommy Walters was there, playing with a couple of other boys and she called, 'Have you seen Angel?'

'Yeah, she was with us till a little while ago, but then she said she was going to see someone.'

Sally's stomach did a somersault. Angel had been whining for days that she was missing her dad, and not stopping to think about it she chased after her daughter, hoping to catch up with her before she reached Maple Terrace.

There was no sign of Angel and breathless, Sally stopped outside the flat. She didn't have her handbag and without keys she was forced to ring the bell, shocked when Patsy opened the door.

'Hello, Sally. Have you come round for your daughter? We were a bit surprised when she turned up on her own.'

'Yes, I've come for Angel,' Sally said, fighting the urge to dig her fingernails into Patsy's face. Holding her head high and hardening her voice, she added, 'Tell her that I'm here to take her home.'

'Don't you want to come in?'

'No, I don't! Now please tell my daughter that I'm waiting.'

'But she wants to see her daddy and there's no harm in her staying for a little while.'

Sally's back was rigid. She wouldn't give Patsy the satisfaction of seeing how upset she was. Instead she spat, 'I don't want my daughter associating with the likes of you.'

'There's no need to be nasty. We've just had our dinner, and I was about to start rearranging the furniture when the kid turned up. Arthur was dead chuffed to see her.'

Sally felt the blood drain from her face. So, Patsy was already making herself at home. She was planning to shift the furniture, change the room that Sally had so carefully arranged, and what was more, it seemed Arthur was allowing it. 'Get my daughter,' she demanded. 'I'm taking her home.'

'I think you'll find that Arthur has a right to see Angel.'

'No, he hasn't. He lost any claim on her when he had it off with you!' Sally knew she sounded coarse, but didn't care; in fact, if she had to look at Patsy's smug face for much longer she'd go for her, she really would.

'If that's your attitude it seems your divorce will be nasty. I think you'll find that Arthur's solicitor will insist that he has access to Angel.'

Sally's mind reeled. Divorce! It had come to that. Her teeth clenched. 'A divorce suits me,' she ground out. 'Now, as I said, tell my daughter I'm waiting!'

'All right, keep your hair on,' Patsy said, as she turned to go back inside.

Only moments later Angel appeared and seeing Sally she held back. 'No, Mummy, I don't want to come home yet.'

'Come here!' Sally demanded and, grabbing her daughter's hand she pulled her over the threshold and along Maple Terrace.

Angel was dragging her feet, still protesting, but Sally hardly heard her. Arthur wanted a divorce and, at the finality of the thought, Sally's shoulders slumped.

Patsy smiled happily as she closed the door on Sally. What a bit of luck. She had popped down to see Arthur, only to find that

232

he was talking about getting Sally back and inwardly she had fumed.

Hiding her feelings she told him that the time wasn't right. It was too soon and it would be better to give Sally a bit of space, she'd advised. Despite this, he still wanted to go to Candle Lane, but thankfully Angel had forestalled him by knocking on the door.

By calling round to collect her daughter, Sally had played right into Patsy's hands and she felt a surge of glee. It hadn't taken much to hint that she was living with Arthur and the silly cow had taken the bait. Now, with a few choice words to Arthur, she could push the pair of them even further apart. Her lips curled with satisfaction. Yes, with luck, she'd be able to snare Arthur soon. They were already having sex frequently, the man insatiable, but he'd baulked at her sharing his bed. Well, that was about to change, Patsy decided.

She composed her face, looking sad as she walked into the living room. 'I'm so sorry, Arthur. I did try, but Sally refused to let Angel stay. In fact she was really annoyed that Angel came round here on her own and said that she's going to see a solicitor first thing in the morning.'

'A solicitor! What for?'

'She's going to file for a divorce, and not only that, she intends to make sure that you never see your daughter again.'

Arthur's face flushed with anger. 'I'm not standing for that! I'm going to see her, and right now!'

'You'd be wasting your time. She won't talk to you and made that plain. I did try to persuade her to come in, but in no uncertain terms she refused. If you want to make sure you get access to your daughter, you'll need to see a solicitor too, and as soon as possible.'

'Are you sure she's filing for a divorce?'

'Yes. She said that the next time you hear from her, it would be through a solicitor.'

233

'She can't keep me away from Angel!'

'I know, but you've got to face it. Sally won't take you back and you must take steps to see that you don't lose your little girl too.'

Arthur slumped back on the sofa, his eyes dark with anger. 'The bitch! If this is the way she wants to play it, fine. I'll see a solicitor first thing in the morning.'

Patsy sat beside him, hiding her triumph. Arthur was a proud man, and now there was no way he would crawl to Sally begging for forgiveness. He suddenly grabbed her, fury still evident in his eyes and, as his teeth sank into her neck, Patsy groaned with pleasure. He was taking his anger out in sex, but she didn't mind. Thanks, Sally, she thought, smiling wickedly.

Later, they lay back, both spent, Patsy nestling close to Arthur. Maybe tonight, she thought, maybe tonight he'd let her stay and in the morning she'd be there to see Joe's face when he came to pick Arthur up for work. She pictured the special underwear she had upstairs, imagined wearing it when she opened the door to Joe, and smiled. He would see what he'd let go and it would serve him right. It wasn't that she was interested in him now, after all, Arthur was the one who could please her, but if Joe was jealous it might stir things up a bit between the two men. They might be in partnership when it came to work, but she certainly didn't want Joe calling round socially.

'Won't you give Arthur another chance?' Elsie asked, as she and Bert sat in the kitchen.

'He has Patsy living with him now,' Sally told them, the events of the afternoon still vivid in her mind. She loved her in-laws, yet when they had called round less than ten minutes ago, she had been in no mood to talk.

Angel was still upset, wanting to go back to see her daddy, but had brightened up when Elsie and Bert arrived, especially when they'd given her a present. She had looked at the new box

234

of paints and colouring book with delight, almost immediately beginning to fill in one of the pictures.

'Sally, I'm not defending what my son has done,' Bert said, 'but you've only just broken up. I can't believe that he's moved that girl in already.'

'He has. I saw it with my own eyes.'

'You must be mistaken,' Elsie protested. 'I'm sure it was only a one-off thing with Patsy.'

'Don't like Patsy,' Angel said, her brush poised as she abandoned the painting to listen to the conversation.

Sally frowned, recalling that Angel had said that before. Had her daughter foreseen this happening? She saw how Angel's ears were pricked, and not wanting her to hear any more of this conversation, she said quietly, 'Elsie, I'd rather not talk about this in front of Angel.'

Bert frowned, and then crossed the room to Angel. 'How about coming for a ride in Granddad's car?'

'Can we go to see my daddy?'

Sally tensed, relieved when Bert said, 'Maybe another time, but right now I thought we might go to the park and you can have a ride on the swings.'

Angel scrambled to her feet. 'Will you push me really high?'

'Of course I will. Now run and get your coat.'

'Thanks love,' Elsie told him, smiling warmly at her husband. 'Sally's right, we shouldn't talk in front of the child. I'll be back in an hour and then I'm going to have a word with my son.'

Angel ran back into the room, her coat clutched to her chest. 'I'm ready, Granddad.'

Bert leaned down, his huge form towering over his granddaughter as he helped her put on the coat. 'Right, see you later.'

'I dread to think what Bert will have to say to Arthur,' said Elsie when the coast was clear. 'He was furious when I told him and wanted to see Arthur straightaway. I managed to talk him out of it, telling him that we shouldn't interfere. Now, though, I doubt there's much chance of keeping them apart.'

'Sally, what's this about Arthur moving that girl in?' Ruth asked. 'I know you were upset when you came back with Angel, but I thought you were just annoyed that she'd gone round there.'

'I didn't want to talk about it, Mum, and I still don't.'

Elsie shook her head. 'I still think you're mistaken, love.'

'No, I'm not. Patsy was there when I went to get Angel, but I don't want my daughter anywhere near the likes of her. Arthur wants a divorce, our marriage is over, and as far as I'm concerned, now that Arthur has moved Patsy in, he's forfeited any right to see his daughter.'

'Sally, I know you're angry and I understand, really I do, but you can't keep Angel away from her father.'

'You just watch me.'

Sadie leaned forward in her chair, speaking for the first time. 'Sally, listen to me. I know you're hurt and at the moment swamped with bitterness, but Elsie is right and no matter what Arthur has done, you can't keep Angel away from him. Little girls cling to their fathers, and if you stop her from seeing him it'll rebound on you. She'll come to blame you. Surely you realise that.'

Sally reared to her feet. 'I don't care! Just leave me alone, all of you,' she cried, fleeing the room. She was deeply shocked by Arthur's betrayal and wanted him to suffer too. To that end she would use the only weapon she had. Angel.

'She's in a terrible state,' Elsie said, distressed, as the door slammed behind Sally.

'What do you expect?'

Sadie exhaled loudly before speaking. 'To save the marriage I was prepared to have a go at talking Sally round, but not now, not when he's moved that girl in.'

'I still think that Sally is mistaken. In fact, I think I'll walk round there now. When Bert comes back, will you tell him where I am?'

'I think I'll come with you,' Ruth said.

'It would be better if I spoke to Arthur on my own.'

'Maybe, but I want to see for myself if that girl has moved in. If she has, then as far as I'm concerned, Sally has made the right decision.'

'All right, come on then. You'll see it's a load of rubbish.'

'Sally!' Ruth called. 'Me and Elsie are popping out for a while. You'd better come down and sit with your gran.'

Both women now marched along Candle Lane, hardly speaking during the walk to Maple Terrace.

It was Elsie who banged on the door and when Arthur opened it she barged in. 'What's this about you and Sally getting a divorce?'

Arthur's half smile was more like a sneer, his voice sardonic. 'Hello, and it's nice to see you too, Mum.'

'Don't be funny with me,' Elsie spat, and indicating that Ruth should follow her, they made for the living room.

Arthur followed behind and as he took a seat, Elsie spoke again. 'Now, son, I asked you a question. Are you getting a divorce?'

'Yes, I am, and I don't appreciate you barging in here as if you own the place.'

'Got something to hide, have you?' Ruth scowled. 'Are you frightened we'll catch you with your fancy woman?'

Arthur's chin rose. 'Your daughter left me. What I do now is none of her business, or yours.'

'She had good reason to leave you.'

'Maybe, but if she'd been a proper wife when I came home from hospital, I wouldn't have slept with Patsy. I'll tell you something else – she has no right to keep my daughter away from me.'

'I don't blame her, not when she saw that you've moved that tart in.'

'Is that what she told you? And I suppose the lying bitch said she'd caught us at it again.'

'Don't you dare call my daughter a bitch!'

'If the cap fits,' he drawled.

'That's enough, Arthur,' Elsie said sharply. 'Are you trying to tell us that you haven't slept with that girl again?'

Both women saw Arthur flush, his guilt obvious, but it was Elsie who now spoke, her voice high with shock. 'My God, son, you should be ashamed of yourself.'

'Well, I'm not! Unlike my wife, Patsy wants me and has made that plain. Now I suggest you both leave, and Mum, if you come here in future, make sure you ring me first. After all, I might be busy with Patsy and you wouldn't want to walk in on us.'

Ruth saw the distress on her friend's face and said angrily, 'How can you talk to your mother like that, you rotten sod!'

'Leave it, Ruth. Come on, let's go,' Elsie said, but not before throwing her son a look of disgust.

For a while Elsie was quiet as they walked along Maple Terrace, but then she turned to Ruth, her eyes moist with tears. 'I can't believe this! How could my son talk to me like that? He's become like a stranger to me.'

'I don't know what's come over him, but Sally's right. He does want a divorce.'

'I know, and I dread to think what Bert is going to say.'

Elsie said nothing to Bert until they left Ruth's house and were getting into the car. 'Bert, while you were in the park with Angel, Ruth and I went to see Arthur.'

'Did you? Why didn't you wait for me?'

'I wanted to find out if it was true that he had that slut living with him.'

'And?'

'He didn't deny it, and not only that, he's going to divorce Sally.'

'We'll see about that. We're going round there now and I'll have a few words to say to my son.'

'No, Bert, leave it. It'll be best to wait until things have calmed down a bit, and anyway, Arthur said we have to ring him first before going to see him.'

'He what?' Bert exploded. 'What the hell's come over him?'

'I don't know. I hardly recognised him. He seemed so hard, so cruel . . .' and unable to hold back her tears any longer, Elsie started crying.

Bert's face reddened with anger. 'First, Arthur sleeps with another woman, moves her in, and now says that we have to make an appointment to see him, upsetting you in the process. Right, that's it, Elsie. From now on he's no son of mine.'

'Oh, Bert, don't say that.'

He didn't answer, only putting his foot down on the accelerator in anger as he roared along Candle Lane, whilst Elsie sat beside him, tears still rolling down her cheeks.

Arthur sat back on the sofa, still furious. What right had his mother to barge in here like that, Ruth with her? It was Sally who wanted a divorce, not him, yet he had borne the brunt of their anger. Yes, he had slept with Patsy again, but it wouldn't have happened if Sally hadn't left him. And to top it all, the bitch had told them that Patsy had moved in.

Well, that was it, the last straw. His anger continued to mount, festering inside. Sally had turned everyone against him and Arthur slammed his fist on the arm of the sofa as he vowed to see a solicitor the next day.

He was still fuming when he picked up one of his crutches and stood up, banging the other one on the ceiling. Patsy wanted him, in fact she wanted him all the time, and though he didn't love her he had to admit the sex was terrific. Yes, there was a woman who found him irresistible, and from now on, he'd show Sally that he didn't give a damn.

Patsy walked into the room now, smiling as she said, 'You rang, sir? Or should I say, you knocked?'

'Yes, I did. Come here, you little minx.'

Thirty-Four

A month had passed and the May weather was lovely, but it didn't cheer Laura Walters as she gazed at the grainy black and white photo. It was all she had left of her bonny daughter. An image – a moment frozen in time.

She had tried to stay off the booze, she really had, but it was her only way to drown the pain. If Denis hadn't left her, maybe she could have kept it up, stayed sober, but she was lost without him.

Laura returned the photograph to the tin and picked up another, this one of her wedding. Denis was smiling into the camera, and even in profile, she looked equally happy as she gazed up at him. Scathingly she flung it aside and reached for a glass of cheap cider.

For a moment she looked at the amber-coloured liquid, wishing it was gin, but there was no money for spirits. Laura thought she heard a knock on the door, but ignored it as her maudlin thoughts turned to her parents. She had been a late and unexpected baby, born with a heart defect when her mother was menopausal and her father fifty-three. They had been more like grandparents and she'd hated the restricted life they had forced her to lead. No running, no playing, no excitement.

She had an elder brother, but Andy was already a man when she'd been born and with such a huge age gap, there was little connection between them. On becoming a teenager she'd run away from home and it was many years later, when Tommy had been born, that she'd contacted her parents. She'd had no time to tell them that they were grandparents, her mother refusing to speak to her and her father saying that they would never forgive her for the worry she had caused them. With that the telephone had been slammed down, and it was the last time Laura had tried to contact them.

When Tommy was a year old, Laura felt a yearning for her kin again, but rather than risk the same response she had sent a letter to her brother. He had responded and travelled to London to see her, but the meeting had been strained. Just like her parents, Andy was a worry guts, telling her she shouldn't have risked having a baby. Laura had flared up and yelled that Tommy had been worth the risk.

They had parted on bad terms and though Andy had written to her, Laura hadn't answered it. She was glad she hadn't now. She didn't want anyone in her family to see this house in Candle Lane – to find out how low she had sunk.

There was another knock on the door. 'Laura! Laura! Let me in!'

Denis – it sounded like Denis! Laura rose unsteadily to her feet, finding that the room swam before her eyes. It took her a moment to find her balance and open the door. 'So, you've come crawling back, have you? Where's your key?'

'I don't know,' Denis said, stepping inside.

'Who said you can come in?'

'Come on, Laura,' he wheedled. 'I came back, didn't I, and I've got a few bob.'

Laura found she had difficulty focusing, but wasn't drunk enough to miss the fact that he'd returned with money. 'Why did you go off without a word?'

'I couldn't face it,' Denis said.

'Face what?'

'Losing you.'

Laura continued to stare blearily at her husband, her mind

refusing to function. 'But I got over the heart attack and you'd gone when I discharged myself from hospital.'

'Think, woman! Are you forgetting your problem?'

Laura couldn't stay on her feet and flopped onto a chair, shaking her head to clear her thoughts. Yes, she had a heart defect, but despite the doctors telling her she should never have children, she had borne two bairns. Bloody quacks, she thought, reaching for the cider again.

Denis grabbed her hand, forcing it away from the bottle. 'You got over your heart attack this time, but if you keep drinking, for how long?'

'Leave it out. You sound like my parents. They tried to wrap me in cotton wool and it drove me mad. Anyway, why nag me about drinking now? You drink too, and you haven't exactly been a caring husband. In fact, you hardly came to see me when I was in hospital.'

'I know, but that's because I didn't think you'd survive and couldn't face it.'

'You're just making excuses. You don't care about me, so why have you come back?'

'I do care, and I realised that running away doesn't solve anything. Our marriage was fine before our little girl died, but then we both lost our way and started on the booze,' Denis said, rubbing both hands across his face. 'Laura, things can be different. I've turned over a new leaf and I haven't had a drink for a fortnight. You can stop drinking too.'

Laura laughed derisively as she picked up the bottle of cider again, this time successfully. 'I did stop for a while, but didn't enjoy the experience. Do you want a glass of this?'

'Christ, woman, haven't you heard a word I've said? You've got to stop drinking or it'll kill you!'

Laura stared at her husband, but the need to have a drink was too strong. She poured another glass of cider and gulped it down.

For a moment Denis just looked at her, but then his expression hardened. 'That'll be the last drink you have. I'll see to that.'

Next door in number five, Sally clutched the solicitor's letter confirming that divorce proceedings were in progress. She hadn't wanted to seek legal advice, but Arthur had left her no choice.

Time hadn't eased Sally's heartache and she still felt sick at the thought of Arthur and Patsy together. Not only that, the rift between Arthur and his parents showed no sign of mending and her heart went out to her in-laws. Bert continued to disown Arthur and, though she appreciated their support, she knew Elsie was taking it badly.

Apathy gripped Sally, and though she went through the motions of living, inside she was dead. There was a rap on the letterbox, and when Sally opened the door, her face stretched in amazement. 'Aunt Mary,' she cried, 'you've come home. Oh, it's wonderful to see you.'

'It's lovely to see you too,' and as she stepped inside, Sadie came out of her room. Mary greeted her softly, 'Hello, Mother.'

'So, you're back then.'

'Yes, I was missing you all. How are you?'

'I'm fine,' Sadie said, but then she reached out and took Mary in her arms, her voice cracking with emotion. 'I can't believe you've come home.'

For a moment the two women remained entwined, whilst Sally stared at her aunt, thinking she looked incredible. Mary was tanned and trim, her eyes sparkling with health, her stiff, formal hairstyle and attire gone, replaced in favour of soft waves and garments. She looked the younger sister instead of the elder, and Sally wondered what her mother would make of Mary's appearance.

Sadie finally let Mary go, sniffing and wiping her eyes as she said, 'Come on, let's go into the kitchen. I want to hear all about your travels and that job you took in Spain.'

'You look as brown as a berry,' Sally said.

'The sun shines more often in Spain, even through the winter months, hence the tan, but no doubt it'll soon fade.'

Sally made them a drink, and listened to her aunt's adventures, amazed by all she had seen and done. For a while it distracted her, but then seeing the solicitor's letter on the table, her face saddened.

'Enough about me,' Mary said. 'I'm glad to see you looking so well, Mum, but I'm not so sure about you, Sally. You look dreadfully thin. Why have you lost so much weight?'

Sally felt a lump forming in her throat and, barely able to speak, she croaked, 'Gran, will you tell her what's happened?'

'Yeah, all right, love.'

With her head down, Sally listened to her gran's words, each one like a fresh blow to her heart. 'And to top it all,' Sadie continued, 'Arthur's got his fancy piece living with him.'

'No!' Mary gasped. 'I can't believe it. None of you mentioned this in your letters.'

'I asked them not to tell you,' Sally said. 'You were happy in Spain and I didn't want you to feel you had to come back.'

'Oh, Sally, I'd have jumped on the first plane. I can't believe this of Arthur and I could kill him, I really could. I'm so sorry, my dear. You must be absolutely devastated.'

Sally had bottled her feelings, hiding her pain in an attempt to protect Angel, but now she broke down and as her aunt stood up to hold out her arms, she ran into them. Mary patted her back, her voice a soft murmur of condolences.

Her gran's wasn't so soft. 'That's it, girl,' she said, 'it's about time you gave vent to your feelings.'

Sally did, crying out her pain until at last she drew in great, juddering sobs. She stepped out of her aunt's arms, managing to gasp, 'I'm sorry, this isn't much of a homecoming.'

Mary brushed her apologies away, and soon they were sitting again, Sadie back to asking more about Spain while Sally felt so tired that she just wanted to close her eyes and go to sleep.

Sally was upstairs bathing Angel when Ruth came home that evening, and seeing her sister's shocked expression, Mary smiled.

'Well, who'd have thought it?' Ruth said. 'I've just heard that Denis Walters is back, and now you've turned up too. Is this just a visit or are you here for good?'

'I'm here to stay. It was lovely in Spain, but my family is here and I missed you.'

'Look at you. You're so brown, and what have you done to your hair?'

'I let my perm grow out.'

'You should have done it years ago. It looks much nicer.'

'What's this about Denis Walters?' Sadie interrupted.

'Tommy collared me on the way home to tell me that his dad is back, and he looked as pleased as punch. Perhaps Denis will be able to sort Laura out.'

'He's as bad as her, so I doubt it.'

Ruth sighed as she sank onto a chair, kicking off her shoes. 'I know you've got your flat, but I doubt you'll get your old job back.'

'It doesn't matter. I'll find something else.'

'Where's Sally?' Ruth said, as though just aware that her daughter wasn't in the room.

'She's upstairs getting Angel ready for bed.'

'Poor Sally, she looks awful and so thin,' Mary commented. 'This break-up has obviously knocked her for six, but isn't there anything we can do to get them back together?'

'Leave it out, Mary. Now that he's moved that tart in and filed for a divorce, Sally's better off without him.'

'Arthur's a good man and I still find it hard to believe.'

'Good man! I used to think so too, but not after this.'

Mary frowned as she listened to the explanation of the

246

break-up, but none of it made sense. She would go to see Arthur, and if all that had been said was true, she'd have a few choice words to say to him.

Arthur winced as he shifted in his chair. He had been determined to get used to his prosthesis, and now managed at times without a stick, but today he had slipped awkwardly while checking a delivery and it had left his stump a bit sore.

When they arrived home from the site, Joe had insisted on coming in, going on to cook them both a meal. He was now in the kitchen, saying he'd wash up and make them a coffee before he left.

Arthur took off his prosthesis and was rubbing his stump when Joe came back into the room. 'Arthur, I'd prefer it if you'd use your cane on site. It'd be safer. I don't know why you're in such an all-fired hurry to get rid of it.'

'I want to show her that I'm not a cripple.'

'I suppose you mean Sally. You're getting a divorce, so why do you care what she thinks?'

'I just do!'

'So why let her, and your parents, think that Patsy has moved in with you?'

'Because it was Sally who told my parents, and they chose to believe her over me. I'm their son and they should know me better than that, but as they've made up their mind that I'm the guilty party, sod them!'

'It sounds like your pride talking.'

'Now look, Patsy hasn't moved in, and I have no intention of letting her. Yet I was condemned without a hearing.'

'You're still seeing her though.'

'Yes, I am, and so what? Are you jealous?'

'No, I'm not. I only took Patsy out a few times and soon found she wasn't the girl for me. I still can't believe you prefer her to Sally.'

'Sally doesn't want me, and I'm not a flaming monk. Now come on, let's change the subject.'

'All right,' Joe said, swallowing his coffee and preparing to leave when someone rang the doorbell. 'Stay put, Arthur. You need to rest that leg.'

As Joe opened the front door, Arthur heard a woman's voice and for a moment his heart leapt. Was it Sally? He felt immediately deflated when Mary walked into the room, and forcing a smile, he said, 'Hello, Mary. So you've come home.'

If she'd been in better humour Mary might have told Arthur that she wasn't an optical illusion, but instead, ignoring the other man in the room, she said, 'Can we talk?'

'Joe, this is Sally's aunt and she's just returned from Spain. Though I doubt she's called round to tell me about her adventures.'

'Pleased to meet you,' Joe said, as he proffered his hand.

Murmuring a greeting, Mary shook it, but with Sally's heartbreak heavy on her mind she hadn't come here to socialise. She'd come to see for herself if Arthur had another woman, and so far there wasn't any sign of one.

'Arthur, I'd best be off,' Joe said.

'Yes, all right, mate. I'll see you in the morning,' Arthur replied, and as Joe left the room he added, 'Mary, do you mind sitting down? It's making my neck ache looking up at you.'

Taking a seat, she said without preamble, 'I can't believe what I've been hearing and I came round here to see for myself.'

'See what?'

'This young woman I hear is living with you.'

Arthur's lips curled back into a sneer, his annoyance obvious. 'As you can see there isn't a woman here. Yet even if there was, Sally has filed for a divorce so I don't see that it's any of your business.'

'Sally only sought legal advice after hearing from your solicitor.'

248

'Is that what she told you? Another lie – but of course everyone believes precious Sally.'

Mary was about to ask him what he meant when the living-room door opened. She had her back towards it, and hidden in the wing-back chair, she heard a female voice.

'Thank God that stuffed shirt has gone, I'm fed up with him looking at me like I'm something he's stepped on.'

'Patsy,' Arthur said, his voice holding a warning.

'What?'

Mary stood up, and, startled, the girl's eyes rounded as she said, 'Oh, I didn't see you there!'

'Obviously not. So, it's true, Arthur. You have got someone else living with you?'

His voice was thick with anger as he replied, 'So, just like the others, you've jumped to that conclusion.'

'What else am I supposed to think?'

'Think what you bloody well like. Now I suggest you leave.'

'I'm not going anywhere until I sort this out! What do you mean about Sally filing for divorce first? And is this girl living with you or not?'

'Now look here, I don't have to answer to you, and you needn't stand there looking like some sort of avenging angel. You've already had Sally's version of the truth, so like everyone else, I doubt you'll believe mine. Now as I said, I want you to leave.'

Mary's jaws tightened, but there was no arguing with the finality of Arthur's words. She snatched up her handbag and marched from the room, slamming the door behind her.

It was only when Mary reached the end of Maple Terrace that she began to think logically again. Arthur was under the impression that Sally had filed for divorce first, but why? And what did he mean about Sally telling lies? Of course she wasn't, and anyway, she had seen Arthur's girlfriend for herself.

Though Mary had enjoyed her cruise, and then working abroad, the pain of losing Leroy was still there. For Sally the heartache was still fresh and her heart went out to her niece. In the face of Arthur's intransigent attitude, she doubted there was any way to save her niece's marriage and Mary felt utterly helpless.

Thirty-Five

Another two weeks passed, and Angel became increasingly sulky and demanding, 'I want to see my daddy!'

'Well, you can't,' Sally said tiredly.

'I hate you, Mummy.'

With arms akimbo and her hands on her hips, Angel glared at her indignantly and Sally closed her eyes against the sight, no longer seeing the stance with humour.

'You should let her see her father,' Sadie said.

Sally's eyes widened. 'What?'

'You heard me, Sally. I've said it before and I'm saying it again. I know you think you're punishing Arthur by keeping them apart, but Angel is suffering too and it isn't right.'

'But he doesn't deserve to see her.'

'Maybe not. However, it's Angel who concerns me. I'm not condoning what Arthur has done, but he is her father.'

'Mummy, pleeease,' Angel appealed.

'Go on, Sally. Let her see him, if only for a little while,' Ruth urged.

They were both nagging her now, Sally thought, and wondered angrily whose side they were on. She said curtly, 'I said no.'

'I hate you, Mummy!' Angel cried again, running into Ruth's arms.

There was a moment of startling clarity as Sally watched the scene. What sort of mother was she? In her desperation to punish

251

Arthur, she had used the only weapon she had – her daughter. Worried that Angel might try to go to Maple Terrace on her own again, she kept her in whenever she thought that Arthur would be at home, and Angel was chafing at the restriction.

Sally swallowed, sickened by her self-centred behaviour. She held out her arms. 'Angel, come here, darling.'

'No, I don't want to,' the child said, burrowing into her grandmother.

'Oh, Angel, I'm sorry, darling. Of course you can see your daddy.'

The child lifted her head. 'Really?'

'Yes, really, and I'll give him a ring now to make the arrangements. It's Sunday so he'll be home, and if you like, you can go to see him after dinner.'

'Yippee,' Angel cried, pulling away from Ruth and doing a little jig.

As Sally rose to her feet, her gran touched her arm. 'I'm glad you've come to your senses.'

'I've been awful, Gran.'

'You're hurting, love, and it's understandable, but I knew you'd come round eventually.'

Sally sighed, dragging her feet as she went into the hall. She didn't want to talk to Arthur, didn't want to hear his voice, but for Angel's sake she had to. There would be one stipulation though, Sally decided as she dialled the number. One she hoped Arthur would agree to.

'Hello.'

On hearing Arthur's voice, Sally froze for a moment, the pain of his betrayal still unbearable. 'Arthur,' she said quietly.

'Is that you, Sally?'

'I've just rung to say that I've decided to let you see Angel.'

'I should think so too, especially as you had no right to keep us apart in the first place. She's my daughter too.'

'I know that and she's missing you. However, I don't want her to see you with Patsy.'

252

'Really, and why not?'

'I should have thought that was obvious. Angel is already upset that we're living apart, and it would only add to her confusion if she sees you with another woman.'

There was a silence and then she heard a loud sigh. 'At some point she'll have to get used to it, but for now I'll make sure that Patsy stays out of the way.'

Sally's stomach twisted, still unable to bear the thought of them together. She took a deep breath, steadying her voice. 'Our Sunday lunch is almost ready, so how about I fetch Angel round for an hour afterwards? Say at three o'clock.'

'An hour! Surely she can stay longer than that?'

'All right, two hours, but then I'll return to pick her up.'

'Fine.'

Sally's goodbye was clipped, finding as she dropped the receiver into its cradle that she had to fight her feelings. She wouldn't cry, she wouldn't, and as she returned to the kitchen Angel looked at her expectantly. Sally forced herself to smile. 'I'll be taking you to see your daddy after dinner.'

Angel ran a little circle around the room, cheering loudly, until Sadie snapped, 'For Gawd's sake, pack it in, child. You're giving me a headache.'

'Sorry, Gamma.'

'Why don't you go out to play?'

'Can I, Mummy?'

For a moment Sally hesitated, but Angel knew she would be seeing her daddy later so was unlikely to wander off. 'Yes, I suppose so, but stay in Candle Lane, or else.'

As the door closed, Sally sank onto a chair again. When she took Angel to see Arthur, she would have to see him again, and she dreaded it.

When Arthur walked into the living room, Patsy could see that he was fuming.

253

'What's the matter, darling?'

'That was Sally. She's agreed to let me see Angel at last.'

'Oh, that's nice.'

'You won't say that when you hear the rule she's laid down. She's got a bloody cheek.'

'Calm down, love. What rule are you on about?'

'I can see Angel, but only if you're not around.'

Patsy hid her feelings, saying calmly, 'That's not a problem. I'll just make sure I'm upstairs while the child is with you.'

'Thanks, love.'

'Does Sally still think that I'm living with you?'

'Yes, I think so, and so do my parents, but I've no intention of putting them straight. If that's what they choose to believe, sod them.'

With her head lowered, Patsy's mind raced. She had tried every trick in the book to take the relationship further, but to no avail. Arthur wanted her for sex, and plenty of it, but he still wouldn't let her stay the night. She had a feeling that, despite his protestations, he wanted Sally back.

Patsy's eyes narrowed. She'd have to think of something, some mischief to keep them apart.

Ruth watched as Angel picked at her food and wondered if Tommy was getting anything to eat. Denis Walters said that he'd stopped drinking and that Laura had too, but Ruth doubted it. When she saw Tommy he still looked neglected, dirty and poorly-fed, and it broke her heart. She longed to feed him, but Denis had taken Laura's side, telling her not to interfere.

'Angel, eat your carrots,' Sally said.

'Don't want them.'

'There are starving children in the world who'd be glad for the food on your plate,' Ruth said.

'They can have it.'

'Angel, don't cheek your nanny,' Sally snapped.

Ruth was unable to help the comparison. When she'd fed Tommy he scoffed it, eating anything that was put in front of him. Angel on the other hand was picky, but with a small shake of her head Ruth knew it was their fault. They had all spoiled the child, but now as her granddaughter gave her a heart-stopping smile, Ruth grinned back. She was adorable.

Sadie smacked her lips. 'That was smashing, Ruth. I love a nice bit of lamb with mint sauce.'

'I'm glad you enjoyed it,' she replied, pleased that her mother was so much better nowadays. Ruth knew that she was happier too, though she had to hide the fact. When Sally and Angel had moved to Maple Terrace, she'd missed them so much. The house had felt empty and desolate without them. Now, though, they were back, and though she played the part of being sympathetic, secretly she was hoping there would never be a reconciliation.

She had supported her mother in persuading Sally to let Angel see her father, but now hoped it wasn't a mistake. She didn't want Sally anywhere near Arthur, not if there was the slightest chance of them getting back together. Ruth lowered her eyes. She shouldn't think like that, it was selfish, but then with her next thought, she justified her attitude. After what Arthur had done, he didn't deserve Sally.

At three o'clock, Sally took Angel's hand and walked her to Maple Terrace. It was now early May, the temperature warmer, and if she hadn't been so tense she might have enjoyed the walk; instead her teeth were gritted as she rang the doorbell.

It was some time before it opened, and despite everything, her heart leapt when she saw Arthur. He stood straight and tall, with no sign of a cane.

'Daddy,' Angel cried, running joyfully forward.

Arthur smiled down at his daughter, and then moving sideways he beckoned her inside. 'Hello, princess. Come on in?'

'Mummy too?'

'No,' Sally said hastily, 'but I'll be back to pick you up in a couple of hours. Be a good girl.'

Angel looked bewildered, but stepped inside, and as Arthur closed the door, tears welled in Sally's eyes. It had been so hard to look at Arthur again, and though she had tried to harden her heart towards him, Sally now knew that it hadn't worked. She still loved him. She walked away, her shoulders hunched, and with her eyes down she didn't see Patsy until she nearly bumped into her.

'Hello, Sally, I've just been to get a bit of shopping in. Thank you for letting Arthur see Angel. He's been missing her.'

Sally said nothing, only struggled to hide her feelings and she was about to walk past when Patsy spoke again.

'Arthur's been practising for hours to walk without a stick,' she said, 'and all because he doesn't want to walk with a limp when we get married.'

'Married! You're getting married?'

'Well, yes. Didn't he tell you?'

Sally shook her head, her voice a croak. 'No.'

'Men!' Patsy exclaimed. 'Still, no doubt he'd have got round to it eventually. Of course we'll have to wait until your divorce comes through and I know all the legal stuff takes ages. In the meantime at least we're together.'

Sally felt sick, and while still fighting to hide it, Patsy chirped on, 'Oh yes, and as you can see I'm keeping out of the way while Angel's with Arthur. I've agreed to that for now, but if you ask me it's a bit daft. Arthur and I are living together and it would make more sense for Angel to get used to the idea. After all, you can hardly expect me to disappear every time she comes round.'

Anger dispelled Sally's nausea. 'I don't give a damn if you're inconvenienced. In fact, the longer I can keep my daughter away from you the better,' she spat, marching off with her head held high. To think she had once believed that Arthur loved her. Their marriage meant nothing to him – something easily pushed aside

– so much so that he could even propose to Patsy before their divorce had come through.

It was then that a hard shell began to form around Sally's heart, one that she was determined to keep in place.

Later that afternoon, Ann turned up just as Sally was due to collect Angel. 'I hope you don't mind, but I wanted to see you. Dad dropped me off and he's picking me up in an hour or so.'

'I'm just about to go out,' Sally said, stonily.

'What's wrong, Sally? Is it that you'd rather not see me?'

'No, it isn't that.'

It was Ruth who offered Ann an explanation. 'Sally took Angel round to see Arthur. She bumped into Patsy and the girl told her that she and Arthur are getting married as soon as the divorce comes through.'

'No, you must have got it wrong, Sally. Arthur would have told us.'

'I haven't, but I can't talk about it now as I'm off to collect Angel. I shouldn't be long so I'll see you when I get back.'

'I'll come with you, and if this is true I'll have a few words to say to my brother.'

'Don't bother on my account,' Sally said. 'In fact, I'd rather you said nothing in front of Angel. I don't want her upset.'

Sally didn't feel like talking, but answered Ann's questions as they walked to Maple Terrace. 'Yes, I'm sure they're getting married. I heard it from the horse's mouth. Patsy was full of it.'

Arthur's eyes widened when he opened the door. 'Well, well, hello, sis. I wasn't expecting you. Are you both coming in?'

'No,' Sally said bluntly. 'I've just come for Angel.'

'If that tart's in there, I'm not coming in either,' Ann said.

'If you're talking about Patsy, she isn't a tart, and I won't have you calling her one,' Arthur said, obviously annoyed. 'Wait there. I'll get Angel.'

'Hold on a minute,' Ann said. 'I hear congratulations are in order.'

'What are you talking about?'

'Sally tells me that you and Patsy are getting married.'

Arthur seemed to stretch, his neck rising out of his collar. 'That's another of her lies.'

'No, it isn't,' Sally protested, about to say what Patsy had told her when Angel appeared, grinning when she saw her aunt.

'Hello, Auntie Ann. Are them boys with you?'

'No, darling. They're with Nanny Elsie.'

'Come on, Angel, it's time to go home,' Sally urged.

'I want to stay with Daddy.'

'You can see him again next week,' Sally cajoled, anxious to be away. Arthur had accused her of lying and her fists were clenched into balls, her nails digging into her palms in an attempt not to have this out in front of Angel.

'Well, Ann, it was nice to see you and thanks for the congratulations, even if they are misplaced,' Arthur said, a hint of sarcasm in his tone.

'For the sake of *you know who*,' Ann said, nodding towards Angel, 'I'm saying nothing, but I intend to get to the bottom of this.'

'As long as you listen to *her*, you never will,' Arthur countered, 'but you're right, this isn't the time to sort it out. Off you go, princess, and I'll see you next week.'

As they walked away and out of Arthur's hearing, Ann said, 'Don't you think it was funny the way Arthur reacted when I congratulated him? He said that you were telling lies and I wonder now if you've got the wrong end of the stick.'

'It's what Patsy told me, and if you don't believe me, ask her yourself.'

'I don't want to talk to that bitch, but I'll certainly talk to Arthur,' Ann said.

They were quiet then, Angel skipping beside them, and they

had only just reached Candle Lane when Bert turned up. He said a quick hello, but didn't get out of the car. 'Sorry, the boys are running Elsie ragged and I can't stop. Come on, Ann, we'd better get back before your mother reaches the end of her tether.'

They said goodbye and as they drove away, Sally's eyes darkened. Why had Arthur denied that he was getting married? What was the point of that? She was unable to find an answer.

When the telephone rang that evening, Arthur removed his arms from around Patsy and went to answer it.

His sister's indignant tone rang down the line. 'Arthur, what's going on? Sally tells me that you're going to marry Patsy, but you made out that she's telling lies. I don't know what you're playing at, but after what you've done, don't you think Sally has suffered enough?'

'That says it all and I can see where your sympathies lie. Well, Ann, if you choose to believe everything Sally tells you, more fool you. Now, if you don't mind, I'm busy,' he snapped, slamming down the receiver.

His face was grim as he went back into the living room, and though Patsy looked inviting with her top off and skirt up round her thighs, his passion had died. It had been great to see Angel that afternoon, but it served to emphasise how much he was missing her, and, if truth be known, Sally too. He'd blown it, blown his marriage, but why did Sally have to turn everyone against him?

'What's the matter, darling?' Patsy asked and, as he sat beside her, she reached out to stroke his inner thigh.

'That was my sister. It seems that Sally has told her another cock and bull story.'

'Really! What has she said this time?'

'She's told them that we're getting married, and it seems that everyone believes her.'

'Did you tell your sister that it isn't true?'

'No, I didn't. Like my parents she's chosen to believe what Sally tells them, so sod her. Sod them all.'

'Never mind, darling,' Patsy said, her voice honey soft. 'They'll come round in time, I'm sure of it, and in the meantime . . .'

Her lips covered his, warm and moist, and wanting to forget his pain, Arthur gave himself up to the sensations she aroused. Patsy too gave herself up to the passion, relief coursing through her body that the plan had worked.

Telling Sally that she and Arthur were getting married had been a risky thing to do, but desperate times called for desperate measures. It could have gone badly wrong, but thank goodness for Arthur's pride. By not denying it, there was now a further wedge between him and Sally.

Thankfully there was a wedge between Arthur and his family too – one that she hoped would stay in place for a long time. His pride was something she could use against him, and with any luck it would cause him to propose soon. She wasn't stupid and knew he didn't love her, but what did love matter? If he asked her to marry him to get back at Sally, that was fine with her, and she'd say yes like a shot.

Thirty-Six

On a Thursday morning nearly a fortnight later, two things happened in quick succession in Candle Lane. The postman delivered a letter to every door, and before he had reached the last house, street doors were opening as neighbours converged.

Nelly Cox, her face white with shock, hurried to number five, and as Sally answered the door she bustled inside.

'Ruth, have you had a letter?'

'Yes, so I can guess why you're here.'

'I don't care what they say, I ain't leaving Candle Lane.'

'As they're pulling all the houses down, you won't have any choice.'

'They can demolish mine around me, but I ain't shifting.'

'You might get offered something better.'

'What, in one of them matchbox blocks that are going up! No thank you, I ain't going in one of them. If they want me out, they'll have to bleedin' carry me.'

'We've been scheduled for redevelopment before and it didn't happen,' Sadie said. 'Maybe the council will defer it again.'

'I doubt it,' Ruth murmured, but then Nelly swayed on her feet. 'Sit down, love. You look fit to drop.'

Sally too saw the agitated state Nelly was in, her mother now urging, 'Quick, Sal, make a pot of tea. I think Nelly's in shock.'

Sally did her bidding while her mother gently touched the old woman's shoulder saying, 'I'm sorry, love, but I've got to

261

leave for work or I'll be late. We'll talk again when I come home this evening.'

'Yes, get yourself off,' Sadie urged. 'We'll look after Nelly.'

Sally called goodbye to her mother as she hurriedly made the tea, making sure that it was good and strong. 'Don't worry, Nelly. It might be ages before they can re-house us all. The letter only says that we're scheduled for redevelopment again, but it doesn't say when.'

Nelly's hands were shaking as she lifted the cup to her lips, and Sally found that she too began to worry about leaving Candle Lane. Would her mother be re-housed in a place large enough for all of them? If not, she'd have to find a flat, but with rent to pay she'd have to be sure of a weekly income from Arthur. So far she had drawn what cash was needed from their bank account, but was worried that Arthur would close it soon. If he did, until she received some financial settlement, she'd have no money.

Nelly swallowed the last of her tea, colour now returning to her cheeks. 'You could be right, Sally. We could be here a long time yet.'

'Yeah, maybe,' Sadie said, 'but our turn will come round eventually. The lane is going to be demolished, and that's that.'

'Over my dead body,' Nelly cried with renewed vigour. 'I don't care what they say. I ain't going. I'm staying put.'

'Don't be daft,' Sadie retorted. 'When that huge ball starts swinging and knocking down the walls, you'll be out of your place like a shot.'

'No, I won't! If we all refuse to shift, what can they do? In fact, I think I'll go and have a word with everyone in the lane. If we stick together, we might be able to beat the buggers,' Nelly said forcefully as she rose to her feet, something to act on giving her new strength.

'Dream on, Nelly Cox,' Sadie called, but the door had already closed behind the old woman.

'Gran, do you think the council will offer us a three-bedroom flat?'

'Blimey, I dunno, love. There's only your mum and me down as living here now, so I doubt it. Mind you, she could inform them that you're staying with us and it might make a difference. Have a word with her when she comes home.'

'I'll do that, but I'll take Angel to school now or she'll be late.'

As Sally left the house with her daughter, she saw that Nelly was already knocking on doors.

In the Walters' house, the second traumatic event was unfolding.

'Dad! Dad!' Tommy shouted.

'Wh . . . what?'

'Dad, wake up! There's somefing wrong with Mum.'

Denis Walters' eyelids felt like they were stuck together with glue as he forced them open. He had worked late, coming home to a house that looked like a bomb had hit it. He'd searched in all of Laura's usual hideaways, even finding empty bottles hidden in the boy's room, and presenting her with the evidence, they'd had a stinking row. The stupid woman denied that she was drinking, yet she stank of booze, and he was just about ready to give up. Unable to face sharing her bed that night he'd fallen asleep on the sofa, but now his neck felt stiff as he struggled to sit up. 'All right, son, I'm coming. Just give me a minute to get dressed.'

'Hurry up, Dad. I can't wake her up.'

Tommy's words had him shooting to his feet and, quickly pulling on his trousers he took the stairs two at a time, bursting into the bedroom.

Denis blanched when he saw his wife's face, knowing instantly that she was dead. With his stomach turning he said quickly to Tommy, 'Run to the doctor's, son. Tell him to come right away.'

'Is Mum all right?'

'Do as I say,' Denis yelled, and as soon as his son had scampered downstairs he sank onto the side of the bed. Oh, Laura, Laura! If he hadn't slept downstairs, would he have been able to save her? Had she died in pain, calling for him? Please, no, he thought, let her have gone in her sleep. The house felt strangely silent and he had no idea how long he sat there, gazing at his wife, his eyes burning, but dry. Eventually there were sounds in the hall, and Tommy walked into the room, the doctor behind him.

'Tommy, go back downstairs,' Denis ordered.

'No, I want to see me mum.'

'Do as I say!'

The doctor pushed past the boy, shaking his head as he looked at the bed. 'Close the door, Mr Walters,' he said, eyes flicking behind him to make sure that Tommy was safely outside.

Denis did as he asked, and after a quick examination the doctor spoke again. 'I'm sure you've realised that your wife is dead, Mr Walters, and it was probably another heart attack. I'll arrange for her body to be moved, but in the meantime I suggest you find someone to look after your son.'

His mind in a blur, Denis thanked the man and then grimaced. Christ, he'd thanked the doctor for telling him that his wife was dead. How bizarre was that? His mind jumped. Tommy, yes Tommy, the boy would have to be told, and then got out of the way while Laura's body was taken out of the house.

Denis followed the doctor downstairs, dreading the task ahead of him as he showed the man out.

'What's wrong wiv me mum?'

'Tommy, come here,' Denis said, bracing himself as he placed his hands on the boy's shoulders. 'I'm afraid your mum has passed away.'

'What's passed away? Did she faint?'

'No, lad, your mother's dead.' Denis hated the brutality of the words, and as Tommy's face crumbled he ineffectually pulled him into his arms, something he hadn't done in years. The boy smelt musty, of unwashed clothes and an unwashed body.

264

As the child sobbed, Denis wondered how he was going to cope with him now. How could he work and look after a child? Christ, what was the matter with him? His wife had just died and here he was fretting about the future when she hadn't even been buried yet.

Bloody hell! How was he going to pay for a funeral? They had no life insurance, no savings. Denis closed his eyes in despair.

Sally was on her way back from taking Angel to school when she saw the doctor leaving the Walters' house. She wondered if Laura was ill again, and had only been indoors for a few minutes when someone knocked.

Denis stood on the step, his expression agonised. 'What is it?' she asked. 'Has something happened to Laura?'

Tommy shot out from behind his father, throwing his arms around Sally's legs. 'Me mum's dead. Where's Ruth? I want Ruth!'

'You'd better come in,' Sally invited, her arm automatically going around Tommy's shoulders.

Denis shook his head, leaning forward to whisper, 'The doctor is arranging for my wife's body to be taken away. Can I leave Tommy with you until she's gone?'

'Of course you can, and if there's anything else I can do, please let me know.'

'Thanks,' the man said and, as though unable to cope with his son's grief, he quickly left.

'Come on, Tommy,' Sally said, leading him into the kitchen.

As soon as Sadie saw the boy, she asked sharply, 'Why ain't you in school?'

'Me . . . me muvver's dead,' he cried, throwing himself onto the sofa as his thin body shook with sobs.

'Blimey, Sal, the poor little sod. His mum was so young too.'

Sally sat beside Tommy, pulling him into her arms, finding that her own tears were mingling with his. For the first time in ages Sally forgot her own pain as she gently rocked Tommy back and forth.

When Ruth arrived home from work, Tommy was back with his father, but on being told the news she was knocking on Denis Walters' door minutes later.

The man opened it, his eyes shadowed with grief. Then, hearing her voice, Tommy scooted in front of his father, throwing himself at Ruth. She crouched down, holding him tightly, her heart aching for this little ragamuffin that she had come to love.

'Come in,' Denis said.

Ruth stood up and, holding Tommy's hand, she followed Denis into the kitchen. It was in a disgusting state again and her nose wrinkled with distaste. It wasn't right. Tommy shouldn't have to live like this. 'Denis, would you like Tommy to stay with me until you get things sorted out?'

'I can't ask you to do that.'

'I don't mind. He's no trouble, and no doubt you have arrangements to make.'

'What do you think, son?'

Tommy looked from one to the other, his face wet with tears. 'I don't 'spect you want to be on yer own, Dad. If you like, I'll stay with you.'

Denis gulped, obviously touched by his son's words. 'There's no need, son. I've got things to do, and you might be better off with Mrs Marchant.'

Ruth too was amazed at Tommy's sensitivity, the child then saying, 'All right, I'll go with Ruth, but you will come to see me, won't you, Dad?'

'Of course, and when I've sorted things out you can come home.'

'You'd best get yourself a few things, Tommy,' Ruth urged. 'Some clean clothes and underwear.'

'I ain't got any clean clothes.'

'Then bring your dirty ones and I'll wash them.'

As Tommy ran from the room, Denis said, 'Laura loved the boy, she really did, but the booze changed her personality. I tried to stop her drinking, but I had to work and couldn't watch her for twenty-four hours a day.'

Ruth nodded sympathetically, but her mind was elsewhere. Was Denis capable of looking after the boy? And as though Denis was aware of her thoughts, he spoke again.

'I don't know how I'm going to cope with him now.'

Tommy came back into the room, clutching a bundle of clothes to his chest. Rags, Ruth thought, they all look like rags, but she smiled gently as she took them. 'Right, come on, love, let's get you next door.'

'Bye, Dad,' Tommy said, surprising them both when he threw his arms around his father.

Denis impatiently pushed him away. 'Off you go, son.'

Ruth's lips tightened as she led Tommy out and, unbeknown to him or his father, there was one thought that kept going round and round in her mind. She loved the boy, and if Denis agreed, she'd welcome Tommy into her home, and her heart, permanently.

Later that evening, Nelly Cox stood on her doorstep, leaning against the stanchion. She had tried everyone in Candle Lane, but other than two or three people, none of the others were interested in mounting a protest. The young couples welcomed the demolition, saying they'd be glad to get out of this dump and were hoping to be re-housed in a better place.

Nelly looked down the lane. There were no trees, no front gardens, just flat-fronted terraced houses. She didn't care. It might not be a pretty place, but it was her home and all her memories were here.

There had been sad times, but none of these came to mind as she looked back on the years. She recalled street parties, and would never forget the dancing in the lane at the end of World War Two. Another party had been arranged for Queen Elizabeth's Coronation, and though it couldn't compare to the end of the war celebrations, she had vivid memories of doing a knees-up with her neighbours.

Nelly's eyes came to rest on the Walters' house, newcomers like most people in the lane now, but she'd been saddened to hear of Laura's death. In the old days all the neighbours would have banded together to help. A collection would have been arranged for flowers, and food organised for the funeral. Those days were gone, and instead of popping in and out of each other's houses for a good old gossip, doors were locked and families sat in front of their televisions for hours on end.

Had anyone been to see how Denis Walters was coping? Yes, probably Ruth or Sally, but she doubted anyone else had bothered. A small voice whispered in Nelly's conscience, and realising she hadn't made the effort either, she quickly hurried to knock on the door.

'I'm sorry to hear about your wife,' she said as Denis opened it, saddened to see the pain in the man's eyes. 'I've come to see if there's anything I can do.'

'Thanks, do you wanna come in?'

She followed Denis into his dirty kitchen, asking, 'How's Tommy?'

'He's taken it badly and is next door with Mrs Marchant.'

'Ruth's a lovely woman. She'll take good care of him.'

'I know.' A small silence fell but then Denis blurted out, 'I don't know what to do. I ain't even got the money to bury my wife, and how can I work with Tommy to look after?'

'Haven't you any family who can help?'

Denis shook his head. 'My parents are dead, and I've no brothers or sisters. Laura's parents may still be alive, but they severed all connection with her.'

'That's awful. Why did they do that?'

268

'Laura had a heart defect and as a child she'd been fiercely protected. Her parents constantly worried and treated her like an invalid. When she was old enough she ran away from home, and they never forgave her.'

'Ain't there anyone else?'

'There's Laura's brother, and at one time they exchanged letters.'

'You should get in touch with him, let him know that his sister has passed away and, if they're alive, her parents too,' Nelly said gently. 'Who knows, they may be able to help.'

'You're right. They ain't short of a few bob. I'll have to find his letter, see if there's a telephone number.'

'I'll leave you to it, and don't forget if there's anything I can do, you only have to ask.'

'Thanks,' Denis said, already rifling through a drawer as Nelly bustled out.

It took Denis an hour but at last he found the letter and number, clutching the piece of paper as he hurried to the nearest telephone box.

Nelly Cox was right, Laura's family had to be told, and they might offer to help. Would they stump up money for the funeral? He hoped so. Laura deserved a better send-off than one the National Assistance would provide.

'Hello,' a voice said, the soft Scottish burr making Denis gulp with pain. When he'd first met Laura, she too had had those soft tones. She'd been working as a chambermaid in a hotel, but wanted to be a receptionist. To gain promotion she had worked hard to remove all trace of her Scottish ancestry.

'Hello,' Denis choked. 'Is that Andy?'

'Yes, and who's this?'

'It's Denis, Laura's husband. I'm ringing to tell you that . . . that she's passed away.'

For a moment there was silence, but then Andy said, 'No, no, I can't believe it. What happened?'

269

'It was her heart,' Denis told him. 'She . . . she died at home.'

There was another moment's silence, and then his voice husky with distress, Andy said, 'I . . . I'll have to tell my parents and then come down for the funeral. When is it?'

'I dunno. I haven't made any arrangements yet and I can't until I somehow get the money to pay for it.'

'I see,' he said, but then his voice became brusque. 'In that case I'll sort things out with my office and then get the first train to London in the morning. Are you still at the same address?'

'No, we live in Battersea now,' and after giving him the new address, they said their goodbyes, Denis feeling a sense of relief as he replaced the receiver. It seemed Laura's parents were still alive, so surely they, or Andy, would sort out Tommy's future. The boy was part of their family after all, and deserved a better life than this.

As Denis walked home he admitted where his thoughts were taking him. He'd been a useless father and knew he wouldn't be able to cope with the boy. He'd taken no interest in his son since losing his daughter, drowning his pain with drink, and though he'd stopped boozing, it hadn't made any difference. He still hadn't been able to save Laura.

Denis stopped off at the off-licence. He had found another reason to drink again. When Andy arrived, he'd see what a useless drunk he was, and with any luck he'd take Tommy back to Scotland with him. The boy would have a good life there and would be well provided for.

At home again, Denis drank deeply. He wasn't doing this for himself. He was doing it for Tommy.

Thirty-Seven

Though a school holiday, Sally didn't have a problem with looking after Tommy. The boy was subdued, and Angel oddly quiet too as though aware that Tommy wasn't himself. The Friday morning passed without any problems. However after lunch the boy said, 'I want to see me dad.'

'He may not be in, Tommy. He . . . he has a lot of things to sort out,' Sally said, avoiding mentioning the funeral arrangements. 'But come on, we'll go and see. Won't be long, Gran,' she called, taking Angel along too.

Denis was in, but swayed as he opened the door, his hand reaching to cling to the frame for support. 'I thought you were Andy,' he slurred. 'I'm eshpecting him.'

'Yer drunk,' Tommy said, his mouth set in a scowl as he looked up at his father.

'Just drowning me shorrows. You can't blame a man for that.'

'Come on, Tommy, you can see your dad later,' Sally urged.

'Yeah, go with Shally,' Denis agreed.

'Who's Andy?' Tommy asked.

'He's your uncle, but we've got things to talk about before you meet him. Now bugger off, son.'

Sally's lips thinned and she placed an arm around the boy's small shoulders to lead him away. With Denis in that state Tommy was better off out of the way, but they found Sadie snoozing, and Sally was worried that the children would wake her.

271

'You can play outside, but Tommy, leave your father in peace.'

'Yeah, all right.'

Angel grabbed her marbles, challenging Tommy to a game, and after warning them to stay in the lane, they ran out, leaving Sally to sink into a chair. She was disgusted with Denis Walters and felt heartsick for Tommy. With his father on the booze again, what sort of future did the poor lad have?

Sally didn't get the chance to sit for long, her gran waking up and asking for a drink. This was followed by a visit from Nelly. 'I saw the kids playing outside. How is Tommy coping?' she asked.

'He slept with Mum last night and she said he had a good cry, but now his father is back on the booze.'

'That doesn't surprise me,' the old lady said, greeting Sadie with a grin as they walked into the kitchen. 'Hello, mate. How are you?'

'I'm fine, and what are you looking so cheerful about?'

'I'm moving out of Candle Lane in a couple of weeks.'

'Well, you've changed your tune. I thought you said they'd have to drag you out kicking and screaming.'

'Yeah, well, I've had the offer of a place in Osborne House.'

'What! But that's an old people's home.'

'Yeah, I know, but I've been to see it and it looks lovely. I'll have me own room, and I've decided it would be better to be amongst people of me own age than stuck alone in a tower block. It's all right for you, Sadie, you've got your family around you, but me, well, I ain't got anyone.'

Sally gulped, feeling sorry for Nelly, and vowed to visit her regularly.

'Come on, Tommy, let's play tag,' Angel urged. 'I'm fed up with playing marbles.'

'All right, but I want to keep an eye out for me uncle.'

They played the game for a while, but then both out of breath they sat on the kerb. Tommy suddenly spotted a man with ginger hair turning into the lane, but with no idea what his uncle looked like he said, 'Angel, do you fink he's me uncle?'

'He might be,' Angel replied. 'Come on, let's ask him.'

The two children ran up to the man, Tommy saying, 'Are you me Uncle Andy?'

'Well now, I held a baby called Thomas many years ago, but surely this big strapping lad in front of me can't be him.'

'Thomas,' Angel spluttered, liking this man with his funny way of talking. 'He ain't Thomas. His name is Tommy.'

The man smiled, but there was a tinge of sadness in his eyes. 'And what is your name, lassie?'

'I'm Angel.'

'And a bonny Angel you are too.'

Tommy tugged on his arm, asking again, 'Are you me uncle?'

'If you're Tommy Walters, then yes I am. Now, how about we go and have a word with your father?'

'He's in there,' Tommy said, pointing to his front door.

'Aren't you coming in with me?'

'Nah, me dad's pissed and told me to stay out of the way. Since me muvver died, I've been sleeping next door in Angel's house.'

For a moment the man looked shocked, but then he crouched down in front of Tommy. 'I'm sorry to hear about your mother, lad.'

Tommy lowered his head, his little teeth biting on his bottom lip. The man pulled the boy into his arms. 'There's no shame in tears,' he murmured.

Angel hovered as Tommy settled against his uncle for a while, but then the man said, 'I must talk to your father, lad.'

Tommy cuffed his face, both children watching as his uncle knocked on the door. Denis Walters opened it, and after inviting the man in, the door closed abruptly.

'He seems nice,' Angel said.

'Yeah, but don't you dare tell me mates that I cuddled him.'

'Why not?'

''Cos I don't want them to think I'm a cissie.'

Angel looked bemused, but said, 'All right, but I want a suck on your gobstopper.'

Tommy sprinted off, shouting, 'You've got to catch me first.'

'Have a seat, Andy,' Denis slurred.

'Only Laura called me Andy,' he said sadly. 'I can't believe she's gone.'

'Nor can I,' Denis said, taking a swig of whisky.

'I can understand you having a drink or two. I didn't take it well when I lost my wife.'

'I didn't know, and I'm shorry to hear that.'

'I did write to Laura but she never replied. Mind you, I wrote to your old address so she may not have got my letters.'

'Yesh, that's probably it. Do you want a drop of whisky?'

'No thanks. I saw Thomas outside, he's a nice-looking lad.'

'He ain't a bad kid, but he's had it rough for a while.'

'Rough! What do you mean?'

Andrew listened as Denis began to speak, the man often stumbling over his words, and found that he had to fight his growing anger. Denis was moronic, bemoaning his life, and it soon became obvious that he was after money. Maybe it was the drink talking, but when he insinuated that he couldn't look after his own son, Andrew didn't want to hear any more. 'Listen, man, let's try to sober you up. We can't talk while you're in this state.'

'I'm all right,' he said, his hand reaching for the bottle again.

'No,' Andrew said sharply, 'you've had enough and I think you had better sleep it off. Where is your bedroom?'

Denis protested, but the drink overcame him and he allowed himself to be led upstairs. When he saw the bed he backed away. 'No! No.'

Andrew ignored his protest, pressing him down, Denis

274

mumbling as he fell on his side, 'Laura, Laura,' and then clutching a pillow he almost immediately passed out.

The room looked spartan and Andrew shook his head. Who'd have thought his sister's life would come to this, living in poverty in little more than a hovel? The kitchen had been bad enough, but this room was even worse. Guilt flooded him and he cursed himself for not keeping in touch. Laura may have run away, may have married a useless waster, but she had deserved better than this.

He'd been saddened when Denis had told him that their little girl had died, but also angry. The man had known that Laura had a heart defect, and that she shouldn't have children, but he'd done nothing to prevent it. The strain of having another child must have been enormous on Laura's heart, and extra damage must have been done.

Denis slept on, snoring loudly, and downstairs, Andrew opened the street door to see if his nephew was still around.

There was no sign of him, the lane dismal, and though he had just arrived, Andrew was already longing for home, though as he'd told Denis, he had no wife to welcome him back. Not that Moira would have greeted him with open arms, Andrew thought. Moira and her family had lived close by and they had sort of fallen into courting, getting married six months before the war. She had become pregnant almost immediately, but then he'd been called up, his son nine months old before he was given leave.

His mind shied away from the intimate side of his marriage and the disappointment of a cold wife and he focused instead on his son. Donald was a grown man now, married to a lovely girl, and his first grandchild was on the way.

However, before returning to Scotland Andrew wanted to see a bit of his nephew and now wondered if the boy was next door. He'd have a quick wash and then go to the house, hoping that they wouldn't mind the intrusion.

* * *

The children had scooted in, Angel saying, 'Mummy, we saw Tommy's uncle and he's nice. I want one.'

'Sorry, darling. I'm afraid I was an only child so there's no chance of that. You have got an auntie though. Your Aunt Ann.'

'It isn't fair. I want an uncle too.'

'I only saw him for a minute or two,' Tommy complained. 'He's been in with me dad for ages.'

A knock on the door interrupted Tommy and going to open it, Sally said, 'Yes, can I help you?'

'I'm sorry to disturb you, but if Tommy is here, would it be all right to see him?'

'Oh, you must be his uncle.'

'Yes, that's right, Andrew Munro, but please call me Andrew. I'm pleased to meet you.'

'Come on in,' Sally invited.

He seemed to study her face for a moment, but then Sally led him to the kitchen and as soon as Tommy saw the man he ran up to him. 'Watcha, did me dad say I can come home now?'

'I'm afraid not, he's asleep, but no doubt it won't be long before he wakes up. In the meantime, laddie, I thought we could become better acquainted.'

'You don't 'arf talk funny.'

'So do you, lad,' he said, smiling with amusement.

Sally introduced him to Sadie, and then offered the man a drink. He spoke mostly to Tommy, though of course Angel refused to be left out, and then after half an hour he stood up. 'Well, Tommy, I'd best get back to see if your father is awake. We've got a lot to sort out, but no doubt I'll see you again soon.'

He said goodbye to them all, and as Tommy ran with him to the door, Angel said, 'Mummy, something is happening.'

'What do you mean?'

'I dunno, but it's like I'm having a dream and my head feels funny.'

Sally knelt beside her daughter, aware of the street door closing

276

as Tommy's uncle left. Then Angel asked, 'Will Nanny be home soon?'

'Yes, in about half an hour,' Sally said, bewildered when her daughter shook her head as though to clear it.

Angel smiled. 'I feel all right now.'

'Are you sure?'

With an affirmative from her daughter, Sally stood up. She had no idea what had just happened, but with her mother due home soon she'd better make a start on their dinner.

Thirty-Eight

Ruth turned into Candle Lane, her feet throbbing. Tommy had been on her mind all day and she was worried about his future. After giving it a lot of thought, as far as she was concerned there was still only one answer. Denis was incapable of looking after his son, and surely he would see the sense of letting Tommy live with her. It wouldn't be easy, but with Sally's help it would work out all right. She would wait until the funeral was over and then have a talk with the man. Surely he'd see things her way?

When she walked in, Angel came running up to her. 'Nanny, Tommy's got an uncle.'

'What's this, Sally?'

'He turned up today and he seems nice.'

'You like him, Nanny.'

'No doubt you mean I'll like him when I meet him, but that remains to be seen,' Ruth said.

Tommy pushed in to cuddle her and Ruth held him for a while, but then Sally said, 'Dinner's nearly ready. Angel, go and wash your hands, you too, Tommy.'

When the children returned, Ruth helped Sally to dish out the food, but her head shot up when Tommy spoke to her. 'Me Dad's on the piss again.'

Ruth looked at Sally and she nodded. 'He was sleeping it off when Tommy's uncle called round.'

With eyes down to hide her true feelings, Ruth said, 'In that case, I think you should stay out of his way until tomorrow.'

'But I want to see me uncle again.'

'In the morning,' Ruth insisted, and though Tommy argued, she wouldn't be swayed.

Later, when Ruth put Tommy in her bed, she stroked his hair for a while until at last he fell asleep. She then went back downstairs, deciding to voice her thoughts as she sat with her feet on the fender. 'I've been thinking about Tommy's future and I reckon he'd be better off living permanently with us.'

'Don't be daft, Ruth, the boy belongs with his father,' Sadie protested. 'Not only that, you're at work all day so it'll be Sally who gets saddled with looking after him, not you.'

'Sally won't mind, will you, love?' Ruth asked, as she looked at her daughter.

'No, not really, but I can't see Denis agreeing to it. There's his uncle too, and I don't know why, but I have a feeling that he's going to figure in Tommy's future.'

Ruth didn't like the sound of that and said sharply, 'Right then, I'd better meet this uncle.'

Still in her tatty slippers, Ruth knocked on Denis' door and when he opened it she could smell the alcohol on his breath. Were both men boozing, Tommy's uncle a drinker too?

'Watcha, Ruth,' Denis slurred. 'Are you coming in?'

'You're drunk,' she said with disgust as she followed him inside.

'Yeah, but don't look at me like that. I've had enough of it from Andy. He doesn't approve either, but it seems the pair of you have forgotten that I've just lost my wife.'

Ruth ignored the barb, only saying, 'I've heard that Tommy's uncle is here. I was hoping to meet him.'

'He got some grub in earlier, but then took one look at the cooker and said he'd go out for a meal.'

'Is he close to Tommy?'

'He hardly knows the kid. He hasn't seen Tommy since he was a baby.'

Ruth's mind raced. Surely Denis would see that even if the boy's uncle offered him a home, it would be like living with a stranger. Should she make her offer now? She was about to speak when there was a knock on the door.

'That's probably Andy. I'll go and let him in.'

Blast, Ruth thought. She had missed her opportunity.

Denis came back into the room, a man behind him, and even after all these years the recognition was instantaneous. 'No! Oh no,' she gasped, 'it can't be!'

The room began to tilt and she had a vague notion of him moving towards her, his voice barely reaching her ears as blackness descended.

'Ruth. My God! Ruth!'

When Ruth opened her eyes she saw Andrew leaning over her, his voice concerned as he asked, 'Are you all right?'

Her vision cleared, the question bursting from her lips, 'Andrew! How . . . how did you find me?'

'Ruth, I wasn't trying to find you. I'm here for my sister's funeral and had no idea that you lived in this area.'

Denis now spoke, his expression puzzled. 'How do you two know each other?'

'It's a long story,' Andrew said, 'but for now would you do me a favour? Would you go out for a drink or something? Ruth and I need to talk in private.'

'I suppose so, but I've no money.'

Ruth saw a flicker of annoyance in Andrew's eyes, but then he pulled out a note, thrust it into Denis' hand and said, 'Here, but it might be a good idea to stay off the hard stuff.'

Her mind was still confused. Andrew said he was here for his sister's funeral. Laura! Surely he didn't mean Laura? It seemed impossible to comprehend. Of all the places in London, Andrew's sister had ended up living in Candle Lane.

When Denis left, Andrew turned to face her again and Ruth's breath caught in her throat. No wonder she had been so taken with Tommy. It was so obvious now, the family resemblance plain to see.

'This has been a shock for both of us,' he said, sitting down beside her and smiling faintly. 'Do you know you've hardly changed, yet it must be well over twenty years since I last saw you.'

'You haven't changed much either. Maybe a bit less hair, but I knew you instantly. You said you were here for your sister's funeral. Surely you don't mean Laura? She was only in her early thirties.'

'My parents had her late in life and there was a huge age gap between us.'

Ruth's mind was still reeling. Andrew hadn't come looking for her. Why would he? He had no idea. When Laura's funeral was over he'd go back to his wife and son in Scotland. If she told him the truth he'd probably be furious and it would only cause more problems, more heartache.

'As you can see,' Andrew now said, 'there's a lot to sort out, which means I'll be here for about ten days or so.'

'T . . . ten days,' Ruth squeaked.

'Yes, but don't look so worried. Denis doesn't need to know about us, and surely after all this time you're not worried about your husband?'

'Husband!' Ruth blurted out. 'But I haven't got a husband. We divorced many years ago.'

'So, you're divorced. I'm on my own too. I lost my wife just over a year ago.'

'I'm sorry to hear that,' Ruth said, her mind jumping again. Andrew was a widower. Did that make a difference? She needed to be on her own, to have time to think. Andrew's closeness was having an effect on her, one that after all these years, she was surprised to feel.

She rose unsteadily to her feet. 'I must go, but if you're going to be around for over a week, perhaps we can talk another time.'

'I'd love to see you again. Can I take you out to dinner one evening?'

Ruth gulped. 'I . . . I'm not sure,' she stammered.

'Ruth, where do you live? Is it close by?'

'Live? But I thought you knew. I've been looking after Tommy. I live next door. I must go now. I . . . I'll let you know about dinner,' and with that she hurried home.

'Well, what did you think of Tommy's uncle?' Sally asked as soon as Ruth walked in.

'He . . . he seems all right.'

'Mum, you look a bit odd. Are you feeling all right?'

'I've just got a bit of a headache,' Ruth blustered. 'I think I'll have a bath and then an early night.'

It didn't help. At eleven-thirty Ruth was still awake, unaware that next door, Andrew was too.

With Denis drunk again and snoring in the next room, Andrew was unable to sleep in his nephew's lumpy bed. He got up and went downstairs, hoping that one of the fireside chairs might prove more comfortable.

He heated some milk and then with a blanket wrapped around his legs, sat dwelling on Ruth. He'd been amazed to see her, and equally amazed to find the old attraction still there. Over the years he'd occasionally thought about her, and though their time together had been short, her face remained vivid in his memory. Compared to his wife, Ruth had been full of fun, her laughter infectious, and she had loved to dance.

As his eyes roamed the kitchen, Andrew's thoughts turned to his sister. He flung off the blanket and stood up, absent-mindedly fingering Laura's few cheap ornaments on the mantelshelf. An old biscuit tin, the lid depicting a Highland scene, caught his eye, and opening it he saw it contained photographs, the top one of his sister's wedding.

Andrew carried the tin to the table and took out the photograph. Laura looked so happy and he felt a surge of pain. She was his sister, yet they had become like strangers. He put the photograph to one side and took out another, this an old sepia photo, cracked with age. It was one of his parents, his mother smiling, looking young, and pretty, but then Andrew's eyes widened in shock. His mother looked nothing like that now, but he had seen that young smiling face somewhere, and recently.

Comprehension dawned, along with anger. Why had she lied to him? If it wasn't so late he'd confront her now, but he'd definitely have it out with her first thing in the morning!

Dawn couldn't come quickly enough for Andrew.

Thirty-Nine

Waking with a start, Ruth found that she had her arms around Tommy. She was glad that she'd decided to put him in with her, the boy finding comfort in being cuddled. But what had woken her? Had someone knocked on the door? She glanced blearily at her bedside clock, saw it was only just after six and frowned when there was another loud knock. Who the hell was calling this early on a Saturday morning?

She eased herself away from Tommy and threw on her dressing gown, still cursing as she went downstairs. 'Andrew!' she cried, stepping back as she registered the anger on his face.

'You lied, told me it was a false alarm. Why?'

Ruth shot a look over her shoulder. 'Please,' she begged, 'keep your voice down. You'll wake everyone up.'

'I asked you a question and I'm waiting for an answer.'

'I don't know what you're talking about.'

'Don't act the innocent. I can't believe I didn't see it immediately. Does she know?'

'We need to talk, but please, not . . . not here,' Ruth stammered, her eyes wide with fear.

His face suddenly softened. 'Ruth, don't look at me like that. I'm not a monster and I'm sorry for shouting, but this has knocked me for six. Look, Denis isn't up yet and I doubt he'll surface for some time. Why don't you get dressed and come next door?'

'All right, give me ten minutes.'

Ruth closed the door quietly and crept upstairs, relieved that she was the only one awake. It was amazing that her mother hadn't heard the racket, but so far there wasn't a sound from anywhere in the house. She dressed quickly, snuck back downstairs, and left a note on the kitchen table in case anyone got up before she returned.

At her soft knock, Andrew opened the door immediately, and when she followed him into the kitchen, he handed her a photo. 'My mother,' he said. 'And as you can see, the resemblance is remarkable.'

Ruth studied the face, her voice quaking. 'I'm surprised you didn't notice straightaway.'

'Something niggled at me as soon as I saw her, but I just couldn't figure out what it was until I saw that photograph. It's obvious that she's mine.'

Ruth did her best to explain, often faltering as she tried to find the right words. 'When my husband came home on leave and found me pregnant with your child, he . . . he begged me to stay with him, and promised to bring her up as his own. I didn't know what to do, Andrew. Ours was a brief affair, and though I thought the world of you, Ken was my husband.'

'I still had a right to know.'

'I did what I thought was for the best. You had a wife and child of your own, and whether I was having your child or not, you'd still have gone back to them after the war.'

For a moment he was quiet, but then he said, 'I couldn't have left my wife and son, but I still had a right to know about my daughter. I could have seen her occasionally, watched her grow up and been a part of her life. She's beautiful, Ruth.'

'Yes, she is, and I can only say I'm sorry. I did what I thought was for the best, but it turned out to be the biggest mistake I ever made.'

'Why, Ruth?'

'Ken never accepted Sally as his own and he made both our lives a misery.'

'My marriage wasn't happy either.'

'Wasn't it? I'm sorry.'

His face softened a little, and he said, quietly, 'Does Sally know that your ex-husband isn't her father?'

'She does now, but I didn't tell her the truth until he left me.'

'And when she found out, did she ask about me?'

'Yes, but I knew so little about you. I knew what regiment you were in during the war, but that was all. It wasn't enough for her to trace you.'

'It sounds like you didn't want her to find me?'

'I had no idea how you'd react, or even if you'd accept her, and Sally had faced enough rejection. Not only that, how would your wife and son have felt if she'd turned up on your doorstep?'

'I wouldn't have rejected her, but as for my wife, you have a point. I doubt she'd have taken it well. However, things have changed and there's no reason why I can't get to know her. Please, Ruth, tell her who I am. I think you owe me that much.'

Ruth stared into Andrew's eyes, saw his plea, and knew she owed it to both him and Sally. 'All right, come on then. There's no time like the present.'

Sally had only just got up when her mother came in, Tommy's uncle with her. She looked at them, saw that her mother's hands were shaking and asked, 'What is it? What's wrong?'

Her mother hesitated, looked at Tommy's uncle, and then said haltingly, 'Sally, I . . . I have something to tell you. Andrew is your . . . your father.'

Sally couldn't believe her ears, and astounded she squeaked, 'My . . . my father?'

'Yes, Sally.'

She found herself dumbstruck, waiting to feel something, but

286

she just felt numb. Ever since she'd found out that Ken Marchant wasn't her real father she had dreamed of this moment, dreamed of finding her dad and being swept into his arms.

Why couldn't she react? Why couldn't she move? He was looking at her, his expression soft, and a spark of recognition ran through her. She could see it now, see this man's resemblance to both her and Angel – and it wasn't just his red, curly hair. My God, he's Angel's grandfather!

She stiffened as he began to walk towards her, but then his eyes seemed to fill and with a watery smile he held out his arms. Sally didn't know how, but the next minute she was in them, being held tightly as his soft voice murmured in her ear, words that made her own tears fall. 'Hello, my bonny lass.'

'Why are you cuddling Sally?'

They pulled apart, both now looking at Tommy. His hair was standing up like a brush, and suddenly the family connection and all it entailed, hit Sally. Laura Walters had been her aunt, and this little boy, the one she had once rejected, was her cousin!

As if reading her thoughts, Ruth said, 'Sally, don't say anything for now. There'll be enough time later.'

Sally still couldn't take it all in, and finding she was gripping her father's hand she turned to look at him, his smile making her heart leap.

His kindness became obvious too as he released her hand and squatted down in front of Tommy. 'Now, lad, you can't blame a man for cuddling a beautiful woman. Tell me, how are you?'

'I'm all right, but where's me dad?'

'He's still asleep, but you'll see him soon. In fact, why don't you get dressed and we'll see if he's up and about?'

Tommy nodded, and as he ran from the room, Ruth shook her head worriedly. 'I'm only just beginning to see how difficult this is going to be. There's going to be a lot of explaining to do.'

'Yes, but for now I'd like to concentrate on my daughter. Are you all right, lassie?'

'It's been a bit of a shock, and my head is still spinning.'

'I hope it's been a pleasant one. You and I have a lot to catch up on.'

'I'll have to tell my mother,' Ruth said. 'In fact, I'll see if she's awake.'

She was about to leave the room when Angel burst in. 'Mummy, tell Tommy! He won't let me in the bathroom and I want to pee!'

There was a stifled, choking sound, but then Andrew's laughter rang out, filling the room. Sally found it infectious and grinned, whilst Angel stood hopping, her face indignant as she said, 'Mummy, it's not funny. Tell Tommy!'

Sally took her daughter's hand, still hearing Andrew's laughter as they went upstairs. My father, she thought. That man's my father, and suddenly it was wonderful.

When Andrew finally stopped laughing, Ruth said, 'You do realise that Angel is your granddaughter?'

'What did you say?' a voice boomed.

'Mum! I was just coming to see you.'

'Did I hear you say that this is Angel's grandfather?'

'Yes, he is. Sit down before you fall down, Mum, and I'll tell you all about it.'

Ruth only just had time to tell her mother before Tommy dashed back into the room, and hoping that Sadie would have the sense to keep quiet, she said hurriedly, 'That was quick, love. Are you ready for your breakfast?'

'Can me uncle have some too?'

Andrew shook his head. 'I think Ruth has enough mouths to feed. Have your breakfast, lad, and then come next door. I'm sure your father will be up by then.'

'Can't I come now?'

Andrew looked at Ruth and seeing her quick nod he said, 'Yes, all right. I'm sure I can rustle up something for us both to eat.'

Ruth accompanied them to the door, whispering, 'Thanks, Andrew. My mother's still in shock and I don't trust her to keep her mouth shut.'

'They'll have to be told.'

'Yes, and soon, but give me time to draw breath first.'

'Told what?' Tommy asked.

'Little pigs have big ears,' Ruth said, smiling down at the boy.

'I ain't a pig!' Tommy said indignantly.

'I know you aren't. Now go on home with your uncle and I'll see you later.'

'Ruth, we'll talk again soon,' Andrew said, 'but Denis and I have got a lot to sort out today. The funeral,' he silently mouthed. 'Will it be all right if I send the boy back in about an hour?'

'Yes, of course it will,' she said, hiding her worries as she closed the door. It had gone well, and Sally had taken to Andrew immediately, yet as she had watched their growing closeness, her mother's words came back to haunt her. She was right – girls did cling to their fathers.

Ruth remembered her own father, her devastation when he died, and now shivered. Andrew would be going back to Scotland soon, his home a long, long way from London. Had she set Sally up for more heartbreak?

Andrew was glad he'd got a little food in and after scrubbing a saucepan and then doing the same to the grill pan, he managed to rustle up beans on toast. He chatted to Tommy as the boy cleaned his plate finding that he was a nice lad, a bit rough round the edges, but his intelligence shone through. In some ways he reminded him of his own son at that age, both having the same quick mind.

He wondered how not only Donald, but his parents too, would take the news about Sally. He wanted her to be a part of his life, to make up for all the missing years, and not only Sally, his granddaughter too.

It was another half an hour before Denis got up, scratching his head, his face showing the ravages of drink when he walked into the kitchen and said hoarsely, 'Any tea in the pot?'

'Yes, but I doubt it's still hot.'

Denis didn't seem to care as he poured himself a cup, then asked, 'Did Ruth send you home, Tommy?'

'No, Uncle Andy came and fetched me.'

'How come you know Ruth?' Denis asked.

'It's a long story. We'll talk about it later.'

'You fobbed me off yesterday. What's wrong with now?'

'I said later, man. For now we've got a lot to sort out, arrangements to make, so I suggest you get ready to go out.'

'Yeah, yeah, all right.'

'Can I come wiv you?'

'No, you flaming well can't,' Denis snapped.

Andrew ruffled Tommy's hair. 'We won't be long, lad, but for now run on back to Ruth.'

Tommy hesitated and Denis yelled, 'Do as you're told!'

'There was no need to shout,' Andrew said, as Tommy ran out. 'You seem to be forgetting that the boy has just lost his mother.'

'Yeah, well, he's better off with Ruth for now,' Denis said, 'and as I asked before, how come you know her?'

Andrew decided that with Tommy out of earshot he might as well get it over with. 'I met Ruth many years ago, in fact during the war, but haven't seen her since.'

'I see, like that was it? I've heard stories about the things that went on during the war. What was that little ditty? Oh, yeah. "When their men were away, the wives went out to play."'

'Shut up! It wasn't like that. Ruth hadn't heard from her husband for a very long time and thought he'd been killed in action. You have no idea what it was like. Bombs rained down almost every night and Londoners were going through hell. Many thousands were killed or lost their homes, and with strict

290

rationing they were on near-starvation diets. All right, Ruth and I met, and yes, we had an affair, but those were desperate times. People lived for the day, knowing that it might be their last.' Andrew stopped speaking, annoyed with himself for justifying what happened.

'All right, keep your shirt on, mate.'

'That isn't the end of the story, and when you hear the rest I don't want any more derogatory remarks.' Andrew took another steadying breath. 'You see, Ruth's daughter is my child.'

'What! Sally Marchant is your daughter! Blimey.'

Andrew watched as Denis digested the news and waited for him to take on board the implications.

He didn't have long to wait as the light dawned in Denis' eyes. 'Bloody hell! This means that Tommy is related to the Marchants. I can't believe this. It's amazing.'

'Listen, I don't think Tommy is ready to hear any of this yet. He's just lost his mother and it would be too much for him to take in.'

'I dunno. He's very fond of Ruth and it might help him to know that he's a part of her family.'

'You may have a point, but do you mind if I consult with Ruth first? Angel will have to be told too, and maybe Tommy at the same time.'

'It's funny really. This makes me Sally's uncle and she must only be a few years younger than me. I know I'm not her blood relative, but Laura was. Laura would have loved that.'

Andrew's stomach tightened with guilt. Once again he knew that despite their differences he should have kept in touch with Laura. Instead he now felt he'd abandoned her. All he could do now was to see that Laura had a good send-off, a decent funeral, and urged, 'Come on, get yourself ready now. We've got a lot to sort out today.'

Once the arrangements had been made, Andrew would have to ring his parents. They weren't in good health and wouldn't be able to undertake a journey to London, but they would want to send flowers. It had been so hard to tell them about Laura's death, the news hitting his mother and father hard.

Now Andrew had other news to break, but he felt it best to tell them about Sally face to face. How would they take it?

Forty

That same day, Joe was sitting in his car, his eyes fixed on the street door through his wing mirror. He'd been adding things up and was determined to check up on Patsy, sure that she wasn't all she pretended to be. He found her finances a mystery, a mobile hairdresser who didn't seem to work that many hours, yet who could afford the rent on her flat, along with expensive clothes. Then, when he'd given her the elbow, she had set her cap at Arthur. If she was looking for a meal ticket, why make it difficult for herself by choosing a married man? Was it that she saw Arthur as an easy target?

Joe had hoped that the break-up between Sally and Arthur would be short-lived, that Arthur would come to his senses and finish with Patsy, but the opposite had happened, Arthur had turned it all on Sally.

With a glance at his watch, Joe worked out that Patsy had been in the house for nearly half an hour, but with no idea how long it took to do a woman's hair, he settled back to wait.

Only ten minutes later the street door opened, and adjusting his mirror, Joe stared uncomprehendingly at the man who was seeing Patsy out. He was bald, totally bald, and at least seventy years old. Joe had intended to follow Patsy, to see just how many clients she had in one day, but now waited until she was out of sight before getting out of the car. There had been something

293

strange in the old chap's attitude towards the girl, something almost intimate.

Joe straightened his tie and buttoned his jacket before approaching the house. He then knocked on the door, wondering what on earth he was going to say to the man when he opened it.

As soon as the old chap saw him standing on his step his face showed alarm. 'Yeah, what do you want?'

'I'd like to ask you some questions about the young lady who just left.'

'Blimey! Are you CID?'

Joe blinked, wondering what made the man think he was a police officer, but quickly realised he could use it to his advantage. 'That's right and I'm investigating that young lady's activities. Now, as I said,' he stated officiously, 'I'd like to ask you some questions.'

'I won't have to come down to the station, will I?'

'I could interview you in your own home, but it depends on how cooperative you are.'

'Come in,' the man invited, obviously eager to avoid a trip to the station.

Joe followed him down the narrow hall to a room at the back, and took a seat, still trying to sound officious. 'Can you tell me why the young woman was visiting you?'

The man's face flushed crimson. 'If you're investigating her activities, surely I don't have to spell it out.'

'I'd still like you to tell me.'

'She . . . she's a prostitute. Look, I don't know anything else about her. I've got her phone number, passed on to me by a mate, but that's all.'

Joe felt the colour drain from his face and fought to hide his shock, only managing to murmur, 'I see.'

The man's eyes narrowed suspiciously. 'Here, hold on, I'm not sure you're CID. Show me your warrant card!'

Joe rose quickly to his feet and before the man could react he dashed down the hall and out of the house. Then, almost leaping the last few feet to his car, he jumped in and drove off, his hands moist with sweat as they gripped the wheel.

As he drove a little further, Joe had a thought and chuckled, berating himself for running off like that. After all, it was unlikely that the old man would complain to the police – not after entertaining a prostitute.

He still couldn't really take it in. Patsy a prostitute! Who'd have thought it? Yet somehow it all made sense, Arthur a meal ticket to get her out of the game. Somehow he had to break the news to him and he wasn't looking forward to it.

With most of the arrangements made, Andrew and Denis returned to Candle Lane. Denis was maudlin, saying he needed a drink and soon after went off without thought of going to see his son.

Andrew was hungry and went to a nearby café to have an evening meal before going to Ruth's, warmed by the pleasure he saw in her eyes when she let him in. 'I know we can't talk in front of the children so I waited until I felt they'd be in bed,' he told her.

Sally greeted him with a huge smile and then asked, 'Did you manage to sort out the funeral?'

'Yes, it's on Friday.'

'No, no, it's Tommy's birthday on Friday,' Ruth protested.

'Are you sure? Denis didn't mention it.'

'I can't believe that the man forgot his own son's birthday.'

'Nor can I, but we'll just have to hope we can change the date.'

'What about your parents?' Ruth asked. 'Will they be travelling down?'

'I'm afraid not. They aren't in the best of health.'

'Have you told them about me? About Sally?'

'Not yet. I'd prefer to tell them face to face.'

'I've just realised something,' Sally said. 'They're my grandparents.'

'Yes, that's right and you are very much like my mother. I rang my son too, but as his wife is close to having a baby he needs to stay with her and won't be able to attend the funeral.'

'Your . . . your son,' Sally gasped. 'But that means he's my half-brother!'

'Sally, I'm sorry. Of course . . . you don't know about Donald. I should have thought before I spoke.'

'Stone the crows! This gets more and more complicated,' Sadie said. 'I'm beginning to lose track.'

'Andrew,' Ruth said, 'I think it would help Sally, and my mother, if you tell them about your family.'

'Yes, I think you're right,' he agreed. 'Now, where shall I start? My father, Duncan Munro, was a surveyor and I took over the firm when he retired. My mother's name is Jane, and she was a McFarland before she married my father. They had two children, myself and Laura, and we grew up in a hamlet just outside of Edinburgh.'

'And Donald?' Sally asked.

'I married Moira and we had one son. My wife died just over a year ago.'

'Is Donald older than me?'

'Yes, he was born in nineteen-forty.'

'Do . . . do we look alike?'

'No, not really. Donald takes after my wife, though he does have auburn hair. In fact, it's rather like Tommy's.'

'Blimey,' Sadie said. 'I wonder what your son will make of having a skin and blister?'

'Skin and blister?'

'Yeah, it's cockney rhyming slang for sister. There are lots of them. Apples and pears for stairs and—'

Ruth broke in, 'Andrew, have you told Denis?'

'Yes, and he wants Tommy to know that you're related. What do you think?'

It was Sadie who answered. 'I don't think it would hurt.

296

Kids are more resilient than we give them credit for. While he's just lost his mother, it might help him to know he's got other family.'

'I think my mother's right,' Ruth said. 'I'm very fond of the boy, and since Laura died he's clinging to me.'

'All right, if you think it's for the best, perhaps we can do it tomorrow. Is that all right with you, Sally?'

'Yes, it's fine.'

'Sally, I hope you don't mind me mentioning this,' Andrew said, 'but I haven't heard any mention of Angel's father?'

Sally started hesitantly, telling him why her marriage had broken up, and Andrew was unable to miss how wounded she looked. He was angry that Sally had been driven out of her home and said, 'He should have been the one to move out, not you.'

'I couldn't live there again, not after seeing him with Patsy. When Mum gets re-housed, if there's no room for me I'll find another flat.'

'Re-housed! What do you mean?'

It was Ruth who took over then, telling Andrew that Candle Lane was scheduled for demolition.

'When are you moving?'

'We don't know yet.'

'I just hope they don't stick us in one of them bleedin' tower blocks,' Sadie exclaimed.

While walking around with Denis to make the arrangements for the funeral, Andrew had seen the council estates and nodded in agreement. 'I can't imagine anything worse, it's a shame you have to live around here. There are parts of England that are lovely, and of course Scotland is beautiful.'

'I've never been out of London, not even during the war and I don't intend to leave it now. What part of Scotland do you come from?'

'Edinburgh and it's a bonny place.'

'You . . . you live so far away,' Sally said and paling she fled from the room.

Andrew was dismayed and rose to his feet to follow her, but Ruth's voice stayed him. 'Leave her, Andrew. She's only just found you, and now she has to accept that soon you'll be leaving again.'

Andrew sank back onto the chair, realising that Ruth was right. They lived so far apart, and he too was saddened.

Forty-One

Arthur opened his door on Sunday morning, surprised to see Joe. He looked worried and said, 'Hello, mate, can we talk?'

'Of course,' Arthur agreed, getting the man a beer before they both sat down. 'Now then, what's the problem?'

'I found something out yesterday, but I've only just plucked up the courage to tell you.'

'Spit it out then.'

'Arthur, Patsy isn't all she pretends to be.'

'What's that supposed to mean? Never mind, it doesn't matter anyway, if you must know I'm getting fed up with her. I keep telling her that I don't want to take things further, but she won't listen and is constantly pressuring me to move in. It's getting on me wick, and I don't know why she's in such a hurry. She's got a decent flat upstairs and we see a lot of each other, but she's getting more and more possessive.'

'Yeah, well, I know why.'

'All right, tell me.'

Arthur's jaw dropped as he listened to Joe, at first unable to believe what he was hearing. 'All right, she sees me as a meal ticket, but I can't believe she's a prostitute. That bloke told you a pack of lies.'

'Arthur, he was as bald as a coot and she certainly wasn't there to cut his hair.'

If Arthur had any strong feelings for Patsy, he might have

been deeply upset, instead he only felt bewildered. His stomach churned. He'd been sleeping with a prostitute. Bile rose in his throat and he stood up abruptly. 'I'm going to have it out with her.'

'Do you want me to join you? I'd love to see the look on her face.'

'All right.'

It wasn't long before Arthur was thumping on Patsy's door, glowering when she opened it. 'You bitch!' he spat. 'Thanks to Joe, I've found out what you do for a living.'

Her eyes widened and she poked her head out to look up and down the terrace, saying quickly, 'Look, you'd better come upstairs.'

'What's the matter? Don't you want the neighbours to hear this?' Arthur asked sarcastically as they followed Patsy up to her living room.

'Right, what's all this about?' she asked.

'You're a prostitute.'

'How dare you! I'm no such thing.'

'Don't bother to deny it,' Joe said. 'I followed you, spoke to one of your clients, the daft old sod took me for CID and spilled his guts.'

'Who the fuck are you to spy on me?' she screeched, her veil of innocence dropping. 'What I do for a living is none of your business.'

Patsy's mask had well and truly slipped and once again bile rose in Arthur's throat. 'It make me sick to think that I slept with you. How many men have been there before me? No doubt hundreds, you filthy bitch.'

'Yes, and all of them were better at it than you. Now get out of my sight, you bloody cripple, and take your so-called mate with you.'

Arthur blanched and as soon as they were back in the flat Joe asked, 'Are you all right?'

'She's the first person to call me a cripple and it wasn't pleasant.'

'Patsy's just ignorant and what she says isn't worth worrying about.'

'Yeah, I know,' Arthur said, yet despite his bravado her words kept echoing in his head. 'I'm well rid of her.'

'You sure are, mate, and I had a lucky escape too.'

Arthur only nodded. Yes, he was well rid of Patsy, and Sally too for that matter. Women, he was sick of them. Patsy had turned out to be a prostitute, and his wife a bloody liar.

'I'm sorry, Arthur, but I've got to go. My mother's expecting me for lunch, but I can ring her to put it off if you need me to stay.'

'There's no need, I'm fine,' Arthur insisted, his anger calming and when Joe left he sat pondering all that had happened. It wasn't long before he found himself thinking differently. Yes, Sally had turned his parents and sister against him, but she had probably done it out of a need for revenge. He couldn't blame her for that, and let's face it, he could have put his family straight. Instead he'd let his stubborn pride get in the way.

It was time to mend bridges with his parents, to tell them the truth, but there was no way he was going to admit why he'd broken up with Patsy.

They arrived an hour later, and after listening to what he had to say, his mother cried, 'Why didn't you tell us this before?'

'You all chose to believe Sally, and I was angry, Mum. You condemned me without a trial.'

'What do you expect?' his father snapped. 'You'd hardly been home for five minutes before you slept with that girl, you can't deny that.'

'I'm not denying it, Dad, but despite what Sally told you, I didn't move her in.'

'You carried on sleeping with her though.'

There was no way Arthur could refute that, but how could

he tell his parents that the sex with Patsy had become like an obsession, that for a while he couldn't get enough of her? A wave of nausea made him gulp. 'Anyway, I've broken up with Patsy now.'

'What? But Sally said you're going to marry the girl.'

'It's another one of her lies, and as I said, it was her idea to get a divorce, not mine.'

'I can't believe it. It's so unlike Sally.'

'I think it was her way of getting revenge.'

'But that isn't like her either,' Elsie said, as she ran a hand through her hair. 'It was Patsy who said to Sally that you're getting married.'

'What? I didn't know that.'

'Well she did, and let's think about something else. Did Sally tell you that she wants a divorce, or did that come from Patsy?'

At his mother's words, Arthur hung his head, his thoughts racing. 'Come to think of it, Mum, yes, it came from Patsy.'

'Bloody hell, son,' his father snapped. 'It sounds like that girl has been stirring things up, probably to keep you and Sally apart, and you were a mug to believe her.'

'I'm starting to realise that, Dad.'

'Then get yourself round to Candle Lane and sort things out.'

'She'll be bringing Angel round this afternoon, so there's no point in going there.'

'You can't talk properly in front of Angel.'

'Dad, what's the good of trying to sort things out? Sally still finds my leg repulsive.'

His mother leaned forward, speaking earnestly. 'She denied that and I'm sorry, son, but I'm inclined to believe her. I think you must have been imagining things.'

'I don't think I was.'

'Talk to her, son. The least Sally deserves is an apology.'

'She'd only throw it in my face. We're getting a divorce and our marriage is in the hands of our solicitors.'

'Come on, Elsie. If this is his attitude we might as well go,' Bert snapped.

Arthur was relieved to see them leave, yet thinking of all that had been said, he had to face the truth. Patsy wasn't just a prostitute, she was a mischief maker too, and he'd been too wrapped up in anger and pride to see it. What had happened to him since he'd come out of hospital? What sort of man had he turned into? He'd let Patsy manipulate him and looking up at the ceiling he scowled, hating that she was living just above him.

Unable to settle down, Arthur went to the pub for a lunchtime drink, finding that he couldn't get any of it out of his mind. He had to go to Candle Lane, and speak to Sally alone. Swallowing the last of his pint, Arthur set off.

When he knocked on the door, Sally opened it, looking shocked to see him, but she quickly recovered. She stepped beyond the door and pulled it almost closed, blocking off any view of the hall. 'If you've come to collect Angel, it's too early. She's still eating her dinner.'

'It's you I've come to see. I want to apologise and to ask you to come home. I've finished with Patsy, and though I know she told you that she'd moved in and that I wanted a divorce, it was all lies.'

'You're forgetting that I walked in on you. I saw you together with my own eyes.'

'I can't deny that, but I promise you, she didn't move in.'

'So you say, but you still carried on with her, still slept with her.'

Arthur lowered his eyes, fighting to find words. 'Sally, please, I'm sorry. I really did think that you couldn't stand the sight of my leg, and well, Patsy threw herself at me.'

As soon as he saw the expression on her face, Arthur knew he'd said the wrong thing and braced himself as her lips curled.

'That's rubbish and something you've conjured up as an excuse for carrying on with Patsy. As for her throwing herself at you, why didn't you say no? You may have lost part of your leg, but you've still got your tongue! Go away, Arthur.'

'Angel . . .'

'You can forget seeing her today,' and at this Sally abruptly went back inside.

Arthur found the door slammed in his face. For a moment he stood motionless, but then he turned and walked away. Sally would never forgive him, had made that plain, and with sickening clarity now, Arthur knew it was no more than he deserved.

What was taking Sally so long at the door? Ruth wondered. She rose to her feet when she heard the door slam, just in time to see Sally dashing upstairs.

Ruth followed her and as Sally threw herself across her bed she asked, 'What's wrong, Sally? Who was that at the door?'

'It was Arthur. He's finished with Patsy and came round to apologise.'

'What did you say to him?'

'I told him to clear off.'

'Good for you,' Ruth said, 'but isn't he supposed to have Angel for the afternoon?'

'Yes, but I told him to forget it,' Sally said, her eyes filling with tears.

'Don't let him get to you,' Ruth urged.

'Mum, please, I need to be on my own for a while.'

'Sally, you're forgetting that your father is downstairs, and so is Denis. We're supposed to be talking to the children after dinner.'

'All right, I . . . I'll be down in a minute.'

Ruth shook her head but as she returned downstairs her mother was waiting at the bottom.

'What's going on?'

Quietly Ruth said, 'Arthur just called round to see Sally and she's a bit upset.'

'What did he want?'

304

'He's finished with Patsy and came to apologise. Huh, as if that's enough to get Sally back.'

'If Sally still loves him maybe the marriage is worth saving.'

'After what he's done you can't expect Sally to take him back.'

'Angel adores him, Ruth, and she needs her father.'

'What for? Sally did all right when Ken left, in fact she was better off without him, and with Arthur sleeping around she's better off without him too.'

'Ken wasn't Sally's father, and before you condemn Arthur, you should think about the old saying. Those who live in glass houses shouldn't throw stones.'

'What's that supposed to mean?'

'Are you forgetting that you had an affair, and the man who fathered Sally has just turned up again? He's sitting in our kitchen as bold as brass and sharing our Sunday roast.'

'Shush, Mum, he'll hear you,' Ruth hissed, and as her eyes flicked towards the kitchen, Andrew appeared on the threshold.

'Is there a problem?' he asked.

'Sally's husband has been round and she's a bit upset. She just needs a bit of time on her own, that's all.'

'Where's Mummy?' Angel asked.

'She's got a bit of a headache and she's having a lay down,' Ruth said. With her dinner now cold she cleared the table, and then cut up the apple pie into portions before serving it with custard. 'Here's your pudding.'

'Cor that looks good, Ruth,' said Denis, tucking into his, sober so far, but Ruth wondered how long it would last.

When they had finished, there was still no sign of Sally, and as the children left the table Andrew said quietly, 'Perhaps we should put off talking to them until later.'

Ruth nodded her agreement. 'It wouldn't hurt to leave it for an hour.'

'Well then, Denis, I don't know about you, but after that wonderful dinner I could do with a walk. It might be nice to get

305

the children out from under Ruth's feet. Is there a park or something nearby?'

'Yeah, but I ain't in the mood for walking. I'd rather have forty winks.'

'I think you should spend some time with your son for a change.'

'I just have, but now I'm off for a kip.'

Andrew looked less than pleased, but with the children looking on he said, 'Right then, bairns, let's find the park.'

'I know where it is,' Tommy told him.

When they left, Sadie sighed with relief. 'Thank Gawd for that, a bit of peace at last. Maybe I should go up to have a word with Sally.'

'No, leave her,' Ruth said quickly. She didn't want her mother advising Sally to go back to Arthur. She wanted to keep her close, Angel too.

Ruth was washing up when she heard the rattle of the letterbox, and sighing at the intrusion she went to see who was at the door.

'Ruth, can I have a word?'

'Yeah, come in, Nelly.'

'Blimey, bang goes our bit of peace and quiet,' Sadie complained. 'What do you want, Nelly?'

'Now then, Sadie, there's no need for that. I'll be leaving the lane soon and as I can only take a few bits and pieces to Osborne House I've popped along to see if Ruth wants any of me furniture.'

'Sorry, Nelly, take no notice of me. It's just that we've had a houseful and they've only just left. Sit down, love.'

Sally came into the room, her face blotchy from crying, and Nelly asked worriedly, 'Are you all right?'

'She's fine,' Ruth said, answering for her. 'It's just that Arthur's been round and she's a bit upset.'

'Did he ask you to go back to him, Sally?'

'He came to apologise, but it's too late for that.'

Nelly sat quietly for a moment, but then said, 'I felt like that too, but I'm glad I forgave George.'

'What!' Sadie spluttered. 'You're not saying that George had another woman!'

'Yes, he did. We'd been married for about six years at the time and he had it off with the barmaid in the George and Dragon.'

'Never! I can't believe it.'

'It nearly broke us up, but I'm glad it didn't. It was my old mum that talked some sense into me.'

Ruth listened in amazement. Nelly had been married for over forty years and her husband had been devoted to her. It seemed impossible to believe that he'd been unfaithful. 'What did your mum say, Nelly?'

'She said I had two choices. I could chuck him out, or I could take him back. Then she made me look at the alternatives. I loved George, but if I chucked him out I'd be miserable, my marriage over. On the other hand, George had made one mistake, and if I could forgive him we could go on to have a happy marriage.'

'I don't think it's as simple as that,' Ruth said.

'George was so ashamed and promised he would never do it again, but you're right, Ruth, it wasn't that simple. Despite his promise it took a long time before I could trust him again, but I never regretted my decision. My mum was right. I'd have been as miserable as sin without him.'

'Well I never, Nelly Cox. You're full of surprises,' Sadie said.

'I've never told anyone until now. but I thought it might help Sally to know that she isn't the only one whose husband has strayed.'

'How can I forgive Arthur? He made love to Patsy in *our* flat, on *our* sofa and I saw them! No, that wasn't love, it was lust! I can't forgive him, I just can't,' and with that Sally ran out of the room.

'Oh dear. I thought telling Sally about George might help,' and then looking heavenward she added, 'Sorry, George, but I know you'll understand.'

'Nelly Cox,' Sadie said, her eyes narrowing suspiciously, 'I think you made it up. Your George was never unfaithful.'

'Well, not as far as I know.'

'You crafty moo, but thanks for trying,' Sadie said.

'You never know, when Sally's had time to think it over, it still might work,' Nelly said. 'Now then, Ruth, about me furniture.'

Ruth hoped it wouldn't work and impatient to get rid of Nelly she said, 'It's good of you to offer, Nelly, but I can't think of anything I need. I'm sure there are others in the lane who could make use of it.'

'All right, I'd best knock on a few doors then, but will you tell Sally that I'm sorry, that I didn't mean to upset her?'

'I'm sure she knows that,' Ruth said, glad to see Nelly out. She then glanced upstairs wondering if she should go up to have a word with Sally, but then her daughter appeared. Ruth felt that sympathy would only bring tears again so she said brusquely, 'Come on, I could do with a hand with the washing up. Your father will be back in about half an hour and we've still got to talk to the children.'

Forty-Two

When Andrew returned with the children, his eyes went straight to Sally. 'Are you all right, my bonny lass?'

'I'm fine,' she said, but that was far from the truth.

'If you feel ready to tell the children now, I'll go and fetch Denis.'

'Yes, all right.'

It was fifteen minutes before he returned, a dishevelled-looking Denis with him, but at least the man was still sober. Tommy looked from his father to Andrew, and when they sat on the sofa, he squeezed between them.

Sally waited, but when nobody spoke, she asked, 'Do you want me to tell them?'

'Yes, lassie, that's fine with me. What about you, Ruth, and you, Denis?'

Both told her to go ahead and taking a breath, Sally said, 'Tommy, Angel, I've got something to tell you.'

When she had finished speaking, Tommy looked bewildered, but Angel took it all in a very matter-of-fact manner, almost as if she had already sensed the connection. She looked at Andrew, then at Tommy, smiling with satisfaction before saying, 'He's only your uncle, but he's *my* granddad.'

Sally saw the crushed look on Tommy's face. 'That's enough, Angel!' she rebuked.

Ruth held out her arms, beckoning Tommy to her. 'Come here, love, because there's something else I don't think you realise.'

She waited until the boy was in her arms and then turned to Denis. 'Do you want to explain it to him, or shall I?'

'You do it.'

'Tommy, sweetheart, I'm very fond of you, we all are . . .' Ruth said, then floundered, unsure how to explain. 'Err, and well, it isn't surprising that we love you because, you're part of our family. Sally is your cousin.'

'My cousin? My real cousin?'

'Yes, darling, and that makes me your auntie.'

Tommy stared up at her, his eyes wide as he said, 'Blimey!'

They all laughed and it broke the tension, but as Ruth looked at Denis she saw a calculating look in his eyes.

'Well, isn't this nice?' he said, smiling slyly. 'One big happy family. It's nice to know that Tommy will always have someone to look after him when I'm at work.'

Ruth's smile was guarded. She still wanted to take Tommy on permanently, but this wasn't the time to broach the subject. 'Yes, Tommy has us now, and we'll make sure he's treated right.'

Arthur had gone home again, but found the empty flat depressing. He made himself a sandwich and switched on the telly, but nothing held his attention. At seven he decided to see if Joe was back from seeing his mother. If he was home and had nothing else to do, they could go out for a drink. Boy, Arthur thought, he needed one.

Thankfully Joe answered the telephone. 'Yeah, a drink sounds good. I'll come and pick you up.'

'No, it's about time I saw your place, I'll come to you for a change.'

'How will you get here?'

'I can get the tube to Earls Court, or I might come in a cab.'

'Arthur, that's daft. Surely it would be simpler if I drive over.'

'No, I'll come there. See you soon,' Arthur said, and before Joe could argue he replaced the receiver.

He decided on a taxi, but didn't find one until he reached the main road. 'Earls Court, mate,' he told the driver, giving him Joe's address.

Arthur then sat back, watching the passing scenery, doing his best not to think about Sally. When the taxi finally pulled up outside an imposing house, his eyes widened. Blimey, fancy Joe living in a posh place like this. He pulled a face at the fare, thinking it astronomical, and after paying the driver, climbed the wide staircase to Joe's front door. He looked for a bell, but instead of just one he saw at least eight. Finding one for Somerton, he rang it, waiting ages before Joe appeared.

'Wotcher, mate, I'd invite you in, but I'm on the top floor and it's five flights of stairs to get there.'

'Blimey, Joe, what sort of place are you living in?'

'It's a sort of bed-sit with a kitchenette. I like the area and it's fine for now. One day, when we've made a mint, I'll find something better.'

'I'm glad you said when we make a mint . . . not if. Now, where's the nearest pub?'

'Just around the corner and by the look of you I think you need something stronger than beer.'

'What do you mean?'

'Come off it, Arthur, we've been friends too long for you to fool me. You're upset about something. Let's get to the pub and you can tell me all about it.'

With a pint soon in front of him, Arthur said, 'I went round to see Sally. I tried to apologise, but she wouldn't have it. She'll never take me back, Joe, and I've got to accept that, but it doesn't stop me from wanting to drown my sorrows. In fact, along with this beer, I think I'll have a double whisky. Do you want one or are you frightened I can drink you under the table?'

'Right mate, if you want a contest, you're on.'

The two men matched each other drink for drink, until at

ten-thirty they staggered out of the pub, singing their heads off as they clung to each other.

Joe was marginally less drunk than Arthur and when he saw a taxi, he raised his hand to flag it down. 'Come on, Arthur, I've found you a cab,' he said. But when the taxi driver saw the state of them, he drove off again.

Joe grinned lopsidedly. 'Well, mate, it looks like you might have to kip down in my place for the night.'

'All right,' Arthur said, reeling so badly that he ended up on the road.

'Whoops,' Joe said, grabbing his arm and pulling him back onto the pavement.

Arthur giggled inanely, unaware of the danger he'd been in as his voice rose in song. It took a while, but Joe finally found his place, though he had a job to fit the key in the lock. 'Brace yourself, Arthur, we've got a lot of stairs to climb.'

Arthur looked up at the first flight, his eyes barely able to focus, and began to stagger up. On and on the two men went, but luckily for Arthur he was so drunk, he couldn't feel any pain in his prosthesis. He began to sing again, an old Gracie Fields song, maudlin now, 'Sally . . . Sally . . . pride of our alley.'

Joe joined in, both men impervious to the shouts that rang out in the building for them to shut up. 'You're more than the whole world to me.'

Forty-Three

During the next few days, Andrew got to know his daughter, finding to his surprise that, like his mother, she had the gift of healing.

It hadn't taken him long to work out that Sally had no life of her own. He had wanted to take her out whilst Ruth was at work, but with Sadie to look after it proved impossible. It didn't seem right and he found himself increasingly annoyed. He knew Ruth had to work, understood her financial constraints, but even so, the burden shouldn't fall only on Sally.

Andrew's thoughts turned to Angel and he smiled. Since finding out that Tommy was her cousin, she now treated the boy as if she owned him. When she bossed him about, Tommy took it well, but Andrew could already see rebellion on his face. Tommy loved being part of the family and was obviously testing the water, but sparks would fly soon, he was sure of it.

Yes, Andrew thought, smiling softly, Angela was rather bossy and spoiled, but even so he was falling under her spell. She was a delight, and he was already becoming very, very fond of her.

His thoughts now returned to his nephew and his approaching birthday. Thankfully they had been able to change the date of the funeral, and it was now being held on Monday.

With only a couple of days left to buy the lad a present, he glanced at the clock. Denis was still in bed. Had the man got anything for his son? Andrew doubted it. With this in mind he decided to try to make it up to Tommy and buy him something a little bit special. He'd pop round to ask Sally for suggestions.

'Hello, lass,' he said as she opened the door. 'I'm just off to find something for Tommy's birthday. I'm not sure what to get him. Do you have you any ideas?'

'Come in, Dad,' Sally invited, 'I'll put my thinking cap on.'

Dad! For the first time she had called him Dad, and Andrew smiled with pleasure.

'Hello, Sadie,' he said, his smile still wide as he walked into the kitchen.

Sadie just grunted a greeting and Sally pulled a face. 'Gran's not in the best of humour today,' she whispered.

'I may be old, but I ain't deaf,' the old woman snapped.

Andrew had come to recognise that Sadie could sometimes be testy, and though Sally said it was rare, he didn't know how she put up with it.

'Dad, how about a train set?'

'What? Sorry, I was miles away.'

'I suggested a train set for Tommy.'

'Yes, good idea, and where will I find one?'

'There's a large department store at Clapham Junction. It's called Arding & Hobbs and is right on the corner, you can't miss it.'

'Right, I'll try there.'

Andrew kissed Sally on the cheek, called goodbye to Sadie, getting only a grunt in reply, and made his way to the bus stop, wishing he had his car. It had made sense to travel to London by train, but nowadays he was unused to public transport.

As he stood waiting for a bus his eyes were once again scanning the area. He would miss his new-found family when he went back to Scotland, but seeing the huge factories belching out smoke, he certainly wouldn't miss the polluted air.

At six-thirty that evening, when Joe dropped Arthur off outside his flat he said, 'You don't fancy a drink tonight, do you, Joe?'

'No thanks, mate. I haven't recovered from last Sunday yet, and still can't remember getting home.'

Arthur managed a smile. 'When I woke up in your flat it gave me a bit of a turn. Christ, mate, it's a dump and I reckon you should find something better.'

'I will, one of these days. See you in the morning.'

'Yeah, see you,' Arthur said, his mood low as he walked into the flat. After a day on site he hated coming home to emptiness, and even though he hadn't liked living with Sally's mother in Candle Lane, it was better than this. God, he missed Angel, missed the way she always ran to greet him, her cheeky little face lighting up in a smile.

As he flopped onto a chair, Arthur's head sank to his chest. It wasn't just Angel he was missing, it was Sally too. Memories of the happiness they'd shared plagued him. Her joy when he came back from Australia, their wedding, and then the excitement of moving into their first home.

Things had started to go wrong when they'd moved back to Candle Lane. There had been no privacy and with Angel in the same bedroom, no sex. Then there had been his prolonged stay in hospital, and the loss of his lower leg. He cursed himself for misjudging Sally, and now squirmed in his chair. She had always been intuitive and now he wondered if she'd picked up on his phantom pains, mistaking them for real ones. If that was the case, no wonder she had kept a distance between them in bed. Once again he cursed himself for not speaking to her, but he'd been afraid in case she really did find him repulsive.

The telephone rang. It was his mother. 'Hello, Mum.'

'Arthur, I just rang Ruth and she told me you went to see Sally on Sunday. I'm surprised I had to hear it from her.'

'There was no point in telling you. Sally won't come back.'

'Don't give up, son.'

'Mum, my marriage is over and I've got to accept that.'

'Arthur, Sally has got a lot on her mind at the moment and

315

it may be that you just went to see her at the wrong time. Didn't she tell you that her father has turned up?'

'No, she didn't, but I bet Ruth soon showed him the door.'

'No, love, I don't mean Ken Marchant. I mean Sally's real father.'

'Really! I bet that was a shock.'

'According to Ruth, he's a lovely man and he and Sally hit it off immediately. The only problem is that after Laura Walters' funeral, he'll be returning to Scotland.'

'Hang on, Mum, you've lost me. What has Sally's father got to do with Laura Walters?'

Arthur listened to his mother's explanation and his jaw dropped. It sounded too fantastic to be true, a chance in a million. 'So this means that Sally is Tommy's cousin.'

'Yes, but Arthur, as I said, with all this going on you probably caught Sally at a bad time. Now that things have settled, go to see her again.'

'No, Mum, it'd just be a waste of time.'

'If you love Sally, you can't just give up. Can't you see that you have to put up more of a fight if you want her back?'

'Mum, don't go on about it.'

'All right, I'll say no more, but sometimes I could kick you, son.'

'Thanks, Mum, and if that's all, I'll say goodbye now.'

'I've said my piece. Bye, Arthur.'

As Arthur replaced the receiver he wondered if his mother was right.

He went into the kitchen to make himself something to eat, and as he prepared a meal, Arthur decided to give it one more try. He'd go to see Sally again, but not yet, not until he'd properly rehearsed what he was going to say.

Joe didn't drive to Earls Court; he was on his way to Clapham Common. He was still sure that Sally and Arthur would get back together, unable to believe that two people who so obviously loved each other could remain apart. It had been a bit sticky when Arthur had asked him out for a drink again, but he'd managed to fob him off, and was now on his way to meet Patsy. Even if Arthur managed to get Sally back, he doubted she'd return to Maple Terrace with Patsy living upstairs, but that was something he hoped to remedy.

Patsy had been surprised to hear from him, and at first she'd been hostile, but he knew her now, knew what buttons to push, and finally she'd agreed to meet. Joe sat in the pub, eyes on the door, brows lifting when she walked in. There was no getting away from the fact that she was a stunner, her dainty innocent looks giving no clue to her occupation.

'Hello, Patsy. What would you like to drink?' he asked, as she sat beside him.

'A vodka and lime,' she said curtly.

He went to the bar and was soon back, placing her drink on the table. 'Thanks for agreeing to meet me.'

'Well, I must admit I was surprised.' And getting straight to the point she added eagerly, 'You said something about a proposition?'

Joe's face hardened. 'Yes, that's right. I'm proposing that you move out of your flat.'

'Move out of my flat! But why should I?'

'I should have thought it was obvious.'

'Not to me, it isn't.'

'Sally won't move back while you live upstairs.'

She shrugged her shoulders. 'That's just too bad.'

'Does your landlord know what you do for a living, Patsy?'

'What's that got to do with anything?'

'A lot. I wonder how he'll react when I tell him that one of his tenants is a prostitute who uses the flat to entertain men.'

'But I don't!'

'It would be your word against mine, Patsy, and what about

317

the neighbours? When I tell them what you do for a living, I'm sure they'll complain too.'

'You bastard!'

'It takes one to know one, Patsy. Now I'll give you until the end of the week, but if you're not out by then I'll make it my business to spread the word.'

She jumped to her feet, livid, and snatching up her glass of vodka she threw it in his face. 'All right, you win, but you can stick your soddin' drink.'

As Patsy marched out of the pub, Joe pulled out a handkerchief, hastily wiping his face. A few customers were looking at him, doing their best to hide their smiles, but Joe ignored them. As long as Patsy left the flat, that's all that mattered, and then he was struck by another idea. Arthur had suggested he should find somewhere decent to live, and with the flat above him in Maple Terrace now becoming vacant, maybe he'd approach the landlord. It was certainly better than his place in Earls Court.

Forty-Four

On Thursday evening Andrew was ready to take Ruth to dinner. She wasn't the same woman he remembered, one who had been so full of life. It was as if Ruth had been through so much that all the fun had been knocked out of her. Yet even so, when Andrew saw the love she showered on Tommy and Angel, he saw a warm, caring, affectionate woman. Unlike Moira, he thought, remembering his late wife's cold and distant nature.

'Are you ready?' he asked when she opened the door.

Ruth looked a bit pink and flustered as she said, 'Yes, nearly. I just need a minute. Come on in.'

'Hello, Sally,' Andrew said, as they walked into the kitchen. 'I hope you don't mind that I've invited your mother out to dinner.'

'Why should I mind? The children are asleep,' and nodding in Sadie's direction she added with a wry smile, 'Gran too.'

'No, I'm not,' Sadie protested. 'I was just resting me eyes.'

'I wonder who was snoring then,' Ruth said, then turned to smile at Andrew. 'I won't be a tick.'

He nodded, looking at her legs appreciatively as she hurried from the room. Once again he was struck by how little she had physically changed in over twenty years. Her figure was still trim, her skin wonderful, and there were no signs of grey in her hair.

'Angel is still bossing Tommy around,' Sally said.

'She seems pleased that I'm her grandfather, but it was a shock

319

for Tommy to find out that you're his cousin. Once he gets used to the idea he'll find his feet, and woe betide Angel then.'

'Yes, I think you're right, but I doubt he'll pick on Angel. If anything he's always been protective of her. It's strange really, almost as if he sensed the connection between them.'

Andrew grinned. 'I don't know how you can say it's strange, especially with the gifts that you and my mother have.'

'Right, I'm ready,' Ruth said.

Andrew smiled at the pretty picture she presented in her flowery summer dress, topped with a lace cardigan. 'Right, bonny lass, let's go.'

As they walked along Candle Lane, Andrew impulsively took Ruth's hand, and she turned to smile at him, her eyes sparkling. For a moment he saw the happy young woman he remembered, one who loved to dance the night away. 'Do you recall doing the jitterbug with me, Ruth?'

'Of course I do. We had a lot of fun in those days.'

'It was certainly fun when I flipped you over. I don't think I'll ever forget the sight of your frilly French knickers.'

'Andrew!' Ruth said, looking horrified, but then she giggled. 'It's just as well you weren't wearing a kilt or I'd have got my own back.'

'My goodness, woman. You'd have seen more than you bargained for. Scotsmen don't wear anything under their kilts.'

'Oh, I think you'll find I saw enough,' she said, going pink again.

Andrew squeezed her hand, remembering their lovemaking. It had been a passionate affair, their time together snatched, and little had he known that Sally would be the result. 'Our daughter's a lovely girl,' he murmured.

Ruth returned the pressure of his hand, and when they reached the restaurant they sat gazing at each other until the waiter brought the menu.

They chatted throughout the meal, at ease in each other's

company. They were on their final course before Andrew raised the subject that was heavy on his mind. 'Ruth, I'd like to do something to help you, and by doing so it will help Sally too.'

'Help me in what way?'

'I'd like you to accept a monthly allowance, enough to enable you to give up work.'

'Forget it. I can't accept your money.'

'But why? Sally is my daughter and I've provided nothing for her upbringing.'

'What is this – guilt? If so, there's no need. I chose not to tell you that I had given birth so you have nothing to feel guilty about. Sally is no longer a child now, she's a grown woman, and I don't need your money for her upkeep.'

'I know that, Ruth, but you're being selfish. If you'd accept my financial help you could stay at home to look after your mother. Instead you're laying the burden on Sally.'

'How dare you say I'm selfish? When Ken left I had to work full-time to earn enough to bring Sally up, and without my mother's help I don't know how I'd have coped. She contributed most of her pension, and looked after Sally while I was working my socks off. Now my mother is ill and the role is reversed, but Sally loves her and she doesn't mind.'

'Are you sure about that? Have you asked her? She's a young woman, tied to the house all day, and if you ask me, it's your duty to care for your mother.'

Her eyes flashing with anger, Ruth said, 'I'm not listening to any more of this! You've been here for less than a week and already you think you can tell me how to run my life.'

'I'm not doing that. I'm just trying to help, and as I said, it's your duty—'

Ruth's chair scraped against the floor as she got to her feet, face white with anger. 'Duty, you talk to me of duty, you sanctimonious git! I've done well enough without you for over twenty years, and I can take care of my own affairs. In future, I suggest you keep your nose out and . . . and you can stick your money up your arse!'

With this Ruth stormed out of the restaurant, the other customers trying to hide their amusement as Andrew threw down his napkin. 'Waiter,' he called, 'the bill, please.'

Ruth practically marched all the way home, seething with indignation. How dare Andrew call her selfish? She had worked hard to bring Sally up when Ken had left her, with no further help from him, or any man!

What an idiot she'd been. When Andrew had asked her out to dinner, she'd felt like a young woman again, all those feelings she'd harboured for so long rising to the surface.

She was crazy and realised that now – crazy to expect that he still had feelings for her. She had imagined his looks of affection. All he had been interested in was the welfare of his daughter.

As Ruth neared Candle Lane, Andrew's words played over in her mind. He'd called her selfish, but flaming hell did he really think that she enjoyed going out to work? When Sally was a child she would have loved to be a stay-at-home mum, but she'd had no choice.

As she arrived home, Ruth hesitated before putting the key in the lock. Sally would wonder why she was home so early and she wasn't in the mood for explanations. Andrew had said it was her duty to look after her mother, that the burden shouldn't be Sally's, but was looking after her gran so bad?

No, Ruth decided as she quietly crept upstairs to her room. Of course it wasn't.

322

Forty-Five

Friday morning saw Sally up earlier than usual. It was Tommy's birthday today and she was going to prepare a special tea for when he came home from school. The jelly would have to be made now if it was to set in time and she wanted to do it before the children got up.

There had been a debate about the birthday tea, Sadie saying it wasn't right when the boy's mother hadn't been buried yet.

Ruth argued that Laura would have wanted to celebrate Tommy's birthday. There would be enough tears on Monday, she insisted.

Sally had been torn between both points of view, but in the end had sided with her mother, much to her gran's disgust.

Only half an hour later, Ruth appeared, but she looked morose as she walked into the kitchen.

'Are you all right, Mum?'

'Yeah, why shouldn't I be?'

'You look a bit down in the mouth.'

'I'm fine,' she said shortly.

Sally knew from past experience that her mother could be stubborn and that it would be pointless to press her. 'Right then, I'll go and get the children up.'

Shortly they were washed and dressed, and then when they went downstairs, Sally smiled when she saw how Tommy's face lit up.

'Wow!' he yelled, looking in wonderment at the parcels. 'Can I open them?'

'Of course you can.'

Tommy grabbed the largest, tearing off the paper, and said joyously, 'Look, Angel. It's a train set from my dad and Uncle Andy.'

'It's not fair. I want one too,' Angel scowled.

Ruth's smile was strained, but she spoke at last. 'Wouldn't you rather have a nice new doll?'

'I don't like dolls. I want a train set.'

'Now then, miss, it's Tommy's birthday today,' Sally admonished, 'and I don't want any sulks. When it's your birthday you can choose what you want, but until then I think you should wish Tommy a happy birthday and give him our present.'

Angel ran to the dresser and taking out a parcel she handed it to Tommy. 'I chose these, and you've got to let me play with them.'

Tommy took the package, eagerly tearing off the paper, his face lighting up when he saw the contents. There was a net bag of marbles, cigarette cards, the latest edition of his favourite comic, *The Beano*, a jigsaw puzzle, and a box of jelly babies. 'Cor, fanks.'

'And this is from me,' Ruth said, holding out yet another package.

'Blimey, this is me bestest birfday ever,' Tommy said, once again ripping off the paper. 'Cor, fanks!' he cried, pulling out six little boxes containing Dinky cars.

'I want some cars too,' Angel said, pouting.

After admonishing her daughter again, Sally spoke to Tommy. 'When you come home from school we'll have a birthday tea and I'll ask your father and uncle to join us.'

'Fanks,' but then his expression changed to one of sadness. 'I wish me mum could see me new toys.'

Angel wrapped an arm around him, and Sally was touched as her daughter said, 'Never mind, Tommy. You can share my mummy.'

'I can't. She's me cousin.'

Sally bent to ruffle his hair. 'That's right and a cousin who loves you very much.'

He brightened a little and began to play. Angel joined in and said, 'I want the red car.'

Sally looked at her mother. She had hardly spoken to Tommy. 'Mum, are you sure you're feeling all right?'

'I've told you, I'm fine, but unlike some people, I have to get ready for work.'

Why had she said that? Sally wondered as her mother stomped out from the room.

That afternoon, Andrew found the birthday tea a success, with Denis sober and on his best behaviour. After the children had consumed copious amounts of food, including jelly and ice cream, he set up Tommy's train set, joining the children on the floor and regularly winding up the clockwork engine. After a while, unable to resist, Denis joined in too.

When Ruth came home from work the atmosphere immediately changed. She was unsmiling, and her eyes barely met Andrew's as she took in the scene. He stood up, and walked over to her, saying quietly, 'Let's not spoil Tommy's party. Can we go somewhere and talk?'

'I suppose so,' she said, walking into the hall.

Andrew followed her, and as Ruth went into Sadie's bedroom she kept her back to him, her arms folded defensively as she gazed out of the window. He had been cursing himself since last evening. Ruth was right, he shouldn't try to interfere in their lives. She had brought Sally up on her own, and had made a good job of it, but instead of praising her, he had called her selfish. In his desire to help Sally he had hurt Ruth.

He went up behind her and placed his hands on her shoulders. 'I'm sorry. I had no right to call you selfish.'

She turned, eyes moist as she looked up at him. 'I've done the best I can, but I've been thinking about what you said all day. Sally offered to look after my mother when she had her stroke and she's never complained. But maybe you're right, maybe it isn't fair on her.'

'Ruth, I had no right to interfere, and if Sally is happy to look after her grandmother, that's fine. If she isn't, my offer of financial help, enabling you to stay home, stands.'

'I really don't want to take your money, Andrew, but I suppose it's only fair to ask Sally how she feels about it.'

'Good, and now that we've sorted that out, can we be friends again?'

She smiled up at him, and once again Andrew saw the girl he remembered. The memories flooded into his mind, of holding her, touching her, and before Andrew knew it he had bent down to kiss her.

Ruth didn't resist, her lips soft as her arms slipped around his neck, and when the kiss ended, Andrew continued to hold her in his arms. 'How about dinner again tonight,' he whispered, 'and this time we won't talk about Sally.'

When her parents returned to the room, Sally saw her mother smiling happily. 'Andrew has asked me out to dinner again,' she said. 'Is that all right with you, Sally?'

'Of course it is. As usual I have nothing planned, but I'm thinking about offering healing at the hall again.'

'Good idea. It'll do you good to get out of the house.'

'Right,' Denis said, 'I'm off, and Tommy, it's about time you packed that train set away. It's taking up too much room on the floor and someone might step on it.'

'No, leave it out, Tommy,' Angel demanded.

'No, it might get broken.'

326

'Course it won't.'

'I'm putting it away,' Tommy insisted, beginning to pull the track apart.

Angel jumped up, kicking the engine in the process. As it fell to its side Tommy glared at her, red-faced with anger. 'You did that on purpose!'

'No, I didn't.'

'Yes, you did,' and standing up he gave Angel a shove. She fell backwards on her bottom, Tommy looming over her as he yelled, 'Don't touch my train set again!'

'I will if I want,' Angel cried as she scrambled onto her knees, and snatched the engine, poised to throw it.

'Angel!' Sally shouted. 'Don't you dare!'

'That's enough, lassie,' Andrew said as he swiftly picked up his granddaughter. He took the engine from her hand, handing it to Tommy. 'Now then, Angel, what sort of behaviour is this? Tommy was kind enough to let you play with his train set, and instead of thanking him, you try to break it.'

'I want a train set too.'

'I don't think you deserve one. Now say sorry.'

'No.'

Andrew sighed, and placed Angel back onto the floor. 'I'll leave you to sort this one out, Sally, but I think this little girl deserves a smack.'

'Yes, and she'll get one if she doesn't apologise to Tommy.'

Angel's eyes flicked around the room, and seeing all their stern faces, she said, 'Sorry, Tommy.'

Tommy said nothing as he dropped to his knees, once again packing away the train set.

'Have you had a nice birthday?' Ruth asked, as she bent to help him.

Tommy kept his head lowered, but Ruth noticed a quiver in his shoulders. 'Oh, love, it's all right. Angel didn't mean it,' she said, pulling him into her arms.

'I don't care about the train. It's me mum. It's me birfday and I want me mum.'

Ruth rocked the child and, glancing at Denis, she saw that he too looked distressed. She didn't have much time for the man, but when all was said and done, he had just lost his wife. However, Tommy was her main concern and she had yet to talk to Denis about taking the boy on permanently.

At seven-thirty, Sally put both children to bed whilst her mother got ready to go out. When Andrew came to collect Ruth at eight, Sally watched them leave and was about to settle in front of the television with her gran, when someone knocked on the door.

'Bloomin' hell, me favourite programme is just starting,' Sadie complained.

'I'll see who it is,' Sally said, her stomach knotting when she saw who it was. 'Go away, Arthur.'

'Sally, please, I want to talk to you.'

'We have nothing to say to each other.'

'Please, just hear me out for five minutes.'

'No,' she said, making to close the door.

His hand stretched out, holding the door open. 'I won't leave until you agree to listen to me.'

Sally could see that he meant it and her mouth tightened. 'All right, but five minutes, and no more.'

'Can we talk in private?'

'All right, I suppose we can use my gran's room.'

Sally stood back to let Arthur in and as he followed her into Sadie's room, she turned abruptly, her arms crossed defensively.

Arthur's eyes held an appeal. 'Sally, won't you give me another chance?'

'I can't. I could never trust you now.'

'I'll never do it again, I swear I won't. Please, Sally, don't throw our marriage away over one mistake.'

'One mistake! You slept with Patsy more than once and from what I saw that first time, you loved it.'

He flushed, lowering his head. 'If you hadn't left me, it wouldn't have happened again.'

'Oh, so now it's my fault that you couldn't keep your hands off of her!'

'No, I didn't mean it to sound like that, but when you left, Patsy was there, and she kept on throwing herself at me.'

'Huh, and you couldn't say no?'

'I know now that she lied to keep us apart, but at the end of the day it was just sex, that's all. It meant nothing.'

Sally found her fists clenched, nails digging into her palms. Whilst she'd been crying night after night, he'd been fine, sleeping with Patsy and having a good time. She felt sick at the thought of Arthur touching Patsy, of the intimacy they'd shared. 'The sex may have meant nothing to you, but as far as I'm concerned you betrayed me, and our marriage. Just go, Arthur.'

'Sally, please, I love you.'

'Love! You don't know the meaning of the word. Just get out. I'll never forgive you, Arthur, and as far as I'm concerned, our marriage is over.'

'What's going on?' Sadie said sharply, as she came into the room.

'Nothing, Gran. Arthur is just leaving.'

'Sally . . .' he began.

'I said get out,' she yelled.

Arthur shook his head, but then swung round to leave, and when Sally heard the door closing behind him she flung herself across her gran's bed, giving vent to her feelings, the pain of his betrayal still unbearable.

She felt the bed dip beside her, and then her gran's hand stroking her hair. 'Come on, love,' she cajoled. 'If you carry on like this, you'll make yourself ill.'

'Oh, Gran, I can't bear it.'

329

'Can't you find it in your heart to forgive him?'

'No, I can't. Every time I think of him with Patsy it turns my stomach,' Sally croaked, cuddling closer to her gran. The pain was still there and she began to wonder if it would ever go away.

Forty-Six

On Monday, Laura's funeral was a sad affair, and to Andrew the bright, sunny, June day seemed incongruous. The sky should be grey, as grey as his mood. There weren't many in attendance, just himself, Denis, Ruth and a few neighbours.

Andrew rose to his feet as the service ended and they left the small chapel to see scant floral tributes laid on the ground outside.

'I'm sorry for your loss,' a woman said, and Andrew turned to look at her.

'Thank you, and thank you for coming. I'm sorry. I don't know your name.'

'It's Jessie, Jessie Stone, and like Nelly over there, I live in Candle Lane.'

'Well, thank you again for coming,' he said before Jessie moved on to offer her condolences to Denis.

Andrew walked over to Ruth, saying quietly, 'I still think that Tommy should be here.'

'It was his father's decision to send him to school, but I must admit, it feels strange that the boy has no idea that his mother is being buried today.'

'Denis seems to think that he's too young to understand.'

'I doubt that. Tommy is astute for his age. Still, we'd best make our way back. Sally has laid on a little spread.'

Andrew took Ruth's arm. He'd be leaving tomorrow, but so

much had been left undone. He was worried about Tommy and as Denis was drinking heavily, he wondered what sort of future his nephew would have. At least the boy had Ruth. Tommy clung to her, and in time he felt that Ruth would in some ways become a surrogate mother.

'Ruth, as I'm leaving tomorrow, will you have dinner with me again this evening?'

'Yes, of course I will.'

He squeezed her hand and then after a short journey they were pulling up in Candle Lane, walking into the house to see a lovely spread on Ruth's kitchen table. Andrew looked at the neatly-cut sandwiches Sally had prepared, but found he had no appetite.

A hand touched his arm, and he saw that Sadie had come to his side, her voice soft. 'I'm sorry I wasn't there, love. I'm feeling much better nowadays and could have gone to the chapel, but as usual I'm being mollycoddled. I tried to talk Sally into going, but she insisted on staying here with me.'

'She worries about you,' Andrew said, his mood low. 'I wish I'd shown more concern for my sister.'

'She's in a better place now, love.'

Andrew found no consolation in Sadie's words. Guilt still plagued him. He suspected it always would.

An hour passed, then Jessie Stone left along with another woman from the lane, but Nelly Cox stayed behind to help with the clearing up.

'There's hardly a sandwich left,' Andrew said, managing a smile for Sally. 'Thanks for the lovely spread, lassie.'

She smiled back at him, but the smile didn't reach her eyes. His daughter was unhappy, Andrew knew that, but because Sally had insisted that her marriage was over and wouldn't let him intervene, he felt helpless. Ruth told him that it was for the best, that Sally would eventually get over it, and he hoped that she was right. In the meantime he'd learned his lesson about keeping

332

in touch, and was determined not to make the same mistake again. Somehow he would see Sally regularly, despite the difficulties and distance between them.

'I need a drink,' Denis said. 'I'll see you later.'

Unsurprised, Andrew nodded, and in this instance he felt that he needed a dram of whisky too. 'I'll come with you,' he said, calling goodbye.

Sally was glad of the help as they cleared up. Heavy on her mind was her father's departure tomorrow. She was going to miss him. In the short time that he'd been in her life she had come to love him, Andrew being everything that she had dreamed of in a father.

It was strange to think that she had paternal grandparents and a brother, and Sally wondered if she'd ever meet them. She had wanted to ask her father, but in the early stages of their relationship she still found herself a little reticent.

'Did you see the way Jessie Stone scoffed the ham sandwiches?' Sadie said. 'If her mouth had been a bit bigger she'd had shoved them in two at a time.'

'Yeah, I saw,' Nelly said. 'She's a greedy cow, but enough about Jessie. I've got something to tell you.'

'Spit it out then,' Sadie urged.

'I'm moving into Osborne House the day after tomorrow.'

'Oh, Nelly,' Sally said sadly, 'Candle Lane won't be the same without you.'

'I'll be sorry to leave, but the lane won't be standing for much longer.'

'Nelly, I'm gonna miss you,' Sadie said, and reaching into her apron pocket she pulled out a handkerchief, dabbing at her eyes.

'Gawd blimey, you're crying, Sadie.'

'Of course I ain't. I've just got something in me eye.'

'Yeah, right,' Nelly said, 'and pigs might fly. I didn't know you cared.'

'Who said I do?'

Nelly chuckled. 'We go back a long way, you and me. If I remember rightly, you moved into the lane just before our Queen's Coronation.'

'Yeah, that's right, and a lot of water has passed under the bridge since then.'

'It has, Sadie, it has,' Nelly said. She sat down opposite Sadie and the two of them started reminiscing with Ruth chipping in now and then.

After an hour, the old lady rose to leave. 'Nelly,' Sally said, 'I'll come to see you in Osborne House.'

'Yeah, I will too.'

'Are you sure about that, Sadie? They might take one look at you and not let you out again.'

'Maybe that wouldn't be such a bad idea. At least I wouldn't be a burden to Sally.'

'Don't say that, Gran. You're not a burden and never will be.'

'Count your blessings, Sadie. You're lucky to have a loving family.'

'I know, Nelly, I know.'

Sally walked Nelly to the door where the old woman paused. 'Sally, I know it's none of my business, but I was hoping to see you and Arthur back together before I left.'

'There's no chance of that, Nelly. My marriage is over.'

'Are you sure, love? Are you sure that you really want to spend the rest of your life without Arthur?' and with that comment, Nelly continued on her way.

It was nearly eight o'clock and Andrew was zipping his bag. He was packed, ready for his journey home in the morning, and now, glancing at his watch, he saw it was time to take Ruth out to dinner. Denis was upstairs drunk, sleeping it off, but Andrew suspected that he'd be off to the pub again as soon as he woke up.

Andrew walked next door, Sally answering his knock. 'Come in, Dad. Mum's nearly ready.'

He stepped inside, and then paused to lay a hand on Sally's arm. 'Listen, lassie. I know I'm leaving, but I'm on the end of a telephone. If you need anything, just let me know. I'll ring you often, and as soon as I can, I'll be back to see you.'

'You're coming back?'

'Of course I am. It won't be for a while as I'll have a lot of work to catch up on, but as soon as I get the chance, I'll come down to London again.'

Sally was about to speak, but then Ruth appeared on the stairs. 'Hello, Andrew. I'm ready.'

Andrew smiled up at her, thinking how lovely she looked, and then turned to speak to Sally again. 'I'll be round to see you before I go.'

'All right. Bye, Dad,' she said, but Andrew could see the strain on her face.

As they left the house, Andrew took Ruth's hand. There was a growing intimacy between them, but so far she hadn't mentioned his offer of financial help. 'Ruth, have you asked Sally how she feels about looking after her gran yet?'

'Yes, and she was adamant that she doesn't mind.'

'Are you sure?'

'Yes, I'm sure. Now can we please drop the subject?'

Andrew sighed heavily. He had done nothing for Ruth, or his daughter, and it weighed heavily on his mind. 'I feel I should be helping you in some way.'

'For goodness' sake! Not again! As I told you before, I chose not to tell you about Sally. So will you stop trying to salve your flaming conscience.'

'That isn't what I'm trying to do.'

'Andrew, I'm sorry. Look, it's your last evening in London so let's not fall out.'

'All right, Ruth, but can I just say that if you need anything, anything at all will you let me know?'

'If it will make you feel better, then yes, I'll do that.'

They reached the restaurant and after ordering their meal, Andrew said, 'I hate to see Sally so unhappy. She tries to hide it but I can see it in her eyes.'

'Me too, and I could kill Arthur for what he's done to her.'

'He wants her back.'

'There's no chance of that. Arthur was unfaithful, and worse, Sally caught him at it.'

'I have a feeling she still loves him.'

'He doesn't deserve her,' Ruth said as the first course arrived and after a few mouthfuls she changed the subject. 'Are you still going to tell your parents about Sally?'

'Yes, of course. I'll tell my son too. Secrets have a way of coming out, and meeting you again has proved that.'

'How do you think they'll take it?'

'I don't know. My parents will be shocked, and I've no idea how they'll react. As for Donald, I'll just have to wait and see.'

'Sally is going to miss you.'

'As I told her, I'll come back to London as soon as I can, and it won't only be to see Sally.'

'Won't it?'

'I want to see you again too.'

'Really?' she said, her face going pink.

'Yes, really.' And as Andrew said these words, he knew he meant them.

Forty-Seven

On the train to Scotland the next morning, Andrew felt torn in two.

It had been a difficult parting. He had hated saying goodbye to Sally, Angel too, both of them breaking down in tears as he left. He was amazed at how quickly he had come to love them. Yet he had to return to Scotland; his life was there, his parents, and his son.

Andrew's thoughts turned to Ruth, and he examined his feelings. There was no doubt that the spark was still there, and he was sure she felt the same, but with him in Scotland, and Ruth in London, there was little chance of their relationship going any further.

The journey seemed endless; the sound of the wheels riding over the tracks was making Andrew sleepy and he began to doze. Hunger eventually drove him to the dining car, and as he ate, he gazed at the passing scenery, his thoughts continually turning to those he'd left behind.

At last they reached Edinburgh, and leaving the train Andrew grabbed a taxi, sinking back in the seat with a sigh. He looked out of the window, and as the rolling countryside came into view, his heart lifted. He was home.

The house felt damp and empty as he walked in and there was no one to greet him. However, the furniture shone and he eyed

337

it with appreciation, pleased that his cleaner had kept the place up to scratch.

Leaving the hall he went into the large reception room, finding that after the small cramped house in Candle Lane, his home seemed enormous.

Andrew walked over to the telephone, dialled his parents' number and told them that he'd be round to see them soon.

'Hello son,' his mother said, when he walked in an hour later. 'You look tired. Did . . . did our flowers arrive for the funeral?'

'Yes, and they were lovely.' He saw his mother's eyes fill with tears, and going to her side, he took her hand.

'Oh, Andrew, I can't believe I'll never see my daughter again.'

'Now don't get upset again,' Duncan Munro cajoled.

She dabbed at her eyes, then said, 'And . . . and Laura's son?'

'He's a fine boy, Mother, and as bright as a button.'

The tears began to run down her cheeks. 'He's our grandson, but we've never seen him.'

'That can be remedied. I'm sure he'd love a holiday in Scotland.'

Duncan Munro cleared his throat, his voice husky. 'Donald rang earlier, and when I told him you were coming to see us, he said he'd pop round too.'

As if on cue, the doorbell rang, and Andrew went to answer it. 'Hello son. Any sign of my grandchild yet?'

'No, Dad. I think he's so comfortable in there that he doesn't want to come out.'

'Oh, it's a boy, is it?'

'I hope so, but then again,' he mused, 'a girl might be nice.'

As they walked into the sitting room, Andrew saw that his mother was dabbing her eyes. He wanted to tell them, to get it over with, but would the shock be too much for her? She brightened when she saw Donald, and it was then that Andrew made up his mind. 'I'm glad you came round, son. I have something to tell you all, and I might as well do it now.'

'You sound a bit ominous, Dad. Is it bad news?'

'I hope not, son.'

Donald looked puzzled but sat down, and after a pause Andrew began to speak, doing his best to be brief. There was a gasp from his mother, a grunt of annoyance from his father, and Andrew found he couldn't look at his son. It sounded terrible, he knew that. A wartime affair, a child he didn't know he had, and now a granddaughter too.

The room was hushed as he finished speaking, but then his father's voice broke the silence. 'And you're telling us that Laura lived next door to this . . . this woman!'

'Ruth, Father. Her name is Ruth.'

'Oh, Andrew,' his mother gasped. 'I can't believe you did such a terrible thing.'

'It was a wartime affair and those were extraordinary times. I was very young, away from my family for the first time, and well . . . it happened.'

'Humph,' his father grunted. 'You were a married man, and Donald here must have been just a baby. You should be ashamed of yourself.'

'I'm certainly not proud, but on finding I have a beautiful daughter and granddaughter, I can't regret it either.'

'Dad,' Donald said, speaking for the first time, 'this means I have a half-sister.'

Andrew braced himself and turned to look at his son. He dreaded the censure he would see in his eyes, but to his surprise Donald was smiling. 'Yes, it does, and as I said, her name is Sally. I . . . I'm sorry, son.'

'Dad, you don't have to apologise to me. I loved my mum, but I knew you weren't happy.'

'Did you? I thought I hid it from you.'

'I know you tried, but I'm not blind. Anyway, you and Mum

had separate rooms so it didn't take much working out. I also heard her talking to a friend once and she was making it plain that she found *that* side of marriage distasteful.'

'Donald!' Jane Munro snapped. 'I don't think this is a subject for the drawing room.'

'Oh, Grandmother, this is the nineteen sixties.'

'Nevertheless, these things should not be spoken of so openly.'

'All right, I'm sorry,' Donald said, then turning to Andrew and asking eagerly, 'Can I meet her, Dad?'

'Meet who?' Andrew asked.

'My sister.'

'Err . . . yes, I suppose so. Perhaps when I next go to London you could come with me.'

'If I can get away I'd like that, but in the meantime, tell me about her.'

'Well, like me, she has red hair, but facially she's a mirror image of your grandmother, and also has her healing gifts.'

'Does she?' Jane Munro said, her face softening. 'And – and her daughter?'

'Angel has red hair too, and again there's a resemblance to you.'

'Angel! What a strange name.'

'It's Angela really, but everyone shortens it,' Andrew said, smiling as he thought about his granddaughter. 'She's a little tomboy, but adorable with it.'

He saw his mother's eyes fill with tears again and with a small sob she said, 'If I have learned anything from Laura's death, it's that I was an unforgiving fool. I cut her out of my life, and now it breaks my heart to know I'll never see her again. Don't lose touch with your daughter, Andrew. See her as often as you can and perhaps bring her to Scotland to see us. I . . . I'd love to meet her.'

'Things are a little difficult for Sally. She cares for her elderly grandmother and has little freedom, but don't worry, I'll find a way.'

His mother suddenly paled and Duncan Munro rose to his feet, shuffling to her side. 'I'm sorry, but I think your mother needs to rest.'

'Yes, come on, Dad,' Donald said. 'This has all been a bit of a shock for them and it's time we left.'

Andrew nodded, once again appreciating his son's maturity and common sense. His parents were elderly, and of course they were shocked, but they had taken it better than he'd expected.

'How about coming round to dinner tomorrow night, Dad? Maureen would love to see you.'

'Yes, I'd love to,' and as they parted, Andrew wondered how much longer it would be before his daughter-in-law gave birth to the baby.

In Candle Lane the following morning, Nelly Cox was almost ready to leave, and now bustled along to number five to say goodbye.

'Oh, Nelly, are you sure you're doing the right thing?' Ruth asked. 'The council might have offered you something other than a tower block.'

'Yeah, maybe, but it still wouldn't be the same. I'd be living amongst strangers, and to be honest, I can't face it. At least in Osborne House I'll be amongst people of me own age, and they lay on a lot of activities.'

'We're going to miss you, Nelly,' Sally said, flinging an arm around the chubby old lady.

'I thought you said you'd come to see me.'

'We all will, won't we, Mum?'

'Definitely,' Ruth said.

'I'll come even if they have to carry me,' Sadie said, sniffing as though close to tears.

'That's good, and you had better keep me up with the gossip,' Nelly said, her face strained and it was obvious that she too was fighting tears. 'I'd best be off. I thought I'd leave in style so a taxi is coming to pick me up.'

'What about the few bits you're taking with you?'

'They're already gone. That nice young chap at number twenty offered to take them in his van.'

'Oh, that was good of him,' Sadie said.

'Yeah, some of the newcomers to the lane ain't too bad.'

'Newcomers!' Ruth protested. 'They've been living here for five years.'

'That still makes them new,' Sadie said.

The two old ladies gave each other a watery smile, and as Nelly turned to leave, Sadie croaked, 'Take care, love.'

Ruth hugged her, and then Sally did the same, feeling a sense of unreality. It didn't seem possible that Nelly Cox was leaving. She had been a part of their lives for so long, and always ready to lend a hand to anyone in trouble.

'Please, don't see me out. It'd be my undoing,' Nelly begged.

'All right,' Ruth choked.

Nelly threw one last look at them and then closed the door behind her, and as Sally let the tears flow, it was as though a chapter had closed on their lives.

In Scotland, during the rest of the week, Andrew threw himself into his work. He dreaded going home, finding the house empty and unwelcoming, something he hadn't noticed before his trip to London. For the first time since his wife's death he found himself lonely, his thoughts revolving around Ruth, his daughter, granddaughter and Tommy.

He saw his parents frequently and had dinner with Donald and Maureen again, his daughter-in-law impatient for the baby to be born. She was huge and walked around with her hand permanently cradling the small of her back, amused when he suggested a run round the block to start things off.

On Thursday evening, over a week since his return, Andrew rang London. Ruth answered the phone and sounded pleased to hear from him. 'How are you?' he asked.

'Fine, we all are – well, except for Denis that is.'

'What's the matter with him?'

'He's drinking heavily and is hardly home.'

'But what about Tommy?' Andrew asked worriedly.

'Don't worry. He spends nearly all his time with us. In fact, if I can catch Denis when he's sober, I'm going to suggest that we have Tommy permanently.'

'Ruth, that's good of you, but now you really must let me help financially. I doubt you'll get anything from Denis for his keep.'

'There's no need. He's only one small boy and will hardly eat us out of house and home.'

'Why do you have to be so stubborn? Tommy is my nephew and I want to help.'

'I'll think about it.'

Andrew sighed, knowing it would be a waste of time to push her. Even so he would see that he provided something towards Tommy's upkeep and now asked, 'Have you heard anything from the council about re-housing?'

'No, not yet, but I doubt it'll be long.'

'I just hope you get offered something decent.'

'So do I, but tell me, Andrew, how did your family take it when you told them about us?'

'At first they were upset about our affair, but they came round, and I know they'd love to meet Sally, Angel and Tommy. Maybe they could come up here during the school holidays.'

Ruth was quiet for a moment, but then said, 'Yes, I'm sure they'd love that.'

They continued to chat, but Andrew could sense something different in Ruth's tone and after a while he reluctantly said goodbye.

With a heavy sigh he went to his study, picked up a folder and began to prepare a client's overdue structural report. With pen poised, Andrew tried to concentrate, but found his thoughts going back to Ruth.

Forty-Eight

Andrew kept at it, and by the time another week had passed, he had begun to catch up on his work. He'd spoken to Ruth on the telephone again, and then Sally, inviting her to Scotland to meet his family when Angel and Tommy broke up from school.

It hadn't been easy to arrange, Sally saying she couldn't leave her gran, but then he'd spoken to Ruth again and she'd agreed to take a week's holiday from work to look after Sadie. A date had been set for the first week in August, less than a month away, and he couldn't wait. And it seemed his parents couldn't either. When he'd told them they were thrilled.

Andrew flexed his arms, and stretched his back, feeling the stiffness easing. He'd had a lot to do since returning to Scotland and could do with a break, but then his secretary put another call through.

'Dad, it's a boy!' Donald cried.

Andrew could hear the excitement in his son's voice and grinned. 'That's wonderful, and is Maureen all right?'

'Yes, she's fine.'

'I'll be there as soon as I can.'

Andrew shouted a hurried explanation to his secretary before running out of the office. The hospital wasn't far away and he was soon in the maternity ward, staring down at a bonny, bouncing boy who had weighed in at nearly eight pounds.

His eyes grew moist as he looked at his new grandson. He

had a shock of red hair, a screwed-up little face, and both parents were bubbling with happiness. 'Well, son, what are you calling him?'

'He's to be Andrew Duncan Munro, after you and Grandfather.'

'Thank you,' Andrew choked, his voice thick with emotion.

'Well, Dad, there's nothing to keep you here now. Your grandson finally decided to come into the world, and as you can see, he's a healthy wee lad.'

'What do you mean?'

Maureen smiled gently. 'Every time you've been to us for dinner, you have talked non-stop about Ruth.'

'Have I? I wasn't aware of it.'

'You've told us that she's a fine woman, warm and caring, not to mention attractive.'

'So what are you waiting for?' Donald asked.

'I don't understand.'

'Dad, I don't want you to spend the rest of your life alone, rattling round in that great empty house. We can tell you're fond of Ruth, maybe more than fond. If she feels the same about you, why don't you marry her?'

'Marry her! Oh son, I don't know about that.'

'Don't let your marriage to Mum ruin the rest of your life. You deserve a bit of happiness.'

Yes, Andrew thought, he was fond of Ruth, but shook his head at the thought of marriage. 'It's too soon, and we hardly know each other.'

'Then go back to London and get to know her better.'

'I can't do that. I still have work to do, and anyway, Sally will be coming to Scotland with Angel and Tommy soon.'

'Yes, Sally, Angel and Tommy, but what about Ruth? She must feel left out.'

'She has to stay behind to look after her mother, but maybe I'll invite her at a later date.'

345

Donald laid a hand on his arm. 'Dad, you have a way of letting things slide, of burying yourself in work. If you leave it too long, Ruth will think you aren't interested, and if she's as attractive as you've told us, you could lose her to someone else.'

'Donald's right,' Maureen said. 'Work can wait. Your heart can't.'

Andrew gazed at his grandson, a fine sturdy lad who would grow up in clean, fresh air. He thought about Angel, his lovely little granddaughter, living in totally different conditions, and it was then that he made up his mind. If he married Ruth it could solve all of their problems, and surely fondness was something to build on? 'Yes, you're right. I'll go back to London tomorrow.'

'And will you ask Ruth to marry you?' Donald asked.

'I think so, but she may say no.'

'I doubt it, Dad, but you won't know unless you ask.'

Andrew bent down to plant a kiss on his grandson's head. 'Have you spoken to your grandparents?'

'Yes, after ringing you. They're as pleased as punch to have a great-grandson, and don't worry, we'll keep an eye on them whilst you're away.'

'Thanks son, and now that you've both sorted out my life, I'd best be off. I'll be back as soon as I can.'

Andrew hugged both happy parents, and then almost ran from the hospital. It was already four o'clock, but with any luck, he'd be in London by tomorrow evening.

On Friday evening, Ruth's face was a picture when she opened the door. 'Andrew!'

'Aren't you going to invite me in?'

'Yes, of course, but why didn't you let us know you were coming?'

'It was a last minute decision and I thought I'd surprise you.'

Andrew found his heart thumping. Now that he was face to face with Ruth again, he began to recognise his feelings. Yet surely it was too soon to know? She smiled at him and his stomach flipped. There was no denying it. He wasn't just fond of her – he loved her, and prayed she felt the same.

'Dad!' Sally cried, as he walked into the kitchen. 'What are you doing here?'

'I've come to see you of course, but first I want to speak to your mother. Ruth, will you come out to dinner?'

'But you've only just arrived.'

'I know, but I have something important I want to talk to you about, and it can't wait.'

'Is something wrong?' she asked worriedly.

'No, nothing at all,' he said, smiling softly.

'Oh, Dad, Angel's going to be thrilled to see you,' Sally cried. 'She hasn't stopped talking about you since you left and is so looking forward to our holiday. We didn't expect to see you before then. How long are you staying?'

'I'm not sure, but I hope Denis can put me up again.'

Ruth frowned. 'You'd be better off on our sofa. As I told you on the telephone, Denis is drinking heavily and rolls home at all hours. Nine times out of ten, Tommy sleeps here, and that suits me fine.'

Andrew fought to control his annoyance. There'd be enough time later to sort Denis out, but for now he had other things on his mind. 'Well, Ruth,' he said, 'will you come out to dinner?'

'Yes, but give me five minutes to get ready.'

'You look fine as you are.'

'At least let me put a bit of powder and lipstick on.'

Ruth was digging in her handbag for her compact, whilst Andrew turned to Sally. 'My daughter-in-law just gave birth to a bonny wee boy.'

As comprehension dawned, Sally's face filled with light. 'That means I'm an auntie.'

'Yes, it does, lassie, and your new nephew has red hair too.'

'I can't wait to see him.'

347

'I'm ready,' Ruth said, fluffing her hair as she looked in the mirror.

Andrew kissed Sally's cheek, saying goodbye to her and Sadie, but as he led Ruth outside, he found his stomach fluttering with nerves. It wouldn't take long to reach the restaurant, and he was desperately trying to rehearse his words.

They sat at a small table by the window, and as he took the menu, Andrew found his palms sweating.

'Are you all right?' Ruth asked.

'Yes, I'm fine. Now what shall we have to eat?'

They gave their order, and as the waiter walked away, Andrew gazed at Ruth. Should he ask her now, or perhaps wait until the final course? She was gazing back at him. Was that affection he saw in her eyes?

Nerves held him back. For so many years his late wife had rejected him, scorned his affection, and he dreaded facing that again. Was he ready to risk marriage again? He toyed with his napkin, remembering how lonely he had felt in Scotland, and berated himself. Of course he was ready, but later, he'd ask her later.

'You're quiet, Andrew. Why don't you tell me what's on your mind?'

He grasped for something to say. 'Sally has Tommy to look after while you're at work now, as well as her grandmother. How is she coping?'

'Oh my God!' Ruth cried. 'So that's why you came rushing back again. You're worried about Sally and want to tell me I'm a selfish mother again?'

'No, of course not. I understand that you have to work, but I think I have the perfect solution. You see—'

Ruth cut in, hand up, her palm facing him. 'If you've travelled all the way from Scotland to offer me money again, you've wasted your time.'

'That wasn't what I had in mind. Please, Ruth, let me finish,'

348

Andrew urged. 'I know you're to be re-housed soon, but I think I have a better suggestion. You see I have a large house in Scotland, left to me by my grandparents. It has six bedrooms and a small annexe. There's room enough for all of us, Tommy too if his father will agree. You could give up work to care for your mother, and Sally could live in the annexe with Angel.'

'What! You want us to move to Scotland?' Ruth stared at him in shock, but then her eyes narrowed. 'What are you asking of me, Andrew? Am I to be your servant? Or perhaps your kept woman?'

'No, no! For goodness' sake, what do you take me for? Oh, hell, I've made a mess of this. What I'm trying to do is ask you to marry me.'

'Ma . . . marry you?'

'Yes and as soon as possible. It would solve all our problems. I can't bear the thought of being so far away from you all, but I have to live in Scotland. As I said, you're due to be re-housed, and Sally has no home of her own. Can't you see it's the most sensible solution?'

Andrew watched the range of emotions that ran across Ruth's face. When he'd proposed he thought he saw joy, but now he saw doubt, consternation, and then worry.

'It isn't that simple, Andrew. I'm not sure that either Sally, or my mother, would agree to move to Scotland.'

'Why not? I live in a beautiful area with clean, fresh air, and plenty of space for Angel and Tommy to run around. Surely that's better than the grim, dirty streets they play in now?'

'When you put it like that it sounds wonderful, but my mother is a born and bred Londoner and would never leave.'

'Ruth, it's you I'm asking to marry, not your mother. If your answer is yes and she wants to continue to live with you, she'll have to agree.'

'Andrew, I know you see my mother as a difficult woman, but before her stroke she was a different person. Now though she's in bad health and such a big move might be too much for her.'

349

'Wouldn't Scotland be better for her than the possibility of being stuck in a council tower block?'

For a moment she stared at him, doubtfully, and as he reached out to grip her hand Andrew pleaded, 'Ruth, I'm comfortably off, so much so that I can support you all. Please say yes.'

She pulled her hand from his grasp. 'You haven't mentioned one very important thing.'

'What's that?'

'You've asked me to marry you, and have pointed out how sensible it would be, but . . . I need more than that.'

Andrew gazed at her, saw her eyes lower, and then the penny dropped. He was a complete and utter fool. He'd forgotten the most important thing of all. 'Ruth, finding you again seems like a miracle to me, and though we've only just got to know each other again, I can't deny my feelings. I love you. In fact I don't think I ever stopped loving you. Please say you'll marry me.'

She smiled at him now, joy in her eyes, 'Oh, Andrew, I love you too . . . and . . . and my answer is yes.'

Andrew grinned with delight, but then his face sobered as Ruth said, 'I still don't think my mother, or Sally, will move to Scotland.'

'Well, darling, there's only one way to find out. As soon as we've finished our meal we'll go and ask them. Don't worry, I can be very persuasive.'

'I hope so,' she said, relaxing a little, and for the next hour they excitedly discussed their wedding plans.

When her parents arrived home, Sally saw they were holding hands, but her breath caught in her throat when her father announced they were getting married. With hardly time to take it in, her mother then told them that they could all move to Scotland.

'Are you bleedin' mad!' Sadie spluttered. 'Scotland! I ain't living in Scotland.'

Andrew crouched down by Sadie's chair, speaking gently. 'Please, don't just dismiss it out of hand. I have a large house, in a lovely area, and Ruth will be able to give up work to look after you.'

'I don't need looking after and I'm sick of saying that. You go, Ruth, but I'm staying here.'

'Sally,' Andrew said, moving from Sadie's side, 'what about you? Would you like to live in Scotland?'

'I . . . I don't know. It's all a bit sudden, but if my gran won't go, then I can't leave her.'

'Lassie, I've only just found you, and I hate us being so far apart. When I travel back to Scotland I'd like you all to come with me.'

'When are you leaving?'

'As soon as possible.'

'And when are you and Mum getting married?'

'I've told your mother that I'd like my family in Scotland to be at our wedding, and she's agreed to be married in Edinburgh. We haven't set a date yet, but hopefully soon.'

Sally's mind was reeling. She was pleased that her parents were getting married, but moving to Scotland? A holiday, yes, but this was something else.

'You go, Sally, but I'm staying put.'

It was no good – with Sadie still protesting loudly Sally couldn't get her thoughts into order. 'Mum, Dad, I'm going to bed. We . . . we can talk about this again in the morning.'

Andrew placed an arm around her shoulder. 'Goodnight, my bonny lass. I'm sorry to spring this on you so suddenly, you too Sadie, but if you both decide to come, I promise you'll be happy in Scotland.'

Sally nodded, and after saying goodnight she made her way upstairs. If her gran wouldn't go, there was no way she could leave her, but with the flat in her mother's name, would the council re-house them?

* * *

Saturday morning dawned clear and sunny, but as Sally awoke, her eyes felt sticky. She rubbed at them impatiently, and seeing that Angel was asleep she crept downstairs. 'Gran, you're up early. It's only six o'clock. Are you all right?'

'I'm fine, but I didn't sleep well.'

'I thought Dad might stay here last night, but he must have gone next door.'

'Yeah, he wanted a word with Denis.' Sadie shifted in her chair, then said, 'Sally, how do you feel about moving to Scotland?'

'I don't know, but I wouldn't go without you.'

'I tossed and turned all night, weighing things up, and then I came to a decision I didn't expect to make.'

'Really, and what decision is that?'

'Nelly Cox has moved into Osborne House, and I rather fancy joining her.'

'Gran, please, don't do that. I'll stay here and we can live together.'

'No, I've made up my mind. Now then, let's talk about you. I had hoped you and Arthur would get back together, but as you're adamant that you won't, then I think you should move to Scotland. I don't like the thought of you living alone in London and your family will be there.'

'You won't be, nor will Aunt Mary.'

'Scotland isn't in Outer Mongolia. You'll be able to travel down to visit. Flaming hell, Mary! She doesn't even know that your mother is getting married again.'

'Yes she does, I rang her last night before I went to bed,' Ruth said, yawning as she walked into the room.

'Gran said she's going to move into Osborne House. Do something to talk her out of it, Mum.'

'If you think I'm going to Scotland without you, Mum, you've got another think coming. In fact, I'm not going anywhere unless the pair of you agree to come too.'

'Now you're being silly.'

'No I'm not. Now what's it to be? Have I got to call off my wedding or are you coming with me?'

'Now you're resorting to emotional blackmail,' Sadie complained, 'but as Andrew seems a good man and you deserve a bit of happiness, I suppose I'll have to move to Scotland with you. What about you, Sal?'

'Yes, I'll come too.'

Ruth grinned. 'Thank goodness for that. Now I'm off to get dressed and then I'm going next door to tell Andrew the good news.'

She hurried from the room, and half an hour later they heard the door close behind her. With a small shake of her head, Sadie said, 'It's nice to see my daughter so happy. I just wish I could say the same about you.'

'I'm all right, Gran,' Sally lied, as she looked out of the window. They were going to live in Scotland and it felt so unreal, like a dream.

Ten minutes later, Ruth returned with Andrew, her eyes alight with pleasure. 'Denis has agreed,' she cried, 'Tommy can come too.'

Angel came into the room, her eyes sleepy, but they lit up when she saw Andrew. 'Granddad!' she cried, running up to him. 'You've come back.'

'Hello, my beauty,' and turning to Sally, he added, 'This one will have to be told too.'

'Told what, Granddad?'

Tommy appeared then, puzzled to see them all, and sitting both children down, Sally crouched in front of them as she tried to explain the move to Scotland as simply as possible.

'My dad said that men wear skirts in Scotland. I'm not doing that,' Tommy scowled.

'They aren't skirts, laddie. They're kilts.'

'Don't care, I ain't wearing one.'

'Is my daddy coming with us?' Angel asked.

'No, darling, but you'll still be able to see him. There'll be weekends, and school holidays.'

'What about my dad? Is he coming?' Tommy asked.

Ruth answered, 'No, love, but I'm sure he'll come to Scotland as often as he can, and like Angel, you'll see him during school holidays.'

'That's all right then,' Tommy said. 'What's for breakfast?'

Ruth chuckled and went to pour out some cereal, whilst Sally, finding that her daughter had gone strangely quiet, gazed at her worriedly. Angel's eyes looked unfocused and strangely distant, but just when Sally was about to give her a little shake, Angel's head tipped to one side as though she was listening to something.

Angel then smiled and gave a little nod before saying, 'When are Nanny and Granddad leaving?'

'We'll all be leaving at the same time,' Sally told her, 'but I'm not sure when. You had better ask your granddad.'

'Well now, let me see,' Andrew said. 'It's Saturday today, so how about Tuesday?'

'Andrew, that's impossible,' Ruth spluttered. 'There's too much to do.'

'Like what? You'll have no need to bring any furniture so will only have to pack your personal things.'

'We'll have to do more than that. There's the house to close down, the meters to be read, and what about the children's school?'

'I live in a lovely little hamlet with a good school for the children, and they can go there when the new term starts in September. As for the utilities, I can sort those out by telephone.'

'I ain't leaving my bed behind,' Sadie protested. 'It's all I've got left of my home with Charlie. I've slept in the same bed since the day I got married, and I ain't going without it.'

Andrew smiled gently. 'In that case I'll lay on a small removals van.'

'Thanks,' Sadie said. 'Tuesday it is then.'

Andrew grinned with delight, and picking Ruth up he swung her round. 'Start packing your cases, woman. We're all going to Edinburgh.'

At the thought of packing, it finally hit Sally. They were leaving on Tuesday, and she would have to tell Arthur.

Forty-Nine

On Sunday things were still frantic. Ruth was in her bedroom, clothes strewn everywhere as she sorted her wardrobe, bemoaning having to discard things she had hoarded for years. She held up a halter neck dress; the style was too young for her now, but she hated to throw it away. With a last rueful look, Ruth threw it on the pile of rejects, and then began to empty her chest of drawers.

Sally was glancing nervously at the clock. Arthur would be calling for Angel soon, and she would have to tell him. This was a meeting she wasn't looking forward to and she was dreading his reaction.

Soon after, when she heard Arthur's knock, Sally straightened her shoulders, but despite the pretext of bravado, she was still trembling as she let him in. 'Err . . . I need to talk to you in private. Would you come into my gran's room?'

He looked surprised, and as she stood aside to allow him to walk ahead of her, Sally saw no sign of a limp, no sign that he had an artificial leg. He turned to face her, looking tall and handsome, and her stomach lurched. Chiding herself, she fixed her mind on what he'd done, hardening her heart against her feelings.

Tommy was next door with his father and Andrew, whilst Angel was in the yard, absorbed in a game of make-believe shop. Sally faced Arthur. 'I . . . I have something important to tell you. We . . . we're all going to live with my father in Scotland.'

He frowned. 'Scotland! No, Sally . . .'

'My father and mother are getting married,' Sally interrupted, suddenly aware of how strange that sounded. 'He . . . he has a large house with room for all of us, and . . . and I've agreed to go. Angel and I will live in the annexe.'

'Don't be silly. You can't take Angel to Scotland. When would I get to see her?'

'Occasional weekends. School holidays.'

Arthur's face suffused with colour, his voice now rising in anger. 'I'll fight this, Sally. You have no right to take my daughter so far away.'

Sally found her own anger mounting. If she remained in London it would mean finding a flat to rent, and bringing her daughter up alone. Instead her father had offered her a home, a wonderful place to live. 'I have every right! You were the one who committed adultery and caused the break-up of our marriage. If you want to try to stop me, go ahead! I'll see you in court!'

The colour now drained from Arthur's face, and instead of anger she saw pain. 'One mistake, Sally. I made one mistake and I've told you it will never happen again, I swear it. Please, don't go to Scotland. Come back to me and let's make a fresh start.'

There was the sound of footsteps, then Angel's voice as she burst into the room. 'Daddy!' she cried, running up to him. 'I thought I heard you.'

Arthur swept her up, but his eyes were still on Sally. 'Please,' he whispered.

Sally hesitated, but then shook her head decisively, 'No. Never.'

His face crumbled in defeat, and as he lowered Angel to the floor his voice sounded strangled. 'Come on, I'll find a taxi. We're going to Wimbledon to see your nanna and granddad.'

After kissing Angel goodbye, Sally watched them leave, trying to deny her feelings. It was no good, despite everything, she still loved Arthur. The question whirled in her mind. Could she go back to him?

Sally went upstairs. She needed advice, someone to talk to, and went into her mother's room.

'Mum, Arthur's just been to collect Angel and he's asked me to go back to him again. What do you think?'

'What! After what he's done?'

Sally sat on the side of her mother's bed, her head low. 'I still love him, Mum.'

'Now you listen to me, my girl. Arthur had only been home from hospital for five minutes when he had it off with that tart. To top it all, when you left him, he didn't even bother to come after you. No, instead he carried on sleeping with Patsy. Christ, Sally, you'd be mad to trust him again.'

She took in her mother's words and the pain of Arthur's betrayal became fresh again. Yes, she still loved him, but what he'd done was unforgivable. 'Yes, you're right,' Sally said, her shoulders slumped as she left the room.

Had Sally looked back, she would have seen the look of triumph on her mother's face.

Elsie could see that something was wrong as soon as Arthur arrived, so after cuddling Angel for a while she then urged her into the garden with her grandfather.

'Right, son. Tell me.'

He did and Elsie was devastated. 'Scotland,' she cried. 'They're all going to Scotland! But it's so far away!'

'I tried to talk to Sally, but she wouldn't listen. I blew it as usual.'

'Arthur, start at the beginning. What have you said to Sally?'

'The first time I tried to talk her into coming back to me, I made a right mess of it. I said it was her fault that I'd slept with Patsy again and that it wouldn't have happened if she hadn't left me.'

Elsie could guess how Sally would have reacted to that. She loved her son dearly, but he rarely took the blame for anything

358

and always tried to find a scapegoat. He'd been the same as a child. Yet he had so many wonderful qualities, ones she felt made up for this one flaw in his character.

'Arthur, when are you going to take responsibility for your own actions?'

'Don't start, Mum. I know it was my fault and I'd do anything to turn the clock back.'

'We'd all like to do that, but don't give up, Arthur. If you want Sally back, you must try again.'

'It's no good. Sally was adamant, and now that she's moving so far away, I'll only see Angel during school holidays.'

'Oh, God, this is awful. I'm going to miss Angel too, but not just my granddaughter, I'll miss all of them. Ruth and I go back a long way,' Elsie said as she rose to her feet. 'I must go to see her, and perhaps talk to Sally at the same time. She might listen to me.'

'I doubt it, Mum.'

Elsie ignored this and went to the back door, calling to Bert. When he came inside she said hurriedly, 'I want you to run me to Candle Lane.'

'What? Now?'

'Yes, it's important. I'll tell you all about it in the car.' She then turned to Arthur. 'Make some sort of excuse to Angel, and stay here until we come back.'

Arthur nodded, rising to his feet and walking out to the garden. Elsie watched for a moment as he crossed the lawn towards his daughter. Angel was playing with the cat, pulling a piece of string and giggling as the animal tried to catch it. Her red curls were bouncing, the sun enhancing the fiery colour, and she saw Arthur sweep the child up into his arms. How must he be feeling? He had lost his wife, and now must feel that he was losing his daughter too. There had to be something she could do, there just had to. 'Come on, Bert, let's go,' she urged, anxious now to get to Candle Lane.

* * *

Ruth's bed was still strewn with clothes when she heard a knock on the door. She thought it was Mary and hurried downstairs to let her sister in.

'Elsie! Bert!' she said, startled to see them instead of Mary.

'Arthur has just told me that you're all going away. We've been friends for years, since our children were small and I had to come to see you. I can't believe you're getting married.'

'You could have knocked me down with a feather when I saw Andrew again,' Ruth said, as they followed her inside. 'He's wonderful and just as I remembered him.'

'I'm pleased for you, even though it seems a bit quick.'

'I know, isn't it amazing? If Andrew didn't live in Scotland, I'm sure we'd have taken things more slowly. Still, quick or not, I'm over the moon. I'm sure we're all going to love living there.'

Elsie's stance stiffened. 'What about Arthur! Sally's taking Angel such a long way away and he's in a terrible state.'

'When my daughter caught Arthur with that girl, she was in a state too. It's his fault that the marriage broke up, and seeing what Sally has been through, I can't feel sorry for him.'

'Ruth, please, Arthur made a terrible mistake, but he loves Sally, and I'm sure that deep down she still loves him too. Isn't there something we can do to get them back together?'

'No, I'm afraid not. She's made up her mind and is coming with us.'

'Is she in? Maybe I could try talking to her.'

Ruth lowered her eyes. She was getting married, going to Scotland, and when Sally had agreed to go with them, her happiness had been complete. The last thing she wanted was Elsie putting a spoke in the wheel. 'Sally is upstairs and I think she's had enough upset for one day.'

'But—'

Another knock on the door cut off Elsie's protest. Ruth went to answer it, hoping it was her sister this time as that would give her an excuse to get rid of Elsie. 'Mary, come in.'

Mary greeted Elsie and Bert, but then Ruth said, 'As you can see, my sister had just arrived and we have family business to discuss.'

Bert's voice suddenly boomed. 'Fair enough, but we'd like to see Sally before we go.'

'I heard your voices and was on my way down,' Sally said, as she walked in.

Ruth's lips tightened. This was the last thing she wanted. 'Elsie and Bert are just leaving.'

'Sally, I can't believe you're going to Scotland,' Elsie said, ignoring the hint. 'Arthur is in a dreadful state.'

'It's no more than he deserves,' Ruth told them.

Bert walked up to Sally, taking her hand in his. 'I know you've been badly hurt, but Elsie is right. I've seen the state my son is in. Can't you find it in your heart to forgive him?'

'Please, Sally,' Elsie urged.

Ruth held her breath, her heart thumping as she looked at her daughter. *Oh, Sally, don't go back to him,* she silently willed.

'No, it's too late now,' Sally told them, and Ruth's breath left her body in a rush of relief.

'Do you still love him?' Bert asked.

'Please, I don't want to talk about it any more,' she said, tears suddenly filling her eyes.

'I told you I didn't want my daughter upset again,' Ruth cried. 'She's been through enough. Now I don't want to be rude, but I think you should go.'

Sadie came into the room. 'What's going on?'

It was Elsie who answered. 'We just came to talk to Sally and to say goodbye to you all.'

'I hate goodbyes,' Sadie said grumpily, as she shuffled across to her chair.

Elsie pulled Sally into her arms. 'I'm sorry we've made you cry. It's the last thing we wanted to do. I know you're leaving soon, but will you keep in touch?'

Sally dashed the tears from her eyes and with a watery smile, said, 'Of course I will, and . . . and you'll still see Angel. I'll bring her down to visit as often as I can.'

Elsie was close to tears now, and seeing her distress, Ruth felt awful. This was her friend, a woman who had helped her when she was in need. She ran across the room, wrapping her arms around her friend. 'I'm going to miss you, Elsie.'

It was Elsie who pulled away first, sobbing now as Bert led her from the room.

'That was awful,' Mary said. 'The poor woman was so upset. Mind you, I'm going to miss you all too.'

'You can come to visit us as often as you like. Andrew has a large house so there'll be plenty of room.'

'Have you set a date for the wedding?'

'No, not yet. Everything is happening so fast, but when we do have a date, you will come, won't you?'

'Yes, of course. Wild horses couldn't keep me away.'

Both looked at their mother when she spoke. 'I never thought I'd leave London. Even when bombs were falling during the war, I stayed put.'

'You could live with me, Mum.'

'Don't be daft,' Ruth protested. 'You have to work and Mum still can't be left on her own.'

'Sally could stay with me too.'

'You haven't got room,' Ruth pointed out, annoyed at her sister's suggestion.

Mary sighed. 'I know, and to be honest I'm just being selfish. You're all moving away and it feels like I'm losing my whole family.' And as though fighting her emotions, Mary's voice became brusque. 'Anyway, where's Andrew? I've yet to meet him.'

As if on cue, there was a knock on the door. 'I expect that's him now,' Ruth said, soon leading him into the kitchen. 'Andrew, this is my sister, Mary.'

'Hello,' he said, reaching out to shake her hand.

'So, you're going to marry my sister.'

'Yes, and I hope you'll come to our wedding.'

'As I told Ruth, I'll definitely be there.'

Sally was hardly listening, her mind drifting and her head beginning to ache. 'If you don't mind, I'd best start sorting my things out,' she said, glad to leave the chatter of voices. Her heart was heavy as she went upstairs, and instead of packing she flung herself across the bed.

She had made her decision, she was going to Scotland, but now, as Sally turned over to stare up at the ceiling, tears once again flooded her eyes.

Fifty

Monday morning dawned bright and clear, but when Arthur climbed into the car, Joe could tell by his friend's face that something was wrong. 'What's up, mate? You look down in the dumps.'

When Arthur told him why, Joe's jaw dropped. Until this moment he'd been sure that eventually there'd be a reconciliation, but instead Sally and her family were moving away. 'Christ, mate, I can't believe it.'

'Neither could I at first, but she's definitely going.'

'Bloody hell, mate, that's a crock. I've got a bit of news too and at least it means I'll be around to help you to drown your sorrows. You once suggested that I should find somewhere else to live, and now that Patsy has moved out, I'm taking her flat on.'

Arthur smiled wryly. 'Well, at least there's no chance that I'll be accused of having it off with you.'

During the rest of the journey Arthur hardly spoke and sat slumped in his seat. Joe tried to lift his spirits, but his replies were monosyllabic.

When they arrived at the site it was full of activity and once again Joe felt a thrill of excitement. The development was taking shape, and soon he hoped they'd see a large return on their investment. 'It's looking good, Arthur. The first house will be finished in another month or two and we'll use it as the show house. Mind you, we'll need to get the décor right.'

'Sally would have been great at that. She's got an eye for interior design.'

'Talk to her again, Arthur. She may still change her mind.'

'No, it's too late. She's leaving for Scotland in the morning.'

Joe sighed, wishing Arthur would put up more of a fight. He was about to voice his thoughts, but his friend had already climbed out of the car, his face etched with sorrow as he headed for the site office.

They had only one visitor in Candle Lane that evening. Mary called round to say goodbye. She couldn't get time off work in the morning and now clung to them. 'What time is the van coming?'

'It'll be here at eight, but it won't take long to load. There's only Mum's furniture, a couple of cartons and our cases.'

The telephone rang and Sally went to answer it. It was Arthur's sister, Ann.

'Sally, I can't believe you're doing this,' she said, without preamble. 'All right, what Arthur did was terrible, but you can't take Angel away from him.'

'I'm not. I'm only moving to Scotland and he can still see her.'

'Huh, it'll be once in a blue moon.'

'Ann, I'm doing what I think is best.'

'I can't see how taking Angel away from her father is for the best.'

'She'll be living in a better environment, with her family around her.'

'Your family, not her father's. Sally, don't do this. My brother made a mistake, a stupid mistake, but he's told me that Patsy meant nothing to him. It's over with, finished.'

'So is our marriage, Ann.'

'Sally, you're being unreasonable.'

'*I'm* being unreasonable!'

'Yes, I think you are.'

Sally clenched her teeth. 'I wonder if you'd say the same if it was your husband who'd been unfaithful.'

'I think I'd be more forgiving.'

'Well, Ann, I hope you never have to put that theory to the test,' Sally said. She'd had enough and didn't want to talk any more. 'I'm sorry, Ann, I don't want to argue with you, and I must go.'

'All right, go then, but I still can't believe you're doing this to my brother.'

She felt a surge of anger and slammed the receiver down, only for it to ring again a few seconds later; this time Elsie was on the line. She could hear the pain in her mother-in-law's voice, and when the phone was passed to Bert, his voice was thick with emotion too.

Sally spoke to them for a while, her voice cracking, and when the receiver was finally replaced she felt completely shattered.

More followed when Mary rose to leave at ten o'clock. It was an emotional goodbye for all of them, and unable to stand any more, when the door closed on her aunt, Sally went to bed.

An hour later and Sally was still awake, wishing the spiritual presence would come to comfort her, but she saw only shadows cast by the moon. Turning over her eyes drooped, but behind closed lids she recalled the pain she had seen in Arthur's eyes. Was she being unreasonable? Was this her way of getting her own back for the hurt he'd caused?

Sally's mind turned to all the things that had been said; Arthur's words, those of her in-laws, and lastly, Nelly Cox. She had forgiven her husband and gone on to have a happy marriage.

There was also Nelly's question. The old woman had asked if Sally really wanted to spend the rest of her life without Arthur.

Sally felt as if she'd only been asleep for minutes when her mother was waking her up again.

'Come on, Sally, it's six-thirty.'

Blearily she opened her eyes and with a small nod, sat up. So this was it, the day had arrived. In just a few hours they'd be leaving Candle Lane. It was going to be a long day for all of them, and as Angel was still asleep, Sally decided to leave her for another half an hour.

Gran was up when she went downstairs, and as her mother made a pot of tea, she was smiling happily. 'What do you want for breakfast, Sally?'

'Nothing, Mum. I'm not hungry.'

'You should try to eat something. We've got a long journey ahead of us.'

Sally sat down, Nelly's question still on her mind and as her mother handed her a cup of tea, she stirred it absent-mindedly. Unbidden, tears welled in her eyes. 'Oh, Mum.'

'Sally, don't start. There's no time for tears. We've got too much to do this morning.'

'I'm not sure I'm doing the right thing, if going to Scotland is the right choice.'

'Don't be daft, of course it is. We'll all be out of this dump, and living in Edinburgh will be so much better for Angel. She'll thrive there and I know that Andrew will see that she wants for nothing.'

Sally stood up, her shoulders hunched. 'All right, I'll go and get washed and dressed before getting her up.'

'Good girl, but don't spend too much time in the bathroom. I'll need to sort Tommy out too.'

Another hour sped by, and now Andrew had joined them. Moments later, Denis called round, looking hung over as he said goodbye to Tommy. 'Now be a good boy and I'll come up to Scotland to see you whenever I get the chance.'

Tommy didn't seem concerned when his father left, the parting surprisingly easy, and now Ruth began to run around like a headless chicken, checking drawers and cupboards for anything she might have failed to pack.

'Calm down, darling,' Andrew said. 'Look, here's the removal van.'

Sally felt as if she was in a dream, her head woozy. They were going. They were really going.

Whilst the removal men were shown Sadie's furniture, Sally stepped outside, memories flooding back as she looked along Candle Lane. In her mind's eye she could see herself as a child, playing with Ann. She could picture Arthur too, a cheeky boy who often teased her, but he'd grown into a handsome man who'd stolen her heart.

As though her thoughts had bidden him, Sally saw someone turn into the lane. Arthur! She watched him walking towards her, her tummy feeling as though it had turned a somersault.

'Sally, I had to come, had to see you. Please don't go,' he begged. 'Please give me another chance.'

As she stared up at him, Nelly's question filled her mind again. Could she put it behind her? Could she trust him again?

'Sally, I love you, and I swear I'll never be unfaithful again.'

Her throat constricted with emotion, they gazed at each other, and as Sally took a hesitant step forward, Arthur swept her into his arms. It felt right. This was where she belonged.

'Please, Sally, please come back to me.'

'Nelly Cox asked me a question and now I know the answer.'

'What question?'

'She asked me if I really wanted to spend the rest of my life without you.'

'And?' he asked, eagerly.

'No, I don't.'

He lifted her up, his voice loud with joy as he shouted, 'Nelly Cox, I don't know how you did it, but I love you.'

'I don't think she can hear you,' Sally said, smiling now. 'Nelly left Candle Lane and she's moved into Osborne House.'

'Then I'll go to see her with the biggest box of chocolates I can find.'

Sally's face sobered. 'Arthur, I must tell my parents, and not only that we had better stop the removal men before they put my cases on board!'

They walked into the kitchen, hands clasped. 'Mum, Dad, I'm sorry, but I've changed my mind. I won't be coming to Scotland.'

'Daddy!' Angel squealed, running up to her father. 'I knew you'd come. I knew we wouldn't be going to Scotland with Nanny and Granddad.'

Arthur swept her up into his arms. 'How did you know?'

'The lady told me.'

'What lady?' Sally asked, but somehow she already knew the answer.

'The one who comes in the lovely light.'

Andrew spoke, his voice full of wonder. 'My mother sees something similar.'

'Me too,' Sally said. 'And now it seems my daughter will be following in our footsteps.'

Ruth spoke at last, her eyes sad. 'I can't believe you're not coming.'

'We'll visit you as often as we can.'

Andrew moved to Ruth's side, taking her hand. 'I know you're upset, but take a good look at our daughter. She's happy, and that's what matters.'

'Yes, but for how long? You're out of your mind, Sally. What if he hurts you again?'

'Ruth, I won't,' Arthur said. 'I'll never make the same mistake again.'

'See that you don't, laddie,' Andrew growled.

Tommy looked bewildered, his little face puckering. 'Ain't you coming wiv us, Angel?'

'No, I'm staying with my daddy.'

'I don't wanna go then. I wanna stay here too.'

Ruth knelt down in front of him. 'Listen darling, if you want to stay, you'll have to live with your daddy. If . . . if that's what you really want, then . . . then of course you don't have to come with us.'

Tommy's lower lip was trembling, his eyes full of confusion. Ruth hugged him to her, then said, 'It's up to you, darling, but I . . . I love you and would hate to leave you behind.'

Tommy looked at Ruth, his uncle, and then with his head down he plucked his earlobe, obviously deep in thought. The room was hushed, even Angel was silent, and then with a grin the boy looked up. 'All right, I'll come wiv you, Auntie Ruth.'

They all heard her sigh of relief, and, after giving Tommy another hug, she turned to look at Sally, her eyes full of unshed tears. 'Oh, love, I'm so sorry for being selfish. You're my daughter and I wanted you with me, but I was only thinking of myself. I can see now how happy you are, and . . . and I'm pleased for you.'

Sally ran across the room, wrapping her arms around her mother. 'You're not selfish. You're the best mother anyone could have and I love you. I'm going to miss you so much, but you're getting married soon, and no matter what, I'll be there. We all will,' she said, turning to look at Arthur.

He nodded, and now Sally went across to her gran, kneeling by her side. 'I'm going to miss you too.'

'And I you, but you're doing the right thing.'

'The van's loaded,' a voice said.

'Right, thanks,' Andrew replied brusquely. 'And if I'm not mistaken, that sounds like our taxi.'

Sally's breath caught in her throat and rising to her feet, she found herself in her father's arms. 'Be happy, my bonny lass.'

He let her go abruptly, his eyes moist, and Sally watched with tears as they all said goodbye to Angel. Her daughter looked upset, and as Arthur swept her up again, she clung to his neck.

Arthur crooked her with one arm, whilst he took Sally's hand. 'Come on,' he urged, leading her outside.

Sally watched as her father helped her gran into the taxi, then

Tommy climbed in, followed by her mother. She felt torn in two, one part of her wanting to be here with Arthur and Angel, the other half wanting to dive into the cab and go with her family. 'No, no,' she cried, unconsciously moving forward.

Andrew came to her side, hugging her again. 'I know how you're feeling, lassie, but I can see that your heart is here with your husband. We'll all see each other soon, so hang on to that.'

He then turned swiftly, climbed into the taxi, and as the door closed behind him, the engine started.

They were all waving as the car pulled away, Sally watching and waving back until it turned the corner.

Arthur took her hand. 'Don't cry, darling. As your father said, we'll see them all again soon.'

Sally drew in juddering breaths. She looked up at Arthur, saw the love reflected in his eyes, and knew that she had made the right decision.

Her place was here, with her husband. They loved each other, and just like Nelly and George Cox, many happy years stretched ahead of them.

Read on for Kitty's memories of growing up in Battersea

The Battersea I see now is different in some ways to the one I grew up in, yet in others there is much that is still familiar. Battersea Town Hall as I knew it then is still there, but is now an Arts Centre. Battersea Power Station is a landmark, though it wasn't visible from where I lived, nor was the Dogs' Home.

All the shops I remember on Lavender Hill are gone, but when I was sent to do my mother's shopping it was a trip to the butcher's, the grocer's, baker's, greengrocer's and the ironmonger for paraffin. Now of course we can buy all we want under one roof in a supermarket. I was always in trouble for eating the crust off one end of the freshly baked bread before I arrived home, and worse, one Easter I picked all of the fruit out of several hot-cross buns.

It was mostly a working class area, and the streets were our playground, along with bombsites left over from World War Two. We had Clapham Common close by, and a little further away, Battersea Park where there was once a funfair and small zoo. I loved the park and spent many hours playing there, though I rarely had the entrance fee for the funfair so I had to stick to the swings.

My parents worked in local factories and I became a latch key kid. I don't remember feeling deprived, after all, our friends and neighbours were in the same boat, and in fact I felt we were rich when we got a black and white television in 1953, just in time to watch the Queen's Coronation. We didn't have a telephone, nor did any of our neighbours, and of course mobiles didn't exist.

It's only in retrospect that I realise what a hard life my mother had, working full time and then coming home to cook and clean for a family of five without all the wonderful gadgets we have nowadays. There were no ready meals or microwaves, and mostly everything had to be prepared from fresh produce. To give my mother a break from cooking we occasionally had fish and chips, or I would be sent to the pie and mash shop with a jug which they would fill with green, parsley liquor.

Our kitchen was nothing like the fitted ones seen nowadays. There was just a sink in one corner, and a cooker in the other, with a large cupboard for a larder. We mostly lived and ate in this room, with the sitting room kept for best.

Of course I remember lovely summers, but I also recall cold winters, coal fires, and without heating in our bedrooms, there would be ice on the inside of the windows every morning. No duvets either as they were unheard of, just blankets, and for extra warmth I had my dad's old army overcoat thrown on top.

Washing was put in the bath to soak and then came what must have been a backbreaking job of rubbing it up and down on the scrubbing board, let alone all the rinsing and wringing out before it could go on the line. A little later my mother got a Baby Burco boiler complete with electric mangle and she felt very modern.

I came into contact with many local characters, from my extended family to those that lived around us, and of course they are an inspiration for my books. I tend to use just one trait, like an old lady who used to mix up her words and appeared in one of my books, to a man who used to abuse his wife.

We heard stories of the Kray brothers in East London, but in our area, South London, it was the Richardsons who were considered the local villains. All I heard was gossip and none of these characters touched my life. On the whole the locals were a mixture of good and bad, funny and sad, and all, I am sure, had stories to tell.

It's their stories that I imagine, that I draw my inspiration from, and so a little of each of them goes into every book.